D0966129

# NEVER TURN BACK

## ALSO AVAILABLE BY CHRISTOPHER SWANN

*Shadow of the Lions*

# NEVER TURN BACK

A NOVEL

## CHRISTOPHER SWANN

CROOKED LANE

NEW YORK

Published in the United States by Crooked Lane Books, an imprint of The Quick Brown Fox & Company LLC.

Crooked Lane Books and its logo are trademarks of The Quick Brown Fox & Company LLC.

Library of Congress Catalog-in-Publication data available upon request.

ISBN (hardcover): 978-1-64385-537-0
ISBN (ebook): 978-1-64385-538-7

Cover design by Melanie Sun

Printed in the United States.

www.crookedlanebooks.com

Crooked Lane Books
34 West 27th St., 10th Floor
New York, NY 10001

First Edition: October 2020

10 9 8 7 6 5 4 3 2 1

For three storytellers gone too soon:
To my grandfather, Henry Conkle, for sharing with me his love of
narrative and English literature;
To my father, David Swann, for all of his stories that are now
family legend;
And to Jim Barton, my friend and colleague, for teaching the
power and enchantment of storytelling to so many students,
including my youngest son.

# PART I

What's done cannot be undone.
—Lady Macbeth, *Macbeth* (5.1.68)

# CHAPTER ONE

I'M AT A TRAFFIC LIGHT DOWNTOWN ON PEACHTREE STREET AT EIGHT AM on a Friday, the sky far too blue and sunny, and as I sit in my Corolla in last night's clothes, waiting for the light to change, the headache buried in my skull sends out a single red tendril. I need coffee and a shower and a handful of Advil. To distract myself, I think about Marisa, the woman I met yesterday at the English teachers' conference and drank with at the hotel bar, the woman with whom I spent the night. But now the headache is unfurling behind my forehead and I just want to get home and climb into bed and sleep for twelve hours.

At the thought, as if *sleep* is a key that unlocks the vault of my memory, I can hear my mother quoting Robert Frost: " 'The woods are lovely, dark and deep, / But I have promises to keep, / And miles to go before I sleep, / And miles to go before I sleep.' " That was one of her favorite quotes, reflecting her extraordinary commitment to my father, no matter how difficult that commitment became. My father had a rather different take on the issue. Once, after he had returned from Iraq, I complained to him about a promise that a schoolmate had broken, and he gave me a lopsided smile. "The best way to keep your word is not to give it," he told me. Which, even then, I knew was a pretty cynical thing for a father to say to his thirteen-year-old son.

The twin memories of my parents are like a pair of blades scissoring my heart, and I'm grateful to be distracted by the light changing. I'm a dozen cars back from the light, so I take a moment to close my eyes and picture an actual steel vault, the door massive and open. I'm holding an old shoebox, stuffed near to overflowing, a thick rubber band securing the lid, and I place the shoebox into the vault, push the door shut with a loud clang, and spin the wheel, locking it. Then I open my eyes and drive forward, through the intersection and on to home.

MY HOUSE NEAR Chastain Park is less than ten minutes from the school where I teach but over half an hour from downtown, even going against traffic. Halfway home I pull into a Starbucks drive-through, another willing victim of globalization and convenience, and order a large latte and a croissant. I suck down the latte and manage to get croissant flakes all over myself and the interior of my Corolla, but I don't run into a lamppost or another vehicle, which I take as a win.

I live in a two-bedroom cottage tucked behind a much larger and more imposing house owned by Tony and Gene, who rent the cottage to me. Built a year before the Japanese bombed Pearl Harbor, the cottage has cedar-shingle siding, dusky blue shutters, and three concrete front steps leading up to a covered concrete porch the size of a postage stamp. There are garages in Chastain larger than my home. But the neighborhood is a suburban enclave of trees and lazy, winding streets anchored by a huge public park, complete with a golf course and sports fields. My house is within ten minutes of work, a Korean dry cleaners, a neighborhood Publix, a Target, and several decent bars and restaurants, all without having to get on Atlanta's nightmarish interstates.

By the time I get home, Tony, one of my landlords, is crouching in the flower bed on his front lawn. He's wearing an enormous straw hat the color of a ripe avocado, and he waves at me as I turn into my driveway, which runs along the edge of his lot. Sometimes he and his partner Gene bake me chocolate chip cookies or invite me to watch movies in their in-home basement theater, which has reclining leather seats, a wine fridge, and a sound system you could hear on the moon. Tony runs some sort of IT consulting business from home, and Gene is a real estate agent who drives a new Mercedes every year. Last summer they got married and threw a post-wedding bash for all their friends and neighbors that would make Gatsby's soirées look like a five-year-old's birthday party. Robert Frost wrote that good fences make good neighbors, but so do kindness and empathy. I don't always return those in kind, and today I don't stop and make small talk like I should because I'm dirty, slightly hungover, and more than a little embarrassed that Tony is seeing me coming home after a late night, but I'm lucky to have such nice neighbors, and I need to let them know it.

I make my way slowly up the pine-shrouded driveway in my Corolla, the asphalt buckled by tree roots so that I dip and pitch my way to the end. Brown pine needles blanket the asphalt and even the roof of the cottage. *Need to get up there with a leaf blower*, I think, and I take undue pride in the observation, as if I were acting like a responsible adult rather than slinking away from a one-night stand and skipping the final day of a conference my employer paid for. Nothing worthwhile happens on the last day of a three-day conference, especially not on a Friday when everyone is itching to get home for the weekend, but that doesn't keep me from feeling guilty. Then comes a memory like an echo: wet lips, a hungry mouth, a gasp followed by a throaty chuckle, Marisa's dark hair playing across my face as she rose above me. Even hungover as I am, for a moment I feel desire slowly stirring. But overlaying this is a worn yet familiar sense of sadness. This is not the first time I have hooked up with a stranger at a conference. I've found it's easier than maintaining an actual relationship. Better to make a quick exit than a prolonged goodbye. Or so I tell myself.

I walk up the steps, reaching for my house keys. Wilson is inside whining at the door. "Hold on, boy," I say, trying to get the key in the lock. My dog is housebroken, and Tony and Gene said they would let him out yesterday—I make a mental note to get them a bottle of wine—but I know Wilson must be hungry at least.

When I get the door open, my miniature dachshund is dancing on the carpet. Usually he almost bowls me over as he runs out the front door to relieve himself on the front lawn. Today he barks at me, twice, then turns and runs to the back of the house, into the tiny hall that separates the two bedrooms. The one on the left is officially the guest bedroom but has no bed and is essentially a storage closet. Wilson turns right, into my bedroom, his paws scrabbling on the hardwood floor. He yips excitedly.

"Wilson!" I call. The last thing I need is for him to pee all over my room. I drop my workbag and follow him. "Wilson, come!"

I walk through the doorway of my bedroom and come to a dead stop. Wilson is prancing around at the foot of my bed like he's just treed a squirrel. A woman is lying on top of the covers, looking up at the ceiling, her hands clasped over her stomach. *Marisa*, I think, and I am startled and excited and freaked out all at once. Immediately I realize it's not Marisa. This woman is wearing jeans and has bare, filthy feet, and her short hair is a shade of magenta that doesn't exist anywhere in nature.

"You named your dog Wilson?" she says, still looking at the ceiling.

Wilson glances up at the bed, then back to me, a low whine in his throat. I reach down and rub his ears and get a rapid licking from a tiny, rough tongue in response. "Good boy," I say.

She sits up on her elbows to face me. "You did *not* name him after the volleyball in *Cast Away*," she says.

"Tom Hanks got an Oscar nomination for that," I say, still rubbing Wilson's ears.

She laughs. "Jesus, that's pathetic."

I sigh and straighten up. "Good to see you too, Susannah."

"Suzie," she says. With that, Susannah hops off the bed. She's wearing a tight black T-shirt with the words *Get Up the Yard* slashed in white across the front. "Got anything to eat?" she says. "I'm starving."

"And apparently shoeless."

"My feet hurt. Plus I stepped in dog shit when I took *Wilson* outside for you. You're welcome."

"Where've you been, Susannah?"

"It's *Suzie*," she says. "Seriously, I'm fucking dying of hunger over here."

DON'T GET ME wrong, I'm glad to see my sister. It's just that her sudden reappearances can be jarring. She operates on her own timetable, rarely calls or emails, and disappears for months at a time, so seeing Susannah in the flesh is really the only confirmation I ever get that she's even alive.

Whenever I would complain about something Susannah had done, like taking my books from my bedroom without asking or eating the last pack of peanut butter crackers in the pantry, Mom would commiserate, but she always ended those talks the same way. "I know it's hard having a little sister," she would say in her Irish lilt. "But she's *your* little sister, Ethan. She's the only one you've got."

This was a refrain both of my parents often used to impress upon me the importance of being Susannah's big brother, the unique role I was to play in her life. But once she was old enough to ride a tricycle, Susannah came to feel insulted by the idea that she could possibly need me to protect her. I was inclined to agree. People who messed with Susannah were more likely to need me to protect them from her. When I was twelve and Susannah was nine, a budding bully in our neighborhood named Jake called my curly-haired sister Brillo Head. The next day, Jake was riding his bike, a red Diamondback Octane, when the brakes failed to work and he crashed into a utility pole, breaking his forearm and collarbone. When Jake's little brother Tommy told the rest of us on the cul-de-sac about Jake's accident, I looked at Susannah. She gave me a ghost of a smile only I could see. More chilling than that smile was the pair of needle-nose pliers I found sitting on my dresser that evening, the perfect tool for snipping a brake line on a bike. I put the pliers back where they belonged, in the toolbox in our garage, but said nothing, partly because

I couldn't prove anything but also because I didn't want to upset Mom and Dad—Mom because she would cry, Dad because I didn't know how he would react.

A year after the bike incident, we were orphans.

SUSANNAH EATS A cheese-and-mushroom omelet and three pieces of toast. I settle for a glass of orange juice and more coffee. Afterward we sit on my front steps in the warm late morning and sip coffee as we watch Wilson explore the yard and chase chipmunks.

"Gotta love Atlanta," Susannah says. "Middle of January and it's like sixty degrees outside."

"Global warming."

"It's a lie."

"Global warming is a lie?"

"Straight-up liberal propaganda."

"You know, I've never understood that," I say. "The whole global warming conspiracy idea. What would be the point?"

"Political control. People who want to crush capitalism and introduce a world government. There're documentaries and everything."

I never know whether Susannah believes what she's saying or not. I've found it's safer to just listen and try not to start an argument.

"So, where've you been?" I ask.

She shrugs. "Around."

"Around Atlanta?"

"Hell no." She takes a sip of her coffee. "Nashville. Cleveland for a little while. Saint Louis. Wanted to head out west, maybe Montana."

"You didn't?"

She shakes her head. "Didn't feel right. So I ended up back here." She speaks as if she has been on a summer road trip. I haven't talked to her in over a year, haven't seen her in two.

"You planning on staying for a while?" I ask, trying to sound neutral.

She shrugs. "Don't know. Maybe. Need to find a job. Your school need a substitute teacher?" When I look at her, she holds a hand up, palm forward. "Relax. Just kidding, Professor. Sheesh." She takes out her phone and starts tapping at it.

"What are you doing?" I ask.

"Looking for a hardware store," she says, still looking at her phone. "You need new locks."

"Why do I—?" I stare at her. "Did you *break into* my house? I thought my neighbors let you in!"

She shakes her head. "Got in really late last night, figured you'd be home." She looks up from her phone. "Speaking of, looks like somebody did the walk of shame this morning."

"I was at a conference," I say, feeling my cheeks redden. "There was a get-together last night. I stayed out late and crashed in someone's hotel room."

She smiles. "You're a terrible liar. Relax, I don't care. And I didn't break anything. You just have shitty door locks. Oh, there's an Ace Hardware just down the street. Perfect." She slides her phone back into her pocket and looks expectantly at me.

AFTER I TAKE a shower, I walk over to my neighbors' house to ask Tony if it's okay for me to replace the front and back door locks at my expense. I tell him my sister's visiting and she gets anxious about home security. Tony says sure, no problem, come over for a drink later if you want. I beg off, as I have no intention of introducing Susannah to anyone, let alone to Tony and Gene over drinks. Instead I bundle Susannah into my car and we drive to Ace Hardware, where Susannah—who insists that I call her Suzie, which I refuse to do—examines every dead bolt and door lock until she pronounces one brand acceptable. I buy two sets and spend the rest of the afternoon installing the things and doing what passes for my weekend housecleaning while Susannah washes a duffel bag of laundry and plays with Wilson.

Despite the fact that it's a small house, we manage not to talk a lot to each other during the day, aside from the usual banter and bickering. Susannah is like a rare and edgy bird of prey—say the wrong thing and she'll either claw you or take wing and vanish. I get the sense that she is tired and might like pretending to be domesticated for a couple of nights, so instead of inviting her to stay, I just assume that she will and don't bother asking. But I am waiting for the right moment to ask her what's going on, if she has any plans for the near future, and I figure dinnertime is it—she'll be more relaxed, less likely to attack or bolt.

Dinner turns out to be pizza from Double Zero, which Susannah orders, has delivered, and pays for with cash, a gesture I appreciate. We eat on the couch, listening to the Lumineers and drinking beer. Wilson lies on the floor, happily exhausted from chasing his rope bone, which Susannah threw for him all afternoon.

Susannah is lying back on the couch, feet on the coffee table, eyes closed. I swear she's even smiling. "So," I say, deciding to tiptoe into this particular minefield, "you seen Uncle Gavin lately?"

Susannah snorts. "Fat chance. Thinks I owe him money."

"You did take his car."

Her eyes open and she sits up. "I *borrowed* it, for Christ's sake! I just needed a ride to Athens to see Dirt Plow. How did I know I'd get pulled over?"

"The police thought it was stolen."

"*Borrowed.*" She emphasizes this by poking me in the shoulder.

"Ow."

"Toughen up, buttercup," she says. "What about you? You seen him?"

"No. Dirt Plow? Who was that, your boyfriend at the time?"

"They were a *band*, dumbass."

"I'm the dumbass? The band's name was Dirt Plow."

"They were good, asshole. That was their last show before they broke up. They were reinventing grunge. Very earthy."

"I'll bet," I say. "Did they play on farm equipment? Use a tractor as a drum?"

"Tommy Mojo was their guitar player. *He* was a freak."

"No doubt."

"You wouldn't know a good band if it farted in your bathtub."

"That doesn't even make *sense*."

Susannah glances at her phone. "Shit, it's almost seven thirty."

I groan.

"Come on, Ethan." She grabs my TV remote. "It's time for *Jeopardy!*"

Susannah's version of *Jeopardy!* is simple: you have to verbally guess the correct question before the contestants or any other opponents— meaning me—do, and if you guess the correct answer first, you win the cash amount for that question. You have to answer in the form of a question, of course, and you cannot write anything down—you have to keep track in your head of how much money you've won. She has played this with me since she was ten.

On the television, Alex Trebek stands behind his *Jeopardy!* lectern, looking like a televangelist about to gently admonish some wayward teens. The categories appear on-screen, and as usual the titles are somewhere between geeky and twee: MAPS, ATTILA THE HUNGRY, THE 1860s, COMIC STRIPPERS, PRESIDENTS BY FIRST NAME, and MYTHELLANEOUS. The computer programmer contestant starts with Mythellaneous for two hundred and Trebek reads out the answer, about Laocoön and a wooden horse.

"What is Troy?" Susannah shouts out before I can even open my mouth. "Boom!" She mimes throwing down a mike. I roll my eyes.

At the end of the first round, Susannah is winning, but I've answered five straight in a row and am feeling good enough to get us each another beer at the commercial. "Comic Strippers was so lame," I call out from my kitchen, popping off the bottle caps.

"That's just because you couldn't get that one," Susannah says.

"You mean the one you thought was *Family Circus* instead of *FoxTrot*?" I say, grinning.

She flips me off but takes a beer from me when I walk back in, all without taking her eyes off the television, where Alex Trebek has reappeared with a new board: AMERICAN WRITERS, FOUR-LETTER STOCK MARKET WORDS, PEOPLE ON POSTAGE, ANCIENT CIVILIZATIONS, SCIENCE, and YOU KNOW, THE MOVIE WHERE . . .

"Science?" I scoff. "Stupid title."

"Here's a better one—*what is potassium?*" Susannah belts out before Alex Trebek is even halfway through the first question. She gets it right, and naturally it's worth two grand.

Nine minutes later the second round is over and we are virtually tied within a few hundred dollars of each other. Susannah bares her teeth at me. I offer a sneer in return. "For our final round," Alex Trebek says, and we both lean forward in anticipation. With a *ding*, the final category appears: SHAKESPEARE'S WOMEN.

"Yes!" I lift my clenched fists over my head.

"Jesus Christ," Susannah says.

Quickly we grab our phones and type out how much we want to bet, which we will show each other at the end to prove who the winner is. Susannah is muttering to herself. I try to calculate how much I can bet without going bankrupt. My sister is brilliant, but this is my game, my question. I bet half of what I have. We both put our phones on the table, facedown, just as Alex Trebek reappears.

"And the answer is," he says gravely, just before it appears on-screen:

The last words spoken by this character are
"What's done cannot be undone: to bed, to bed, to bed."

"One of your students, maybe?" Susannah says.

I flip her off—*nice try*—as I read the words. The answer skates around my brain, too quick to comprehend. Not Gertrude, not Juliet, not Portia . . . I almost have it, my lips forming the answer.

"More like whoever you banged at your conference," Susannah says, and her comment sweeps through me like a winter blast, clearing my head of everything except an image of Marisa, her lips on mine, our bodies tangled together in that hotel room. My heart contracts, squeezed in a fist of granite. Susannah takes advantage of my hesitation and shouts, "Who is Lady Macbeth?" Which is, of course, the correct answer. Triumphantly she picks up her phone and displays how much she bet: everything.

IT'S LATER AND we are sitting on my couch in the dark, the blank screen of my TV facing us. In his bed in the corner, Wilson sighs, a single huff, and then goes back to sleep. I lift my beer to my lips, but the bottle is empty, like the many bottles littering the coffee table. "I need to go to bed," I say.

Susannah stirs. "I'll sleep on the couch."

"No," I say, followed by a molar-cracking yawn. "You get the bed. I'll take the couch."

"I like the couch."

"Seriously, Suze, take my—"

"I'm sleeping on the goddamned couch, Ethan."

"Okay, fine. Jesus."

Susannah *hmm*s.

I try to read her expression, but I can't make out her face in the dark. I yawn again, my wits fading. I feel as if I'm turning to stone, that come morning I'll be a statue of a man sitting on a couch.

"You gonna go back to therapy?" I ask. It's a risky question, but it just popped into my head, and I'm too tired to care.

To my surprise, Susannah *hmm*s again.

"Is that a maybe?" I ask.

"I don't know," she says. "Maybe. Yes."

Wilson whimpers in his sleep.

"I gotta go to bed," I say again, without moving.

Susannah says, "Do you ever think about that night?"

I hold in my words along with my breath. There is only one night she could be talking about. I try not to think about the shoe on the walkway, or Susannah's bedroom light, the one she turned on, a beacon in the dark to the growling car. "No," I manage.

"I do," she says. "All the time." And then she says nothing else as I sit there in the dark next to her. From the street, a passing car's headlights sweep across the window, glinting off the beer bottles on the coffee table, and then they slide away, leaving both of us stranded in the shadows.

# CHAPTER TWO

THE NIGHT MY PARENTS DIED I WAS TAKEN TO THE HOSPITAL, WHERE, AT some point, bathed in a twilight haze of painkillers, I realized that a man wearing a flat tweed cap was sitting in a chair across from me, reading a newspaper. He glanced up as if he knew I was awake, and his eyes were black as tar. "You look like you're trying to give me a Nazi salute," he said.

Slowly, I turned my head to look at my right arm, frozen in a full cast up to my armpit and raised up on a stack of pillows. "*Sieg Heil*," I murmured. My lips were dry, and my tongue pushed out between them, fat and rubbery, unable to wet them enough.

The man put his newspaper aside, stood up, and walked over to me. The first thing I noticed was that he was short. The second was that he held a blue plastic cup in his hand. He shook the cup and it rattled. "Here," he said. "They said you could have this." He held the cup to my mouth, and I managed to open my lips. A few crushed pieces of ice slipped into my mouth.

"Not too many," he said. His voice was odd, a thin southern accent overlaying something hard in the vowels.

I sucked on the pieces of ice as if they were peppermints. "Where are my parents?" I managed. "My sister?"

"The doctor's coming," he said. "You hold on."

"You're from Ireland," I said. That was what I'd heard in his voice. *The dohkter's comin'.* It was a version of my mother's accent. A memory surfaced: I was in a hospital room with Mom and Dad, meeting Susannah just after she was born, and a man appeared in the doorway, holding a wrapped present. Dad wouldn't let him in. He was shorter than Dad and wore a flat cap and coat—Susannah was born in February—and he looked at me over Dad's shoulder with a pair of deep, dark eyes. The same eyes that were looking at me now.

"Are you my uncle?" I asked him.

He nodded, once, then turned his head to the door. "Need a doctor in here," he said, not shouting but something close to a bark.

"That's the first thing . . . you say to me?" I asked. He turned back to me, and I continued, "I look like a Nazi?" It was stupid—hysterical, even. *Heil Hitler.* I started to chuckle, and even though I could see the alarm in his face and felt tears on my cheeks, I didn't want to stop laughing, because if I did I'd have to acknowledge that this was my uncle Gavin, my mother's brother, and if he was here that could mean only one thing. But then a nurse swept in and leaned over me—broad face, professional concern in her gaze, her voice kind and soothing—and everything was sucked down a gray whirlpool that went black.

When I next woke up, sunlight streamed through the thin curtains shrouding the single window. Uncle Gavin was sitting in the same chair, leafing through a magazine. He'd taken his cap off, and his hair was a tangle of black with a touch of gray at the temples. I managed to clear my throat, and he looked up. No gray in those eyes—just deep, deep black. "Ethan," he said. "How are you feeling?"

"Never better," I croaked.

He glanced at my arm in its cast. "The doctor says you'll be in the cast for a few weeks," he said. "Then rehab. But there shouldn't be any permanent damage."

I took a breath, released it. "I was shot," I said.

He gave me a careful look of appraisal. "It was clean," he said. "The wound. Bullet went right through. Broke the bone in your upper arm, two inches below your shoulder. You'll have some nice scars to show off."

"I got shot in my humerus?" I said. "Hilarious." I took another breath, aware of a distant pain in my upper arm if I breathed too deeply. "Susannah?"

His face closed up, though his eyes were the same liquid black they had been. "Hanging in there," he said. "Touch and go for a while, but the doctor says she'll make it."

"My parents are dead, aren't they," I said.

Another appraising look, as if he were calculating how much grief I could manage. "Yes," he said.

I closed my eyes and nodded, then leaned my head back against my pillow. Once, I'd helped my mother make spaghetti squash, scraping the steamed squash out of the gourd with a fork. I felt like that squash, scraped and set aside on the counter.

"There . . . was a girl," I said. "She lost her shoe." There was more, I knew, just around the slippery corner of my memory, but the shoe was the important point. That and the fact that my parents' deaths were my fault.

*Mine and Susannah's*, a voice said in the back of my head.

*Shut up*, I said.

"Ethan?" I opened my eyes to see Uncle Gavin frowning. Had I spoken aloud?

"Did the police," I said, then swallowed. "Did they find who . . ." I could not complete the sentence.

Uncle Gavin shook his head. "Not yet." Another pause, and something gathered in Uncle Gavin's face, hard and threatening. "But if they don't find them," he said, his voice lower still, his dark eyes fixed on mine, "I will."

SUSANNAH'S INJURIES WERE far worse than mine. The doctors had explained that the bullet had so damaged her that she would never have children, but that seemed too ridiculous a concept to worry about right now—her lower body being swathed in bandages was a more immediate concern. The nurses had told me that she was on pain medication and so might not be fully alert. In her hospital bed, she looked so small and pale, the skin under her eyes bruised. "Hi," she managed.

"Hi," I said.

I was in a wheelchair, my cast-encased arm now in a sling. Susannah took this in with a long, slow look. "So we both got shot," she said.

*Because both of us fucked up,* I wanted to say. Instead I nodded.

She lay her head back, looking at the ceiling. "Mom and Dad are dead, huh?"

Any resentment or anger I felt toward her at that moment drained away. Her hollow voice was more devastating than tears. My own eyes watered. I was getting sick of crying. "Yeah," I said, wiping the back of my arm across my face. *Orphans,* I thought. I looked at my sister, pale and distant, practically mummified by her bandages. What were we going to do?

"You should've shot the other guy first," Susannah said. Then she fell back asleep.

THE DOCTORS RELEASED me the next day, but I wouldn't leave Susannah, who had to remain "for observation," which I read as code for *she still might die.* I'd like to think that I wanted to stay because of filial loyalty. Looking back, however, I realize it was also fear. Leaving the hospital would mean that I was walking away from my previous life with my mother and father and heading into a new, frightening world without them. It would be an acknowledgment that my parents' deaths were real. So I remained stubbornly at my sister's bedside. It was only when Susannah finally told me to get out of her room so she could get some sleep that I left. But as Uncle Gavin steered me and my wheelchair out of Susannah's room and down the hall to the elevator, I couldn't shake the feeling that I was deserting my post.

I probably should have been more freaked out by leaving the hospital with Uncle Gavin, who was a virtual stranger. All I knew of him was that he, like Mom, had been born in Ireland and that he had brought her with him to the United States after their parents died in a car accident. On the rare occasions Mom or Dad had mentioned Uncle Gavin, it was always to say he had "gone down the wrong path" or "made bad choices" or "had to lie down in the bed he'd made." He was a sort of family bogey-man, an avatar of wickedness. *What* wickedness my uncle had suppos-edly done was never made clear. As far as Susannah and I could piece together from the rare instances when we overheard our parents talking about Uncle Gavin, somehow Mom felt she had failed as a sister, allowing Uncle Gavin to wander off into corruption and degeneracy. Of course, Susannah and I wanted to know all about him, to hear stories about bad old Uncle Gavin and his iniquity, but Mom refused to discuss it with us in any detail, and Dad forbade us from bothering Mom about him. And now he was rolling me out of the hospital. By all rights I should have been worried, but somehow I felt . . . not *cared for*, exactly, but *protected*.

Uncle Gavin drove a black Lincoln Navigator, which, while upscale and tricked out in leather and wood trim, left me disappointed. I'd imag-ined Uncle Gavin driving some sort of bad-boy car, like a Shelby Mus-tang or maybe a Ferrari. Instead, he was driving the kind of SUV that Buckhead mommies dropped off at the valet at Phipps Plaza. I got into the passenger seat, Uncle Gavin closing my door with a heavy *whunk*.

"Where are we going?" I asked once Uncle Gavin got in the driver's seat. I wanted so badly to go home, except my home no longer existed. Now it was only a house with bloodstains.

Uncle Gavin looked at me with those dark eyes. "You're coming home with me," he said.

UNCLE GAVIN LIVED in Grant Park, a gentrified neighborhood in southeast Atlanta near the zoo. The northern suburbs, seated on the gentle heights of tree-topped hills, gazed down on the glass and steel towers of Atlanta from a distance. Grant Park was older, grittier, a stone's throw from downtown. It was also a neighborhood getting a facelift. Every third block or so revealed a boarded-up house, a weedy lot strewn with rubble, or brand-new construction.

Uncle Gavin's house was a remodeled Victorian bungalow that sat up from the sidewalk, stacked-stone walls flanking stairs up to a gate in a wooden fence that surrounded the property. An oak tree shaded the tiny yard, which had more boxwoods than grass, but everything looked tidy.

As we pulled up to the curb by the front steps, I saw a woman standing on the front porch, smoking a cigarette. She wore a pink tank top and painted-on jeans, and her chestnut hair was piled in a messy updo. When we got out of the Lincoln, the woman dropped her cigarette and stepped on it to put it out, then chewed her thumbnail.

I stopped at the bottom of the steps. "I don't have any clothes or anything," I said.

Uncle Gavin held up a duffel bag. "I got you some things from your house," he said.

We looked at each other. I imagined Uncle Gavin walking into my house, where his sister had been killed, and going down the hall to my room to get me jeans and shirts and underwear. The scene hurt so much, so quickly, that I mentally pulled a garage door down, closing it off.

"You okay?" Uncle Gavin asked, and when I nodded he led the way up the stairs, holding the gate open for me. We climbed the wooden steps to the porch, where the woman was waiting. "Supper?" Uncle Gavin asked her.

"On the stove," the woman said. She had the kind of Southern accent I associated with NASCAR and country music stations. "Oh, honey, how's your arm? Bless your heart." It took me a moment to realize she was talking to me, but before I could say anything, the woman had enveloped me in a hug, careful not to jostle my slinged arm. Two things registered simultaneously: her hair smelled like coconuts, and she had enormous boobs.

"Fay, this is my nephew Ethan," Uncle Gavin said. "Ethan, this is Fay." He offered no other information, although very soon I realized Fay was my uncle's girlfriend.

Fay released me and bent down a bit to look me in the eye—she was taller than me, almost a whole head taller than Uncle Gavin. She was younger than him, too. I tried not to look at her impressive cleavage. Fay was tanned and her face was striking, but there was something slightly off about her, a rabbity nervousness about her eyes and nose. "You have been through an awful thing," she said. "I am so sorry."

I'd about lost it right there, blubbering all over the front of Fay's tank top, when Uncle Gavin stepped forward. "All right, let the boy alone, now. Ethan, I'll show you to your room, and then we'll have supper." I don't know if he wanted to save me from any further grief for the moment, or if he wanted to avoid having an emotional teenage boy on his front porch, or if he just wanted to eat. But Uncle Gavin's comment gave me time to pull myself together and walk into his house.

# CHAPTER THREE

On Saturday morning, yawning and not a little hungover, I walk into my den and stop dead. Susannah is in purple leotards and a blue exercise top, doing a downward-facing dog pose, her butt facing me. Wilson is lying on his pillow, staring at Susannah in adoration. He gives me a tail wag but then returns his attention to Susannah.

"That's not how I like to wake up in the morning," I say.

Susannah, her head pointed to the floor, looks back between her legs at me. "A cute girl in spandex? Perish the thought."

"My sister exercising in my den is what I meant."

Susannah walks her hands back toward her own feet, bent almost in half, and then stands straight up, the movement graceful and fluid. "You should try it," she says. "All that sitting around will kill you."

I move toward the kitchen and coffee. "I take Pilates," I say.

She raises her eyebrows. "Oh, *Pilates*," she says, holding one hand to her chest in mock surprise. "I'm sorry, I wasn't aware I was speaking to a *Pilates* student."

I flip her off without turning to look at her.

"What do you call yourselves, anyway?" she calls after me. "Pilatites? Pilatizens?"

I ignore her, and it's not just that I'm hungover or that her perkiness is especially annoying. Susannah has dislodged some memories that I had carefully packed away. Not Ponytail—he's a regular visitor in the dead of the night, stalking my dreams in his black vest and white T-shirt. No. This is something I tied to a concrete block and dropped in the depths of my memory, but now it's rising to the surface, slimy and mottled and smelling of rotten fish. It's a nightmare of fragmented images: kudzu in the night, plywood over a hole in the wall, screaming in a pitch-black house. I want to banish it, force it away, but it's a memory, a biochemical encoding in my brain, and it's not a single remembered event tucked in a file that theoretically I could delete but a series of smaller memories distributed across my brain, like strands that form a web, a web that has now trapped me. I am again in Frankie's car—God, Frankie—as he drives down the darkened streets, both of us peering through the windshield, looking for Susannah, riding to her rescue, ha, good one, *rescue*, like we'd ever had a hope of rescuing her, like my sister hadn't been lost to us from the start—

"Ethan," Susannah says now. She's in my kitchen doorway, looking at me.

I realize I am standing at my sink, the water running, empty coffeepot in my hand. "Yeah," I say, turning off the water. "I'm fine. What?"

"You okay? You just . . . zoned out for a minute."

I blink at her, then look at the coffeepot in my hand. Coffee. Right. I turn the water back on and fill up the pot. "Just tired," I say, and I offer her a smile. "And maybe hungover. Can't hang with my little sister anymore."

Susannah looks at me for another moment, then smiles back. "Getting old, big brother. You have enough coffee for two? I'm going for a run."

I raise the pot. "On it." I put the pot in the coffeemaker, then start looking for a filter and grounds. When I glance up at the doorway, Susannah is gone. I pause and place my hands on the counter, closing my eyes for a moment's peace, trying to visualize that mental vault, the place where I keep the past locked away. But it's as if the vault door is open and leads to a dark cave at the back of my brain, full of twisting tunnels and passages where I've tried to lose all those memories, and there are things in there that I've kept hidden for a long time, that I cannot allow to come out into the light. So I reach back into that cave and take out a different set of memories, still painful but less raw, in an effort to keep the truly dark ones at bay.

IN THIS MARGINALLY safer collection of memories, Susannah comes home from the hospital.

When we picked Susannah up from the hospital, she stared out the car window for the entire ride, despite Fay's brittle attempts at conversation. Once we reached Uncle Gavin's house, Susannah moved slowly and stiffly up the front steps, like a woman ten times her age. Her room was at the back of the house, across the hall from Gavin and Fay's, a guest bedroom that was bigger than mine but with all the sterile personality of a motel room—brown comforter, gray curtains, a dusty-looking throw rug on the hardwood floor. Fay had tried, decorating the room with new frilled sheets, some pink-and-white throw pillows, and a *My Pink Pony* poster on the closet door, but it was an embarrassing sitcom failure of a little girl's room.

When Susannah first shuffled in, she looked around her new room, then at me, then at Fay, who stood smiling nervously in the corner. "What fresh hell is this?" Susannah said, directly to Fay.

Uncle Gavin strode across the room and slapped Susannah across the face. Fay gasped. I flinched as if Uncle Gavin had struck me instead. Susannah's face was now pale as paper, except for the reddening handprint across her cheek.

"Don't speak to Fay that way in my house, and not anywhere if you know what's best for you," Uncle Gavin said. "You've lost your parents, and I'm sorry. But you won't give her any cheek in my home. Understand?"

Susannah glared at Uncle Gavin, who glared back. Standing there, useless and frightened and utterly confused as to what to do, I thought of the whole irresistible-force-meeting-an-immovable-object scenario. Susannah was a champion at this kind of standoff, but Uncle Gavin stood before her, unbending, his black eyes fixed on hers. And then Susannah's mouth tightened as if she had made a decision, and she said, "Yes, sir."

I let out a ragged, astonished breath.

Uncle Gavin nodded. "Then let's get you settled in," he said.

Later than night, I knocked on Susannah's door. She was sitting in bed, reading one of the Harry Potter books. I noticed the *My Pink Pony* poster was gone from the wall. After reading for a few more seconds, Susannah looked up from her book. "What?" she said.

I sat down on the edge of her bed. "Are you okay?"

"I got shot in the uterus, Ethan."

"I don't mean that, I mean . . . Uncle Gavin."

She frowned. "What? You mean earlier? Yeah, I'm fine."

"I should have done something," I said. I hated how pathetic I sounded.

Susannah raised her eyebrows. "Like what? Hit him over the head with a lamp?" She closed her book. "It's okay. Now I know."

"Know what?"

"Where I stand with Uncle Gavin."

# CHAPTER FOUR

The Monday after Susannah appears on my doorstep, I go to work.

The Archer School originally occupied a single stone house built in the 1930s, but since then the school has expanded to include state-of-the-art science labs, an enormous gym, playing fields, a dining hall, a fine arts center, and new classroom wings. The private-school market in Atlanta is rich with choices, each school trying to create and market its own niche, and Archer has staked its claim on an egalitarian ethos that is open, tolerant, and comprehensive in its curriculum. It's an ethos I appreciate, or perhaps it's more accurate to say it's an ethos I aspire to follow. Archer is a place that has accepted me, which is more important than anything else.

Hanging above the glass front door of the Stone House is the school seal, an emerald *A* in a white circle bordered by the school motto: *Mente, Corpore, et Anima*—"With Mind, Body, and Soul." Like an ecclesiastical hall monitor, Father Coleman Carter, bald and built like an ex-linebacker, holds the door open for me. "Abandon all hope, ye who enter here," he says, grinning.

"That's pretty cynical for a priest," I say.

Coleman's blue eyes glint. "You're pretty observant for an English teacher."

I walk inside and Coleman matches my stride, letting the door shut behind us. Coleman is blunt, occasionally profane, and delights in mischief. He teaches history and comparative religion. We became friends about a minute after I first arrived on campus for an interview, four years ago.

"What did you think of the conference?" Coleman asks.

I shrug. "Got a nice tote bag out of it."

"Missed you Friday morning," he continues. "Did you go to the breakfast?"

"Nope," I say. "Stayed home. Caught up on my grading."

Two freshmen boys pass us in the hall. "Mr. Faulkner, Father Carter," one says, nodding.

Coleman has an impressive vocal range, and now his words ring out like sharp notes from a horn. "For the love of God, son, I'm an Episcopalian. Use the name my mother gave me. It's Father Coleman. Carter is my surname." He looks at me. "You *teach* them what a surname is, don't you?"

I shrug. "I'm an English teacher, not a genealogist."

Coleman's face is large and expressive, with a potato for a nose and ears like flattened leaves of cabbage. I like provoking Coleman because his face will stretch into all sorts of contortions. Now his eyebrows lower in a frown and his mouth puckers up like he is about to either kiss me or spit. He turns to the two wide-eyed freshmen. "I want you boys to witness this," he says, his voice vibrating with the first tremors of outrage. "This is the death of American education, right here. I look at Mr. Faulkner, and I despair of the future. When an *English* teacher fails to inform his students of the meanings of basic vocabulary words, I begin looking for the four horsemen of the apocalypse."

I say, a bit defensively, "I teach vocabulary."

Coleman's eyebrows rise comically. "Where do you find the time, in between standing on your desk and inspiring your students with Walt Whitman quotations?"

"*Dead Poets Society* is so clichéd," I say. "Nowadays we hold hands in a circle and listen to the beauty of words and weep."

Coleman's laughter fills the hallway, to the marginal relief of the two freshmen staring at us. "You bunch of effete academics," he says, still laughing. He then looks at one of the freshmen as if sighting him through a targeting scope. "Mr. Deal," Coleman says, and the student jumps with surprise. "Do you know that word, *effete*?"

The freshman licks his lips. "I think . . . does it mean clever, or something about an accomplishment? Like, a feat of strength?"

Coleman closes his eyes. "Jesus Christ, it's worse than I thought," he says. He opens his eyes and glares at the boy. "No, Mr. Deal, it doesn't mean *like* anything, nor does it mean clever or anything about an accomplishment. It means weak or enervated, or delicate due to a pampered existence. It can also mean effeminate, but I do not use the word in that manner, as I dislike gender stereotypes about as much as I dislike the New England Patriots. I would suggest that you run, *run* to the nearest classroom and find a dictionary, or look one up on the internet if you must, and begin reading as if your life depended upon it. Go."

The two freshmen go.

"That was a nice little teachable moment," I say. "Very pastoral."

Coleman harrumphs. "All I did was ensure that those young men know what the word *effete* means. I can guarantee you they'll remember it."

"Yeah, about that. What's with calling me effete?"

"You love poetry, I thought of John Keats, ergo effete."

"*Ergo*? Keats wasn't effete. The man wrote some of the greatest poetry in the English language while he was dying of tuberculosis, and he only lived to be twenty-five. Ergo, Keats was a badass."

Coleman shakes his head, scowling, but I know I've pleased him. He appreciates wit and enjoys locking horns in argument. The people who are frightened of him—and there are more than a few—don't realize how much of Coleman's behavior is an act. The man uses bluster as a way to engage with the world because, at heart, he doubts both the world and himself and longs for assurance that all will be well, which perhaps explains why he is a priest. I have learned that such assurance is hard to find, and harder to keep.

"I got coffee," Coleman says as we walk down the hall toward his classroom. "Not the swill in the lounge, the real stuff."

"What, you import it from Colombia?" I say. "Grind it by hand?"

"It's Starbucks in a French press, as you know very well."

In Coleman's classroom, Betsy Bales is sitting at Coleman's desk, typing on her laptop. She gets to her feet as we enter, all five foot two of her. Her short height accentuates how enormously pregnant she is. "There you are," she says, brushing her blonde hair off her forehead.

"Here I am," I say.

Betsy quirks an eyebrow. "I was talking about Father Coleman," she says.

Coleman frowns. "You just want coffee," he says.

Betsy lays a hand on her belly, which is roughly the size of a pumpkin, and gravely tells him, "Only your coffee. And just half a cup."

Coleman grumbles but moves to a table at the back of the room, where he has a large French-press coffeemaker. Betsy follows him, giving me a smile over her shoulder.

Coleman pushes down the plunger on his already-steeping French press, then pours Betsy a chipped mug of coffee, another for me, and a third for himself. He holds up his mug. "Onward and upward," he says, and we clink our mugs and sip. Coleman pauses and sighs contentedly. I look at Betsy and roll my eyes, causing her to stifle a giggle.

Betsy, who teaches European history, has been team teaching with me this year under Coleman's guidance as part of a new Humanities course, combining English and history. At the end of last spring, Betsy found out she was pregnant. She taught all fall, her body slowly growing until she resembled the world's most adorable Weeble, but now she is supposed to go on maternity leave this week. However, her long-term sub, a retired teacher who's been scheduled since last October, emailed last week to say her husband had—honest to God—won a cool million playing the lottery and they were moving to California immediately. Now we are scrambling to find someone before Betsy gives birth in the classroom.

"So," Coleman says, "what are you kids teaching today?"

"Ethan's wrapping up *Macbeth*," Betsy says, taking a sip. She sighs, supremely content with her coffee.

" 'Double, double, toil and trouble,' " Coleman says, waggling his free hand as if conjuring something. Nodding toward me, he says to Betsy, "How is he?"

Betsy looks at me over her mug, considering.

"Brilliant," I say. "The word you're looking for is *brilliant*."

"Not bad," she says.

Coleman grins.

Indignant, I say, "You've been teaching with me for more than a semester now, and the best you can say is I'm 'not bad'?"

"I've seen worse," Betsy says.

"Getting Mark Mitchell engaged in class conversation is a lot better than *not bad*." I insist.

"That's funny," Betsy says. "I never have trouble getting Mark to talk in class."

"That's because he loves you," I say.

Betsy dismisses this with a wave of her hand. "You just need to know how to engage them, get them to do what you want."

"I'm a teacher, not a psychologist."

Betsy frowns in mock puzzlement. "There's a difference?"

Coleman noisily sips his coffee. "This is cute and everything," he says, "but I was actually asking because I'm going to need your observation notes before you go on maternity leave."

"About that," Betsy says. "Any luck finding a sub yet?"

Coleman's phone makes a loud *ding*, interrupting whatever response he's about to make, and with an irritated grunt he pulls it out of his pocket and glances at his screen. "Speak of the devil," he says. "Got a teacher interested in a long-term sub position who just showed up at the front desk."

"Please, Baby Jesus," Betsy says.

The bell in the hallway chimes, signaling five minutes before class starts.

"I'll check on the sub and fill you in later," Coleman says. He motions us out with his coffee mug. "Go on, go mold young minds."

"More like scrape the mold off of them," I say. "I'll bring your mug back later." I go to the door and hold it open. "Come on, young Jedi."

Betsy picks up her workbag. "Whatever, Yoda," she says.

THE WHITEBOARD AT the front of my classroom has the words EVIL, TEMPTATION, and DISRUPTIVE written in red marker. I circle EVIL and then draw lines from it to each of the other two words. This is what my student Sarah Solomon has dubbed the Trinity of Terror. I turn to face my AP English students, who are all seated in a half circle before me in their school uniforms: white button-down shirts, gray flannels for the boys, plaid skirts for the girls. Their laptops are open on their desks, their copies of *Macbeth* balanced on their knees. "So," I ask, "what's Shakespeare saying about evil and Macbeth?"

Mark Mitchell stirs, his moon face rimmed by blue-black stubble. "He likes it. Being evil."

Sarah Solomon squints behind her cat-eye glasses. "Does he?" she asks. "He freaks out after he murders the king, he keeps getting frustrated by the witches—"

"The man's complicated," Mark says.

I tap the whiteboard under the word TEMPTATION. "So what tempts him?"

A pause as my students reorient themselves to the class discussion. Then Mark shrugs. "He wants power and his wife's a psycho."

I shake my head. "True, but that's not enough." I start pacing back and forth in front of the whiteboard. "He's not some greedy pushover who gets bullied by his wife. He wouldn't be a compelling character if he were. It's not just ambition. Macbeth *knows* he's doing something wrong. He murders the king of Scotland in his own home, then frames the king's sons for it and takes the throne. He sends murderers to kill his best friend and his friend's son. He has Macduff's entire family slaughtered. He ends up literally alone in his castle at the end, no friends, his wife dead, facing Macduff. He never convinces himself that anything he does is the right thing to do. He *knows* it's wrong, the entire time. So why does he do it?"

My students look at me, an audience awaiting a revelation. I have them hooked. I'm good at this, good enough to know that I shouldn't do the whole sage-on-the-stage thing all the time. But there are times it works well. Like now.

I stop in the center of the horseshoe of desks. "Because he wants to," I say. "He knows it's wrong, and he does it anyway."

My classroom door opens again, but I don't look to see who's coming in. All my students are present. It's probably Coleman dropping by to watch me teach; he does that occasionally. Besides, I'm in the flow, onstage, before my students, and I don't want to lose my momentum.

"The witches plant an idea in Macbeth's head that he knows is dead wrong, and he can't shake it loose," I continue. "He cannot stop imagining himself as king. And he murders the king, literally has his blood all over his hands. He commits himself to evil. And he pays a high price for it—he can't sleep, he's shaken with fear, he isolates himself from the rest of humanity. Lady Macbeth goes mad and kills herself. But Macbeth goes on. He self-destructs, but he does it on his own terms. It's awful and awesome in the original sense of the word—inspiring fear and wonder. Look at his last words to Macduff. He realizes all is lost, and Macduff even offers him a way to surrender, but Macbeth throws his shield forward. 'Lay on, Macduff, / And damned be him that first cries, "Hold, enough!" ' "

I stop. My students sit unmoving, caught up in this vision of Macbeth. Even Mark looks intrigued, nodding in agreement.

I turn toward the doorway, ready with a smile or a quick retort if it's Coleman. Coleman is there, all right, leaning against the wall and smiling. But it's the woman with him who brings the world to a temporary stop. The last time I saw her, she was facedown on a hotel bed, naked, sleeping. Now, in a navy-blue pantsuit, Marisa Devereaux stands in my classroom, hands clasped, and gives me the smallest of smiles, applauding my performance.

# CHAPTER FIVE

"Sorry to interrupt," Coleman says in a stage whisper. He's smiling like a man who just learned his earlier diagnosis was wrong and he doesn't have cancer after all. "I just wanted to introduce you."

Marisa gives me a proper smile now, professional and courteous. I stand for a moment just looking at the two of them, flummoxed. *Why is she here?* I'm surprised and self-conscious and also feel the pleasant buzz of attraction.

I realize I'm standing there like a schmuck, my students looking at me and Father Coleman and Marisa, so I tell my class to get started on their homework and I step out into the hallway with Coleman and Marisa. "Hi," I say, taking Marisa's hand. It's soft and smooth and well manicured. I realize I don't know whether I should refer to having already met her or introduce myself as if for the first time.

Marisa solves the problem for me. "Nice to see you again," she says. "Did you enjoy the conference?" She continues to smile, but there's no suggestive tone, no sly wink or quick squeeze of my hand. She lets my hand go.

"Yeah," I say. "Yes. It was good."

"Marisa met Byron at the conference," Coleman says. Byron Radinger is Archer's assistant head of school. "She's looking for a position," Coleman adds, raising his eyebrows at me. "Byron was impressed and invited her to visit."

I turn back to Marisa. "You're the sub?"

Marisa looks a little bashful. "I'm sorry I didn't call first to make an appointment," she says. "I was heading up to Kennesaw State this morning—there's an adjunct instructor position there—but traffic was so bad I called to tell them I'd be late. They said 285 was shut down, so they rescheduled me for tomorrow. So I got off the highway and realized I was right near Archer, and I remembered talking with Ethan"—she turns to me—"about how you all needed a long-term sub, and since I was already dressed for an interview, I just took a chance."

We talked about the sub position at the hotel bar on Friday night. It was early in the conversation, only one drink in. Marisa had asked about Archer, and I had mentioned Betsy Bales and the long-term sub debacle. That was before we ordered more drinks and started flirting and wound up in bed together.

Coleman smiles. "I, for one, am glad you took that chance," he says. His relief is clearly palpable.

We all stand there for a moment, smiling at each other, while I try to wrap my brain around the idea that Marisa might end up being Betsy's sub. Might? Coleman looks like he would hire her on the spot. "So, where are you teaching now?" I ask.

The smile on her face falters a little. "I was teaching at the Hastings School up in Connecticut until last summer. I came back to Atlanta to help take care of my mother—she's had some medical issues. But she's better, and so I'm back out on the job market."

"I'm sorry to hear about your mother," I say, and Marisa nods in appreciation.

"Ethan, I'll let you get back to your class," Coleman says, "but I'd like you and Betsy to talk with Marisa after lunch. Tell her about the position, get a sense of whether or not this would be a good fit."

"Betsy's got a doctor's appointment at one," I say.

Coleman looks at his watch. "I'm trying to get Marisa to meet with Teri and Byron and a few other folks this morning," he says. "Guess it'll just be the two of you, then."

Marisa turns to me with a smile and a slightly raised eyebrow.

"Sure," I say, trying to ignore the nervous flutters in my stomach. "You bet."

AFTER TEACHING CLASSES all morning and grabbing a quick lunch in the dining hall—a cavernous room of long tables, wooden beams overhead, and high windows that the students have dubbed Hogwarts— I return to my empty classroom to find Marisa sitting in the front row, looking at her phone. She puts her phone down and stands, smiling. "Hey," she says.

"Hey," I say. "How was your morning? They run you through the gauntlet?"

She holds up her hand and ticks off her responses one by one. "Assistant head, principal, athletic director, dean of students, and lunch with a few student council kids. Pretty comprehensive."

"That's Archer." I pull a chair around to face her, and we both sit down.

"How long have you taught here?" she asks.

"This is my fourth year," I say.

"You like it?"

I nod. "It's a good place. The coffee is terrible, but Coleman supplements that with his own supply. What do you think so far?"

She considers the question. "The adults seem to care a lot," she says. "The students seem bright, mostly eager, polite. As for the coffee, Coleman's is fine."

We smile at each other. I realize I'm fidgeting with a pen and put it down on the desk. In college, whenever you hooked up with someone and had to sneak out the next morning, it could be awkward later running into him or her between classes or in the student center. Sometimes a relationship would form, either casual or serious. Other times you'd cut your eyes away and avoid future one-on-one encounters. That was the route I usually took. Except now I'm interviewing a woman I slept with four days ago, a woman I could very well end up co-teaching with.

"So," I say, thinking I'll ask her about the classes she's taught.

"So I wanted to—" she says at the same time. We both stop.

"Go ahead," I say.

"No, you—"

"Please," I say, gesturing with an open hand.

She smiles, looking down at her desk, then looks back up at me. "I wanted to say I enjoyed seeing you teach this morning."

"Oh," I say, flattered and embarrassed. "Thanks. I found that lecture on *Macbeth* online somewhere. I didn't come up with it."

Marisa shakes her head. "Maybe not, but you're good at this. You aren't just reading some notes off a page to your students." She grins. "Makes sense, I guess. I mean, Faulkner, English teacher . . . you aren't actually related to William Faulkner, are you?"

I smile. "No, but students ask occasionally. My mom taught English."

"She must be proud," Marisa says. "Does she give you tips?"

"She died," I say. "When I was a kid." I'm shocked that I'm saying this, especially to a relative stranger—I've spoken to only two other people at school about my parents—but I feel the urge to share this, to unload a bit of this dark thing I carry around with me.

"Oh," Marisa says, her eyes rounding. She reaches over and touches my forearm, and her touch stirs something in me. Not lust; it's more like gratitude. "I'm so sorry," she says.

"Thank you," I say. She nods and removes her hand, and I'd be lying if I said I don't want her to put it back.

"Well," she says, and she stands up. I get to my feet as well. "I'm sorry to run, but Coleman wanted me to check in with him before school ended." She holds out her hand, and we shake. "I really hope this works out. I know you all are in a bind with your colleague going on maternity leave and the sub having quit on you. But I'd love the opportunity to work with you all."

"Likewise," I say. We stand there for a moment, looking at each other. "Marisa," I say, and I feel like I'm stepping into a field with a deep hole hidden somewhere in it. "About last Friday . . ."

She smiles, a tentative curve of her lips. "I was wondering when you would bring that up."

"I just . . . I'm sorry if that—embarrasses you, or anything," I say. "I know I just left the next morning, and maybe today was a little awkward, but—"

"Ethan," she says, and I shut my mouth. "It's fine," she says. "We're adults. I'm a big girl. It was consensual, and fun. But I'm here for a job, and I don't want to make things complicated for you or me."

"Oh," I say. Oddly, I'm both relieved and just a bit disappointed.

She tilts her head, as if considering me from a new angle. "If me working here is a problem, please, tell me now, and we can work it out."

"No, it's fine," I say, shaking my head.

"Or I can go to Kennesaw State and their lovely adjunct position." She makes a little pout at that.

Now I laugh. "No, seriously, it's fine," I say. "It wouldn't be a problem at all."

She smiles, clearly relieved, and holds her hand out again. I take it and she squeezes softly. "Thank you," she says. "For everything today."

"Good luck," I tell her, and I watch her as she walks out the door. She turns to look back over her shoulder, tosses me one last smile, and she's gone.

# CHAPTER SIX

When I get home from work, Susannah greets me at the door wearing her *Get Up the Yard* T-shirt, artfully torn jeans, and black Doc Martens laced halfway up her calves. "We're going out for drinks and food," she announces. "Pick somewhere that has lots of both. My treat."

I look over at Wilson, who is eyeing me from his bed and thumping his tail. I put my workbag down, walk over, and crouch down to scratch his belly. "What did you do to him?" I ask as Wilson half closes his eyes in doggy ecstasy. "He normally dances around when I come home."

"Took him on a long walk around the neighborhood," Susannah says. "Fed him lots of treats. He's half comatose; he'll be fine. I just took him out to pee. I've been stuck here all day. I even mopped your damn floors, which, by the way, were probably violating an EPA rule."

"I thought the EPA was a bunch of hippies who believe in global warming."

"Come on, Ethan," she says, making a pouty face. "I'm hungry."

Part of me wants to just have a beer and order a pizza and stare at the TV. I still need to process what happened today at work with Marisa Devereaux. But I'm sure as hell not going to talk about it with my sister. "You're so pushy," I tell her.

She grins, a dazzling show of teeth. "I'm assertive and cute."

WE GO TO the Palms, a brewery three blocks up Roswell Road that serves good pub food along with craft beers. They have a pool table in the back, and after Susannah has had a beer, she heads to the pool table and hands me a cue from a rack on the wall. "Age before beauty," she says.

We play a round and I win, sinking the eight ball into a far-corner pocket. "Lucky shot," Susannah says, but she smiles as she says it.

"You're in a good mood," I say.

"Mercury's out of retrograde," she says, taking a sip of her beer. "Hey, I forgot to ask; how's Frankie?"

I bend over my cue, chalking the tip and wishing I could avoid the question. "He's good," I say. I finish with the chalk and put it back on the edge of the table, and when I look up, Susannah is staring at me.

"You didn't go see him," she says.

I sigh. "No, I didn't go see him."

"So when's the last time you *did* see him?" Her stare is getting sulfurous. "Last Thanksgiving? What about the year before that?"

I shake my head.

"You haven't seen him since you and I went together? That's over *two years* ago. What the hell, Ethan?"

I start putting balls into the triangle on the table. "I didn't want to," I say.

"Didn't want to? He's your *friend*."

"I know that."

"Did you feel *guilty*, or—"

"I didn't want to go by myself," I say.

She puts her hand on her hip, her other hand holding the cue with the butt end on the ground, like she's planting a flag. "Don't put that on me," she says.

I roll the triangle of balls on the felt, hearing their muted *clack*, then lift the triangle off and hang it on its hook on the wall by the cue sticks. "You weren't here," I say. "It didn't feel right to go alone."

Susannah narrows her eyes in disappointment. "You think Frankie wasn't alone?"

I lean my cue against the table. "I need to take a leak," I say.

"Yeah, you do that," Susannah mutters, grabbing the cue ball and lining up her shot.

AFTER OUR PARENTS died and Susannah and I moved in with Uncle Gavin and Fay, the world, to my disgust, kept turning. I still went to school. I tried to become invisible and inured to the profound hole in the center of my world. What I really wanted was the opposite, to have someone truly care for me, to let me cry and grieve and grope around in the dark to find hope again. But I was thirteen years old, and although I could understand Shakespeare and algebra and the history of ancient Rome, I had little or no clue about how to act like a human being. This was complicated by the fact that everyone at school treated me as if one wrong word would cause me to either dissolve or explode. So I withdrew into my hooded sweat shirt and walled out everyone. After a few weeks, everyone else in eighth grade quit acting like I was going to have a screaming meltdown in the middle of earth science and they all left me more or less alone.

And then, the summer before high school, I began working at Uncle Gavin's bar, where I met Frankie.

My uncle's bar is in Midtown, at West Peachtree and Eleventh Street. The frontage is all dark green and windows, *Ronan's* etched in glass above the black front door. Uncle Gavin named it after where he and my mother were from, Cill Rónáin on Inis Mór, an island west of Galway. Uncle Gavin thought *Ronan* would be easier for people to pronounce. We always went in a service door on the side, which opened onto a short hallway with worn wooden floors. There was the scent of beer and fried food and the zing of some sort of industrial cleaner. We would pass a private room or two, then go through a swinging door that led past a staircase before entering the kitchen. That's where I worked that summer, and then all through high school, washing dishes.

Uncle Gavin's business partner, Ruben Gutierrez, essentially ran the bar, at least the day-to-day operations. I can remember him standing in the middle of the kitchen in dark slacks, a maroon shirt, and a black fedora pushed back on his head, his hands moving expressively as he talked. The first time Susannah and I met him, soon after our parents' funeral, he gripped my hand firmly, like one adult to another, and he clasped Susannah's hand in both of his, as if about to get down on one knee and propose. Ruben was theatrical, perhaps, but I could see sorrow in his broad face. I was surprised, would continue to be surprised for a time, by being the subject of such sympathy. It's not that I was a cynic—I understood why people were reacting this way to my loss, how it was a kind, human gesture. But I did not know the protocols of grief, or how to react.

Ruben's son, who was my age, also started working at the bar that summer. He was named Francisco, although he told me to call him Frankie. Some people are like a bright flame in a cave, rendering everyone else in flickering shadow, and that was Frankie. Within seconds of meeting him I felt self-conscious about the old pair of Target-brand jeans and the indistinct polo shirt I'd put on. Frankie wore crisp Levi's the color of midnight and a bright-red short-sleeve button-down. He needed only a black fedora to complete the picture of his father. It took me a week to realize that Frankie alternated wearing the red shirt and its identical twins in yellow and green, but he wore the exact same pair of jeans every day. Eventually Frankie told me he washed those jeans every night to get rid of the stink of food, but he washed them in the sink so they wouldn't fade. "Always gotta look good, man," he said. "That's my motto. They'll put it on my tombstone."

As we washed dishes and racked clean glasses and plates, Frankie would talk nonstop about Braves baseball, the *Twilight* movies, crunk music, how there was going to be a Hispanic comic-book Spider-Man, the relative hotness factors of the bar's waitresses, his eternal love for Salma Hayek and Lindsay Lohan, his utter hatred of *The Old Man and the Sea* ("Guy finally catches the fish, and then the sharks *eat* it, the end—*¿qué chingados es eso?*"), and the '71 Pontiac Firebird Trans Am his father was teaching him to repair.

One day, after a couple of hours of spraying pots and pans and cleaning down the grill after the lunch rush, Frankie said, "My dad told me about your parents, man. That sucks."

A sudden sorrow rose in my throat, threatening to squeeze it shut. I pushed a rack of dishes into the dishwasher and pulled the door down, starting the cycle. "Yeah," I managed. My eyes prickled, but I wouldn't cry. I glanced at Frankie. He was looking at me, but it wasn't the look of someone who was waiting for me to share the gruesome details. "Yeah, it sucks," I said.

Frankie nodded. "My Aunt Josie died two years ago. My mom's sister. Mom was brokenhearted, you know? Wouldn't get out of bed."

"I'm sorry," I said. "Was your aunt sick?"

"Drive-by. Wrong place, wrong time." Frankie frowned, stacking clean glasses on a shelf. "My mom's been sick for a while now. Josie was a nurse, would take care of everyone when we got sick. Now . . ." He shrugged, then picked up a stack of plates. "Gonna take these out to the wait station."

"You just want to get a look at Sally's *culo*," I said. Sally was one of the waitresses—cute, blonde, and in her twenties.

Frankie grinned, a flash of big white teeth. "Listen to the *güero* speaking the Spanish!" he said—*güero* meaning "white boy" or "blondie," a joke aimed at my red hair. "I'm so proud." Then he dropped his voice into a Barry White register. "But Sally *does* have a sweet ass." He walked out of the kitchen, still grinning.

I watched the dishwasher vibrate, listened to the water shooting around inside it. Frankie was the first person my age I'd met who had some sort of ability to understand what had happened to my parents, to me. He hadn't pressed for details. And when Frankie had opened up about his aunt and I'd made a lame joke about Sally because I was awkward about sharing anything personal, Frankie had gone along with it. I realized, listening to the dishwasher churn, that Frankie might be the kind of friend you kept for life.

NOW, STANDING AT the urinal in the men's room of the Palms, which is paneled in dark wood and smells of disinfectant and beer, I think about Frankie, Susannah's words echoing in my head: *He's your friend. You think Frankie wasn't alone?* I pee, hoping to void the guilt as well, and mostly failing. Susannah and I had been making a yearly pilgrimage every Thanksgiving to Morgan, Georgia, to visit Frankie in Calhoun State Prison, up until two years ago when Susannah went AWOL. I told Susannah it hadn't felt right to go alone, and that's true, as far as it goes. What I didn't say was that going to see Frankie had become less and less about going to see our friend and more and more about fulfilling a yearly ritual with my sister. With Susannah gone and out of touch for most of the past two years, I'd decided not to drive the three hours alone to see Frankie. I was surprised at how simple that decision had been to make, how easy it had been to justify it to myself, and how hard the backlash of shame slapped me upside my head.

When I finish, flush, and wash my hands and can't skulk in the bathroom any longer, I go back out and head to the pool table. Halfway there I stop. Three guys, maybe college age or a little older, are standing around Susannah, who is leaning over the pool table to make a shot. One of the guys, his red polo shirt untucked from his jeans and his two days' growth of beard trimmed just so, is talking to her while staring down the front of her shirt. I can tell that Susannah is leaning over the table deliberately, hiking her ass in the air and showing her cleavage. Jesus.

"Come on," Red Polo is saying. "Just one game. If I win, you tell me your name."

"And if I win?" Susannah says, still focused on her shot.

"I tell you *my* name," Red Polo says, flashing a high-wattage smile that would not look out of place on a red carpet.

Susannah shoots, the cue ball striking the racked balls with a *crack* that makes everyone blink, followed by a *thok* as she pockets the seven ball in the corner. She stands up, pulling her shoulders back, and gives Red Polo a sad smile that is just this side of a smirk. "You can't sell me something that I don't want," she says.

One of Red Polo's buddies, in a blue polo and glasses, smiles and shakes his head. The third guy, wearing a black T-shirt with the Jack Daniels logo on the front, actually snickers. Red Polo glances at Jack Daniels, his smile dimming, then turns his attention back to Susannah. "Trust me," he says. "You want to know me."

"Okay," I say, stepping forward, and all three guys turn to stare at me. Susannah does, too, but with a grin that's half welcoming, half irritated—I just interrupted her playing time. "Y'all go get a drink and let us get back to our game," I tell the three guys.

Red Polo frowns. "Who the hell are you?" he says.

"Her brother," I say, at the same time Susannah says, "My boyfriend." I resist the urge to close my eyes and groan and instead watch Red Polo and his friends. I'm not big or intimidating, but Red Polo looks at his buddies, nonplussed, then back at me, and shrugs.

"Sorry, man," he says, then turns toward the bar, the other two following his lead.

I let out a breath I didn't know I was holding and start to say something to Susannah, but she's already stalking after Red Polo. "Hey!" she says, and Red Polo stops and turns around, startled. Susannah marches up to him, looking up into his face. "You were all over me at the pool table, but now another dude shows up and you're like, 'My bad, bro, didn't know she was yours'? What am I, property?"

Red Polo stares at her. "What?" he says, sounding lost.

"I'd like an apology," Susannah says.

Red Polo's expression morphs into something between a sneer and a scowl. "What is your problem?"

Susannah takes a step closer to him and, her voice dripping with disdain, says, "You and your *man* act."

Red Polo clearly doesn't like his masculinity being threatened. His half sneer turns into a snarl, and he makes to shove Susannah away. Susannah grabs his wrist with one hand and with her other grips his arm, her thumb digging into the meat above his elbow. He rises on his toes in pain, and when he tries to twist away, she stomps on his foot with her Doc Martens before letting go. "Shit!" he yelps, and then takes a hard swing at her with an open hand. Susannah raises her arm, blocking his slap while bringing her elbow up into his chin, then follows with a palm strike to his eyes. He cries out and staggers back a couple of steps.

Jack Daniels, who is behind Susannah and out of her line of sight, starts to make a move, then stops when I whip a pool cue around so the cue end of it is under the soft part of his jaw. "Uh-uh," I say, pressing into his neck with the cue so he steps back. I glance over at Blue Polo, who raises his hands as if in surrender.

"You fucking bitch," Red Polo says, seething and glaring at Susannah. "You are dead."

A large hand clamps down on the back of Red Polo's neck. The bartender, a big bald guy with a beard and an earring, has decided to intervene. In a deep voice corroded with a lifetime of cigarette smoke, he tells Red Polo, "Get out."

"That bitch assaulted me!" Red Polo says.

The bartender shakes Red Polo gently, like a Rottweiler with a rope bone. "Self-defense," he says. "After you harassed her. Out."

Susannah smiles at Red Polo as if sympathetic. "'Bye, Felicia," she says.

After Red Polo and his posse leave, the bartender, who introduces himself as Jerry, offers us a drink on the house. "Nice job dealing with those assholes," Jerry says to Susannah.

She gives him a little smile. "Instead of a drink, how about a job?" she says. "You need a waitress?"

Jerry grins, an ugly contraction of his face that still manages to be friendly. "I might at that," he says. "You waited tables before?"

"Our uncle—" I start to say, about to mention Uncle Gavin by name, say how both of us worked at his bar, but Susannah interrupts.

"Our uncle made sure we always got a job in the summers growing up," she says, smoothly cutting me off. "I've waited tables."

"You won't have any problems dealing with drunk frat boys, that's for sure," Jerry mused. "Not that we really get a lot of them. Tell you what, you bring me a résumé, and I'll get you started on a couple shifts this week."

Done with pool, we decide we're ready to eat, and we sit in a booth and order burgers and another round of beers. After the waitress takes our order, I say to Susannah, "Why didn't you want me to mention Uncle Gavin?"

She takes a long pull at her beer. "I don't need his help," she says. "Got this on my own. Two days here and already got a job offer. Did you see the look on that preppy boy's face?"

"I tend to remember when people look at my sister like they want to murder her."

"He was being a dick. Nice work with the pool cue, by the way. Thought you were gonna spear that poor guy in the neck."

I frown. She had her back to me when I was holding the Jack Daniels kid at bay. "How did you—" I stop and look over at the bar and its mirrored back wall. "You saw my reflection."

"Elementary, my dear Watson," Susannah says, raising her glass as if toasting me. "See, this is fun."

47

# CHAPTER SEVEN

Fᴇʙʀᴜᴀʀʏ ɪs ᴜsᴜᴀʟʟʏ ᴀ ʟᴏᴜsʏ ᴛɪᴍᴇ ᴏғ ʏᴇᴀʀ ɪɴ sᴄʜᴏᴏʟ—ɪᴛ's ᴄᴏʟᴅ, it rains a lot, and seniors especially are getting antsy. Spring break can't come soon enough. This year, I'm too busy to pay attention. Susannah showing up on my doorstep radically recalibrated things. She's still crashing on my couch, although now she's waiting tables at the Palms and is looking at apartments. She's also started going back to group therapy, and she hasn't brought up Frankie again either. All in all, it's good, or as good as it gets with Susannah.

Teaching with Marisa has been surprisingly nice. She gets the kids, and while there's been a little resistance, simply because they like Betsy Bales so much, they're warming up to her. She's focused and funny, a good combination with teenagers. And she is very careful to walk that line between taking over the class and letting me be in charge of everything. Not bad for only two weeks on the job. Coleman was ecstatic, of course. We were all relieved—no one wanted to hire a babysitter while we looked through whatever résumés we had left on file, scraping deeper and deeper at the bottom of a pretty crummy barrel.

Marisa hasn't mentioned our night together again, and neither have I. Which is good. Except I admit to being distracted sometimes by her hair, or her throaty laugh, or how she walks. It's not professional of me, but it bothers me for another reason.

I got this teaching job on my own. Yes, it helped that my mother was a teacher and that my boss used to work with her. But my uncle had zero to do with it. I've walled off that part of my life and built this new life, carefully, brick by brick. It's mine, and I know every layer and crevice of it.

I've built different walls, too, thicker ones, around myself. I'm no wilting flower, and I'm not an insensitive jackass, either. But like I said before, I've found it easier to casually hook up with women than to create and maintain a relationship. I've told myself it's because I'm young, that I don't want to be tied down, that I enjoy being a bachelor. Deep at night, on the edge of sleep, I can admit to myself that it's because I don't want to get hurt, that I'm afraid of how I would react if I lost someone else I cared about. Breaking up with a girlfriend is not the same thing as losing one's parents to sudden violence. But I dated two women semiseriously, one in college and one after, and when each relationship ended I felt gutted, hollowed out, my first instinct to lash out and make my ex feel the same way. I did that in college when my first girlfriend, Caroline, dumped me for another boy, and I said horrible, spiteful things that made her burst into tears before I marched self-righteously out of her dorm room, slamming the door behind me. When I broke up with my second girlfriend, Dani, it was more of a mutual thing—we liked each other, but neither of us was interested in getting married. There had been no other guy, and Dani had been nice. But despite that, I had the same mean desire to make her feel awful for bringing up a fact that had been true for some time: that we had been drifting away from each other. In that instance, to whatever little credit I deserve, I held my tongue, although I wasn't as warm and understanding as I could have been.

So whenever Marisa smiles at me and my heart seems to turn over in a way that is not unpleasant, I examine the state of the walls I've raised around me, looking for cracks or gaps, and I shore up my defenses as best I can, as if I'm a stone fortress and not a human being.

THE SAME DAY we get word that Betsy Bales has had her baby—a little girl named Allison, seven pounds and healthy—Marisa is in my office after school to go over a reading assignment for our students, Coleridge's poem

"Kubla Khan." She borrows a pen from me to take notes while I give her some background—how Coleridge took laudanum and fell asleep reading about Kubla Khan and had a strange, vivid dream about the Mongol ruler and Xanadu. When he woke up, he had two or three hundred lines of verse in his head and started to write them down. But then someone interrupted Coleridge and he stepped away from his desk for a few hours, and by the time he returned, he found to his frustration that he couldn't remember the dream-vision or the poem. All he was able to write was a weird, fragmented piece of verse about a pleasure dome, fountains erupting out of chasms, sunless seas, demon lovers, visions, repressed passions, and the mad power of art.

Maybe I should blame Coleridge and his bizarre poem for what happens next.

Marisa and I are hunched forward in our chairs, as if conspiring over the poem in her hand. I finish talking, and for a few moments neither of us speaks. Then Marisa leans forward, and when I look up from the poem, her face is perhaps a foot away from my own, her eyes on mine. Everything pauses, like the universe is holding its breath. This close to her, I can smell some sort of underlying spice, a blend of vanilla and pepper. Her lips are barely parted, her eyes wide.

In a low voice, almost a whisper, Marisa says, "Do you want to kiss me?"

"Oh," I say. My brain feels like someone just unplugged it and it's slow to reboot, but it's trying to throw up barriers like it usually does. "I . . . I mean, do *you*?"

Something flickers across her expression—disappointment, embarrassment? She withdraws a bit, increasing the distance between us. "I'm sorry," she says. "I mean, if you don't want to, that's fine; I just thought—"

"No," I say. "That's not—I mean, yes. Yes. I would like that. It's only . . ." I take a breath, let it out. This is stupid. But those damn walls always rise up, boxing me in. "We work together," I say finally. It is a statement of fact instead of an argument.

Her expression relaxes and she smiles shyly. "You're my coworker, not my boss," she says. "And I'm an adult. Consenting." She hesitates, then leans forward. "And if you want to keep it quiet at work, I won't talk to anyone." She holds me in her gaze. "Anyone."

If I was surprised earlier, now I feel like I've been clubbed over the head with a railroad tie. Marisa is wearing an ivory camisole underneath her navy blouse. I think about how the silk would feel in my hands. I try to remember how her mouth tasted, and I want nothing more than to find out again.

"I'm on the pill," she says. "And I've been tested. No HIV, nothing." She lifts an eyebrow. "How about you?"

"Yes," I said. "I mean, no. I mean, yes, I've been tested, but . . . I don't have anything."

Marisa reaches over and drops my pen back into my shirt pocket, her face only inches from mine, and then withdraws, but then she pauses, resting her fingertips on the inside of my wrist. "If you don't want to," she says, "I'll walk away and never mention it again. It won't be a problem." She lightly strokes my wrist. "But I think we would both regret it."

Her eyes are gray washed with green. Athena had those kind of eyes, according to Homer. Bright, all-encompassing. I want to swim in them, in her. And why not? Why the hell not? The walls crack, their foundations crumbling.

She leans forward, hesitates for the briefest moment, and then kisses me, a deliberate, soft pressure of her lips on my mouth. She pulls back and considers me. "Not bad," she says, and then grins, triumphant.

I reach out and cup my hand to the back of her head and return that kiss properly, fully, like I am drinking her in, the last wall collapsing under the spell of that kiss, the taste of her lips, her pepper-vanilla scent twining around us.

THAT SATURDAY WE have a dinner date, and I get to the restaurant about ten minutes early. It's a South African place with a good wine list and spiced chicken and beef dishes that wake up your mouth, just cool and different enough to be impressive without breaking the bank. Susannah, thank God, left earlier to go to a concert downtown with a coworker and said she was going to spend the night at her coworker's apartment in Midtown, so while I was getting ready I didn't have to explain where I was going or answer questions about why I was dressing up for a date.

Right on time, Marisa arrives at the restaurant in an Uber. She didn't want me to pick her up, which is a little odd. I know she moved back home to take care of her mother, and the one or two times she's mentioned it she's seemed upset by it, so I let it go. I wonder if she's embarrassed by her parents. But when she steps out of her Uber, all those thoughts are blown away like so much smoke. Marisa is an attractive woman, but tonight everyone—the valets and the two guys going into the restaurant and even the two girls with them—is looking at her. She's wearing a short black dress that shows off her legs. Her dark hair falls to her bare shoulders, framing her face. "Hi," she says.

"Hi," I say reflexively. I don't swallow, but it's a near thing. "Wow. You look amazing."

She smiles and kisses me on the cheek, sending a pleasant thrill up my spine. "Why, thank you," she says, taking my arm. "You don't look half bad yourself."

We are seated at our table, and our waiter comes and delivers the standard patter about specials and house specialties. Marisa listens to him with a half smile, the candlelight softening her face, glinting off her hair.

"Do you like wine?" I ask, picking up the wine list.

"A day without wine is like a day without sunshine," she replies, and for a second everything skips a beat. A memory as clear and bright as a new coin drops into my head—sitting at the dinner table with my parents, Susannah in a high chair, a box of takeout pizza on the counter, my father pouring my mother a glass of wine. *A day without wine is like a day without sunshine*, he said to her, smiling, and then he kissed her.

Marisa frowns slightly. "Ethan? Something wrong?"

I shake my head and make myself smile. "No," I say brightly. "Not a thing. You like red or white?"

We choose a South African red. The waiter brings it and pours for both of us, then leaves without asking for our orders. That annoys me until I realize the waiter is deliberately not rushing us, giving us time.

The memory of my parents has thrown the evening slightly off-kilter, and I take a breath, willing myself to relax. The red wine helps.

"This is nice," Marisa says, swirling her wine gently in her glass. "But it's a little backwards."

She has caught me midsip, and I swallow my wine quickly. "You don't like it?" I say, indicating the glass in my hand. "We can order a different bottle."

She shakes her head and leans forward a little, looking me in the eye and dropping her voice just a notch. "I mean this. Going out on a date, to a nice dinner, getting to know each other better." She gives the barest hint of a smile, the corner of her mouth slowly rising. "Usually that's what happens before you go to bed with someone."

I wait a beat, watching her smile widen, and then I match it with one of my own. "That's the usual course of events," I say.

She laughs and tips her glass toward me, conceding a point.

DINNER IS GOOD, our conversation easy and pleasant. But beneath it all is a strong current that tugs at both of us, rising slowly like a river we have waded into. It strengthens when we share a dessert, when the check comes and we flirt over who is paying for dinner, when we walk outside and come to that moment where Marisa will need to call an Uber or not.

"I can take you home," I say. "If you want."

Marisa is leaning into me, my arm around her, and that vanilla-pepper scent wraps around me. She turns her head so her lips are at my ear. "I don't want to go home," she says.

The valet brings my car around. I'm not sure how I manage to drive us home, in large part because Marisa rests her hand on my thigh as I'm driving. As it is, when I do get to my street, I go up my driveway fast enough that we bounce over the tree roots and I hit my head on the roof of the car. Marisa laughs, deep and throaty, and when I park the car I reach over and kiss her, hard, her mouth opening to mine and our tongues meeting, exploring. We barely get out of the car and into the house. I think fleetingly of how glad I am that Susannah is out tonight, and that I took Wilson to the vet today for his annual checkup and left him overnight because he loves to play with the other dogs, and then I'm fully swept up in the current that carries us down the hallway, Marisa's lips on my neck, her tongue teasing my ear, my fingers searching for the zipper at the back of her dress, and we are both swept over the edge and fall, limbs and mouths and hair entangled, onto my bed.

"WE," I SAY, a bit breathlessly, and then I have to wet my lips with my tongue because they are suddenly dry. "We need to do that again."

Marisa, having already made a discreet run to the bathroom, stretches luxuriantly next to me and gives an affirmative *mmm*. She nestles next to me, head on my shoulder, one leg over mine. "Definitely," she murmurs. Her hand splays across my chest, stroking gently.

I kiss her forehead. "Slower next time, maybe."

She turns her head to look up at me, her eyes wide and innocent. "You didn't like it?"

I smile and run one hand down her side, the curve of her hip. "I liked it fine," I say. "But I'd like to enjoy it for longer."

"Well, then," Marisa says, and she gracefully throws one leg over me so she's straddling me, arms on either side of my head, face inches above mine. In the dark I can hear the smile in her voice. "No time like the present."

AFTER, BOTH OF us lying on our backs, catching our breaths, I realize we are holding hands, Marisa's fingers entwined with mine. It's curiously more intimate than anything else we've done that evening. Something swells in my chest then, pleasant and warm and golden-light. It takes me a moment to realize it's happiness.

"Be right back," Marisa says; then she lets go of my hand and gets out of bed. I know she's just going to pee, but I don't like the empty side of the bed she leaves behind. I lay in the dark, my head and heart both whirling. *Lucky*, I keep thinking, like a mantra.

A flush, then Marisa padding across my room and getting back in bed. "Cold," she says, snuggling up to me.

"Do you want a T-shirt?" I ask. I feel her head nod against my chest. "Okay." I slide out from the covers and go to my chest of drawers, take out a T-shirt, and carry it back to her. As she pulls it on, I find my boxers and pull them up, then lie back down on my pillow, waiting for Marisa to curl up next to me, which she does. She's warm and smooth and . . . *present*, is the best way I can describe it. She's fully here, with me, my arm around her like it belongs there.

"God, I feel so close to you," she says, her lips brushing my shoulder.

I squeeze her in acknowledgment, my eyes drifting shut.

"It's like we can share anything," she says. "No secrets."

My eyes open.

"Tell me something I don't know about you," she says.

"I'm really, really good at *Jeopardy!*," I say.

She pinches my nipple gently. "Not like that," she says.

"Ow." I swat her hand away playfully.

She raises herself up on her side, looking at me. "Seriously," she says. "Tell me something I don't know about you."

I stare up at the ceiling, feeling as if I've stepped off a cliff and just realized it a split second before I began to fall. "Why?" I ask.

There's a pause, and I lie there in the dark, wondering if I've made a mistake.

Marisa says, "Because I want to know you."

It's a good answer. Part of me would like to ask that question too, although I'm afraid of the answer. "Okay," I say, thinking. "I'm scared that I'm not a good enough teacher."

Another pause. "Seriously?" she says. She sounds genuinely surprised.

"Yeah," I say to the darkened ceiling. "I am."

Another pause. "But you're so good at it," she says.

I shrug, then realize she probably can't see me shrug in the dark. "I've got a good act," I say. "Like a performer. It's not that I'm faking it. I like what I do, and I know things. I just—I don't know."

Marisa seems to hesitate, and then her fingers are brushing my arm, making tentative contact. "Is it because of your mom?" she asks softly.

The walls come up then, thick stone and barred windows. I close my eyes and concentrate, imagining that vault in my head, the place where I can stuff all those unwanted thoughts. "Maybe," I say, eyes still closed. In my mind I'm holding that overstuffed shoebox, now messily wrapped in duct tape, but the vault isn't there; it's some indistinct distance ahead of me. "Tell me about your mom," I say, still concentrating. I'm walking across a desert floor, sand beneath my feet, the shoebox in my hands growing heavier. And then I'm at the vault and I put the shoebox inside and slam the door shut with a *boom* . . .

I open my eyes, coming back to my darkened room, realizing Marisa hasn't said anything. "Hey," I say, turning to look at her. She's still there, lying on her side in my bed. "You okay?"

"I don't want to talk about that," she says, and her voice is flat.

"That's okay," I say, sitting up. "We don't have to talk about anything you don't want to."

I can't see her face clearly, although she's still looking at me. Then she sits up abruptly. "Oh gosh," she says, her voice back to normal. "It's late. I have to get back home."

"What? No," I say. "Please stay. I'm sorry I—"

"No, it's not—you didn't do anything; I just—"

"Come on," I say, reaching for her, but she's already sitting on the edge of the bed, looking for her clothes. I scoot across the bed and put my hand on her shoulder. "Marisa, I'm sorry, you can stay—"

She tenses up when I touch her, tight and coiled as a spring, and I almost take my hand away, but I leave it on her shoulder, touching her but not grasping. Then she lets out a breath, and some of that tension falls away. "It's okay, Ethan," she says, and she turns and kisses me, her lips pressing lightly against mine. "I just really have to go." She sighs. "My mom will need me."

"Okay," I say. "Sure." I take my hand off her shoulder. "I'll give you a ride home."

"No," she says. "I'll Uber home. I want you to stay here." She stands up and removes my T-shirt, and for a second I see her body, naked and pale in the shadows, before she pulls her dress over her head and tugs it down.

"But—" I say, protesting.

Marisa leans across the bed and kisses me, more fully this time. I try to pull her back into the bed with me, but she breaks away. "I really have to go," she says.

"Please let me drive you home."

She puts a hand on my chest and gently pushes me back down onto the bed. "I want you to stay here," she says.

"Marisa—"

"Shh." She lays a finger across my lips. "I want you to stay here, in your bed. And I want you to think about me."

"That won't be hard," I say against her finger.

"Good," she says. Then she gets off the bed, and I see the glow of her phone. "Uber is three minutes away," she says. And then she's gone. I hear the front door open and then shut.

"I'm sorry," I say aloud, without being entirely sure what I'm apologizing for.

I SPEND MOST of Sunday doing my usual chores, grocery shopping and cleaning and getting ready for the week to come, but I'm on autopilot, going through the motions while I try to figure out what happened with Marisa. I parse our dinner conversation like it's the Rosetta Stone, examining every word and gesture. I consider every kiss, every touch, every move we made in bed like a coach analyzing a game video. Was it weird that she wanted me to share something secret? Was it weird that I didn't want to? She brought up my mother, a topic I've almost always considered off-limits. But then I brought up her mother, too, and she closed down, her voice cold as Siberia. Can I blame her for that? But then she suddenly had to go home, and it was strange that she would rather take an Uber than let me drive her home. What the hell was that? Was she embarrassed by her family? Or was it some sort of emotional game she was playing with me? Because I don't need that kind of crap in my life.

These are the thoughts that swirl in my head all day as I wipe off the kitchen counters and clean my toilet and look for cereal and spaghetti at Publix. And I am no closer to a solution after all of that than I was last night.

Wilson does his usual happy dance when I pick him up from the vet, licking me eagerly when I take him home, so there is that.

ON MONDAY, I do not have my shared class with Marisa. Instead I teach my freshmen and catch up on grading and respond to emails and look over a draft of a test I will give my seniors—the usual. It is easier at work to silence the questions in my head about Marisa. But at lunch I find myself looking around for her, both wanting to see her and nervous about it. She isn't in the dining hall. When I ask Coleman if he's seen her, he says she is helping out with a student council meeting, so I let it go.

That afternoon after school, I am reading over some lecture notes about *Frankenstein* when there's a knock on my door, and I look up to see Marisa in the doorway. "Hi," she says. She is holding what looks like a gift bag tied with a green ribbon.

"Hi," I say.

We stay like that in awkward silence for a moment.

She holds out the gift bag. "I wanted to apologize. For how I left."

I stand. "Hey, if I did anything this weekend—"

"You didn't do anything," she says. "Take this, please."

I take the bag. "You didn't need to get me anything," I say.

She smiles. "I know."

I open the bag and laugh. Inside is an Archer coffee mug from the school gift shop, along with a Starbucks gift card.

"I know you like coffee," she says.

"Thank you," I say. "But I'll only accept this if you let me buy you a cup."

She wrinkles her nose, which is almost adorable. "I don't like coffee."

"You don't like coffee? Seriously?"

She raises an eyebrow. "Is that a problem?"

"Total deal breaker. I cannot possibly date anyone who doesn't like coffee."

Now both eyebrows are raised. "Why, Mr. Faulkner, are you asking me to be your girlfriend?"

"Maybe," I say, grinning.

She looks over her shoulder, as if checking, and then walks forward, her hands on my chest and pushing me back across my office. I have a storage closet at the far end of my office, the door now open, and Marisa directs me into the closet until I bump up against the stacked shelves. My hands find her waist, and she raises her arms so her hands rest on my shoulders. "Maybe I can do something to help you overlook my coffee problem," she says, her face lifted up to mine, and then we are kissing, long and lush and deep.

I break away first. "Marisa," I say, looking over her shoulder. No one is there.

She chuckles, then starts kissing my ear.

"Wait," I say. I don't want to wait, not at all, but both my office and supply closet are wide open. "What if someone comes by?"

Marisa slides away, my hands falling from her hips, and walks to the office door, closing it and pressing the push-button lock. Then she walks back to me, pulling the closet door shut partially shut behind her so we are in shadow rather than total darkness, sunlight from the classroom windows barely filtering through. She steps right up to me, placing her wrists on my shoulders so her fingertips are in my hair, her scent surrounding me. My hands find their way to her hips again. "Paulie doesn't come through here until four thirty," she says. Paulie is the custodian on our hallway. Marisa lowers her head slightly, her eyes still on mine. "Want to stop?"

A minute later, Marisa has her legs wrapped around me, her arms up and holding onto the shelves, which groan and shake as we ravish each other.

# CHAPTER EIGHT

"WHAT'S WRONG?" SUSANNAH ASKS.

"It's fine," I say, trying to shift into park. "Gearshift just gets stuck sometimes."

"Gear selector," Susannah says.

"What?"

"It's called a gear selector if you've got an automatic transmission," she says. "Which you do."

"Good to know," I say, struggling to shove the lever—gear selector—up. It doesn't want to budge. Then, with a *thunk* and a plastic crunch, it slides up to park. "See?" I say. "Right as rain."

"That's a stupid saying," Susannah says. "I hate rain."

"Rain is necessary for life," I say. "Plants need it, they make oxygen and feed herbivores, et cetera."

"Rain sucks when you're out standing in it. And there is nothing right about your car."

"What's wrong with my car? You don't like Japanese cars?"

"It could be a Tahitian car and your gear selector would still be fucked up. Take it to the garage."

I gesture out the windshield at the Petco store I've parked in front of. "We have to get food for Wilson."

"Which I'm sure he'll appreciate after we die in a car accident because your Tahitian automatic transmission seized up." Susannah starts tapping at her phone.

"I've got Pilates in two hours."

"Which you can Uber to from the Toyota garage. And the nearest one is like a mile up the road."

"I know. That's my regular garage."

"So let's go." She looks up from her phone. "You don't fuck around with stuff like this, Ethan. Trust me."

I open my mouth to say something snarky, but there's something in her voice, in the way she levels her gaze at me, that makes me stop. "Fine," I say. I put my key back into the ignition and start the engine. "Let Wilson starve."

"I left him half a sleeve of Ritz crackers," Susannah says. "He'll be fine."

"Tell me you're joking."

"What? They're Ritz crackers. How bad could they be?"

"Imagine a dog having violent diarrhea all over your living room."

She pauses, then starts tapping on her phone again.

"Don't look for a vet," I say. "I've already got one. You can pay that bill." I shift the car into drive, and the gear selector makes another ominous *thunk*.

"Think I'd rather get the vet bill than your car repair bill," Susannah says. She gestures lazily. "Onward, Jeeves."

BY THE TIME I get to the garage and explain the problem to Curtis the mechanic, I've already texted my Pilates instructor to tell her I'm not coming. Curtis rubs his beard and makes all sorts of dire predictions about the gearbox. I tell Susannah to get an Uber herself if she needs to go anywhere, but she elects to stay, claiming she can catch up on cable news in the customer lounge. But the one flat-screen TV is turned to the Discovery Channel, some show about a team of urban dog rescuers, and three kids stare openmouthed at the screen. Susannah and I settle in a far corner to wait.

"Bet it's just the lever," Susannah says. "Probably not the gearbox or the whole thing would've frozen up. I bet you got a piece of plastic that fell down in there somewhere."

"Is this like that thing people do during the Olympics, where suddenly they're experts in curling or whatever?" I ask. "Or do you actually know what you're talking about?"

Susannah snorts. "If I had a dime for every time some guy asked me that—"

"You'd have a dime-ond mine," I say.

"That's terrible," Susannah says. "I mean, like legitimately so bad it's almost good."

We sit quietly for a minute, wrapped in our own thoughts. As mine have done recently, they float toward Marisa. Having makeup sex with her in my office closet was insane, even a little disturbing—what if we'd been caught?—but I can't deny how even the thought of it makes my pulse quicken, sends a surge through my spine. But I don't want to talk about her with Susannah, who would latch on to her and suck all the joy and newness out of . . . what do Marisa and I have? Is this a relationship? It's been a sufficiently long time since I have seriously dated anyone that I'm hesitant to use that word, and it's early days yet, but what else would I call it? Not that I'm going to bring this up with my sister—if I mention Marisa at all, Susannah will sense my hesitation and pounce. Hell, she might pick up on my thoughts about Marisa through some sort of telepathic osmosis.

I shouldn't worry, because in true Susannah fashion, without any preamble, she says out of the blue, "You know what I was always jealous about with you and Frankie?"

"Our fly fashion sense?" I reply.

"All the errands you both used to run for Uncle Gavin," she says. "Y'all were out on the street having adventures and doing all this secret brotherhood shit, and I was stuck at the house with Fay."

"Fay took you to the aquarium and the World of Coke," I say. "She didn't exactly chain you to a radiator and make you fold laundry for hours."

"Yeah, but she was a pain in my ass." Susannah is slumped low in her seat, legs spread wide and feet flat on the floor.

"Remember when Fay took us all to see *The King and I* and wanted to make a special night of it? You brought your friend Ashley and snuck in vodka for your Diet Cokes. She threw up all over the front of my shirt at intermission."

Half of Susannah's mouth quirks up in a smile. "Ashley couldn't hold her liquor," she said.

"Fay talked about going to see that play for weeks. And that's the night you pulled that stunt. We had to leave in the middle of the play. And that same night, Fay left. She walked out on our uncle after eight years together." *Because of you*, I almost add, but I don't. I don't need to.

What I most vividly recall from that evening was the fight Uncle Gavin and Fay had when we got home, what they said about Susannah.

"She's cruel, Gavin," Fay said. "She likes being cruel. You saw what she did to her friend tonight. I bet she planned this out from the start, you know? Making Ashley her friend and then ruining it. Ruining *her*. That's what she does, Gavin. She knew that the *one thing* I wanted to do tonight was go enjoy a play and at least pretend we are some sort of functioning family, and she *fucking ruined it*!"

My uncle, with an almost infuriating calm, said, "She doesn't want you to do anything kind for her. She'll take that and turn it around on you like a knife."

"Do you not realize how fucked up that is?"

"She's in pain."

"*So am I!*" Fay shouted.

My uncle did not move or offer any sort of reconciliatory gesture. He simply said, "She's my sister's child, Fay."

The sheen in Fay's eyes broke, and angrily she wiped away her tears. "Well, she's not mine," she said. She stalked across the room toward the front door. When she was about to pass me on the couch, she stopped. "I'm sorry, baby," she said, then bent forward and pressed her lips to my forehead. I closed my eyes to receive that kiss, drinking in the coconut scent of her hair. Then Fay stood and walked past Uncle Gavin and out the door, slamming it shut behind her.

Now, as we sit in the customer lounge of the Toyota garage, Susannah glances at me, then looks toward the TV, where Mama Bone, the leader of the urban dog rescuers, is trying to coax a pit bull out from behind a dumpster. "I actually do feel bad about that," Susannah says.

"Better late than never, I guess," I say.

"Fuck you, Ethan."

"Oh, I'm sorry, you want me to be proud of you for actually feeling guilty?" I'm mad now, but some detached part of me registers how quickly this escalated, how we are at each other's throats.

But then Susannah looks at me, and while she's still slumped in her seat, her glance is searing. "I hated that Fay tried to be our mother," she says, her voice low and almost even. "I was a horrible bitch to her, and I'm sorry. But Mom *died*, Ethan. Basically in front of us. Dad too."

It takes me a moment to find my voice. "I know," I say.

Susannah turns back to face the TV. "I resented her," she says.

After a moment when she doesn't say anything else, I say, "I mean, I get why you resented her. We didn't know her, didn't even really know Uncle Gavin either, and she steps in and—"

Susannah shakes her head. "I resented *Mom*," she says, and that hits me like a baseball bat to the chest. "And you can't resent your *mother* because some asshole killed her," she continues, still looking at the TV. "So I took it out on Fay."

At our parents' funeral, I sat in the front pew with Uncle Gavin and Fay on one side of me, Susannah on the other, and I remember that even in the fog of my grief, I realized Susannah was just staring at the floor the entire service—glaring at it, really, as if concentrating all her anger onto it. She had refused to sit next to Fay, refused to receive mourners at the reception even though she could sit in a chair because of her injuries. And I remember being vaguely pissed off about it but just writing her behavior off as another example of Susannah being an angry bitch. I'd been wrapped up in my own misery and hadn't left room to think about my sister. Surrounded by mourners, many of whom spoke words of kindness and sympathy—*your mother was so wonderful, she's in a better place, your father is still watching over you*—I remember feeling utterly alone. I hadn't even considered what Susannah might be feeling, how her grief might look very different from mine.

I'm sufficiently stunned by all of this that I don't say anything for a while, and Susannah and I sit in silence, not even registering the TV anymore.

"It wasn't very adventurous," I finally say. Susannah turns her head slowly and raises an eyebrow. "Me and Frankie," I say. "That summer. Mostly we just hand-delivered envelopes to people."

Susannah doesn't say anything for a minute, then decides to accept my comment for the half-assed olive branch that it is. "What people?" she asks.

"All kinds," I say. "I remember the first one was Johnny Shaw."

"Uncle Gavin's lawyer?"

I nod. "Had this goon in his office, big guy with a shaved head and no neck, wore a pistol in a shoulder holster under his jacket. Tried to scare us."

"Did it work?"

"He wanted to know our names, so I told him mine was Ernest Hemingway. He said, 'Okay, Mr. Hemingway, you can just leave that envelope with me.'"

Susannah laughs now, bright and startling in the customer lounge. The three kids watching Mama Bone jerk their heads to look at Susannah before slowly returning their gaze to the TV. A man peering at a magazine looks over at us, then goes back to reading. I don't care. It feels good to make Susannah laugh.

"Okay, so what else did you and Frankie do?" she asks.

"That's pretty much it: delivered stuff to people. A diner on Crescent, sometimes. A shoe store in Underground. Once a lady working at the passport service desk in the post office."

"Blank passports, I bet," she says. "So, when did you figure it out?"

"About the blank passports?"

"That Uncle Gavin is what he is."

I pretend to think about her question. I'm really stalling. This isn't a conversation I've ever had, with anyone. My walls are going up, portcullises dropping, searchlights sweeping back and forth over barbed wire. At the same time, though, I feel . . . relief, I guess. A potential unburdening. I've carried around my uncle's secrets—some of them, anyway; not all of them, never all—for years, like a heavy pack I've gotten used to and would only notice when I shed its weight off my back.

"That first summer," I say.

Susannah makes a dismissive *pff*. "I guessed *that*. You're slow, not stupid."

"Thanks?"

"Seriously, what made you figure it out?"

*All the deliveries*, I want to say. Me and Frankie being Uncle Gavin's messenger boys. But that wasn't it, not really.

"Brandon Cargill," I say to her.

Her eyes widen with understanding. "I know who he is. He would come by Ronan's after—" She hesitates for only a second. "After you left, for college. What happened with him?"

Part of me wants to acknowledge that pause of hers, all the unsaid things loaded into that brief moment. Another part of me wishes I had a drink—a cold beer, maybe a double bourbon. Instead I sigh, and then I tell her.

BRANDON CARGILL WORKED out of a garage west of downtown, in an industrial strip sandwiched between the interstate on one side and the neighborhoods of English Avenue and Vine City on the other. Low brick buildings and warehouses alternated with patches of scrubby fields bordered by rusting chain-link fences, the downtown skyscrapers rising on the periphery like sentinel towers. Clusters of power lines strung from poles crisscrossed overhead, a net to keep a boundary on the sky. There were no tourists there, no strolling shoppers, no parks or restaurants. The area had all the charm and functionality of a manhole cover.

ATL Body Shop was a long, white garage with several bays, each with its own pull-down door. Most of the doors were up, revealing cars in various stages of repair. Frankie's father Ruben drove us there—which was unusual, because Frankie and I usually walked or took MARTA when we made our deliveries—and he pulled to the curb, then gestured at the garage as if to say, *Here's your stop; get out and be quick.*

"You're not coming?" Frankie said to his father.

Ruben shook his head. "I'll be right here," he said. I realized he hadn't turned the engine off. Again he waved his hand at the garage. *"Apúrate.* And remember—don't give him that envelope until he gives you one." That was another odd thing—we were exchanging envelopes, not just delivering them.

We stepped out of Ruben's car and crossed the concrete parking lot, wincing at the heat that slapped us, at the air we drew into our lungs like dragon's breath, leaving an aftertaste of gasoline and hot rubber. An old maroon Honda Accord, its rear windshield starred and cracked, sat in front of an open bay as if abandoned, or simply too exhausted to roll forward into the shade of the bay.

I elbowed Frankie, and when he looked at me, I nodded at the Honda. "Think you could fix that?" I asked.

Frankie glanced at the Honda. "Not worth my time, man," he said. "Piece-of-crap purple rice burner from the Nineties—"

There was a loud, explosive crash from the garage ahead that sounded like someone had hurled a metal trash can into an empty dumpster. We froze. Standing in the doorway of the nearest bay was a tall, rawboned man in stained coveralls, a backward Atlanta Braves cap on his head. He held a drop-forged wrench in one hand. It took me a moment to realize he had swung the wrench and struck the side of the garage with it, resulting in that horrible echoing crash.

"You talking about my car?" the man said.

Frankie didn't falter. He beamed a smile bright as the sun. "Sorry, sir," he said. "My apologies."

"Shut the fuck up, Chachi," the man said. Frankie's smile vanished, a total eclipse. The tall rawboned man pointed at me with his wrench. "What you want, kid?"

I glanced at Frankie, then back to the man. "I'm looking for Brandon Cargill."

The rawboned man clenched his jaw, his nostrils flaring. "Brad," he said.

I blinked. "What?" I said.

"It's Brad, motherfucker," he said. He swung the wrench so it banged off the side of the garage, the crash shivering in the air. "Who sent you?"

I glanced at Frankie to get his reaction. *What the hell?* But the man banged the wrench once more. "Don't look at the spic, look at me when I'm talking to you," he said. "Who the fuck sent you?"

I'd heard racist speech and jokes before, but I'd never been confronted by an adult who used such speech so openly. I gaped at the man, who pointed at me again with the wrench. "Who the fuck sent you?"

"Gavin Lester," I said.

The man raised his wrench and threw it. Frankie and I ducked involuntarily. The wrench spun end over end between us and smashed through the windshield of the maroon Honda. Safety glass bounced off my jeans. Before I could move or put my hands up or even breathe, the man was in front of me, close enough that I could see an almost translucent mole on his jaw, just below his left ear.

"The fuck does he want?" the man said. "Shut up," he added as I opened my mouth. "I know what the fuck he wants. You tell him Brad Cargill needs his first."

Frankie held up the manila envelope. Quietly, he said, "I think this is what you want, Mr. Cargill."

Cargill whipped his head around to stare at Frankie, who stood his ground, looking straight back at him, the envelope held between them like a flag of truce. At that moment, I realized Cargill was just *wrong*. He was a stupid, loud kind of wrong, the kind of wrong that would blow his nose in his hand and then wipe it on your shirt with a sneer. The kind that would, with malice and intent, call a Latino teenager a spic, then chuck a heavy wrench through a windshield to make a point. The kind that would walk into your house one evening and blow your life away.

As if he knew what I was thinking, Cargill pointedly looked away from Frankie to me, his eyes round with outrage. "You know who the fuck I am?" he said.

I fought to keep my voice level and mostly succeeded. "You're the gentleman who gets this envelope. Once you give us what my uncle needs."

Cargill worked his jaw as if trying out a few words silently, getting the shape of them in his mouth, before discarding them. "What did you say?" he finally said.

"You're the gentleman—"

He cut me off with a chopping motion of his hand. "About your uncle," he said.

"Gavin Lester," I said. "He's my uncle."

Something seemed to melt away from Cargill then, as if he had shrugged off a coat and left it on the ground. He smiled, revealing a discolored eyetooth. "I'm sorry," Cargill said, and his soft voice, almost a croon, caused my back to crawl like a bag full of live bait. "I just lose my temper sometimes, is all. So Gavin Lester's your uncle, huh?"

I nodded, not trusting myself enough to speak.

Cargill chuckled, then reached out a hand like a spider and ruffled my hair with it. "Gavin Lester's nephew," he said. "Jesus. Well, all right, Gavin Lester's nephew, let's have that envelope."

I looked past that smile at the pale, flat eyes set back into his skull. "Yours first. Sir."

Something shifted in Cargill's face then, like a snake coiling. Then he snickered and clapped me on the shoulder so that I nearly stumbled. "Damn, you got a brass set on you," he said. "Okay, okay." Cargill rubbed his nose, then dipped his hand into a coverall pocket and pulled out a fat, crinkled envelope, the kind you'd put a letter in, except this one wasn't big enough to hold whatever was in it. It looked like someone had shoved a paperback in it and tried to lick it shut.

"Let's make sure it's all here, shall we," Cargill said, tearing open the flap. He pulled out a wad of bills, the kind with Benjamin Franklin on them. Cargill began counting aloud by hundreds, thumbing through the bills, but his eyes kept returning to me, a ghost of a grin dancing around his mouth. When he ran out of bills at ten thousand, he pushed the stack back into the now-ruined envelope and handed it to me. I took the envelope and held it with both hands. Ten thousand dollars. Jesus.

"Thank you," I managed.

Cargill reached out and put a finger on my forehead like he was pressing an elevator button. "Not so fast," he said. He removed his finger. "You and your amigo have something for me."

Dumbly, I nodded and looked at Frankie, who stepped forward and handed his envelope to Cargill, who plucked it so quickly out of Frankie's hand that Frankie blinked in surprise. Cargill hooted with laughter. "*Gracias*," he said with a wink, pronouncing the word *grassy ass*. "Y'all tell Uncle Gavin that Brad Cargill appreciates it. Be seein' you again, prob'ly." He mock saluted us. "*Hasta la vista*, baby," he said. His laughter rose behind us like a flight of crows as we turned and walked back across the broken concrete to the curb, where Frankie's father was waiting for us, beyond the maroon Honda with the shattered windshield.

"HE SOUNDS LIKE a piece of work," Susannah says.

"It's like he was God's first try at a human," I say, causing Susannah to laugh again. "But he was seriously scary. Frankie said he was straight-up evil."

Instantly I regret mentioning Frankie. Guilt washes over me like a tide. But Susannah doesn't say anything at first, just plays with the laces on her Doc Martens.

"I didn't go see him, either," she says. "I left and didn't write him a note or anything for almost two years, just sort of assumed you would go see him. Which wasn't fair to you."

I let her words sit for a moment. "So we both suck," I say.

She shrugs. "He went to prison because of me."

That brings me up short. I lower my voice. "Frankie went to prison for both of us."

She considers this, then nods. "So, yeah," she says. "We both suck."

We look at each other, mutely acknowledging our collective guilt. Then Curtis the mechanic steps into the lounge. "Mr. Faulkner?" he says. "Figured out the problem. Looks like you got some plastic stuck in your gear selector."

I close my eyes in disgust, but not before seeing the triumphant smile on my sister's face.

# CHAPTER NINE

I LIED TO SUSANNAH EARLIER. IT WASN'T BRANDON CARGILL WHO showed me who my uncle is, not really. Cargill was the precipitating event, true. But it was Uncle Gavin himself who told me.

After Cargill threatened Frankie and me with a wrench, Ruben drove "me and Frankie" with "us" back to the bar, where I washed dishes and stacked plates and fought hard to stem a rising tide of anger and resentment. Cargill was one eye twitch away from a straitjacket. And I had no doubt my uncle knew it. That was why he'd told Ruben to drive us over. Fat lot of help he'd been, sitting in the car while Cargill terrorized us with a wrench. Who threw a wrench into a windshield? And he'd deliberately thumbed the stack of hundreds at me and Frankie. Why? To get a response? To show off?

That evening, I planned to lay into my uncle, ignoring whatever look he would shoot at me. But it was one of the days we stayed late, where I ate dinner in the kitchen while Uncle Gavin ate in his office. When he finally walked down the stairs, he was on his cell phone and just waved at me to come on. For the entire drive home that evening, he stayed on the phone, so I seethed in silence next to him while he drove and spoke to someone about renovations he wanted to make to the bar. When he pulled up to the curb outside the house, I got out and slammed the door behind me, then stalked up the steps to the porch. *Fuck him*, I thought. I walked through the front door and marched straight upstairs to my room, where I shut the door behind me and lay down on my bed. I began counting slowly. When I hit fifty-seven, there was a knock, and Fay opened the door. Of course: Uncle Gavin would send Fay rather than knock on his own nephew's door.

"Hey," she said, leaning against the doorframe. She was going old-school tonight, wearing black leggings and an off-the-shoulder pink sweat shirt like some Eighties starlet. I could smell her coconut hair from my bed. Concern wreathed her face like a halo. "You okay?" she asked.

"Right as rain," I said. I swung my feet off the bed and stood up. "Just need to talk to Uncle Gavin." I made for the door without waiting for her response, and she stepped back to allow me out. Walking through a cloud of her perfume, I nearly buckled at the knees from desire, but I made my way past her and went downstairs.

I found Uncle Gavin on the porch with his evening paper, just as I had expected. The sun didn't set until almost nine o'clock in June, and there was still enough light for him to read by. I let the screen door spring back behind me so it smacked the frame. Uncle Gavin glanced at me over the top of his newspaper. I locked eyes with him, determined not to let him hide behind the day's headlines.

"What?" he said after a few taut seconds.

"Brandon Cargill," I said.

Uncle Gavin grinned. "Did he tell you to call him Brad?"

"It's not funny."

"I understand from Ruben he put on a holy show, what with throwin' a wrench through a car window—"

"It's not funny!" I shouted, wiping the grin off Uncle Gavin's face. I didn't care if Fay heard me, or Susannah, or the whole goddamn block. "I thought he would hit me! Or Frankie! With a goddamn *wrench*! Who the hell *was* that guy?"

Uncle Gavin didn't even blink, just sat in his wicker chair, gazing at me with those black eyes.

"Now I get the death stare?" I said. "Did I offend you by cussing? I'm *fucking sorry*." Rage coursed through me, and I began stalking across the porch to the steps and then back to the front door. "Johnny Shaw's gorilla wore a *gun* under his jacket. Are you fucking *serious* with sending me and Frankie to these people? Is this a joke to you? Do you want me to get shot? Have Cargill pull out a, a *shotgun* or something and stick it under my jaw and blow my head—"

"*Enough*," Uncle Gavin said. He didn't shout it, or even raise his voice much, but there was something dark and angry thrumming through that one word that brought my marching to a halt. He folded his newspaper and tossed it down onto the porch. "Jesus," he said, rubbing his face. "Sit down." He gestured at the other wicker chair next to his. "Come on," he said, waving me forward. "Sit."

I walked over and sat on the edge of the chair, too keyed up to sink back into its cushions.

Uncle Gavin pinched the bridge of his nose and sighed. "I'm shite at this," he said.

"At what?" I said.

"Raising a teenager," he said.

"Not gonna argue."

I thought he would get mad, but he just raised an eyebrow. "Maybe you can give me some tips," he said.

"You mean like 'Don't send a teenager into a situation where he might get shot'?"

Uncle Gavin snorted. "No one's going to shoot you."

"No, he'll just bash my brains in with a fucking wrench."

"Language," he said.

I rolled my eyes but nodded in acquiescence. "How do you know he won't do that? Or that Mr. No-Neck at Johnny Shaw's office won't shoot me in the kneecap?"

"Mr. No-Neck? You mean Gus?"

"Johnny Shaw's bodyguard is named Gus?"

"Gus Cimino. And no, he definitely won't shoot you."

"You keep saying that."

"Because it's true."

I raised my voice. "How do you know?"

He fixed me with a look, the same right-in-the-eye look he'd given me in the hospital when he told me that if the police couldn't find the people who had killed my parents, he would. And then, as if someone had pulled the chain on a lightbulb, I understood.

"Oh shit," I said.

"Language."

"Mother*fucker*," I said.

Uncle Gavin raised a flat hand like he was taking an oath. "Hand to God, I'll smack yer gob right off yer face."

"They're scared of you," I said. "Or they know not to mess with you. Because you're . . ." I ran out of words. No, that's not it—I just didn't want to say what came next.

Uncle Gavin dropped his hand and waited.

"You're a criminal," I said. "Aren't you."

Uncle Gavin sat back in his chair. By this point the sun was a ruddy afterthought behind the skyscrapers to the west, and the streetlight cast shadows from the oak tree in the front yard. Shadow leaves dappled Uncle Gavin's face so that I lost his eyes in the dark.

"Do you really want to know the answer to that?" he asked.

"The wrong path," I breathed, almost a murmur.

"What?"

I shook my head. "Nothing."

Uncle Gavin made a hurry-up gesture with his hand. "Out with it," he said.

I hesitated. "It's . . . something my parents would say." I tried to find Uncle Gavin's face in the shadows. "About you."

A pause; then Uncle Gavin leaned forward so the light crossed his face. He looked sallow and grizzled with his five o'clock shadow. But the light didn't touch his eyes. "Your mother said that," he said. It wasn't a question, but I nodded anyway. He sat back in his chair, back into the shadows. I couldn't see his face, couldn't read his expression. Was he angry? Sad? Brooding?

When he spoke, his voice was low and tired but laced with resolve, as if he was determined to say something, no matter how painful. "You know that your mother and I, our parents died when we were young. We were older than you and Susannah, but still. When we came here, to the U.S., we had a duffel bag of clothes and a couple of hundred dollars between us. I wanted to find a job straightaway. Your mother, she wanted nothing more than to go to school and then to university. But we needed money to find a place to live, to eat. So I had to work."

"But why did you come here anyway?" I asked. "I mean, to the U.S.? I know after your parents . . . after they died, you all left Ireland. But why come here? Why not go somewhere else in Ireland, or England or something?"

He paused, then, his face still in shadow. "What did your mother tell you?"

I shrugged. "Not much," I said. "She . . . didn't talk about it a lot. She said you all couldn't stay in Ireland. That's all."

My uncle nodded. "That's about right," he said.

I couldn't help it. "But why *couldn't* you stay in Ireland?"

"That's my business," he said, with as much finality as if he had firmly shut a door in my face. He waited a moment or two to make sure I understood, then continued. "We moved to Atlanta, your mother and I, and I found work wherever I could get it. I saw straight off it would take years to get a green card. And it would take money to send Alanna to school." He gestured at the street, at the city towers rising beyond the trees, bright against the night sky. "There's money in a city. Opportunity. So I found it."

I asked the question that had been lurking in a dark crevice of my brain for a few minutes now. "So, you . . . what? Sold drugs?"

"Jesus, no." Uncle Gavin was shaking his head. "Never. Drugs are like a cancer; they rot everything." He leaned forward, his eyes on me. "In a city, everyone needs something. You need a certain kind of lawyer because your kid got busted with a dime bag and you don't want his future ruined. Or you can't get the city to come out and fix a busted sewer pipe. That's what I do, Ethan. I know things, know people. I help them get what they need."

"For money," I said.

He nodded. "Yes," he said. "For money. Usually. Sometimes I give favors. But yes, I get paid."

I let out a breath. "What about Johnny Shaw?"

Uncle Gavin grinned. "He's been my lawyer for years."

"And Brandon Cargill?"

The grin on my uncle's face shrank, became something harder. "He's the kind of person you have to work with. There are Brandon Cargills everywhere. Easiest way to deal with them is quickly." The grin was gone by then, his face now back to its usual inscrutable look.

A thousand questions filled my head, but they spun by so fast I had a hard time catching one to put it into words. "My mother," I managed to say, and by saying those words, others rose up behind them. "She didn't like what you did."

"No," he said, and there was a world of sadness behind that single *no*, although you wouldn't have known it to look at his face. He simply looked tired. He took in a breath, breathed it out his nose. "She did not. I kept it from her for a long time. But she was so smart. She figured it out. We fought about it. By then she was in college, and she met your da." He shrugged. "From then on, we didn't talk much. Your da met me once at the bar, alone. This was after Susannah was born."

"They wouldn't let you in," I said, remembering my uncle in his flat cap at the door to the hospital room, my father barring the way. "At the hospital, when my sister was born. They wouldn't let you into the room."

"Your da wanted to talk to me about that, after," Uncle Gavin said. "I couldn't tell if he was apologizing or telling me to stay away. Both, I think. I told him I understood and promised not to bother you again, that I would wait for Alanna to call." He paused. I realized with a sharp jab of conscience that my mother had never called, that my uncle would live for that for the rest of his life. "He was a good man, your da," Uncle Gavin continued. "Kind enough to me when he had no real reason to be."

We sat in the aftermath of that story, each nursing a private grief. Down below us, in the dim halos of light from the streetlamps, I could see bats dip and swerve, zigzagging across the sky.

"My parents," I said, and something thick and sorrowful rose up in my throat, behind my eyes. With an effort I forced it down. "You said you would find out who killed my parents."

Slowly Uncle Gavin nodded, once. "I did say that."

"So, have you . . . ?"

"I'm waiting for the police," he said.

I stared at him. "It's been months!" I said. "Almost a year!"

"One thing I've learned," my uncle said, "is patience." I started to speak, and he held up a hand to cut me off. "They're still looking," he said. "The police. I don't want to get in their way."

"Because what? You're scared?"

He ignored the anger in my voice and kept his own voice even. "I don't want to get on their radar," he said. "They expect me to do something. They know what I do. They can't prove it, not in court, but they know. So they watch. And so I wait for them to do the work. And if they don't find what they're looking for—and it's still possible that they will—but if they don't, they'll close the case and move on to the next murder. And then I'll be free to look. The police keep me updated every few weeks." He smiled slightly. "And I have my own sources."

I couldn't contain myself any longer. "And you're okay with that? Just putting it on *hold*? Why can't you just *find* Ponytail and his partner and—" I stopped, not daring to utter the next words. *Kill them.* Something dark uncoiled in my heart at the thought, and I shivered.

In the same even voice, Uncle Gavin said, "I've got you and Susannah to think about now. I can't do much for you if I'm in prison myself."

I felt the weight of that settle on me, my uncle's simple declaration of responsibility for me and Susannah, along with the underlying suggestion that the same unspoken thought of retribution was on my uncle's mind. Then he glanced at his watch and stood. "Time for bed," he said, his tone pleasant enough but also definite, and after a moment I stood too and followed him into the house, our conversation over but not finished.

# CHAPTER TEN

F<small>OR OUR SECOND DATE</small>, I <small>TAKE</small> M<small>ARISA TO SEE</small> R<small>OMEO AND</small> J<small>ULIET</small> <small>AT</small> the Shakespeare Tavern downtown.

The play is good—a couple of local high school students play Romeo and Juliet, and although the actress playing Juliet has a tendency to shout her lines, she does a fine job portraying an idealistic teenager pushed to desperation. Marisa seems to enjoy herself, laughing at the bawdy Mercutio and sighing as Romeo falls utterly head over heels for Juliet. When the play ends, we stand and applaud loudly with the audience, Marisa sticking her fingers in her mouth to whistle when Mercutio returns for his curtain call.

"So you liked it?" I ask as we walk outside.

"It was so good!" she says. "It's almost as good as the Globe in London. I saw *Othello* there a few years ago. Have you been?"

I shake my head and smile, although the question strikes a sour note. My parents never had enough money to take me and Susannah anywhere farther than the beach at Hilton Head, and Uncle Gavin wasn't the vacationing type. "It's on my bucket list," I say.

Marisa must sense something, because she immediately downplays going to the Globe. "It was a short trip, not even a week. My father wrote it off as a business expense. He was trying to get some investors for a project here."

I make a noncommittal noise, then ask, "Your father works in finance?"

She wrinkles her nose. "He's a real estate developer," she says with clear disdain. Then she laughs. "God, I sound like a snob. Sorry. It's just I don't really get along with him. He can be controlling: Mr. Big Shot behind his big old desk."

We are walking south on Peachtree, the downtown skyline looming across the highway. Now that the sun has gone down, I'm reminded that it's only the end of February—there's a chill in the air, like an invisible frost, and occasionally a cold breeze tries to work its fingers under my coat. Marisa shivers, glances at me, and smiles. "I'm okay," she says. "As long as we aren't walking all the way back to your place."

"No," I say. "Actually . . ."

"What?"

I'm afraid this is going to ruin a perfectly good evening. "We can't go back to my house," I say. "My sister is in town, visiting, and she's crashing with me until she gets her own apartment."

Marisa shrugs. "That's cool, I don't care."

"Oh," I say. She doesn't care about going back to my house? Maybe I've misread this entire date. "Okay, that's good."

She looks at me and bursts out laughing. "The look on your face," she says. She stops walking, so I stop, too, and she leans forward and to kiss me. "I meant I don't care that your sister is there," she says. "I'd like to meet her."

"Nope," I say, shaking my head. I start walking again, and Marisa hurries after me. "Not happening."

"Why not?"

I struggle to find words that can adequately explain why not. "My sister is complicated," I say.

"Everyone's complicated."

"Not like my sister," I say. "Look, she won't get home from her restaurant shift for another couple of hours, and she's not the kind of person who comes home discreetly. Plus you've seen how small my place is."

"So we'd all be right on top of each other?" Marisa asks.

"Exactly."

She quirks an eyebrow. "Naughty," she says.

"Jesus Christ," I mutter, and she laughs again so it echoes down the long stone canyon of Peachtree Street.

"Fine," she says when she's recovered. "But it's your loss." And she walks ahead of me, swinging her hips from side to side. And although I laugh as she vamps for me, I also can't help but watch her and stare at the back of her, and I know she knows it, too.

THE SUN DIAL sits at the top of the Westin Peachtree Plaza, a sleek, round tube of steel and glass that rises over seventy stories above the street. We ride to the restaurant in a glass elevator that shoots up the outside of the hotel, all the way to the very top. The outer perimeter of the Sun Dial, with floor-to-ceiling windows, shows off a panoramic display of the city.

A waiter leads us to a reserved table on the northern side, where many of the city's tallest buildings shine in the night sky, a webbed necklace of lights spread out in all directions. A bottle of champagne sits in a sweating ice bucket, and the waiter pours us two flutes and leaves us alone with dessert menus.

"Good call, Mr. Faulkner," Marisa says. "Very impressive."

I raise my glass. "Cheers." We clink and sip, the champagne dry and bubbly, prickling the inside of my nose in a strangely pleasant way.

Marisa sits back and stretches, her arms over her head. It's both cute and alluring. "So, your sister," she says, leaning forward and resting her elbows on the table as she gazes at me. "She have a name?"

"Susannah," I say. "You have any siblings?"

She shakes her head. "Only child. A mixed blessing, although there's not a lot of blessing in it. My father guilts me into taking care of my mother."

I frown. "How's that?"

She picks up her champagne flute, sips, then turns the glass in her hand, considering it. "I mentioned he can be controlling. Everything to him is the next big score. Everything's transactional." She puts the glass down. "My mother's injury doesn't fit into that paradigm. You can't bargain with it or bully it or get around it. So he gets others to deal with it. Like me."

"I'm sorry," I say, and I am. While I would give anything to have both of my parents alive again, I can understand that other people's families are difficult, and I can see that having a sickly mother and a domineering father is hard on Marisa.

Marisa watches me, the nighttime city gleaming behind her. "You didn't ask about my mother," she says.

"Excuse me?"

"My mother. You didn't ask about what happened to her."

I look back at her. "I'm sorry. You said before she had some health issues, but you didn't elaborate. And I didn't want to pry."

"It's not prying," she says. "I want you to know me. I want you to know everything."

I reach for my glass and hold it up. "Now *that* I will drink to," I say.

She smiles and shakes her head. "I'm serious, Ethan. I want us to know each other." She leans forward, her eyes on mine. Those beautiful gray eyes, shot through with green. "It's hard for you to talk about your mother, isn't it?" she says.

I put my glass down. "No," I say. "I just don't want to." I pick up a dessert menu. "Should we each get something different and share—"

"You're avoiding talking about her," she says.

I lower my menu and look directly at her. "Yes," I say. "I am. Because I don't want to talk about her." Marisa opens her mouth, eyebrows curved in sympathy and understanding, and I hold up my hand to stop her. "I don't talk about what happened to her and my father. It's not about you, or me not trusting you. I don't talk about it with anyone. So let's just order dessert, okay? I'm having fun, with you. Can we keep having fun?"

For a moment, Marisa says nothing, her expression blank, and I'm beginning to wonder if I've stepped over a line. But she stepped over a line, too. I have a right to not want to talk about my parents. Suddenly I'm angry, sick to death of being the guy whose parents were killed, the orphaned boy who carries this thing around with him always, whose life seems forever determined by a single act of violence. I don't want to be that boy anymore. And I don't know how to not be him.

Then Marisa takes a breath and closes her eyes and nods, once. When she opens her eyes, they are dark and liquid and she seems to look straight into me. "I'm sorry," Marisa says, her voice low, almost small. "I do this sometimes. I just want in and I push too hard. It's just, I feel . . . I feel close to you. In a way I haven't felt in a long time." She looks down at the table. When she looks back up, the open look of need and hesitation—no, fear—in her face pains my heart.

I reach my hand across the table, and she takes it and squeezes. "Hey," I say. "I'm sorry. I'm sorry, Marisa."

She nods and gives me a tight smile, then relaxes just a bit. We sit there, a thousand feet above the city, gazing at each other and holding hands, until the waiter comes to take our dessert order.

MARISA EXCUSES HERSELF after we finish a shared slice of cheesecake, and when I've paid the bill and finished my cup of decaf, she's still not returned. I'm considering asking for a second cup—and beginning to wonder if she's actually ditched me—when she suddenly materializes, looking slightly out of breath. "Hey," I say, surprised. I stand up. "You okay?"

"Come on," she says, holding out her hand, and I take it. She practically marches me to the elevator. Impatience radiates from her as we wait for the elevator to arrive. When the doors finally slide open, she pulls me into the elevator, stabs the CLOSE DOORS button, and darts a glance at a couple approaching the elevator. "You'll need to get the next one," she says to them, and before I can say anything to the startled couple, Marisa turns and kisses me, her tongue darting into my mouth. I embrace her, as much to hold on as out of passion, as the doors shut.

She pulls away, her breathing ragged, and punches a floor button.

"Marisa," I say, and then she's kissing me again, her mouth hot, urgent. My hands fall to her hips, slide down to cup her ass and pull her toward me. She sighs, then grasps my shoulders and lifts herself up and onto me, legs around my waist. I nearly stagger against the wall of the elevator, holding her, then lean back in the corner.

"Ethan," she breathes, kissing my neck.

"Marisa," I say, and now I'm half laughing. "What are we—"

"Shh," she says in my ear, squeezing me with her legs.

I'm so distracted I don't realize the elevator has stopped until it dings and the doors slide open. Startled, I nearly drop Marisa. The doors open onto an empty hotel hallway. Marisa hops down and pulls me out of the elevator.

"What are we doing?" I say.

She smiles, wickedly. "I like hotels," she says. "As I recall, so do you." We pause outside a room, and she holds up a key card.

I look at the key card, then at her. "You checked in? That's where you went?"

In answer, she slides the key card into the slot by the door handle, then removes the card with a flourish. The door to the room cracks open, swinging inward slowly.

Marisa places her fingertips on my chest and steers me into the room, kicking the door shut behind her. We make our way through the dark room to the bed, shedding clothes along the way. Marisa pushes me so I fall onto the bed on my back, and she crawls on top of me, wearing black silk panties and nothing else. "Touch me," she says, her voice slightly hoarse, and I oblige.

# CHAPTER ELEVEN

I LOVE SHOWING TELEVISION ADS IN CLASS—THE SMART ONES AND THE off-the-wall ones and the sentimental ones that pluck at our emotions like a guitarist tuning his Fender. Ads are great examples of the power of language and imagery to manipulate an audience. And we fall for the good ones every time, even when we know exactly what they're doing. The lonely grandmother, the kind young boy, the lost little girl, the dim but good-hearted father—they are such clichés that we forget they actual work.

The stern but caring teacher, that's another one. My mother played that role quite effectively. Actually, that's not fair; it wasn't a role she played as much as it was honest self-expression. Most kids are great detectors of bullshit and will quickly write off teachers who strike them as fake or insincere. But they loved my mother, at first because she was pretty and witty and spoke with an Irish accent, later because she was compassionate and clever and devoted to her students. Whenever I see an old greeting card ad involving a teacher, it's usually a mawkish affair involving piano music, sunlight streaming through classroom windows, a simple expression of thanks from a student, and the teacher blinking back a tear. And yet I always think of my mother when I see those ads, because she *was* that teacher, the kind who cared and could always turn things around, no matter what was wrong.

Except my father, perhaps, but I'll never know for sure. She wasn't given enough time on this earth to do that.

One Christmas Eve when I was ten years old, I was helping Mom make sugar cookies to set out for Santa. This was something I had always done with Mom. In Ireland, Mom told us, they had left out a mince pie and a bottle of Guinness, along with a carrot for Rudolph, but in America we should leave out cookies and milk. Susannah always wanted to help, but then she would get bored and wander off, trailing flour and candy sprinkles. That particular Christmas Eve, Dad had come home early from the bank—this was the last Christmas before he was sent to Iraq—and gone out in the cul-de-sac with Susannah, where he was watching her ride her bike while Mom and I made the cookies. I'd been wanting to talk with Mom for a couple of days, but I hadn't had the chance to do it without Susannah being around, so I decided to strike while the iron was hot.

"Mom?"

"Hmm?" Mom said, dusting a collection of snowman-shaped cookies with green sugar.

"Is Santa real?"

Mom looked up from the cookies. "Why do you ask?" she said.

I shrugged. "Horace says Santa isn't real and it's just your parents pretending."

Mom put the sugar shaker down and wiped her hands on her apron. "Horace McAllister? Why did he say that?"

"Is he right?"

Mom stopped wiping her hands on her apron. "Do you want me to tell you the honest truth?"

I nodded. She took a breath, blew it out.

"Dad and I sneak downstairs on Christmas Eve and put out all the presents from Santa."

"The stockings, too?"

"Yes, my love."

I considered this. "So you lied to me. To us."

Mom didn't react with shock or dismay, like I'd thought she would. Instead, she looked at me a little sadly, as if disappointed in my response. "Dad and I pretend Santa comes down the chimney and leaves presents for all of us, yes. The same as our parents did with us." She smiled. "You already knew Santa wasn't real before Horace said anything, didn't you?"

This was true, as the previous Christmas I had noticed that the handwritten *To Ethan—Love, Santa* on my stocking presents looked suspiciously similar to Mom's own handwriting. But I had shoved my suspicions into a dusty closet in my mind and ignored them, until Horace had opened his big mouth at recess earlier that week, telling everyone that Santa was a lie. I wasn't sure which was more upsetting: my parents lying to me, or Horace exposing the lie with a smirk on his face, like the rest of us had all been played for suckers.

Mom walked around the island counter and put an arm around my shoulders. "I like to think that Santa is real myself," she said. "That there's someone in the world who loves kids so much that he wants to reward them for their good behavior and spreads joy wherever he goes. It's the spirit of the thing that's true. And pretending to be Santa and seeing you and your sister on Christmas morning . . . that makes your father and me very happy. Does that make sense?"

I nodded. "Yeah, okay," I said. And it did make sense to me. It was the spirit of the thing that was true.

She gave me a gentle squeeze; then a slight frown creased her forehead. "You aren't going to tell your sister, are you?"

"No!" I said. I was actually a bit horrified at the idea, both because I didn't want to ruin Santa for my sister and because I didn't want to deal with whatever infernal plan she would come up with as revenge. "Why would I do that?"

Mom smiled then, a beautiful radiant beaming, and kissed me on the top of my head. "You're a good son, Ethan," she said. Then we hugged and went back to decorating sugar cookies.

That moment has a kind of soft, golden light around it in my memory, like a Hallmark ad, if you will, although Hallmark would never make an ad about a kid learning that Santa isn't real. "You're a good son, Ethan," Mom told me. I had instinctively made the right choice, and my mother praised me for it, and so I tried—for a short time, anyway—to live up to that standard, to make the right choice. I have revisited that memory often, turning it over and over in my mind until it was worn smooth as soapstone.

A far more recent set of memories, darker and disturbing, rubs against that single one of my mother, like bits of gravel in a shoe. Memories and thoughts of Marisa.

Dating Marisa was fun and exciting at first. The sex was—is—fantastic, and left me wanting more. That night at the Westin . . . God. No luggage, no spare clothes—it felt sexy and decadent. The next morning we had to share the hotel's tiny tube of complimentary toothpaste, which made us laugh. One thing led to another, and we barely made the checkout time. When I finally got home, I was able to brush off Susannah's questions and just smiled at her.

Beyond all that, though, I've also felt something else, a kind of connection that usually causes me to bolt. Marisa is a combination of assertive and vulnerable that draws me in, and she seems to understand me on a level most people don't, or can't.

But recently something has shifted between us, as if we have taken a strange turn.

Last week, my AP class was talking about contemporary examples of popular feminist texts, and Sarah Solomon brought up the Disney movie *Mulan* and was all over it when Marisa, in the back of the classroom, started laughing. "Jesus Christ on a merry-go-round," she said. "Mulan? Really? She has to pretend to be a guy to get any respect."

I froze. So did Sarah and most of the other students, although some of them, like Mark Mitchell, looked delighted by the unexpected commentary.

Marisa continued. "I mean, most feminist role models in classic lit are BS anyway, right? Jane Eyre? She ends up married to Rochester, who then recovers his sight. I'm surprised the power of love doesn't help him grow a new hand, too." Laughter from the class. Marisa smiled and kept going. "What about Lizzie Bennet? She falls for that condescending git Darcy. Shakespeare's the worst, though. Ophelia? Total victim. Gertrude? Horny adulterer. Juliet? Kills herself because of a guy she's known for four days."

This is probably when I should have tried to steer the class back in the direction of the original lesson, or openly engaged in a conversation with Marisa. Her going off on a related tangent was fine, but this felt more like a hijacking. But I was so startled and flummoxed that I said nothing, and Marisa took the opportunity to continue.

"Now I can hear Mark"—Marisa pointed at Mark—"saying, 'Hey, but what about Lady Macbeth?' Okay, what *about* her? She calls on the spirits of darkness to 'unsex me here' so she won't have any soft feminine moral compunctions." Mark blushed while his classmates laughed. "Honestly, women get treated terribly in the world, both in real life and in books and movies," Marisa said. "Women aren't weak, but God it pisses me off when people treat us like we are."

"Ms. Devereaux," I said, finally finding my voice. "I hear you loud and clear. Most stories about women don't neatly fit into a feminist paradigm. This includes *Jane Eyre* and the other books you mentioned. So let's talk about that." I open one arm wide to encompass the entire class. "What do you all think?"

"Just one more thing, Mr. Faulkner," Marisa said, and the students swiveled their attention back to her. "You all remember watching *Much Ado About Nothing* last week? Keanu playing some sort of sad pirate villain?" A few chuckles. "There was a line that Beatrice said—I can't remember the actress, the woman who played Professor Trelawney in the Harry Potter movies . . ."

"Emma Thompson," I said.

Marisa nodded. "Yes, thank you. Beatrice has this great line when she's furious with Claudio for publicly humiliating her cousin. 'I would eat his heart in the marketplace.' Now *that's* what I'm talking about. If anyone did anything to try and humiliate me, I would eat his heart in the marketplace." The students applauded, and Marisa smiled and bowed, then gestured to me as if handing back control of the class. The rest of the class went really well, the students buzzing about mixed messages and sexism across texts, but I still felt uneasy about the way Marisa had handled it. And Marisa had embarrassed Sarah Solomon by shutting her down.

I brought this up with Marisa after class, and her eyes grew wide and she seemed upset by the idea that she had distressed Sarah. The next day before class, she pulled Sarah aside and apologized to her. But something about the whole episode stuck with me. Marisa has been doing that kind of thing lately, pushing boundaries. Two days ago, when I passed out essay prompts to my AP students, Marisa was sitting in her usual place at her desk at the back of the room. When I placed the last copy of the essay prompt on her desk so she could better follow along with the class, she took the opportunity to brush her hand up my thigh, deliberately, suggestively. I flinched—I nearly jumped, to be honest—then darted a glance around the room to see if anyone else had noticed. The students appeared to all be looking at their own sheets. I stared at Marisa, who was also looking down at the essay prompt on her desk. Then she smiled, slowly, without looking away from the sheet of paper.

The same evening, I went back to school to watch a volleyball match in the gym, and to my surprise Marisa was there. We watched the match for a few minutes, standing close to each other, me wanting to bring up what Marisa had done earlier that day but feeling awkward about it. When Marisa suddenly said she wanted to talk to me, I felt relieved. She led me out of the gym and into the Stone House and down the Humanities hallway. I assumed we were going to our classroom, but she stopped outside the school counselor's office. "I left something in here that I need to show you," she said. "Do you have your master key?"

I hesitated, then unlocked the office. We both stepped in, and Marisa closed the door behind us.

"What—" I said, and then Marisa was kissing me, guiding my hands under her blouse.

I pulled away. "Marisa, what are you doing?"

"I wanted you," she said, her face tilted up to mine. It was dark in the room, but light from the parking lot next to the Stone House came through the blinds, a false moonlight. "I wanted you today. I'm sorry I startled you in our classroom. I'll be more careful."

I relaxed a bit, my hands at her waist. "Okay," I said. "Thanks for that. It just—caught me off guard."

"Hmm," Marisa said, and her hands slid up the back of my shirt. "That sounds fun."

I kissed her, long and slow. When we finally broke apart, I murmured, "Why don't we go to my place?"

Marisa smiled and took her lower lip between her teeth. "There's a very comfortable couch right over there," she said. She leaned in and whispered in my ear, "Have you ever been fucked on a couch, Ethan?"

Which is how Marisa ended up straddling me on the couch in Cara Delonghi's office, riding me to a shouted orgasm while the entire school cheered in the next building.

# CHAPTER TWELVE

I HAVE BEEN GRADING MY STUDENTS' PRACTICE AP EXAM ESSAYS AND
have just taken a break to search my office for my grade book, which I
have once again misplaced, when there's a knock and Coleman Carter is
in the doorway.

"Father Coleman," I say.

"Have you checked your email?" he asks.

"I'm notoriously bad about checking my email." As I say this, I wake
up my laptop and look at my inbox. There's a message from Jean Edwards,
Teri Merchant's assistant, sent at 9:14 this morning: *Ethan, are you free to
stop by Teri's office at 11:00?* It is now almost a quarter past eleven.

I look at Coleman. "What's going on?"

He shrugs, clearly making a tremendous effort to look clueless. "I'll
walk you over," he says.

I look at him suspiciously. "You're not going to tell me anything, are
you?"

He shakes his head. "Nope."

I stand, lock my office door, and walk down the hall with him. We
take a sharp turn to the left toward the front entrance and then go up
one flight of stairs to the administration level. The door to Teri's office
proper is open, so I walk in. Teri is seated behind her desk, talking to a

student sitting in a chair facing her. The student turns around. It is Mark Mitchell, who bothered to shave today, so his moon face is round and smooth as a baby's.

"Mr. Faulkner," Teri says. Teri Merchant is approaching fifty and looks a bit matronly in her sweater sets, but underneath the professional exterior is a shrewd intelligence that has served her well as a Black female principal in Atlanta's private-school market. "Please. Have a seat."

Behind me, Coleman steps into the office, closing the door behind him with a quiet *snik*.

I sink into the remaining chair Teri indicates, next to Mark. "Mr. Mitchell," I say. "How's it going?" Mark smiles and murmurs something.

"Thanks for coming," Teri says.

"Sure," I say. "No problem. Sorry I didn't read my email earlier."

Coleman settles himself into a wingback chair off to the side, an audience of one waiting for the curtain to rise. I begin to feel uneasy.

"Mr. Faulkner, you've taught here for almost four years now," Teri begins.

"Yes, ma'am," I say, keeping my face neutral. What is going on?

"I have to say," Teri continues, glancing at Mark, then Coleman, "that it is unusual for us to hire teachers fresh out of college. Let alone have them teach an AP course."

Technically, they hired me to teach freshman English my first year. Then the newly hired AP English teacher, Cindy Stone, announced to her class that her job was to see that everyone got an A in AP English. Her students took that as a promise that whatever they did, Mrs. Stone would give them an A, and so she spent the rest of the year trying to get her students to finish their homework and take the class seriously. Her contract wasn't renewed for the following year, and after sending me to an AP workshop over the summer, they gave me the class starting my second year.

Beyond that, Teri Merchant and I had a shared history—she had known and worked with my mother. I'd never had her as a teacher, and when I applied for the job at Archer, I did not realize that Principal Teri Merchant was the same Ms. Merchant who had taught seventh-grade English at Dunwoody Middle.

"We took a chance on you," she says, as if reading my mind. "We could have easily said no and encouraged you to reapply after a few years of experience. But we did not."

For a few seconds I have a horrible thought: someone saw me and Marisa in flagrante delicto at school. While dating a coworker isn't against the rules, I'm pretty sure having sex with a coworker in your closet, or on the school counselor's couch, would be frowned upon, at the very least. My face warms at the thought, and my heartbeat starts to thud loudly in my ears.

Then Teri is looking expectantly at me, a quizzical smile on her face, and I realize she has spoken but I didn't hear her. I clear my throat. "I'm sorry?" I say.

Teri looks at Coleman, who sits up in his chair, about to take on his own role in this production.

"The student council, of which I am the faculty sponsor," Coleman says, "selects one faculty member a year for the Archer Faculty Award, given to the best faculty member as voted on by the student body." He is grinning now and nods at Mark. Mark turns to me, his eyes wide, his face trying to look solemn even though a smile is clearly breaking through, like sunshine through clouds.

In a quiet, almost hushed voice, Mark says, "We voted for you, Mr. Faulkner," and then suddenly we are all standing, and Teri is congratulating me, and Coleman too, and Mark shakes my hand with a crushing grip and his usual half smile, and I'm blushing for real now, overcome with a swelling happiness as if my heart has filled with helium and is carrying me up into the air, away from any earthbound concerns.

I HAVE NO idea how I manage to teach my class of freshmen after lunch. I'm giddy and distracted, and when my freshmen ask once again if we can have class outside—it's a beautiful blue-sky day, the few puffy white clouds for contrast only—I almost say yes. They want to see if I will ever relent, and they also want to hear my usual response: "I don't wear sandals, I don't eat granola, and I don't have class outside." It's stupid, but it usually makes them laugh. Today I just tell them no and have them turn to act 4 of *Romeo and Juliet*, where they act out the scene in which Paris tries ineffectually to woo Juliet and the Friar hovers in the background like the worst match-maker in history. Before I know it, class is over and my students thank me as they leave the classroom. It's something I really enjoy, this spontaneous chorus of thank-yous at the end of each class. It's straight out of a sitcom fantasy of high school, and it always reminds me of how lucky I am to teach here. Today each thank-you feels like a personal tribute. *These kids*, I think, high-fiving one of them, *are the greatest.* When the last student leaves and the door swings shut behind him, I sit at my classroom desk, staring into space with a goofy grin.

I'm not sure how long it is after class is over that the door opens. I'm still sitting at my desk, and at the sound of the door I snap to attention and sit up. Marisa is standing there. "Hi," she says, the door swinging shut behind her. "What's going on?"

"You'll never believe what just happened," I say.

She cocks her head, a smile playing on her lips. "Something about . . . a teaching award?"

I look at her in surprise. "How did you—wait, did Mark say something? Because he's not supposed to say anything until they announce it."

Her smile widens. "I might have had a little something to do with it."

I stare at her. "What?"

She laughs softly. "It wasn't just me," she says. "The Faculty Award. All the students voted. Although I did mention your name to a few people. Primed the pump, so to speak." Now a full, wicked smile from her. "Mark was a sweetheart."

Mark Mitchell, the influential student council president who, despite his semi-slacker pose in class, is smart and dedicated. The same Mark who I've seen watching Marisa, his eyes tracking her around the classroom with something like awe. No, not awe. Infatuation.

My heart drops like an elevator into a coal mine. I stare at her, my earlier feelings of pride dissolving. *This isn't happening,* some part of me insists.

Marisa's smile softens, coming close to an approximation of sincerity. "And you deserved it," she says. "You're such a good teacher, Ethan. Your students know it and wanted to give that award to you."

"You," I begin, and my voice catches, my throat dry. "You . . . told students to vote for me?"

She chuckles. "It's not like I stuffed the ballot boxes or anything. I just made a few suggestions." She tilts her head down flirtatiously. "Maybe we should celebrate."

"You manipulated Mark," I say. "Why would you do that?"

She rolls her eyes. "Oh, please. *Manipulated?* I only told him how important teaching is to you, how much you care about the school." She walks toward me. "I know how much it means to you. It's a *good* thing, Ethan. And your mother would be so proud."

Something in my head gives way at that, some restraint, and I'm flooded with shame. Something else, too—it takes me a moment to realize I'm angry. I stand up. "Marisa," I say, and something in my voice brings her to a halt.

She looks puzzled for a moment, and then her mouth opens in an *ah* of recognition. "You're having an attack of conscience," she says, making it sound like I've got a stuffy nose. "I get it." She takes a step closer. "But you can't tell me you didn't want that award."

"Not like this," I say, and the iron in my voice makes her hesitate. I'm clearly pissed. "You shouldn't have done that, Marisa."

She smiles, slowly, and reaches a hand to my face. I step back. "Don't," I say.

She takes another step—she's close enough for me to touch. "Ethan," she says in a low voice, almost a whisper, "you don't want me to touch you? Don't you think about me, about *us*, together?"

I want her. I admit it. Standing there with her eyes on me, lips parted, waiting for me to reach out and take her, put my mouth on her, slide her skirt down . . .

"No," I say. I lean back against my desk and grip the edge of it.

She stands there, dumbfounded. "What?" she asks, her voice slightly higher, her question raw and direct, and I realize this is the first honest, unaffected reaction she's had since she walked into my room.

I spread my hands, futilely trying to encompass the whole situation with a gesture. "Why would you do this?" I say. "Why would you bring up my mother? You don't know anything about my mother."

"I know everything about your mom," she says. "About what happened to you and your parents. I read the news reports." Her face forms a look of sympathy and concern, her eyes downcast and eyebrows quirked, mouth curved into a slight frown, but I see it for what it is—a construction, a mask. "After we met, I went and found out what happened to you. To your family."

I lean back, horrified. "You *researched* me?"

"It was a home invasion," she says, something like pity in her face. "Two men were chasing a woman who ran to your house. Your father let her in, and they came in after her."

I shake my head, trying to deny her words, but the vault of my memory is open and the images pour out in a flood.

The silver shoe on our front walk.

My mother kissing the top of my head, telling me I was a good big brother.

The growl of the car pulling up in our driveway.

The coppery taste like pennies in my mouth from the adrenaline.

The doorbell ringing and the knocking, frantic, like a child beating at the front door.

Marisa continues, inexorable as night. "Your father let the woman into your house, and the men chasing her found her and came in after her. Those men shot you, and your parents, and your sister." She reaches out and places her hand on my arm. "They hurt you."

I shake my head, wanting her to stop but unable to speak for the moment.

"They hurt you and your family," Marisa continues. "But I knew from the moment we met that I could help you. I did this for you, Ethan. I wish you would trust me. You can tell me anything, Ethan. I would do anything for you. I can help you."

That anger is back again, boiling under the lid I'm keeping on it. It helps me find my voice. "I don't want your help. I don't need it."

Her expression doesn't change as much as freeze in place, although her hand drops from my arm. "Yes, you do," she says. "You do. You have no idea what I would do for you. What I've done."

I step back. "I don't want to do this anymore," I say, and just saying the words makes me feel as if I have been holding my breath, as if now I can finally breathe again.

Marisa smiles like a painting that hangs a little crooked. "Okay," she says. "Obviously you're upset. Let's just take a break. You can go get some coffee, whatever, and then we can talk about—"

"I don't want to do *any* of this anymore," I say.

She stares at me, long enough that I have to bite my tongue to keep from saying anything else just to fill the silence. Finally, her voice low, Marisa says, "Are you breaking up with me?"

"I'm sorry; I don't want to hurt you, but—"

"*Hurt* me?" The scorn in her voice is like knots in a whip lashing into me. Her cheeks are flushed now, her eyes flashing with some barely repressed emotion. "You think you're breaking my *heart* or something?"

"I don't know," I say. "I hope not. But"—and I raise a hand out to her in supplication—"what the hell are you doing, Marisa? Manipulating our students? Getting into my personal life?"

"Your *personal* life?" she says, her voice rising. "I'm sorry, I thought we had a *relationship*, and now suddenly I'm getting up in your *personal life*?"

My voice rises to meet hers. "It's not a relationship if you're playing games and digging into my past behind my back!"

She clenches her fists, her eyes burning with anger. "So now I'm just your whore, is that it? I *embarrass* you, but I'm good enough for a *fuck?*"

I am wholly unprepared for her reaction and just stare at her, shocked, unable to form a response. Then her hands go to her waist and she pulls her skirt down, then yanks her shirt over her head. She stands before me in a bra and black panties, furious, an enraged nymph. "Then *fuck* me, Ethan," she says, sneering. "Fuck me like the whore you think I am. Right here, on your desk. *Do it.*"

I stare at her, dumb in the face of her rage. Then I turn away from her and place my hands on the back of a chair and stand there, hands gripping the chair back, head slightly bowed. Part of me wonders if she'll attack me, snatch the three-hole punch off my desk and bash me in the head. I stand that way, my back to her, for some time, listening. Then I hear my classroom door slam shut. Marisa is gone.

# PART II

The past is never dead. It's not even past.
—William Faulkner, *Requiem for a Nun*

# CHAPTER THIRTEEN

Susannah was refusing to eat again. She scowled across her dinner plate at our mother, who twisted her wedding ring. "Honey," Mom said, "go on and eat your peas."

"They're cold," Susannah said.

Mom glanced at the kitchen doorway. "Please, Susannah," she said. "Your father wants you to eat your vegetables." Something about her voice, a pleading tone underneath her usual Irish lilt, stirred my sense of filial duty.

"Use the microwave, Suzie," I said.

Susannah spat, "Don't call me that."

"Just heat up the goddamned peas, *Suze*."

"Ethan," my mother said.

"You heat them up," Susannah said.

"You're a big girl now," I said. "Toilet-trained and everything. You do it."

It was like arguing with a flat tire. The only way to change Susannah's mind would be to open up the top of her skull and physically remove her brain. Ever since she had turned nine—just after Dad returned from Iraq— she had refused to do anything she didn't want to do, but it had become an annoying game lately; she was trying to see how far she could push us. The game threatened to become dangerous whenever she acted this way around our father. Pushing him wasn't advisable. You never knew which Dad would rise to the surface. Sometimes he would be stern, like the soldier he had been, but otherwise normal. Other times he would just stand there and look lost, a baffled expression on his face. And then there were times when our father could be mean. He had never hit us—*not yet*, a treasonous voice whispered in my head—but he could shout, and he would glower at me and my sister if we were too loud. Once, when Susannah and I were sniping at each other, Dad had snatched the pepper mill from the table and thrown it across the kitchen, putting a dent in the pantry door. I wasn't sure which was worse: seeing Dad turn mean, or not knowing which Dad would be coming home that night.

Like my mother—and I cursed myself for having the same weakness, the same fear—I glanced at the kitchen doorway, the pencil-yellow walls highlighting the empty space there.

Susannah saw me do it, like she saw everything.

"The big bad wolf isn't there, Ethan," she said. "You're safe for now."

"Just shut up," I said.

"*That's enough*," Mom said in the same voice she used to still a classroom of sixth graders. Usually this would be enough to subdue me, and Susannah would grin triumphantly at me behind Mom's back. But something was different that day. Maybe I was sick of Susannah provoking me. Maybe I was sick of seeing my mother's anxiety, of being afraid myself, the fear of my father a bright prison searchlight that stabbed out and pinned us mercilessly to the wall. But I also knew that, somewhere at my core, I was simply angry. I was the older sibling, the only other man in the house. Wasn't I supposed to take care of my mother and sister if my father couldn't—or wouldn't?

So I reached across the table and grabbed Susannah's plate, pulling it to me. Some of the peas spilled onto the table, rolling across the wood surface.

"Hey!" Susannah said.

I shoved my empty plate toward her and began shoveling her peas into my mouth. They tasted like little cold balls of clay.

"Ethan," Mom said, but there was no fight in her voice.

Susannah pounded her fist on the table. "What are you *doing*?" she cried.

"You're welcome," I said through a mouthful of peas.

"Those are *mine*!" She was truly furious.

I was about to make another retort when Mom stiffened in her seat. I looked over my shoulder to see my father standing in the doorway.

"Why are you yelling?" my father said to Susannah in a calm voice that raised goose bumps on the back of my neck. "You know we don't yell at the dinner table."

Susannah's face was bright red. I didn't look straight at her but continued to eat the peas.

"Don't provoke your sister," Dad said, and he sat down heavily in his chair. He was wearing his gray Glen plaid suit with a red paisley tie that was maybe twenty years out of style. Dad sat there at the kitchen table in his unfashionable tie and tired-looking suit, like a stunned commuter who hasn't quite realized he's already pulled into his own driveway, and at that moment my own anger and resentment drained away. He just looked so lost, a sense of confusion tinged with awareness that things were no longer the same but without knowing the precise moment when they had changed. I wanted to give him a hug, but I didn't because I didn't know how he would react—he could be particular about being touched—and because I didn't want to hear Susannah mock me for doing it.

"How was your day?" Mom asked, smoothing out the napkin on her lap repeatedly.

Dad blinked, as if the question had woken him up, then shook his head. "Same old, same old," he said. "Martin was an asshole. Nothing new there." Martin was Dad's boss.

Warily I glanced at Susannah over my last few forkfuls of peas. My father had also begun cursing more freely once he'd come home from Iraq, and Susannah's reactions to that ranged from feigned indifference to puritanical disdain. Susannah, however, wasn't paying attention to Dad. Instead, she was glaring at me as if she hoped the force of her gaze would bore a hole through my head. Then Mom got up to fix Dad a plate of pork chops, and we finished our dinner in a strained but familiar silence.

I WAS READING in bed—*To Kill a Mockingbird*, which I enjoyed, even though it was assigned reading for eighth grade and for some stupid reason you were supposed to hate whatever you had to read for school—when Mom came and stood in the doorway of my room. She was just outside the circle of weak light cast by my bedside lamp, but even then I could see the weariness in her face. Mom was an attractive woman—fair-skinned, red-haired, blue-eyed, all traits I had inherited from her, minus the attractive part—and she had always been slim, but lately she had begun to look tired, worn out.

I closed the book on my finger to hold my place.

Mom crossed her arms and leaned against the doorframe. "Can you do me a favor and take it easy on your sister?" she asked.

I rolled my eyes. "Honestly, Mom," I said.

"I know she can be a pain," she said. "And I know it must be hard having a little sister. But she's *your* little sister, Ethan. She's the only one you've got."

Looking at my mother in my doorway, a soft smile on her tired face, I knew that I couldn't say no to her, that I was bound to carry the cross of the elder brother. I managed a sigh. "Lady, you are the cruelest she alive," I said.

Mom squinted in thought. "*Macbeth*?" she said.

"*Twelfth Night*," I said.

Mom's eyebrows rose.

"What?" I said.

"You're quoting comedies now," she said. "There might be hope for you yet. Even if you called me cruel."

"It was a *joke*," I said.

She walked over to my bed. "You're a good son," she said. "And a good brother."

"Whatever," I mumbled.

She leaned over and kissed me on the top of the head. "I love—"

The doorbell rang, followed by a frantic knocking on the front door. My mother drew back and we looked at each other. It was after nine o'clock, and Mom clearly wasn't expecting company.

"Alanna?" my father called from down the hall.

"I'm in Ethan's room," my mother called back, turning for the doorway.

More knocking, and then the doorbell rang, then again, a frantic pealing like an alarm. I heard my father headed for the front door.

"Jimmy?" my mother called, and she walked out of my room.

I went to my window and looked out the blinds at our front yard. We lived in an old ranch house in a section of Sandy Springs sandwiched between I-285 and Hammond Drive, a major east-west road connecting shopping districts in suburban Atlanta. Driving out of our neighborhood usually necessitated waiting for a break in the long line of cars driving to or from Perimeter Mall, but our cul-de-sac was two blocks from Hammond and got hardly any traffic. So when I looked out the window, I wasn't surprised to see that there were no cars on the street. I couldn't see our front porch from my window—the angle was wrong—but there was something white and shiny on the front walk. It was a shoe, some kind of glittering woman's sandal. It looked like nothing that either my mother or sister would wear.

The front door opened and I heard my father talking, followed by a low wail. It sounded like a girl's voice. Was Susannah awake? I glanced at the closed door to the Jack-and-Jill bathroom we shared, but no light showed below the door. Quietly I stepped into the hallway. Now I could hear my mother; she and my father were apparently both in the foyer with whoever had been at the front door.

"—for God's sake," my mother said.

"Are you hurt?" my father asked. "Can you tell me—"

"Please." This was the new voice, a girl, pleading. "He wants to hurt me. I need help; please help me."

I crept down the hallway, then froze as Susannah's door opened. She stood there, her hair rumpled with sleep. "What's going on?" she asked.

"Shh," I said with a cutting-off motion. "Go back to bed."

"Stop telling me what to do." She looked down the hall. "Is someone here?"

I waved her off, trying to hear my parents, whose voices had lowered to a murmuring. All I could hear was my mother saying "police," and then the girl wailing again—"No, not the police, *please.*"

"Who is that?" Susannah said.

I turned on her. "*Shut up,*" I hissed.

Then my parents walked past the end of the hallway, a third person between them. Not a girl but a young woman. She was shorter than both my parents, with her head bowed as she cried, stringy blonde hair hiding her face. She wore some sort of silvery sequined top and jeans. I also saw she was barefoot. Then they passed beyond my range of vision into the family room at the back of the house. The woman was sobbing now, a low, desperate sound of someone breaking inside, piece by jagged piece.

*That's her shoe outside*, I thought. It must have fallen off her foot as she ran up our front walk. I needed to tell Mom, maybe get the shoe myself. It seemed important that I get it.

Then my father stepped into the hallway, blocking the light so that he loomed like a dark shadow. "Go back to bed," he said. "And turn your lights off."

"Why is that girl here?" Susannah asked.

"*Now,*" my father said in a tone that made me automatically turn toward my room.

Susannah ignored him. "Is she hurt or something?" She craned her neck to try to see around our father. "Do we need to—"

Dad took a step toward her, and for a brief, silver-bright moment, I thought he would hit her. Instead he spoke in a low, terse voice. "She's scared and wants some help. Your mother and I are going to help her. Now *go to bed.*"

"Come on," I said, grabbing Susannah's hand. She tried to yank it out of my grasp, but I pulled her back toward her room. "You heard Dad. We're going back to bed."

"Let *go* of me!" Susannah said, slapping at my arm with her other hand. I managed to open her bedroom door and pulled her inside, then closed the door behind us. As I closed the door, Susannah smacked the back of my head hard enough that stars popped in my vision.

"*Jesus!*" I said.

"Serves you right, you jerk," Susannah said.

I took a deep breath to calm down. "You heard Dad," I said. "He told us to go to bed."

"So go to bed." In the darkened room, Susannah seemed to glow with righteous indignation. "But you can't make me do whatever you want."

"It's what *Dad* wants, you moron."

"Run your own ranch, *Ethan*." This was one of Dad's sayings, meaning mind your own business. Then Susannah sat on her bed and turned on a lamp. Even her hair seemed to flare with resentment, a corona of rage around her pale, scowling face.

"Dad said to turn off the light," I said.

"I'm not sitting in my room in the *dark* with you."

"Why, because you're scared of me?"

She rolled her eyes. "Right. Scared of the boy who's scared Daddy doesn't love him."

"What the *fuck* is your problem?"

"Don't cuss in my room!"

"Fuck, fuck, *fuck*," I said.

"Daddy!" Susannah shouted. "Ethan is cussing!"

I heard the car then, a deep, loud grumbling, like some mechanized dog of war had just arrived on our street. Headlights washed over Susannah's bedroom window. The growl of the engine filled the night air outside. A car door slammed with a solid *thunk*. My spine crawled, and there was a coppery taste in my mouth, like pennies. I was frightened, truly frightened, not the daily, dull red alert of my home life, but a bright flare sent up by my nervous system. *Danger, Will Robinson*, I thought.

"Ethan's cussing!" Susannah shouted again.

I rushed toward my sister and put my hand over her mouth, shoving her back onto the mattress. Between my teeth, I whispered, "Shut *up*."

For once, Susannah didn't argue. She was staring at me, surprised, shocked even, by how I had pinned her onto the bed. But she wasn't afraid. Her stare told me she was assessing, reevaluating, considering next steps. All I wanted to do was hide with her from whatever was coming up the front walk.

"Let go of me," Susannah said from behind my hand.

I shook my head and listened. Someone was climbing the front steps. The car outside growled.

"Right now," Susannah said, her eyes narrowing.

A hammering on the front door—not the frantic knocking from earlier, but physical blows as if someone intended to bash the door in. Then a voice—harsh, male: "Kayla!" Another pounding on the door that made Susannah's window rattle in its frame. "Kayla, I know you're in there!" *How does he know that?* I thought. And then I realized—the girl's shoe. She had lost her shoe running up to our front door. And whoever was out there had seen it, knew it was hers. My stomach, hollow and acidic, clenched like a fist. *I should have grabbed the shoe*, I thought.

Then my mother's voice, piercing, distraught: "Jimmy!" she called out, and right then I knew my father was heading for the front door.

I let go of Susannah and half fell off her bed, then fumbled to open her bedroom door. Dad's angry voice joined the rising chorus—my mother pleading, the man outside snarling, and the girl my parents had let in now wailing and crying in earnest. I couldn't process the words, just the fear and the anger behind them. Senselessly I thought of FDR's famous quote, which Ms. Poorbaugh had written on the board in social studies class: *The only thing we have to fear is fear itself.*

Then the front door was thrown open, followed by the harsh male voice: "Kayla!" And my father bellowed, no words, just an unbottled rage that filled the house so that I thought the walls would explode. *This is a bad idea*, I thought, even as I rushed across the hall into my parents' room. I had to find the flat, wooden box my father had brought home from Iraq.

More shouting from the foyer, followed by a hard *smack* and a bark of pain. Something smashed in the front hall—a plate? No, a lamp. I fell to my knees on the floor of my parents' room and groped under their bed, struggling to reach the box. My fingertips brushed it, almost pushing it away, and then I gripped the box and dragged it out. "The only thing we have to fear is fear itself," I breathed, trying to shut out the other sounds—my mother screaming, my father's incoherent rage, the pounding and stomping of a fistfight in the foyer, the keening wail of the girl, and, in the background, the continuous growl of the car. The box was locked, but I knew my father kept the key in his bedside table. I yanked the drawer out, spilling bottles of pills and loose change on the floor, and I began searching blindly on the floor for the key. "Mother*fucker*!" someone, not my father, shouted in the foyer. Then my fingers found the key, and I shoved it into the lock and turned it, opening the box. Inside lay my father's service pistol, a Beretta M9, a black chunk of metal with a pebbled handgrip and a smooth comma of a trigger. I grabbed the pistol and lifted it out of the box and ran out the door into the hall.

At the end of the hall I saw my father struggling with another man. The man was the same size and build as my father, with a black goatee and acne scars. He was trying to put his hands around my father's neck. Then they stumbled into the den and out of my line of sight.

"Dad!" I shouted, and I ran down the hall with the pistol in my hand.

That's when I saw Susannah's bedroom door was opened, but I was already running in my haste to reach Dad. I saw Susannah in the doorway, saw the furious look in her eyes. I did not see her stick her leg out. I tripped over her foot and went sprawling, the pistol still in my hand. I landed on my stomach in the foyer. When I hit the floor, my hand convulsively squeezed around the pistol and I fired a round into the wall directly ahead of me.

The shot rang in my ears. In the den to my left, I could see my father and the goateed man frozen, still locked in each other's arms, as if the gunshot had signaled the end of a round. Behind them, my mother and the girl, Kayla, hugged each other on the couch. They were all staring at me. Shakily I got to my feet, the pistol still in my hand.

"Ethan?" my father said.

"The fuck?" someone said behind me. I turned to see another man in the open doorway of our home. He wore a black vest over a white T-shirt, and his hair was pulled back in a ponytail. His eyes were wide and frantic. He jerked his hand up—*he has a gun too*, I thought—and there was a loud, percussive *bang* and a hammer blow struck my right arm, just below my shoulder. I staggered back a step, and my arm suddenly felt heavy and senseless. Then I saw Susannah at the edge of the foyer, staring at me. No—she was staring at our father's pistol, which was on the floor between us. I must have dropped it. *Run*, I wanted to say. Then the ponytailed man in the hallway fired again, and then he kept firing, a jagged roll of concussive *bang*s like a string of exploding firecrackers in a metal barrel, and I fell to the floor and squeezed my eyes shut against the shots and screamed.

When I opened my eyes again, I was facedown on the floor, my head turned to face the hallway. Susannah was sitting against a wall, her hands over her stomach, which was red with blood. She was staring straight ahead to the opposite wall. "Susannah?" I managed, my voice thick. She didn't react. I tried to push up off the floor, but I couldn't make my right arm move. I felt weak and nauseous and I was sweating and my arm wouldn't work. "Mom?" I said. "Dad?" I turned my head to look into the den. My mother was still seated on the couch, her head back as if she were looking at the ceiling. Something dark stained the couch. The girl, Kayla, was gone. My father was on the ground a few yards away, on his back, making a horrible gurgling noise. He looked at me.

"Ethan," he managed. "Watch . . . your sister." He paused to say something else. And the pause didn't end, although the gurgling noise did. Dimly I realized that the growling from the car in our driveway was gone too, swallowed up by the night, replaced by the high, thin call of an approaching siren, warning us far too late.

# CHAPTER FOURTEEN

By Friday evening, after confronting Marisa in my classroom, my earlier confidence has dwindled. I meant to come clean to Teri Merchant at the end of the workday, but she wasn't available after school and I had to settle for scheduling a meeting first thing Monday morning. I don't know how I'm going to make it until then. I'm unable to read or watch TV or concentrate on anything except my own vague sense of dread. Marisa's rage unnerved me more than I'd like to admit, but the uncertainty of what she will do next is worse. What if she accuses me of harassing her? Of stalking her? What would she tell Teri Merchant? Susannah is waiting tables at the Palms tonight and won't be home for hours, so with only Wilson for company—he eyes me nervously from his bed—I pace around my house and think about what to do. Should I call Teri now and forget Monday? No, telling her over the phone won't work; it needs to be face-to-face—meet it head on. Or am I just holding off until I lose my resolve and convince myself that I don't need to do this? Twice I pull out my phone, and twice I push it back into my hip pocket. I drink a beer, then another, neither doing anything except making me pee.

What I want to do, more than anything, is walk away from this, just as I walked away from my uncle. But where? A man cannot flee from himself, as Shakespeare himself said. I can't joke my way out of this or try to bargain or fight my way out. I recall my words to my students about

Macbeth, about how he faces his fate, knowing he will lose and die, and how powerfully compelling that is. I laugh at the thought, finish my beer, then throw it into the trash can hard enough that the bottle breaks. The broken glass stays in the can, though. I take it as a sign of what I'm going to do on Monday—I've made a mess, but it will be a contained mess. And then my garbage will be hauled off, leaving me able to start over.

Stupid optimistic metaphors.

ANXIETY IS EXHAUSTING and a bit paranoia inducing. When I roll out of bed Saturday morning, I feel as if I have woken up on a similar but slightly different planet, the lone victim of a vast conspiracy. I've heard nothing from Marisa, but that seems ominous rather than reassuring. Susannah came home late last night and has already left again for her group therapy session, and so I find myself alone in my kitchen, looking suspiciously at my coffee mugs, as if Marisa has planted all of them in my house.

I typically have Pilates class on Saturday mornings, so after I take Wilson outside and feed him, I drive to the gym. But when I get there, the door to the Pilates studio is locked, the studio dark. That's when I recall my instructor, Heidi, texting last week to say there wouldn't be any class today—she was going camping or something with her boyfriend. I stand outside the locked door, annoyed and frustrated that the universe seems to be conspiring against me. And just like that, I decide that's not how I'm going to react. Instead, I head to the nearest row of open treadmills and spend half an hour running in place, knees pumping, arms slicing the air, pushing myself so I am sucking air and darkening my T-shirt with sweat. I try to empty my mind of Marisa and of meeting with Teri and just focus on running until the display shows me that thirty minutes have passed, and then I slow for a few minutes, letting my breathing and my heart rate drop to something approximating normal.

I feel good on the drive home, focusing on the road, the next curve, the faded ROMNEY-RYAN sticker on the car in front of me. The radio is off and I drive in silence. In the afterglow of my run, I feel more certain of my course. Every turn of the wheel is deliberate and smooth, an accomplishment, progress. I'm steering away from the insanity of the past few weeks and onto a saner path. Whatever moral code I operate under is a far cry from when my mother called me a good son; it's cobbled together and inconsistent as hell and maybe even a lie. But I try. That I fail isn't as important as the effort. I tell myself that enough for it to even seem true. Regardless, I am calm and at peace with whatever awaits me on Monday.

The sight of Marisa's red Audi convertible parked in my driveway vaporizes my moment of zen.

My front door is locked, and when I pull out my house keys, they are shaking in my hand. I jam the key into the doorknob and throw the door open so hard that it bounces off the doorstop, vibrating like a tuning fork. Across the den in his bed, Wilson lifts his head up, then scrambles out from underneath his blanket and races over to me, immediately rolling over so I can scratch his belly. "Okay, boy," I say, absently scratching him as I scan the den, the kitchen. No one. "Where is she?" I ask Wilson.

Someone, a woman, says, "What?" I look up and see my sister standing in the hall outside my bedroom. She's wearing a Millennium Falcon T-shirt—*my* Millennium Falcon T-shirt—and a pair of gym shorts.

"You're home early," she says.

"I . . . Pilates got canceled," I say. "Why are you wearing my shirt? What are you *doing* here? I thought you had group."

Susannah grins. "I bailed."

"You bailed. Why did you—?"

Marisa walks out of my bedroom. Her legs are bare, and I'm willing to bet her ass is too. Right now it's covered, just, by a tight black T-shirt with *Get Up the Yard* slashed in white across the front. "Hi," she says, head lowered, smiling.

I stand there, staring. Wilson, forgotten, whines at my feet.

"Yeah . . . so," Susannah says. "Sorry?"

With a soft grunt the air conditioning kicks on, air whirring out of the floor registers.

"Seriously," Susannah says. "I'm sorry. I thought you wouldn't be home for a while."

Marisa steps forward and puts her hand on Susannah's arm, watching me the whole time. She leans her head against Susannah's shoulder. She's still smiling.

"This is Marisa," Susannah says brightly. "Marisa, this is my brother, Ethan."

"Nice to meet you, Ethan," Marisa says. Still looking at me, she takes Susannah's hand and raises it to her lips and kisses it.

Wilson whines, louder, a growl building in his throat. Susannah glances down at him. "Dude, he's gonna pee everywhere," she says. "Might wanna take him out."

I find my voice. It sounds like it's been locked in a basement and beaten for a week, but it works. "Get out," I say.

Susannah frowns. "Hey, look, I'm sorry I didn't ask before bringing her over here. It just, like, *happened*—"

"Fuck you," I say, and the words unlock a white heat that's been building in my chest ever since I saw Marisa's car in my driveway. The shock on Susannah's face is genuine, and I ride it on a fresh wave of anger. "Just fuck you. And *you*"—I point my finger at Marisa—"you get the *fuck* out of my house."

Marisa lets go of Susannah's hand and walks down the hall toward me. Her gray eyes are locked on mine, and now she's grave and imperious and definitely not wearing anything other than my sister's T-shirt. Her voice low, she says, "You don't mean that."

"Wait," Susannah says. She looks from me to Marisa and back again, and I see comprehension unfold across her face. "Oh, *shit*."

"You're upset with me," Marisa says. She bites her lower lip. "You're angry. But you don't want me to leave. You want to punish me."

"I—"

She's in front of me now, so close I can smell her. Vanilla and pepper. She reaches out and takes my hand. "You want to," she says. "I know you,

Ethan. You want to punish me." She grips my wrist and then places my hand to her chest, the swell of her breast in my palm.

"Oh *shit*," Susannah is saying down the hall. She leans against the wall, then slides slowly to the floor. "Oh *shit* oh *shit* oh *shit*, Ethan, I didn't *know*. I *didn't know*."

"It's all right," Marisa whispers to me. She's standing before me in a T-shirt, holding my hand to her breast as if it's an offering. "Do it. Do whatever you want. You can do whatever you want to me, and I'll let you." She's breathing a little more deeply now, and she tilts her head back slightly, her lips parted. I can feel her nipple beneath my hand. Susannah is quietly sobbing somewhere down the hall, but I can't look away from the woman in front of me. A small but insistent voice in my head says *get away*, but there's a darker, voiceless urge. I hesitate, suspended between two wills. "*Do it*," Marisa whispers, closing her eyes. My fingers barely clench, and she smiles, terrible and victorious.

She opens her eyes, wide, her smile gone. "*Shit!*" She glares at her feet. I look down. Wilson, whining softly, ducks his head in embarrassment. A puddle is spreading across the wood floor. Wilson has peed on Marisa's foot.

Marisa's lips curl back from her teeth, and she kicks my dog. He gives a sharp cry and skids a couple of feet across the floor.

Something falls away and in its place is a black revulsion. I shove Marisa away from me, hard enough that she staggers and has to put a hand against a wall to steady herself. I kneel down to check on Wilson, saying "It's okay, boy; it's okay," and Wilson scampers to me and licks my hand feverishly, as if apologizing for being kicked. I don't see any bruising or feel any broken ribs.

Marisa gives a low, disgusted laugh. "Poor puppy."

I snarl, "You so much as *touch* my dog again—"

"I was talking about you." Marisa has regained her composure, arms folded across her chest, T-shirt riding dangerously high. "I *know* you, Ethan. I know who you are. You and your little sister."

Susannah is sitting on the floor behind Marisa, arms wrapped around her knees, crying to herself.

"You don't know a thing about us," I say.

Marisa sneers. "I know *everything* about you," she says. "Poor little tragic orphan, so broken and fucked up you have to sleep with strangers and then pretend you're in love so you can try to feel normal."

There's a blur of movement behind Marisa, and then Susannah is on her. Her first punch glances off Marisa's face. Then she's punching and screaming and trying to rake Marisa's eyes. "You fucking *bitch* you don't *fucking* know anything you goddamned *cunt*—"

I rush forward to pull Susannah off Marisa. My sister is a whirlwind of fists and fingernails and curses. I wrap my arms around her in a bear hug and lean back, trying to lift her off the ground. "Let *go* of me!" Susannah screams, flailing and twisting in my arms. "Put me down, let me go—"

Marisa stands there, her hair disheveled, a bruise on her cheek. She looks slightly dazed, as if surprised at the turn this has taken. Marisa stares at Susannah, who continues to struggle and scream. As small as my sister is, I can barely control her. "Get out!" I shout at Marisa. "Go!"

Marisa looks at me as if she's just now registering that I'm there. The look she gives me is more frightening than anything else that has happened. Her eyes are empty, an utter void . . . no, that's not exactly right. There's intelligence in her look, but it's cold, even malignant. She's looking at me as if sizing up a fetal pig for dissection in freshman biology. Something clicks into place behind her eyes, and she smiles, slowly. "I'll be seeing you," she says. "You can count on that." And she turns and walks unhurriedly down the hallway to my bedroom.

I have to drag Susannah into the den, trying all the while to keep her from scratching my face off. She's cussing and spitting like a cat, and I almost stumble over my coffee table. Suddenly she sags in my arms, breathing through her mouth like she's winded. I tense, my arms still around her. "You gonna be good?" I say.

"Yeah, fine," she mutters. "Just, let go, okay? I'm fine."

I let go of her and take a step back, my arms raised, ready to grab her if necessary. But she collapses onto the couch like she's been deboned. "I'm sorry," she says. "I'm sorry, Ethan; I'm sorry."

"Okay," I say. "Just . . . don't do anything stupid."

She shakes her head. "Is Wilson okay?" she asks.

I look around and see Wilson hunkered down in his bed, gazing at me. He doesn't get up from the bed when I go over to him, but he thumps his little tail. He allows me to rub his ears, then noses me carefully. Then I hear a metallic scrape and I turn to see Susannah walking away from the fireplace, holding the poker that she has taken from its stand. I jump up and run after her into the hall, intercepting her just as she's about to go through my bedroom door and bash Marisa's head in.

I tackle Susannah cleanly, right at the waist, the poker clattering out of her hand as we fall through the doorway into my room. As I lay on top of my sister, trying to keep her pinned to the floor, a sandaled foot edges into my line of sight. I look up to see Marisa standing over us. She's put her jeans on and is still wearing Susannah's *Get Up the Yard* T-shirt. She walks past us as if we aren't even there. I don't turn around to watch her leave. The front door opens, then shuts.

Beneath me, Susannah is crying in hard, silent jags as if something is trying to force its way out of her. Then I hear the patter of Wilson's feet, and soon his frantic little tongue is licking my face. "Okay, boy," I tell him. "It's okay."

"Shit," Susannah says, her voice muffled. "I *love* that T-shirt."


WHILE SUSANNAH TAKES a shower, I put the poker back in its place by the hearth, then strip my bed and stuff the sheets into my closet washing machine. I get new sheets and pillowcases, but I am brought up short by a black thong I see on the floor by the bed. Is it Susannah's? Marisa's? I look at the naked mattress, then at the closed bathroom door, behind which I can hear the shower running. I sigh and put down the stack of clean sheets, then pick up the thong and toss it into the washing machine along with the soiled sheets.

By the time Susannah finishes her shower and appears in my old plaid bathrobe with her hair wrapped in a towel, I've remade the bed and am spraying air freshener around my room. Susannah wrinkles her nose. "What's with the lilac?" she says.

"Wilson had an accident," I say. It's a lie and we both know I'm not trying to cover up any scent of Wilson's. Susannah doesn't say anything, but I still feel like I've been caught cleaning up a crime scene.

"Might need to borrow another shirt," Susannah says.

I pull open a drawer and look for a T-shirt. "How about underwear?" I ask.

She waits a moment before answering. "What did you find?"

"Black thong. I washed it."

"It's not mine."

I pluck a plain navy T-shirt out of the drawer. "Well, I feel so much better now," I say.

"How many times do you want me to say I'm sorry, Ethan? *I'm sorry.*"

I shut the drawer before I turn to face my sister. "I don't want you to say you're sorry. I want you to not do shit like this in the first place."

Her incredulous look lasts only a moment, and then her face tightens, her mouth a cruel line. "What, like sleeping with your secret psycho girlfriend?"

"Wait," I say. "Just wait a minute. How did you even *meet* her?"

She folds her arms across her chest. "In group."

"In *group?*"

"Kinda thinking you don't get to be Judgy McJudgy here."

"Why was she in your *group?*"

"I don't know, Ethan—because she had some *issues* to work out? Like everyone else who's ever been in group therapy? Like *you* would fucking know."

"What does *that* mean?"

"You think I'm the broken one? The same shit happened to you, Ethan. The *same shit.* And you just sail on like nothing happened."

I'm twisting the navy T-shirt in my hands so hard my fingers are beginning to ache. "You think I just *sailed on?* You get shot and Mom and Dad *die*

and I just shrugged it off like, 'Oh, well,' and my life is all fine? After you—"
I stop abruptly, literally biting my lip. Ponytail surfaces in my memory, and
then, at the back of my memory cave, that one night in the Bluff, in the abandoned house with Luco and Frankie and Susannah, stirs and starts to uncoil.
I make a curt gesture with my hand as if to sweep away both memories.

"After I what?" Susannah's voice drops a notch into a calmer register.
"What did I do, Ethan?"

I shake my head, trying to stay focused. "I'm asking about how you
met Marisa in group. You didn't know who she was? You didn't know she
knew me?"

In a flat, disappointed voice, Susannah says, "No, Ethan, I didn't know
she knew you. Do you think I'd bring her here on purpose if I knew?"

"Fuck." I sit down on the newly made bed and put my head in my
hands. "*Fuck*."

After a moment of hesitation, Susannah puts a hand on my shoulder.
"I really am sorry."

"No," I say. "*She* knew."

"What?"

I lift my head and look up at my sister. "This isn't a coincidence," I
say. "She *knew*. Marisa knew you were my sister."

Susannah's mouth opens the slightest bit, a crack in her demeanor,
and her hand falls from my shoulder. I can see her thinking, calculating,
turning over in her mind everything she knows about Marisa.

"When did she join your group?" I ask.

"A month ago," Susannah says. "Maybe a little more."

Soon after she started working at Archer. "How long have you
been—" I say, and then stop, not sure how to continue.

Susannah saves me the trouble. "Sleeping with Marisa? Today was
the first time. But we've been flirting."

"Did you tell her about me? Talk about me in group? About our family?"

"Not by name, no," she says. When I continue to stare at her, she adds,
"I mentioned Mom and Dad, okay? And the fact that I have a brother."

I feel sick and light-headed and want to sit down, but I'm already sitting down. A few months before my parents died, Mom and I watched *Casablanca*, and I remember Humphrey Bogart's hard, wounded despair in reaction to Ilsa's return. Despair is a good way to describe how I feel right now. *Of all the group therapy sessions in all the towns in all the world,* yada yada yada. Marisa found my sister and then latched on to her like a lamprey. And today, the day after we broke up, she jumps in bed with my sister. But *why*? To fuck with me, to manipulate her way back into my house? To show me that she could?

I thought I knew Marisa, understood her as a smart, libidinal woman with a rebellious streak. Now I understand, with bone-chilling certainty, that I haven't known her at all.

AT SOME POINT Susannah hands me a bottle and I drink from it— bourbon, a burnt liquid glow in the throat. We pass the bottle back and forth, sitting on the floor of my bedroom, not talking much, just looking at the wall in companionable silence. Occasionally we speak softly to Wilson, who crawled into my lap earlier and now gazes at both of us like a child must look at parents who aren't fighting right now but could start up again any minute. Susannah and I aren't talking much because we want to maintain this delicate bubble of peace that, sooner or later, will pop. For now, it holds.

Eventually Susannah gets up to go pee, and that's when I realize that the blue-and-green tartan bathrobe she's wearing isn't mine, at least not originally. It's Dad's. It's a bit too big for me, but Susannah looks like an elfin child in it. Sitting on the floor in a pleasant bourbon haze, the memory of Marisa banished for the moment, I look up at my sister, the bathrobe pooling at her ankles, and realize that this is what we all do, eventually— we put on our parents' clothes and try to act like them, like grown-ups.

I hope someone acts like a grown-up soon.

# CHAPTER FIFTEEN

I COME TO IN A TWILIGHT GLOOM, MY HEAD THICK AS A TIRE. I'M IN my bed and my stomach is a heavy, sour medicine ball, and I lie still, closing my eyes, because if I move too quickly that sour ball will start rolling around and I will most definitely be sorry.

"Susannah?" I croak. "Suzie!"

No answer. Then a *tap-tap-tap* on the floorboards and a soft whine from the bedroom door. Wilson. "Okay, boy, coming," I say, managing to put one foot on the floor while still lying flat on my back. The effort required to sit up almost undoes me, but I manage it. Wilson is delighted and prances around my feet while I try to imagine making it to the front door without puking.

I shuffle down the hall and outside into a rose-red sunset, the kind where the clouds seem to be glowing from internal fires. Wilson investigates the yard, occasionally lifting a leg to mark his territory, while I sit on my front steps and endure being somewhere between drunk and hungover. Dimly I note that Marisa's car is gone, although there are tire tracks in my front yard, raw gouges veering away from the driveway and then sharply back toward it. My car remains where I parked it, but now it sports a bright, jagged scar on the passenger door. Marisa must have keyed it on her way out. Uncharitably I think that maybe I should have let Susannah hit her with the poker. That reminds me that Susannah is gone too. Where did she go? And how?

Wilson finally finishes, and after I take him inside and feed him, I see the Post-it note on the television: *Gone running, coming back.* I shouldn't be surprised; when Susannah is pissed off, her reaction is to go exercise herself to exhaustion. And despite everything, I smile—only my sister would leave a note assuring me that she is gone only temporarily, that she is planning to return.

I wander into the kitchen and see an empty fifth of bourbon in the trash can, which about makes me gag. I need to eat something, but toasting a bagel seems too complicated, let alone cooking dinner, so I settle for a dry bowl of Crispix and a cup of instant coffee.

I'm chewing a mouthful of cereal and contemplating another cup of coffee when my phone rings. Susannah. I look around the den for my phone and find it on the table next to the front door. I don't recognize the number, but Susannah constantly loses cell phones and gets new ones. "Hello?"

"Hi, Ethan," Marisa purrs in my ear. "Miss me?"

I almost scream. Instead, I jab my finger at the phone, ending the call. Then I block the number.

I'm on my way back to my bowl of Crispix when there's a *ding*, like when my phone alerts me to a text. But it's not my phone, which is still in my hand. Another *ding*. I slide my phone into my pocket and look around the den some more, checking under a *Moby-Dick* paperback on the coffee table, scanning the furniture. A third *ding* leads me to the sofa, where behind a cushion I find a newer-model iPhone encased in a pop-art-swirl OtterBox. I don't even have to read the messages on the locked screen to know whose phone it is. But when I press the home button to see the texts, I almost drop the phone.

The first text at the top of the list is from **Mom**.

Ethan if u have my phone give it back

I stare at the phone, the back of my neck crawling as the hairs stand on end. There are two more texts, also from **Mom**.

I want my phone ethan
PHONE BACK

When I was a kid, my father let me watch *Poltergeist* on cable, and I remember the glowing vacuum closet and the killer clown doll and the other demonic things plaguing the family in that suburban house, but mostly I remember a slowly mounting sense of dread building up in me and finally crescendoing with the mom falling into the swimming pool with the corpses, sending me into fits of screaming. At the same time, I was utterly unable to turn away from the screen. I feel the same way now, staring at the phone in my hand.

And then, after a few moments, I grow calm, let out a breath I didn't know I was holding, and bring my shuddering heartbeat down several notches. My mother is not texting me from beyond the grave. Instead, these texts are from Marisa's mother, or more specifically from her mother's phone. Marisa must be using her mother's phone to text her own. Still, I look suspiciously at Marisa's iPhone in its pop-art case. I am surprised she left her phone behind. Marisa's phone is her lifeline. The thought that she was flustered or upset enough by our last encounter to forget her phone—and that she's clearly angry that she left it—makes me feel a bit better.

My own phone rings in my hip pocket, startling me. *Shit.* Did Marisa find another phone? Mine rings again, and I pull it out to see who's calling. It says **Archer (Work)**. I hesitate—is she calling me from school?—and then answer, tensing as if prepared to throw the phone away from me. "Hello?"

"Ethan? It's Teri Merchant."

Her calm, professional voice wipes my mind like a blank slate. "Oh," I say. "Um . . . hi. How are you?"

"I wanted to check in with you," she says. "I understand you stopped by my office yesterday after school? Jean said you wanted to talk with me."

At that moment I realize I'm still wearing my gym clothes from this morning and that I smell like a ripe alcoholic. "I . . . yes, I did," I say.

"I mean I do. Want to talk. Actually, that's a great idea." I'm babbling. *Focus, asshole.* "In person would be better," I say. "I mean, not *now*."

"No, tonight isn't great," Teri says. "How about tomorrow afternoon? Say, four o'clock? My office?"

"That's perfect," I say. Tomorrow is Sunday, but the sooner I can talk to her about Marisa, the better.

She pauses. "Are you okay, Ethan?"

I nod. "Yeah, fine," I say. "I mean, I have some family stuff going on. My sister is in town."

As if I've conjured her with those words, through my front window I see Susannah running up the driveway in her workout gear, arms pumping, knees jackknifing, her face red with exertion and running with sweat.

"That's good," Teri says. "It must be nice catching up with her."

Susannah almost makes it up the driveway before she staggers, weaves into the front yard, and pukes all over my lawn.

"It's wonderful," I say into my phone.

ON SUNDAY AFTERNOON, I walk into Teri's office ten minutes early, but Teri is already there, sitting behind her desk. So are three other people. I stop just inside the doorway. Coleman Carter stands off to the side as if trying to blend into the woodwork—he looks about as conspicuous as a boar in a bowling alley. A white-haired woman in a black dress and severe-looking glasses is bending down to speak to a third person in an armchair. When the woman straightens up, I see the person in the chair is Byron Radinger, Archer's head of school.

"Ethan," Teri says, and the other three turn and look at me. "Come on in. Shut the door behind you."

In my head, unbidden, I hear Uncle Gavin's voice. *You've walked into it.*

Then I shut the door behind me and cross the room to stand by the chair in front of Teri's desk.

"Thanks for coming in," Teri says.

"Of course," I say. "Thanks for meeting with me. I . . ." I clear my throat. "I wasn't expecting everyone else. Hello, Byron."

"Ethan," Byron says, standing and shaking my hand. He's a patrician guy from an old family in Charlotte, an East Coast prep-school kid now running a prep school himself.

Coleman smiles at me, but it looks a little sickly. I smile back, then glance at the third person.

"This is Deborah Holt," Teri says. "She's the school's attorney."

*Don't tell her a single word more than she needs to know*, Uncle Gavin insists in my head.

"Mr. Faulkner," Deborah Holt says. Her handshake is firm and dry and perfunctory. We all sit.

"Ethan, before we begin," Teri says, "please know that everyone in this room—myself, Coleman, Byron, Deborah—is your friend."

My heart freezes in my chest for a moment before it resumes pumping. That is the kind of statement someone makes just before he—or she—cuts your feet out from under you.

"I know that, Teri," I say.

Teri glances at Byron, who nods as if acknowledging his own cue. "Ethan, we've received some disturbing information about your teaching and your behavior in class."

The skin on my back crawls. "I'm sorry," I say. "I don't—what's going on?"

Teri turns her laptop around so I can see her screen. "This is your class webpage, isn't it?" she says.

I peer at her screen. "Yes," I say.

Teri clicks the Assignment menu. "Is this an assignment for your AP English class?"

I bend forward to read more closely:

Creative writing assignment: Write about a situation in which one person wrongs another. Like, for example, maybe you were dating someone, perhaps even sleeping with them, and then that person breaks up with you, and it turns out that person has her own history of trauma—a parent badly injured in a car accident, say—and might not even be stable herself. How would you react? Length: 700 words, typed and double-spaced.

I stare at the screen. *Marisa*, I think. My mouth is the Sahara—I would kill for a glass of water. "When . . . when was that posted?" I ask.

"Yesterday," Teri says. "Twelve nineteen PM, to be exact."

About an hour after I found Marisa in my house wearing Susannah's T-shirt. I read the assignment again, confusion giving way to anger. "That's not mine."

"But it's on your class website," Teri says.

"I didn't post that. I didn't *write* that." Then a thought hits me. "Is this still up? Are students seeing this?"

"Coleman took it down as soon as he saw it," Teri says. "This is a screenshot."

I look at Coleman, who clearly wishes to be anywhere but here. "When?" I ask.

He frowns. "When—?"

"When did you take it down? How long was it up?"

"Yesterday," Coleman says. "Around three thirty."

"Ethan," Teri says, "have you received any emails from students about it?"

"I didn't check my email this morning," I say. "Look, this assignment isn't mine. It's . . . weirdly inappropriate—"

Byron leans forward in his chair. "Do you often assign students creative writing exercises like this?" he asks.

"No," I say. "Not like this." I look around at everyone. "What else is wrong?"

Deborah Holt raises one eyebrow a millimeter but otherwise doesn't react. Everyone else looks uncomfortable.

"What makes you think something else is wrong?" Teri asks.

"Because my employer said he had received disturbing information about my teaching and my behavior in class," I say. "This can't be it."

Teri turns her laptop to face her, taps some keys, then turns it back around. Now the screen shows a Twitter page. The handle is EthanF8 and there's an old Archer yearbook photo of me as the profile pic. Below that I read a post: **Getting my students to write creatively ha ha #prepschooltrouble #ArcherSchoolATL**. It's dated one day ago.

"I'm not on Twitter," I say.

Coleman stirs. "Ethan—"

"*This isn't mine,*" I say.

Byron says, "The faculty handbook says teachers will not friend or engage with students on social media."

"I'm not even on social media," I say. "I mean, I have a Facebook account, but I don't go on it hardly at all."

Teri says, "You've got students responding here, Ethan."

I look at the Twitter page and see that the post has comments.

**LOL Mr Faulkner crazy assignment** from scubadood, which is apparently Mark Mitchell's Twitter handle.

**You know it,** EthanF8 responds.

**Is this real?** asks ChristyNewmanCheer.

**TMI,** writes Solomon_Sarah.

EthanF8 replies: **Life's hard, girls—get a helmet.**

"Marisa," I say.

"What?" Coleman says.

"Marisa Devereaux," I say. I look at Teri. "That's what I wanted to talk to you about. We dated, and then I broke it off, and she reacted . . . badly. And now she's doing this."

"You're saying Marisa did this?" Teri says. "That's a serious charge, Ethan."

*Well, it's a good fucking thing we have a lawyer here,* I want to say, but I manage not to. "I didn't write any of these," I say. "Even if I had a Twitter account, I wouldn't post this. And even if I did, I sure wouldn't tag Archer in it. Come on, Teri. This . . . this isn't me. You *know* me."

Teri presses her lips together and pulls open a desk drawer, removing a file folder and putting it on her desk. She flips open the file folder, and inside is my grade book. My name is neatly printed on the cover.

"Where'd you find that?" I ask. "I was looking for it in my office on Friday."

"Someone turned it in to us," Teri says.

"Was it Marisa?" I ask. "Did she take—"

"It was a custodian, Ethan," Teri says. "He found it on the floor near the senior commons."

I sit back. "Oh," I say. That's not good. While this is just a hard copy of the grades I post into our website, it's still bad that it was found where students could have seen it and potentially read all of my students' grades. "I don't know how it got in the senior commons, but if I . . . *dropped* it there or left it, I'll take full responsibility."

Teri gives me a look I can't read, then flips open the grade book. Inside, between two pages, is a photograph. I bend my head to look more closely. It's a picture of a woman, naked from the waist up. I recoil. "What the hell?" I say.

"That was my reaction as well," Byron says.

I stare at the picture. Whoever the woman is, the picture shows her torso, from midthigh up to her neck—there's no head, so no face. It's not Marisa; that I know. It looks like it might be a selfie, given the angle—a digital photo printed on regular computer paper. "You . . . found this inside my grade book?" I say.

"Yes," Teri says.

"I didn't take that picture," I say. "I've never seen it. And I sure as hell did *not* put it in my grade book."

Teri looks at me steadily. I gaze back. *It's not me*, I think.

"I believe you," Teri says.

I let out a breath I didn't know I was holding. Byron makes a displeased sound.

"I believe you," Teri says again, but now she glances at Byron before looking back at me. "But I'm afraid that's not enough."

"Not enough for what?" I ask.

"Ethan," Byron says, "the school needs to conduct an investigation into this. I'm putting you on leave, with pay, effective immediately. If we determine you had nothing to do with any of this, you will be welcome back with open arms. But in light of this troubling evidence, I'm afraid I have no choice but to ask you to stay off campus until such time as we determine you can return."

I GET INTO my car and rest my forehead against the steering wheel. I've been suspended from my job. A job that I love and am good at. Because of Marisa. I slam my fist down on top of my dashboard, then swing my arm and whack the passenger seat, causing my car to rock slightly. I start flailing, kicking the floor, nearly breaking off my rearview mirror. For a few seconds, I must look like I'm engaged in hand-to-hand combat with the interior of my Corolla. When I punch the steering wheel and the horn gives off an alarmed bleat, I'm startled enough to stop, my breathing ragged and heavy.

My phone rings. It's my home number—Susannah.

"Do you need me to come rescue you?" she says.

"Meeting's over," I say. "Marisa fucked me."

She pauses for only a second. "Well," she says, "*technically* that's true—"

Rage floods me, a white-hot neon light. "Shut up, Susannah," I say. "She *fucked* me. She stole my grade book and put a picture of a naked girl in it and dropped it where someone would find it. She opened a goddamned fake Twitter account in my name and posted crazy shit. The school's put me on leave, Susannah. I'm going to lose my *fucking job* because of her."

I hang up and throw the phone at the passenger seat, where it bounces off and hits the dash before dropping to the floor. I want to sob, I want to scream, I want to lie down and go to sleep and wake up to find this was all just a nightmare that's now over. Instead I close my eyes and will my heart rate and my breathing to slow down, and once they do I start the car and drive away.

AT HOME, I find that Susannah is gone. No note on the TV this time, or anywhere else. Her duffel bag is still here, so there's that. She's gone to ground to hide, which she always does in times of crisis. Wilson does a happy dance around my feet, and I take him outside to poop and pee, and then he sits on my lap, allowing me to rub his belly.

Marisa's phone *pings* from the coffee table. I brought it out here earlier. I knew she would text me.

Heard from school yet?
#Fuckyou☺
You still need to give me my phone back
Hellooooo
Must be sad knowing your job is on the line

I don't respond. She's angry enough that engaging with her at this point would be like provoking a snarling dog. I do, however, take pictures of these texts with my own phone. *Document everything*, my dad said once. He was talking about banking, but it's good advice here.

Another text.

I'm going to eat your heart.

Jesus, now she's quoting *Much Ado About Nothing*. I take a picture of that one just before another new text pops up.

You should check out Twitter

I hesitate, then take a picture of the text before it vanishes on her locked screen, like each of the texts before it. Then I go onto Twitter and search for EthanF8's account, where I find this new post, dated forty-one minutes ago:

Someone sent me a naughty picture omg what do I do?

Acid churns in my stomach. I know what picture she's referring to. The one in my grade book. And knowing Twitter, I can guess what's going to happen. Sure enough, Ethan F8 has a number of responses:

Post it
Post that pic
"Naughty" how?
Show me the money Faulkner
Post
Show us the pic
Put it on Insta
Post it
Post it

I feel sick. Thankfully, some people respond by telling EthanF8 to shut up, to stop trying to get attention, to not post any picture. Then my stomach drops when I read an exchange between my student Sarah Solomon and EthanF8 from fourteen minutes ago:

Total bot, Solomon_Sarah posted. You're not Mr. Faulkner.
No bot, EthanF8 replied.
Then a fake.
No fake, either.
Prove it, Solomon_Sarah wrote.

*No, no, no*, I think. *Don't respond.*
I scroll down to the rest of the thread, and I see that EthanF8 has replied.

You write beautiful essays but you hide behind those cat-eye glasses like the world's youngest virgin librarian.

*Shit.*

Maybe that's why you sent this pic

Followed by a copy of the picture Marisa stuck in my grade book, with a black line drawn across the nipples.

"*No!*" I shout, dropping the phone like a burning coal. I jump up and start pawing through my workbag, looking for the school directory, knowing Sarah Solomon's home phone number must be in there. I find the directory, but actually grasping it in my hand makes me pause, though my heart is hammering away in my chest. What am I going to do—call my student to say it's not me posting nasty tweets at her? That I wasn't the one who posted a nude pic and basically accused her of being a stalker? Byron and Teri would love hearing that I did that. Plus I'd probably get Sarah's mom or dad on the phone, and I can easily imagine them calling the police.

So I call Coleman Carter instead.

"It's not me on Twitter," I say as soon as he answers. "It's Marisa. She's bullying Sarah Solomon."

"Slow down," Coleman says. "What are you talking about?"

"On *Twitter*," I say. "That account Marisa opened pretending to be me. She just posted that picture she put in my grade book and basically accused Sarah of sending it to her. Me. Whatever. You have to tell her it wasn't me. You have to call Sarah, call her *parents*, and tell them it wasn't me."

"Hold on," Coleman says. "Sarah who?"

"*Solomon*," I nearly shout into the phone. "Marisa is posting on Twitter as me, but *it's not me*."

On the coffee table, Marisa's phone *dings*. A new text. I glance down at it, and everything stops.

I know who killed your parents

I stand rooted to the floor, staring down at the text on the locked screen. Six short words, and they almost drop me like a heart attack.

I know who killed your parents

Coleman is saying something in my ear. "I'll call you back," I say, and hang up on him.

Marisa's text vanishes from the screen.

"Shit." I swipe her phone and get the request to enter a pass code. "*Fuck!*"

My phone rings in my hand. Another unknown number. If it's Marisa, I'll eat *her* fucking heart over the phone. I answer and shout, "Hello?"

There's some sort of background wind noise, as if the person on the other end is calling me from a racing sailboat. "Ethan?" a voice says unsteadily.

"Who is this?"

A pause, a shifting kind of sound, like the phone is being brushed across something. That rushing, roaring noise continues. "I'm sorry," the voice says. "I just . . . I'm sorry."

Realization forms like a ball of ice in my stomach. "Suze?" I say. "Is that you? Where are you? What's going on?"

A flat, hard sound like a car horn obliterates any reply she makes. Is she on a street somewhere? The sound fades abruptly and Susannah sighs. "I always loved the King and Queen buildings, you know? All lit up at night. Now they're green. Maybe because it's March. Like a spring thing."

The King and Queen buildings are a pair of skyscrapers, glass towers sporting white latticed "crowns," a square one for the King building and a curved one for the Queen. They are a good three or four miles away, just off the Perimeter. "Are you there?" I ask. "Susannah, are you at the King and Queen buildings?"

"So pretty," she breathes, and the finality in her voice, the sense of an approaching end, lights up my spine with alarm.

"Suze, where are you?" I yell, searching around the kitchen for my keys. I snag them off the counter, then start looking for a pair of shoes.

"It's not your fault, Ethan," she says. "I'm sorry."

"Susannah?"

She mutters something; the only words I can clearly make out are "way down," and then the roaring noise increases, only to end in a jarring silence.

"Susannah?" I yell. "Suzie!" There's no sound—the call has ended.

I brace myself against the back of my couch, fighting off a wave of panic, and force myself to think. She doesn't have a car, but she could have Ubered to the King and Queen. But it's Sunday; those buildings wouldn't be open. You can see the towers from lots of places around Sandy Springs. Including the Roswell Road overpass that crosses I-285, about a mile north of my house.

I find my flip-flops under an ottoman, shove my feet into them, and race for the door.

# CHAPTER SIXTEEN

Traffic isn't bad for a Sunday evening, but I weave around
what cars there are on Roswell Road, making liberal use of my horn. A
traffic light turns yellow, and I fly beneath it just before it turns red. But
I have to stop at the light at Glenridge, where the Church of Scientology has taken up residence in an old brick-and-column structure that
looks like the bastard offspring of a Williamsburg mansion and a den-
tist's office. I find myself thinking I will convert to Scientology if I can
get to my sister in time. If I'm not already too late.

The light changes. By some miracle there are no police around as
I gun the Corolla through the intersection, narrowly missing a pickup
truck laden with ladders and paint buckets. Then I'm going down the
long slope toward I-285 and the overpass. Ahead, an orderly array of
red taillights crosses the highway. I blow through another yellow light,
nearly clip a slow-turning SUV, and then I'm racing up the slight rise to
the overpass itself. The sun has dropped below the horizon, but I can see
a figure on the sidewalk, halfway across the bridge, standing at the rail.
The safety barrier, a chain-link fence that usually rises up from the rail
and curves inward, is gone—a few days ago a utility truck overcorrected
on a turn and scraped the rail, tearing a long gash in the fencing. Aside
from a waist-high iron rail and some plastic orange netting above that,

there is nothing between the figure on the walkway and the open air to the highway below.

I pull the car as close to the side of the road as I can, stopping abruptly just at the start of the bridge. I punch on the hazard lights and get out of my car. A UPS delivery van rolls past, giving a quick blast on its horn, the exhaust blowing my hair back.

It's Susannah, all right, thirty feet away, leaning against the railing, peering down at the interstate traffic flowing twenty feet beneath her.

"Susannah!" I call out.

She keeps looking down. I walk toward her slowly, wary of spooking her. "Susannah?" I call out again.

"I dropped my phone," she says, still looking down at the highway. A tractor trailer zooms past below. Absurdly I think of alligators in a moat. "It just . . . slipped out of my hand," she continues. "Almost hit a car. Jesus, that would be a shitty way to go. You're driving along and someone drops their iPhone through your windshield. But it didn't hit anyone."

I come to a stop maybe six feet away, nerves on edge. I hate heights, and I feel if I glance one more time over the rail, I'll either be sick or fall. My stomach clenches at the thought. I swear I can feel the bridge sway ever so gently beneath my feet. Another passing car honks indignantly. In the distance to the east, above the tree line, I can just make out the tops of the King and Queen towers, the greenish glow of their crowns like a pair of spectral eyes observing this family reunion. I try to ignore everything except my sister. She still looks down at the interstate as if mesmerized by what she sees.

"Susannah," I manage to say. I think I sound relatively calm. "What are you doing?"

"Thinking about jumping," she says.

Someone drives past in an SUV, the passenger window down, shouting. All I can hear is, "—you crazy?"

"Susannah," I say. "Suze. Let's . . . let's get in my car. Come on. I'll take you somewhere. We'll get ice cream or something. A beer."

"I don't want a beer," she says. She is still looking down.

"I'll get you whatever you want," I say. "I'll buy you a whole fucking bar. Just . . . don't."

She turns her head to look at me then, and I see tears have tracked down her cheeks. "You know what I want?" she says. "I want Mom."

Her words are a sword through my heart. I open my mouth, close it again.

"I know it's stupid," she says.

"It's not stupid," I say.

She holds a furious grief in her eyes, like an unbearable flame. "I want to jump," she says in a small, tight voice.

"Please don't," I say, my voice cracking. "Don't do that, Susannah. I . . . I don't want you to. Please. We can get you help. I'll get you help."

She leans against the railing as if winded. Below her, traffic streaks by at seventy miles an hour.

"Come on," I say, extending my hand. "Just walk over here. It'll be okay. I love you. It's okay. I love you. Come on."

Slowly, as if she has to decipher the meanings of my words, Susannah frowns, glancing at me. Then, quickly, she straightens up. A bright panic shoots through my heart.

"Okay," she says in the same small, tight voice, as if speaking is painful. And she reaches out and takes my hand, then walks into my awkward hug, leaning against me as I clutch her and choke back sobs. Behind me, cars continue to honk, the passing commuters bearing witness to my sister avoiding death, again.

I DRIVE SUSANNAH to Northside Hospital, the closest ER. It's known as the Baby Factory because most suburban moms in Buckhead and Dunwoody and Sandy Springs deliver their babies at Northside. Both my sister and I were born there. Taking her to Northside makes a strange kind of sense—she was born there and she will avoid dying there.

Susannah sits in the front seat and stares out the passenger window. I don't know what to say and don't want to just babble at her, so I say nothing. Instead I scan the radio incessantly, jumping from Fleetwood Mac to Usher to Selena Gomez to Zeppelin, until finally I just turn the radio off and we drive in relative silence.

I pull into Northside's ER parking lot and head for the gate by the ticket booth, and Susannah stirs, seeming to realize where she is. "Just pull over," she says.

"I am," I say. "Just need to get a ticket and find somewhere to park."

"No, just pull over."

"Susannah, I have to—"

"Goddamn it, Ethan, just pull over," she says, sounding angry and resigned at the same time.

I turn hard right, out of the lane leading into the parking lot, and stop behind a black Lexus in a handicapped spot, just across from the ER entrance. "Okay," I say, turning to Susannah, "what?"

My phone, mounted on the dash, rings. The screen says **Coleman Carter**. I must have hung up on him when I ran out the door to save Susannah. I'll call him back. "Sorry," I say to Susannah. "What is it?"

"I need to go in," Susannah says.

"Well, yeah," I say. "That's why I was looking—"

"I need to go in alone," she interrupts. "Without you."

"What?"

My phone rings again. Coleman. I reject the call.

"I need to do this alone, Ethan," she says.

"Uh-uh," I say, shaking my head. "I'm going in there with you."

"Why?" she says.

"Why? Because I'm your *brother*. Because I want to help."

"I know," she says. "And that's why I have to go in by myself."

"I don't—"

She raises her voice. "I have to do this on my own. My whole life you've had to pick up after me, clean up my shit. I just . . . I need to do this."

My phone rings a third time. *Damn* it. I stab at the answer icon, then put the phone on speaker. "I'm really busy here, Coleman."

"Ethan," Coleman says, and the tone in his voice is like a cold wind on my neck. "I got Sarah Solomon's father on the phone. Her mother found her locked in the bathroom, lying on the floor next to the toilet. She took a bunch of pills."

I stare at the phone, struck dumb by the horror of what he said. "Oh Jesus," I say.

"She'd thrown them up, thank God," Coleman continues. "They don't know exactly what all she took; probably some expired pain meds. They're on the way to the hospital." He pauses. "Sarah had her phone with her when her mom found her. I told her parents it wasn't you on Twitter. I don't think they care much right now—"

"No, that's fine, it doesn't—*matter* now. God. I—is she okay?"

"She should be," Coleman says. "Just wanted to let you know. Are you okay?"

I want to sob. "Yeah," I manage, my voice a bit high. "Yeah. I'm all right. Just—I'm sorry, but can I call you back in just a minute?"

"Yes," Coleman says. "Call me anytime, Ethan. I'm here."

I hang up and briefly close my eyes, then open them and turn to Susannah. "Sorry."

She shakes her head. "It's okay." The look in her face is bleak, her gaze far away. "I'm sorry about your student." She takes a breath. "Marisa did something?" she says, still facing forward.

"Yeah. She posted that picture on Twitter, the one she put in my grade book, said it was my student."

Susannah continues to stare out the windshield. "Was it a naked selfie? No head?"

I frown, confused. "Yeah, but how—"

"It's me." She turns then to look at me, and the look in her eyes is bleak and resigned. No, not resigned. Resolved. "I sent Marisa that picture."

"You sent . . . *why?*"

"Told you we were flirting."

I stare at my sister, unable to think of a response. Someone nearby in the parking lot slams a car door shut.

Susannah nods as if in confirmation, then takes another breath. "Go ahead. I've got this. Really."

I blink, surprised at the shift in conversation, still processing what my sister just told me. "But . . . you don't have insurance; I need to help pay—"

"I'm still on Uncle Gavin's insurance," she says. She looks at me, her face softening a little. "I'll call you later," she says. "Might not be until tomorrow. But if there's a problem or whatever before then, I'll call. Honest."

We sit there in the ER parking lot, looking at each other. My sister's face is pale and tired, mushroom-colored circles under her eyes, but she still has a strength of will that I can see in her glance, a small but resolute flame. Still I hesitate. "You sure?"

She nods, a sad little movement of her head. Then she leans over and kisses me on the cheek. Before I can react, she's out the door, closing it behind her and walking toward the ER. She's halfway across the lot before I think about getting out of the car and following her, but I stay behind the wheel and watch her enter the glass double doors. There's a nurse at the main desk, and I watch Susannah talk to her. The nurse looks out the glass doors at me, and Susannah turns around and gives me a little wave before turning back to the nurse. Then the nurse comes out from behind the desk and leads Susannah into the waiting room, then through it to a doorway leading back to the ER.

I wipe my eyes and take in a shuddering breath, then another as I watch Susannah walk back into the ER with the nurse. As soon as the ER door swings shut behind them, I start my car and drive off, heading home.

WHEN I GET home, I see Marisa has sent a single text:

I'm not going anywhere, Ethan.

*Yes, you are*, I think, and I turn off her phone and put it in a drawer.

I talk to Coleman on the phone that night for a good hour. I know he feels guilty about his role in the meeting in Teri's office earlier today—today? my God, it seems like a thousand years ago—and so listening to me is his self-inflicted penance, but I don't care. He assures me that he doesn't think for a moment that I am capable of doing anything like what Marisa did on Twitter while pretending to be me. I don't tell him the picture is of my sister. Coleman tells me Sarah Solomon had her stomach pumped and has been admitted to Scottish Rite Hospital. Physically she should be just fine, Coleman says. He doesn't say anything about how she's doing psychologically. He doesn't need to. She swallowed a bunch of pills after Marisa bullied her on Twitter.

And circling in the background, like a wolf padding in the shadows just beyond the range of light, is Marisa's claim that she knows who killed my parents.

Somewhere in the middle of the night, eventually, I fall asleep, because my own phone rings and wakes me up late the next morning. It's Monday. I should be at school right now, teaching sonnets. When I answer my phone, it's Susannah.

"I'm at Birchwood," she says.

"You're not at Northside?"

"They transferred me. Bed opened up this morning. My shrink works here."

"Okay," I say, sitting up in my bed. I know Birchwood—it's where Susannah has her group therapy. And she's been admitted there before.

"Are you okay?" I ask. "Do you need anything?"

"A brand-new central nervous system and a box of Marlboros," she says. "But I'll settle for some clean clothes."

THE WAITING ROOM in Birchwood is tastefully decorated with light, muted colors on the walls and carpeted floors. Glossy magazines that are only a couple of months old lie on slim wooden tables. The tables look plastic, but maybe they're made out of actual birch wood, I don't know.

Susannah has voluntarily committed herself. Right now she's in Birchwood's acute inpatient unit. This is the second time she's been here. Birchwood is quiet and clean and the staff are very kind. I hate it. Each time I come in here, I feel like the hospital will absorb my sister somehow, suck her into a back room with strapped gurneys and soulless, smiling doctors who will keep her from ever leaving.

A nurse walks out through a secured door, Susannah trailing him. She looks pale and drawn, but steady. I stand up. "Hey," I say, putting my hands into the back pockets of my jeans.

"You always do that," she says.

"What?"

"Put your hands in your pockets like that."

The nurse stands off to the side like a warder. Which is exactly what he is—making sure Susannah won't make a break for it.

I take my hands out of my pockets and pick up a small duffel. "Got your clothes."

The nurse steps forward, his hand out. "I'll take that, sir," he says. He takes the duffel bag, slings it over his shoulder, and steps back again. That gesture seems to confirm that my sister is, in fact, committed to a mental hospital, and my eyes prick and sting. I blink, determined not to cry.

"Hey," Susannah says. She steps up to me, and the nurse tenses a bit but doesn't move. Susannah wraps me in a hug. I can feel her collarbones press into my chest. "I'll be okay," she says, her voice muffled against my shoulder. I squeeze her and stroke her hair twice, not trusting my voice. She pulls away, gives me a sad smile, and then walks back to the secured door with the nurse, who punches in a code, lets my sister in, and walks in himself, the door closing behind them with an electronic chime.

I know the nurse will look through the bag and remove anything in it that she could use to harm herself, just as they did earlier with her belt. They will place those items carefully into a ziplock bag, which they will mark with her name and file in the appropriate drawer. I wish they could do the same thing with the part of her that drives her to consider jumping from bridges and sleep with fellow group-therapy members. I know they can't, that they will never be able to pluck that out of her like a tumor or a swollen appendix and then discard it tidily, problem solved. Which may be one reason I hate this place, because I feel it's a kind of mental health theater, like removing our shoes in airport security is supposed to make us feel safer when we get on a plane.

I stay in the waiting room for a few more moments, hating to stay and reluctant to leave. The woman at the intake desk told me Susannah has insurance, which I know is supplied by my uncle. But I don't know how much it will cover, or what the limit is for the number of days Susannah can stay, or at what point Susannah will be responsible for costs. All questions that good citizens should be able to answer, and I don't know a clear, definitive answer for any of them when it comes to my sister. I am afraid to ask the intake nurse anything else, to share any information, in case whatever I say conflicts with what Susannah told them. I don't know what, if anything, would happen if I did that. Would her insurance be denied? Would she be thrown out of Birchwood? Or would she remain locked inside, a prisoner of her brother's ignorance and inability to take care of her?

And then there's Marisa, out there somewhere, stalking me through her phone, which is still in a drawer at my house. At what point will she stop terrorizing me via tweets and return to my house to try to get her phone? And what will I do if she does? And how in the name of all the saints and archangels and all the devils in hell does she know who killed my parents?

I take one last look around the waiting room, the soft lighting and the plastic-looking tables and the one couple sitting in a far corner, looking stunned and exhausted, the only other people on this side of the secured door. If this is supposed to be a place of help, then why do I feel helpless?

WHEN I GET home, it's late afternoon, and Wilson is near to bursting his bladder, but he makes it into the yard, where he pees with visible relief. On his way back inside, he gives me only a passing lick, as if withholding affection because I took too long to get home. Then he sticks his snout into his food dish and starts gobbling up the kibble I have given him.

I need to know what Marisa knows about my family, what else she may have done. If her phone weren't screen locked, I could just turn it back on and call "Mom" and demand answers. But even if I could, that feels like rewarding Marisa for bad behavior and would be about as safe as sticking my hand into a bag of snakes. She would just continue to hiss and scratch and laugh, taunting me over the phone. I need a tactical advantage.

Knowing the location of your opponent is a first step. School has been out for nearly an hour, so she should be home. I go online to Archer's website, tap through to the faculty directory, and look up Marisa. The directory lists her street address as Habersham Road, in the heart of Buckhead. Very bougie. There's a phone number, not her cell. I pick up my landline and dial the number. Two rings in, a man answers, formally polite. "Devereaux residence."

"Yes, I'd like to leave a message for Marisa Devereaux, please," I say.

The man—secretary, butler, whatever—sounds as if he spent his undergraduate years practicing elocution at Oxford. "May I ask what this is regarding?"

"I'm a colleague of hers at Archer," I say. "We needed to talk about some lesson plans. If she's at home . . ."

Oxford doesn't take the bait. "Miss Devereaux is not available at the moment."

"Oh," I say. "Shoot. I . . . the thing is, I'm heading to an out-of-town conference tonight and really needed to talk with her before I left. Do you know when she will be back?"

There is the briefest hesitation. "No, sir, I'm afraid I don't," he says, sounding genuinely regretful. "May I take your name and number?"

I hang up. It's possible old Oxford wasn't being truthful and Marisa was standing right there next to him, listening in on the conversation. But something tells me he wasn't lying.

I text Coleman and ask if Marisa was at school today. He responds almost immediately. **No she didn't come in today. Teri was going to talk to her first thing this AM but she never showed.** He follows this with: **You doing okay?**

I text back **Yeah, thanks** and put my phone down. If Marisa isn't at her house and wasn't at school, then she's MIA.

I sit on my couch, doing nothing for a few moments other than looking around my living room.

Wilson finishes his kibble and looks up at me, cocking his head.

I pick up my phone and scroll through my work email until I find one from Coleman back in January where he sent me a copy of Marisa's résumé. I open the attached file and find Marisa's last workplace: the Hastings School. Marisa said she had worked there until last summer. Their website, which is sleeker than ours, shows nine English faculty. The department chair, Niki Simpson, does not have a cell phone listed, although she has an office number. I am about to call her when I go back to the list of English faculty. Of the nine, three are men. One looks to be in his sixties, and the other started at Hastings last August. The third, Todd Jorgenson, has been teaching at Hastings for five years. His photo reveals the smiling good looks of a sitcom star.

A plan dimly takes shape in my head. Before I lose my nerve, I call the main number for the school, hoping they haven't already left for the day, but a receptionist promptly picks up. "The Hastings School; this is Holly."

"Oh, great, I was afraid you'd be closed," I say. "I'm trying to get in touch with Todd Jorgenson?"

"Certainly," says Holly. "I can put you through to his voice mail."

"Actually, Holly, I'm in kind of a bind," I say, standing up from the couch and walking around my den. "Todd's a college buddy and we have plans for spring break, but the airline's canceled the flight."

"Oh no," Holly says.

"Yeah, it's lousy, but we can reschedule. The thing is, I need to know right now what to tell them about the tickets, and I lost Todd's cell. Is there any way you can tell me how to reach Todd directly?"

Holly hesitates and I glance at Wilson, who is still looking at me with a cocked head. *Don't judge*, I want to tell him.

"Well," Holly says, "I'm not allowed to give out personal cell phone numbers."

"Totally understand," I say, nodding as if Holly can see me, although I'm disappointed. Still, I knew this wouldn't be that easy. "I get it." Then I lower my voice slightly. "Todd told me about . . . you know, last year." I pause, but Holly says nothing. "With his coworker," I say, taking the leap. "Sounded awful. I wouldn't want anybody giving out my phone number either."

Another pause. I'm about to hang up when Holly says, her voice lowered to match mine, "It *was* pretty awful. She treated him *terribly*. I always thought she was so nice."

*Me too*, I think. I feel both elated and nauseous. "You can't tell about people sometimes," I manage to say. "If you give me his voice mail, that should be fine, thanks. I'm sure he'll call me right back."

"All right," Holly says, clearly relieved not to be put in a tight spot. "Good luck with your plane tickets! I'll transfer you now."

As soon as she transfers the call to Todd Jorgenson's voice mail, I hang up. Even if Todd would be willing to talk to me, I don't need his story right now. Holly confirmed my suspicions; Marisa has done this before. It's something I can take to Teri Merchant to help me keep my job. But it won't help me right now. Telling Marisa I know what she did at Hastings won't make her reveal what else she knows about my family, and it might just send her completely over the edge of crazy. I need help.

Wilson picks up his rope bone and walks over to me, dropping the toy at my feet. He sits, his tail wagging. I kick the rope bone so it slides across the floor, and Wilson bounds happily after it.

I do not want to call my uncle.

I pick my phone back up and scroll through my contacts until I see the number I need. I hesitate, then touch the screen to call.

The phone rings three times, four, and then it's answered. "Ethan?" my uncle says.

"You have caller ID now?" I say.

"I have a smartphone," he says.

"Welcome to the twenty-first century."

There is a pause, and then, not unkindly, Uncle Gavin says, "What do you need, Ethan?"

I take a deep breath and release it in a shuddery exhalation. "I need help," I say.

"Are you hurt?" he says. "Or under arrest?"

"No," I say. "It's Susannah. And I'm in trouble at work."

He pauses, presumably to take this all in. "Can you come to the bar tomorrow morning?"

"Yeah. Thank you."

"Nine o'clock," he says, and hangs up.

THE NEXT MORNING I take a MARTA train down to the Midtown Station, walk over to West Peachtree, and head north. It's sunny and clear, a typical spring morning in Atlanta. Traffic inches its way along the interstate two blocks to my left. A row of posters on a wall advertises a concert by Balm of Woe at the Tabernacle. It's a short walk, but part of me illogically wishes it were much longer, that I didn't need to make this walk at all.

My uncle's bar appears ahead, on the right, the same paint color and the same signs out front. I turn into the tiny parking lot next to the bar, where there is a side door. The door is ugly and scarred.

It is waiting for me to open it.

# CHAPTER SEVENTEEN

In the spring of our senior year in high school, Frankie and I felt invincible. The future stretched before us, an orchard of possibilities—we only had to stretch out our hands and pluck whichever ripe fruit we wanted.

Except Susannah, then in ninth grade, wanted to burn everything down and leave nothing but ash.

One sunny April afternoon, Susannah vanished from PE class. I knew because a couple of ninth graders, awkward with acne and braces, told me in the hallway that Coach Barnes had been pissed. Frankie and I skipped English class to go look for her, because my sister was not the kind of person to go sit alone on the roof of the gym and write bad poetry when she cut class. True to form, we found her behind the baseball field, crouching in a runoff ditch with three punks who were watching my sister suck on a pipe.

I grabbed Susannah's arm and hauled her to her feet. She squawked, smoke erupting from between her lips, and dropped the pipe.

"Hey!" One of the three punks stood up, his legs unfolding until he stood a head taller than me. Luco was a senior, too, when he bothered to come to school. "Watch out for my shit." He stooped to pick up the pipe.

I said to Susannah, "Stop acting surprised. You knew I was coming when I was twenty yards away."

Susannah grinned, hanging from the end of my arm like dead weight. "Why're you here?" she said, slurring slightly.

"You smoking during school now?" I said to Susannah.

Luco sneered. "You wasn't too good for it yo'self once."

Frankie snorted. "*Caricatura*," he muttered.

Luco put a hand behind his ear, feigning deafness. "What's that, Latrino? Can't hear you, man." One of the other two snickered.

Frankie raised his voice. "I said you're a fucking cartoon. Talking like you're some kind of gangbanger when you just skip school and smoke weed."

"Get up," I hissed at Susannah, who was still hanging from my grip. She glared at me as best she could through slitted eyes.

Luco took a step forward, all laughter vanished from his face. Behind him, his two followers got to their feet. One of them held a wooden baseball bat, a heavy crack splitting it down the middle of the barrel.

"Susannah, Goddamn it," I said.

Luco flexed his fingers like he was trying to remember how to make a fist.

"Ethan," Frankie said warningly. His voice was mostly steady.

Susannah chose that moment to drop to the ground, boneless, tearing herself out of my grasp. I dropped into a crouch alongside her, my hands scrabbling in the dirt. Luco looked down at me. "The fuck you doin'?" he demanded.

My hand found a rock.

"Improvising," I said.

I stood, tossing a handful of dust into Luco's face. Spluttering, he took half a step back, and I used the opening to swing at Luco with the rock in my hand. I hit him in the jaw. Luco howled and clutched his face. I turned just in time to see his friend with the broken baseball bat swing overhead at me like a cheap samurai. I sidestepped, and he stumbled from the follow-through as the bat chopped into the ground and fell from his hands. I was able to kick the bat away before Luco's second minion jumped me.

Frankie and I put up a good fight, but it was three on two, and at the end of it Frankie lay on the ground curled up like he was taking a nap and each of Luco's pals had me by an arm, my feet dragging on the ground.

Luco stood in front of me, a murderous look on his face. I could see the dark, swelling bruise on Luco's jaw where I had hit him with the rock. "Hold him up," he said to his friends. He pointed a fat finger in my face. "Boy, I'm gonna fuck you up, motherfucker."

My left eye was swelling shut, so I had to squint at him. "That's badass," I said. "Very Samuel L. Jackson."

Luco took a step back and then, like he was punting a football, kicked me in the stomach. All the air whooshed out of me, and I retched from the shock and the pain.

Luco was gearing up for another kick when his eyes popped wide open. He stepped back, hands up. I turned my head and saw Susannah standing a few yards away, her feet apart, both hands holding a small pistol aimed at Luco. The two guys holding my arms froze. We all froze.

"Let him go," Susannah said.

Luco was trying to look at both Susannah and the pistol in her hand, his eyes darting back and forth. It would have been funny if I hadn't been struggling to breathe.

The guy holding my right arm said, "That's a two-shot. You gonna shoot all three of us with that?"

"Nope," Susannah. She raised the pistol to aim at Luco's forehead. "Just him."

His voice high, Luco said, "Let him the fuck go."

The two let go of my arms, and I fell to my hands and knees, wheezing and trying not to throw up as I filled my lungs with air again.

"I'll be seeing you, li'l girl," Luco said, somewhere above me.

"Not if I see you first," Susannah said sweetly.

There was a pause, and then I heard footsteps heading away. When I couldn't hear them anymore, I looked up. Susannah was standing in front of me, the pistol held loosely at her side.

"Where the hell did you get that?" I managed to say.

Susannah shrugged. "I know a guy."

"You know a *guy*?"

"Just saved your sorry ass with it."

I stood up, wincing at the pain in my gut and around my eye, which was definitely swelling shut. Behind Susannah, I saw Frankie getting unsteadily to his feet and dusting himself off. "*Hijo de puta* tore my shirt," he said.

"You okay?"

"Better than you." Frankie peered at me. "He gave you a shiner. Gonna be pretty."

Susannah pocketed her pistol and began walking back to school.

"Hey," I said. She paid no attention to me. "Hey!" I shouted. I hurried after her, trying to ignore the pain in my stomach. When I reached her, I grabbed her arm and swung her around to face me. Her expression was equal parts sullen and annoyed. "What is wrong with you?"

"Let me go, Ethan," she said.

"You're skipping school, sucking a pipe with Luco?"

She shot back, "Like you didn't smoke with him."

"Until I realized it was stupid and that I didn't want to go to jail, like he's going to. Like you will if you keep doing this shit."

Susannah wrenched her arm out of my grasp, glaring at me.

"Jesus," I said, understanding. "You're pissed at me."

She folded her arms across her chest and continued to give me a death stare.

"Okay," I said. I wiped my face with both hands, careful not to touch my bruised eye. "Luco is not a good guy. I figured that out like ten seconds after I smoked a joint with him in tenth grade. He's a loser, Susannah. You didn't miss out on anything."

Frankie spoke up. "I told Ethan not to smoke with him."

I gestured toward Frankie. "See? I was stupid and didn't listen. Now Luco is pissed at me because he thinks I dissed him, so he wants to mess with me. How's he going to do that, Suze? How's he going to try to hurt me?"

I stopped and waited for her to figure it out. I didn't wait long. Susannah's expression went from sullen to angry to flushed and back to sullen again in the time it takes to turn a light on and off. She wasn't used to being played.

"Look," I said in a gentler voice. "You showed guts just hanging out with the dude and his two boys. You probably would've stuck that pipe in his eye the second he tried to do anything."

Susannah's face darkened. "Don't try to handle me, Ethan." She walked away, then looked back over her shoulder. "Sorry about your shirt, Frankie," she said, then kept walking.

Frankie stood beside me as we both watched her walk past the baseball field back toward school. "What's wrong with my sister, Frankie?" I said.

Frankie shook his head. "She's too damn smart, and too damn angry," he said. "And she isn't scared of anything."

Susannah reached the parking lot and stepped between two cars, vanishing from sight.

"That's what terrifies me," I said.

TWO DAYS LATER Luco and his friends grabbed Susannah after school and drove off with her. Another kid told us, and I called Uncle Gavin. "He'll hurt her," I said, my voice breaking.

"Go home," he said. "I'll find her."

"I'll go with you."

"Go home, Ethan," he said, and hung up.

Instead, Frankie and I broke into the school's yearbook office and found an old address for Luco. It was in the Bluff, a neighborhood west of downtown that, back in the day, was basically an open-air drug market. Frankie and his dad both had smartphones, so Frankie texted the address to his dad, and then we turned off our phones so we wouldn't hear any calls from his father or my uncle. We got in Frankie's car—the '71 Pontiac Firebird Trans Am his father had taught him to rebuild and that I called the Frankenstein—and drove to the Bluff.

I don't remember much about the drive, except for the fear rising up in me like a dark tide. Luco had taken Susannah and I didn't know where she was, and dear God in heaven I was scared. I was more scared than I had been when two men came into our house and blew my family and my childhood into dust. And I didn't believe in God, but driving to the Bluff in Frankie's car, I told Him that I would do anything, anything to get my sister back; I would switch places with her right now, let Luco do whatever he wanted to do to me, just please don't let my sister be hurt or die, because if there was an afterlife I did not want to meet my father beyond the grave and tell him I had failed him.

It was night by the time we reached the house. The street was hedged in by trees, many overgrown with kudzu, so despite the asphalt and power lines and the Trans Am, the street felt like part of an old civilization being reclaimed slowly by a jungle.

The house was clearly abandoned, the walls tagged with graffiti and the windows boarded up. We snuck into the house through a hole in the back wall covered in plywood. Inside, we found Susannah, sitting in the dark against a wall, eyes closed, face bruised, a fresh needle mark in her arm. Then Luco stepped out of the shadows and cracked me over the head with a pistol before holding us at gunpoint. He had been embarrassed in front of his boys, frightened by a girl with a tiny gun, and now he was relishing his revenge. He had shot heroin into Susannah's veins, and now he was going to shoot both of us and leave Susannah alive so she would know what had happened to us.

There was an electronic squawk from outside, like a klaxon burst. A police car. Uncle Gavin had called the cavalry. Luco turned toward the sound, and Frankie jumped him, causing Luco to drop the pistol. They fought while I scrabbled around on the floor, head still reeling from being hit over the head by the pistol I was searching for. Luco threw Frankie off him and grabbed me just as my hand closed on something—a syringe, maybe the same one he had used on my sister. Luco drew back a fist, and I swung and jabbed that syringe straight into his ear. He shrieked and dropped me, stumbling away and out the front door, then fell down the outside stairs, breaking an ankle.

That's the moment when it should have all gone right, the universe rebalanced, justice served. Frankie and I had gone into the dark cave, fought the ogre, and rescued my sister. We would go home, bruised but alive and victorious. But I should have known, more than anyone, that the universe does not work that way.

Someone stepped into the doorway, blocking the light. It was Frankie, looking out. Blue and red lights flashed beyond him. I could hear Frankie talking with someone. He raised his hand as if he was pointing at something below him. Then a sharp *crack*. Shouts came from outside, and a bright light shone on the front door, revealing Frankie in silhouette, dropping to his knees, hands empty and up over his head.

UNCLE GAVIN PULLED out all the stops, hiring a defense attorney for Frankie and calling in favors. But there were no magic phone calls for Frankie, no councilman in Uncle Gavin's back pocket who could make this go away. Frankie had purposefully shot a man to death in front of two police officers. He was charged with voluntary manslaughter. Later, when he was out on bail, Frankie told me that when he found the gun and stepped to the front door to see Luco writhing in pain on the steps and two police officers getting out of their patrol car, Luco had told him that when he got out of prison he would find and kill all of us. And so Frankie had lifted the pistol and shot Luco in the head, then dropped the gun and raised his hands so the two cops wouldn't shoot him. "It was like you would kill a snake," Frankie said, but his voice trembled when he said it.

When Susannah got out of the hospital, she slept late every morning. Hibernating, she said. She went to outpatient therapy at Birchwood every afternoon, Monday through Friday, for two weeks. In the evenings she slogged through whatever school work she had been sent. She wasn't attending classes, with the school's permission, but Uncle Gavin, who otherwise treated Susannah as if she were made of glass, insisted that she keep up with her work.

One night after dinner I knocked on the door of her room. She was sitting on her bed, doing geometry. "I hate proofs," she said. "I mean hate them. When in my life am I going to need to prove that the sum of the interior angles of a triangle equals a straight angle?"

"Mrs. Markham says geometry is good for sharpening logic and developing your argumentative skills," I said, referring to my English teacher.

Susannah scowled at her textbook. "Mrs. Markham can bite me," she said. "No offense." She wrote something in her notebook, then looked up at me. "What?"

The doctors had told us that they had given my sister Narcan to counteract the heroin in her system and that there had been no permanent damage. They had also told us that Susannah had been raped.

"Nothing," I said. I walked around her room, glancing at her empty desk, the poster of Munch's *The Scream* on her closet door. "Just wanted to see how you're doing."

"I'm even more committed to not becoming a mathematician," she said.

"You know what I mean."

"Worried I'm using heroin?" She turned out her forearms for inspection. "No needle marks, see?"

"Jesus, Susannah."

"If you want to make sure I'm not shooting up between my toes, I can take my socks off."

"All right, enough. God."

She sighed and set her notebook off to the side, then crossed her legs. "I'm fine, Ethan," she said. "I'm pissed off at the world in general and *really* pissed off at Luco, but I'm okay. Really."

"How can you just . . . *say* that stuff so easily?"

She shrugged. "Hours of therapy. And not giving a shit." She considered me. "Thanks, by the way. For coming to rescue me."

"You're welcome."

She tilted her head. "You okay?"

"Me? Yeah. I'm fine."

"Uh-huh," Susannah said. "Your best friend might go to jail for killing someone. You're stellar."

I wanted to wrap my arms around her, but I was torn as to what I would do after that—give her a hug, or strangle her to death. "I worry about you," I said. "Deeply."

"Snafu," she said. I stared at her. "You know," she said, "situation normal, all fucked up."

"I know what *snafu* means."

She punched me in the arm. "Don't worry, big brother," she said. "Ernest Hemingway said we're all broken. That's how the light gets in."

"Hemingway also blew his own head off with a shotgun."

Susannah laughed. "Are you worried I'm going to off myself?" When I continued to stare at her, she got serious. "I won't ever want to kill myself, because I wouldn't give Luco the satisfaction," she said.

"He's dead," I said.

"And I'm not," she said. "Winning."

FRANKIE GOT A plea deal from the DA—ten years, with the possibility of parole after serving three years of his sentence. He took it.

Having my best friend go to prison was devastating. Strangely, aside from Frankie, the person I missed most at that time was Fay, Uncle Gavin's old girlfriend. She would have known what to say to Ruben, or to Frankie. But she had never returned after walking out of the house that night. Uncle Gavin had dated a few women after Fay left, but they rarely stayed at the house—Uncle Gavin would spend the night with them somewhere else—and none of them ever lasted more than a few weeks, let alone showed any genuine interest in me or Susannah. And none of them could cook. We had not had a truly good dinner since Fay left. Even the house missed her, if the state of the windows and the wood floors and the kitchen counters was any indication, but Uncle Gavin and Susannah and I had somehow muddled through. Now, though, it felt as if some black hole of dread had opened up beneath the foundations and was drawing everything into it.

One evening about a week after Frankie began his prison sentence, Uncle Gavin appeared in my bedroom doorway. He rarely came up to the second floor, where I would hole up and do my homework or read or play games on my laptop, a refurbished model that Uncle Gavin had gotten me for school. I was sitting on my bed, blowing off studying for exams and playing Skyrim instead, when Uncle Gavin knocked on the open door. I closed the lid of the laptop. "Hey," I said.

Uncle Gavin came in and sat on the one chair in my room, which was at my little-used desk. He glanced around as if taking in for the first time the bare walls and the piles of mostly clean clothes. "You all right?" he asked.

Since Frankie had gone to prison, I had not talked to my uncle other than saying what was necessary in order to live in the same house. I had not talked to anyone, really, aside from him and Susannah.

"Yeah," I said. "I'm fine."

He nodded, appraising me with those damned dark eyes. "I learned something today," he said.

When it became clear he was waiting for a response, I said, "Okay."

Now my uncle's gaze didn't waver but focused on me. "I told you before that if the police couldn't find those men, I would."

Distracted by Frankie's incarceration, it took me a moment to understand what my uncle was saying. *Those men.* As if from the end of a long corridor in my memory, I heard my father shouting, my mother's scream, gunshots. Something in me stirred, unseen and on the verge of waking. My voice was a dry rasp. "Did you? Find them?"

It was now dark outside, only a streetlamp down the road shining weakly, unable to even cast a shadow across my window. The lamp on my nightstand gave the room a warm, comfortable glow, but I shivered at my uncle's single, affirmative nod.

"Where are they?" I said.

"In Jacksonville," he said.

I shook my head in disbelief. It was so mundane, as if he were telling me where some former neighbors had moved to. My parents' killers should be in prison, or dead. Not in Jacksonville. I tried to imagine what they were doing in Jacksonville, then decided it didn't matter.

"What . . . what are you going to do?" I asked, a bit breathless.

Uncle Gavin considered me for a few quiet seconds. "That depends on what you want," he said finally.

I stared at him. Deep in a cave at the center of my heart, that unseen thing was yawning and about to open its eyes. I knew what my uncle meant. He was asking me if I wanted him to do something about those men. If I wanted him to see to it that those men never left Jacksonville.

In my mind, I saw them both, the one with the goatee and the acne scars who had fought with my dad, and the other one, Ponytail, the one with the gun, and they were both lying on the deck of a boat, bags over their heads, hands tied behind their backs. It was midnight and the boat was speeding out into the open ocean, where under a moonless sky the faceless crew would toss the two men overboard, and they would kick and flail and scream but eventually slip beneath the waves, water filling their mouths and noses and lungs as they sank down, down through the ink-black sea . . .

The scene in my mind was so clear, so visceral, that I gasped and came back to myself a little, sitting on my bed and staring at the dark-blue comforter in front of me. I looked up at my uncle, and he must have seen the horror on my face.

"No?" he asked in a quiet voice.

I couldn't speak, but I shook my head. Uncle Gavin replied with a curt nod and stood, then walked out of my room. The thing in my heart curled itself into a ball and went back to sleep, and I leaned back against my pillows, on the verge of tears and trying to decide if my reaction had been the correct one, and whether or not Uncle Gavin had looked disappointed.

Eight days later, I found a copy of the *Atlanta Journal-Constitution* on my bed. It was folded back to a short article in the Metro section, about a drug bust. I dropped my backpack to the floor and sat cross-legged on my bed to read the article. Two men in a van with Florida license plates had been stopped in College Park on an anonymous tip. In the van, under a false floor, police found a kilo of cocaine. The two were being charged with drug possession and trafficking. A third person was being sought for questioning, according to police sources.

Small photos of the two arrested men accompanied the article. One of them, Jay Gardner, with a buzz cut and a block-shaped head, was unfamiliar. The other one had a goatee and acne scars, the same ones he'd had when he fought with my father in our house, before Ponytail came through the front door with a gun. His name was listed as Samuel Bridges. I looked at his face as he stared insolently at the camera. The article said the charges could bring sentences of five to thirty years in prison. *Longer than what Frankie has*, I thought, and then felt disgusted that my measure for judging jail time was Frankie. Beyond that, though, I didn't know what I felt, or how I should feel. I had a good idea that the same person who had called in the anonymous tip had also left the newspaper on my bed, and was probably at Ronan's right now, talking with Ruben about unreliable vendors or the price of liquor. Should I feel thankful? Pleased that justice had been done? Upset that Ponytail had apparently not been nabbed and was still out there? Angry with and perhaps frightened of my uncle?

Something else bothered me about the newspaper. It felt like an apology, as if my uncle was trying to make amends for failing to keep Frankie out of prison. If that's what it was, I understood the gesture, but it also upset me, my uncle delivering these men, so to speak, to atone for what had happened to Frankie.

In retrospect, it was at that moment, I think, that I realized I had to leave. Not just leave for college, but leave my uncle's house, leave him and his dangerous, shadowy life. I wouldn't be going far away, though. My teachers and a school counselor had told me about college opportunities out of state, with scholarships and financial aid. My AP art teacher, Mrs. Jacobs, had gone to Laguna College of Art and Design in California and knew some of the faculty, and she had offered to write a recommendation for me. "You have an intelligence and a sensitivity that is a gift, Ethan," she had said to me. "Please don't be that boy who wastes such a gift." But as much as I wanted to escape, I couldn't just move to the other side of the country. Later I would weigh that loyalty against a growing sense of regret. But going to California would have meant leaving Susannah as well, and I couldn't do that, not then, not when my sister was trying to put the broken, jagged pieces of herself back together. I would be going to Georgia State instead, right in the heart of downtown Atlanta. But I would not be living with my uncle anymore. I could not unlearn what I now knew about Uncle Gavin and the world he worked in. It frightened me, and especially as Uncle Gavin had been unable to keep Frankie out of jail, I told myself I wanted nothing to do with it. But even worse, a small part of me was drawn to that world, fascinated by it, its rejection of simple morals and right versus wrong.

And so, out of mingled fear and revulsion, I would leave it behind me.

At that moment, though, I did not think all of this out so clearly. Instead, I just sat on my bed, the newspaper in my hand, looking out my window, for a long time.

# CHAPTER EIGHTEEN

THE HALL TO THE KITCHEN IN MY UNCLE'S BAR HAS NOT CHANGED. There are the same bathroom doors, the same private rooms, the swinging door that leads to the kitchen and the stairwell up to my uncle's sanctum sanctorum, the same smell of grease and cleaner and chicken tenders and the loamy undercurrent of Guinness, as if there is a secret river of it flowing beneath the floor. And when I step into the kitchen, I stop so quickly that my shoes squeak on the tile floor, because there is Ruben standing in the middle of the kitchen, in dark slacks and a red dress shirt, although he has misplaced his fedora. But Ruben is dead—he had a heart attack three years ago, right after Frankie's mother died. And then my heart leaps and dies in the back of my throat, because it isn't Ruben but Frankie.

"Holy shit," I say.

Frankie raises his chin at me in a short jerk of recognition. "You too," he says. He puts his hands in his pockets, a studied attempt at ease that doesn't match the set of his jaw or the firm line of his eyebrows.

"I . . . good to see you," I manage.

"You were going to say, 'I didn't know you were out of prison,' " Frankie says.

"Ethan," my uncle says behind me, and I turn to see Uncle Gavin, in his flat tweed cap, walk into the kitchen. He stops outside of hugging distance.

"Hey," I say. I'm still processing the fact that Frankie is here and feel awash in guilt. I'm caught between my uncle and Frankie, like a bit of metal being repelled by two equally powerful magnets. I make my choice and turn to Frankie. "When did you get out?"

"Few months ago," Frankie says. Then he looks past me to Uncle Gavin. "New cook hasn't shown up yet."

My uncle shakes his head. "Give him ten more minutes, and if he shows up after that, throw him out on his ass."

"A few *months* ago?" I say. I look at Uncle Gavin. "You didn't tell me?"

"You never asked," Uncle Gavin says. He seems about to say more when the door swings open and a man walks in, about my height but with broad shoulders, muscled chest and arms, and a waist cinched tight as a ballerina's. My first thought when I see him is that he's a gymnast—he moves like he's walking on an enormous ball, rolling the world beneath his feet. I've seen oiled hardwood floors that are darker than him, but not by much. His head is shaved clean except for a trim moustache and goatee. He frowns when he sees me. "Who is this?" he asks, his voice quiet and unfriendly.

"My nephew," Uncle Gavin says. I don't detect much enthusiasm in his voice.

Now all three of them are looking at me like I don't belong. Then the man pointedly turns to my uncle. "Mr. Lester, do you want to talk in your office?"

"I need to talk to you," I say to Uncle Gavin. "Now. Please."

The man turns back toward me, his frown deepening like an ugly wrinkle.

"Caesar," Frankie says. The man looks at Frankie, who shakes his head. Still frowning, the man crosses his arms and waits.

Uncle Gavin grunts. "Are you okay, Ethan?"

"I honestly don't know," I say.

He considers me, nods, and turns for the stairs. I follow him to the swinging door. Once there, I look back at Frankie. He's still standing in the middle of the kitchen, watching me. Caesar is still to the side, arms folded. "I'm sorry," I say to Frankie. "I just—there's a lot going on. Susannah's in trouble, and I have to find out what this woman—"

"Your sister?" Frankie says. "She okay?"

"*Ethan*," my uncle calls, already halfway up the stairs, and I shrug at Frankie, who motions me to go on and follow my uncle.

MY UNCLE'S OFFICE is upstairs, above the bar. It has bookshelves on one wall and an Oriental carpet and some upholstered chairs, but it is dominated by a massive, claw-footed desk that must weigh a ton. As in all of my memories of Uncle Gavin's office, the top of the desk is a pile of disorder, a blizzard of newspapers, magazines, torn notepad pages, precarious stacks of loose-leaf papers, a food wrapper or two, and two abandoned mugs, both half-filled with what is presumably old tea.

Uncle Gavin sits behind the desk, his chair creaking as he lowers himself into it. "What's wrong, Ethan?" he asks.

I sit in my old place in front of his desk, suddenly uncertain and not a little overwhelmed. "Susannah's in the hospital again," I say, to my surprise.

Uncle Gavin's face is, as usual, inscrutable. "Is she all right now?" he asks.

I rub my face with my hand. "I think so," I say. "She's not . . . she isn't suicidal, right now. I had to talk her off of a bridge."

Silence stretches between us, a spool of wire uncoiled and being pulled taut. Uncle Gavin shifts in his chair, making it creak again. "You said you need help with something," he says.

Some people might think my uncle particularly coldhearted for not expressing more concern about Susannah, or at least asking more about her. They wouldn't be right, exactly. Uncle Gavin has never been an overly warm person, although he can be friendly enough and allows himself to smile and even laugh occasionally. It's more that he is extremely practical, solving problems and moving on to the next bit of business without much sentimentality. Given the nature of his business, his practicality is as necessary as it is fortunate. He asked about his niece and learned she's alive and safe for the moment, so he's on to the next most immediate item of concern.

Haltingly at first, and then with increasing clarity, I tell him about Marisa. He listens behind his desk, those dark eyes of his always on me. Twice—when I talk about her relationship with Susannah, and when I say that I found her phone—I think I detect a flash in his eyes, a sharper awareness, but he says nothing, aside from encouraging me to go on when I occasionally stop to put my thoughts in order. When I'm finished, the silence makes me wish I was still talking.

"Why haven't you gone to the police?" he says.

"And tell them what? This woman is stalking me? They'll have to investigate; it'll take time. She's hurting other people *right now*—students, kids. My *sister*. She's pretending to be me on social media. She's trying to ruin my life." I take a breath. "She knew about my parents being killed. She said she knows who killed them."

Uncle Gavin continues to look at me, unperturbed. "That's impossible."

"It's what she said. It might be bullshit, but I need to know. I need to find her, Uncle Gavin. I need to find out what she knows and keep her from doing any more damage, to me or to anyone else."

Uncle Gavin nods and leans back in his chair. "So what do you need me to help you with?" he asks.

"Marisa's phone," I say, taking it out of my pocket. "She left it at my house. She kept texting me, telling me to give it back. She was taunting me, so I turned the phone off. And now I'm wondering if maybe she sent more texts. Maybe about my parents." The words are heavy and hard to say, and once spoken they seem to lie on the desk between us, ugly and leaden.

"You can't read her texts now?" Uncle Gavin says.

"I don't know her password. I blocked her on my phone, so she started texting her own phone, the one she left at my house. I could only read the texts right when she sent them, and then they'd disappear off the screen."

His eyebrows quirk. "How was she texting her own phone?"

"She had another phone. Her mother's, probably. All the texts she sent came from someone named 'Mom' in her contacts."

Uncle Gavin calls out, "Caesar?" After a few moments, the office door opens and Caesar and Frankie both walk in. They must have both been standing in the hallway outside the office. Frankie looks slightly abashed, as if Uncle Gavin has caught him eavesdropping. He glances at me, then looks away. Caesar maintains his frown.

"I need you to look at a phone," Uncle Gavin says to Caesar. He gestures to me, and I stand and hold the phone out to Caesar.

Caesar doesn't even look at the phone. "Is it turned on?" he asks.

"No," I say.

"Because if it is—"

"It's off," I say. Unless the phone is on or plugged into a power source, it cannot be accurately located.

Caesar gives me a look of disappointment, even disdain, like I'm a promising student who has failed the most basic test. "Next time wrap it in tinfoil," he says. "Blocks the radio signals—"

"Like a homemade Faraday cage," I say. "I know."

We eye each other, like gunslingers waiting for the other to make a move. I'm still holding the phone out to Caesar. Frankie looks from me to Caesar and back again. Slowly, still maintaining eye contact with me, Caesar reaches out and takes the phone out of my hand. He glances at it, then raises an eyebrow at me, presumably because of the pop-art phone case. Then he slides it into a pocket, nods at Uncle Gavin, and walks out the door. Frankie trails him, glancing back at me, and I take that as an invitation to follow them.

# CHAPTER NINETEEN

In the tiny lot beside Ronan's are two parking spots. Uncle Gavin's Lincoln Navigator, a newer model, is in one. To my surprise, Frankie's old Trans Am, the Frankenstein, is in the other. "You kept it?" I say.

Frankie shrugs. "My pop kept it for me," he says. He gets behind the wheel. Caesar opens the passenger door, flips the seat forward, then steps back to let me in, his expression as inviting as a drill bit.

We drive to a refurbished industrial area where Tenth Street dead-ends into the rail yards, old brick warehouses converted into hip new restaurants, art galleries, and furniture stores. Frankie pulls the Trans Am behind one such warehouse, all red brick and black iron, and we get out of the car. At this hour, the area is pretty deserted, the streets filled with heat and light and not much else. I stop midstep as I realize where we are. A mile south of here is the Bluff and the abandoned house where we found Susannah and Luco. I glance at Frankie, wonder if he is remembering that night, but he doesn't seem to be on the same wavelength, instead inserting a key into a padlock on a garage door. He pulls the door up with a metallic ratcheting, and Caesar walks inside. Frankie follows, then halts and beckons me to come in. I step inside, and Frankie pulls the garage door down behind me with a crash.

The room's ceiling is two stories above us, windows high up on the wall letting in the clear morning light. The rough brick walls contrast with the polished concrete floor. A spiral staircase in the corner leads up to a shadowed loft. Caesar flips a switch on the wall, and one of the fluorescent lights hanging from the ceiling illuminates with a harsh hum. Beneath that light on the far wall is what seems to be a workstation, a metal table with a laptop and what looks like a countertop microwave and an assortment of electronic equipment I don't recognize.

Caesar takes Marisa's phone out of his pocket, places it on the table next to the laptop, and sits in a space-age office chair, the back of it a mesh of black webbing and anodized aluminum. "You try the pass code?" he asks me while booting up his laptop. "Or try to jailbreak it?"

"No."

Caesar grunts and starts typing. A window opens on the laptop screen, displaying what looks like machine code.

I look at Marisa's phone and feel the back of my throat go dry. We are about to try to break into another person's phone. *Not we*, I think. *Me.* The fact that Caesar is the one actually doing something with it is irrelevant. "Can you hack it?" I ask, hating the anxious whine in my voice.

Caesar barely spares me a glance before he picks up the phone and removes the pop-art case, then examines the phone carefully. He holds the power button down until the phone lights up, then opens the door to the microwave. Inside, a lightning charger cable sticks out of the back wall of the microwave. Caesar picks up the phone and plugs the lightning charger into it, then puts the phone into the microwave and closes the door. I almost say something, afraid he's going to nuke the phone, but I manage to hold my tongue. Caesar picks up a cord protruding from the back of the microwave and plugs that into a black box the size of a hardback book. Then he takes a USB cable from that box and plugs it into the laptop. As soon as Caesar plugs the box into the laptop, strands of alphanumeric code start cascading down the open window on the laptop.

"This will take a minute," Caesar says, his eyes on the code. I look at Frankie, who motions me to step away with him, and we walk across the room toward the spiral staircase. Underneath the upstairs loft area is a kitchenette with a sink and a refrigerator. Frankie takes a bottle of orange juice from the fridge, hesitates, then holds it out toward me. I shake my head, and he closes the fridge door.

"He likes to work alone," Frankie says.

I look across the room at Caesar, the light from the laptop softening his sharp jawline. I lower my voice. "You trust him?"

Frankie's expression darkens. "He saved my life," he says. "In prison."

I raise my hands as if surrendering. "I'm sorry," I say. "I mean, I'm glad he did. Save your life. I just . . ." I let my hands drop, a gesture in futility. "What happened?"

Frankie takes a sip from his juice, then slowly replaces the cap. "Couple of years ago," he says, "this guy, another inmate, he was annoyed I wouldn't give him my lunch tray, so he threatened me with a shiv. Caesar stopped the guy, did something to his wrist and made him drop it. A week later, the same dude and one of his buddies try to jump Caesar, and I was there and helped fight them off. Got six extra months for it, but from then on Caesar and I had each other's backs." He shrugs.

This makes me feel even worse. Even in prison Frankie was loyal and brave, while I am neither. I'm a yard away from Frankie, but we might as well be on opposite sides of the Grand Canyon. It's been eight years since he went to prison, almost three thousand days. Every one of those days was another opportunity for me to reach out to him, another chance I threw away.

"I'm sorry," I say again. "I'm sorry I stopped coming to see you, sorry I didn't keep in touch. Sorry I'm a shitty friend."

Frankie screws up his mouth, like he is chewing on my words, and he is on the verge of saying something when Caesar calls out, "Done."

We return to the workstation and stand behind Caesar, peering at the screen. I can feel my pulse in my head, a quick throbbing against my eardrums.

"These are the most recent texts sent to this phone," Caesar says. "I wanted to see if she mentioned her location."

On the screen, I read the texts Marisa sent to me on her own phone, starting on Saturday: **Ethan if u have my phone give it back. I want my phone ethan. PHONE BACK. PHONE MFer.** Ridiculously, I feel a slight embarrassment that Caesar and Frankie are reading these.

> I'm going to eat your heart.
> You should check out Twitter
> I know who killed your parents
> I'm not going anywhere, Ethan

"Lovely girl," Caesar says.

"She knows who killed your parents?" Frankie asks, eyes wide.

"I don't know," I say. "But now you see why I want to find out?"

"You don't know where she lives?" Caesar asks.

"With her parents, in Buckhead."

He raises an eyebrow. "But instead of driving to her house and knocking on the front door, you want to break into her phone?"

"She's not home. I called. She didn't show up to work today either."

Frankie asks, "What does she mean about Twitter?"

"She was pretending to be me on Twitter," I say. My stomach burns with acid. "She was bullying students."

Caesar opens a window on his laptop and pulls up Twitter. "What was the handle she used?"

"EthanF8," I say. When Caesar and Frankie both look at me, I say, "I know. It's not me, it's her."

Caesar finds the account, and he and Frankie read Marisa's tweets about the naughty picture.

Frankie lets out a low whistle. "You must have pissed her off."

I close my eyes briefly, as if waiting for someone to stop shouting at me. When I open them, I see what she tweeted to Sarah Solomon:

You write beautiful essays but you hide behind those cat-eye glasses
like the world's youngest virgin librarian
Maybe that's why you sent this pic

And now Sarah is in a hospital. As is my sister. Both women recovering from attempted suicides. Both impacted by Marisa.

I realize Caesar is saying something to me. "What?" I say.

"Her tweets were all posted from Atlanta," he says. "So she hasn't left the city. Or at least she hadn't before her last tweet, which was"—he checks on the screen—"just after four PM on Sunday."

I frown. "When was her last text to me? On this phone?"

Caesar checks the screen. "Six seventeen PM on Sunday. 'I'm not going anywhere, Ethan.' "

She didn't text me anything else about my parents, or about who killed them. An idea strikes me. "Can you figure out where the texts she sent me came from?" I ask Caesar. "Location-wise?"

Caesar shakes his head. "Not from here. If I had the phone she used to send these texts, I could. Or access to that person's cell records." He pauses, considering something, then shakes his head. "Let's see what else we can find," he says. He types and pulls up two windows on his screen. One is apparently her call history, and a string of phone numbers appears, calls Marisa either made or received over the past month. I see my own cell number on there, as well as Archer's main line, and one called Home seems self-explanatory, but I don't recognize the others. The other window shows Marisa's Safari history. Caesar scrolls down past various shopping sites and restaurants, and then he says "Hmm" and pauses on one item from last week: Fulton County Jail.

"Why would she research the jail?" I say.

The website she visited just after going to the jail's website seems even odder: Our Lady of Mercy Monastery.

"A monastery?" I say. "That's the last place I'd imagine her being interested in."

Frankie pulls out his phone and Googles the monastery. It's outside Dahlonega, about an hour north of Atlanta. "Place holds retreats," he says, reading his phone. "Maybe she went to one of those?"

"Like I said, it's the last place I'd imagine her being interested in. At all." I shake my head. "Might just be something she had to look up for work, one of the history classes she's subbing for."

Frankie raises his eyebrows slightly. "Probably not why she's got the Fulton County Jail up here, though, right?"

"Ethan," Caesar says. "You might want to look at this."

I look at the screen, and when I read the headline, my stomach shrinks into a hard ball: DEADLY HOME INVASION—PARENTS KILLED, CHILDREN IN ICU.

"What is it?" Frankie asks.

"It's an *AJC* article," Caesar says. "An old one, about Ethan and his family. Marisa read it twice in the past month."

I'm gripping the back of Caesar's chair so hard that my hand starts to hurt. I let go of the chair and flex my fingers. I don't need to read the article—I already know what it says.

*I know everything about your mom*, Marisa said in my classroom last Friday. *About what happened to you and your parents. I read the news reports. They hurt you and your family. But I knew from the moment we met that I could help you. I did this for you, Ethan. I would do anything for you.*

Frankie is reading the article on Caesar's screen. "Jesus," he says.

"Caesar," I say, "can you—" I clear my throat. My mouth is dry as a stone. "Can you see the rest of her search history?"

He pauses. "I'd have to hack into her Safari account," he says.

"After we've already hacked into her iPhone," I say pointedly. "Can you do it?"

Caesar gives me an inscrutable look, then turns back to his laptop and begins typing.

I SPEND THE next half hour reading through Marisa's search history. I'm splashed all over it. She Googled me the day after we met at the conference and went to bed together. She pulled up my profile on Archer's website, my social media accounts, that *AJC* article about the home invasion and shooting. She even found an old *Northside Neighbor* article about my mother being celebrated for her teaching.

*I know* everything *about you*, she told me with a sneer, in my house.

I feel a terrible emptiness, as if all that's left of me is a scooped-out rind, tossed to the side. And yet somewhere lost in that vast emptiness is a tiny red flame of anger. I can't grasp it yet, but I know it's there. For now, I sit in front of the laptop, numbed, my soul glazed over, trying to understand why Marisa did this. She told me she wanted to help me, to get close, to be with me, so I would . . . what? Love her forever? But it's more like she wanted to solve me, like I'm a Rubik's cube. In all her research, did she somehow truly find out who killed my parents? I parse every conversation, every interaction Marisa and I have had, and now in my memory she looks like someone pretending to be a caring person, someone drawn to broken people, to trauma. To people like me. Until I rejected her. And now she wants to ruin me.

When I'm done looking at her Safari history, Caesar pulls up yet another window. It's Marisa's calendar app. She has a few items for the past couple of weeks, most of them mundane, like a reminder to pick up her dry cleaning. Then I see one scheduled item at ten AM last Tuesday: **J Gardner.**

"Mean anything?" Frankie asks.

I look at the name on the screen. Was J the first initial of the first name, or was J the actual name of the man? In the dim recesses of my memory, something shifts, a ghost barely getting my attention before it floats through a wall and vanishes. "I don't know," I say. "Maybe."

There's nothing else listed for last Tuesday in Marisa's calendar. Then something clicks. "She was out last Tuesday," I say. "She took Tuesday and Wednesday off, said something about her mother not doing well."

Caesar clicks, and the screen now shows Wednesday. She has another entry, also at ten AM: **S Bridges**. That name I recognize—it's like a tuning fork vibrating in my brain. Now I know who J Gardner is as well.

"What is it?" Frankie asks.

My throat is dry and I try to swallow. "Samuel Bridges," I say. "He was one of the men who came into our house. He fought with my dad." In my mind I see that newspaper article Uncle Gavin left on my bed soon after Frankie went to prison, with the pictures of two men who had been arrested for drug trafficking. I look at Frankie. "Bridges went to prison, though. Him and this Jay Gardner guy. My uncle—" I pause. "They got arrested for drugs," I finish. I've never actually confirmed that Uncle Gavin got them both arrested—he's never openly admitted it, at any rate—and so I'm strangely reluctant to broach the subject. And I don't want to admit that my uncle found Bridges and Ponytail, that he made an unspoken offer to have them disappear. That I said no. And that when my uncle called in an anonymous tip, Ponytail escaped arrest.

Frankie frowns. "Why does this woman have their names in her calendar?"

"That's a good fucking question," I say.

There's a low chime from Caesar's phone. He glances at it, then stands up and walks across the room to the garage door. When he pulls it up, he lets in bright sunshine and a shadow-darkened figure. It takes a moment for the shadow to resolve itself as Uncle Gavin, and then Caesar brings the garage door back down with a crash.

"Show me," Uncle Gavin says, and Caesar walks with him toward me and the laptop. I stand, my legs a bit shaky, and step aside. My uncle doesn't sit but leans forward, peering at the screen, using the track pad to scroll and to toggle between Marisa's texts, her tweets, her search history, and her calendar app. I lean against the metal table, arms folded across

my chest, exhausted. Frankie stands off to the side, a loyal soldier awaiting orders.

After several minutes Uncle Gavin straightens up from the screen
and looks at me. "You've read all this," he says, and I nod. To Caesar he
says, "There's nothing else? No final text from her, nothing about what
happened to her?"

I frown. "What do you mean, 'what happened to her'?"

Uncle Gavin looks swiftly at me. "You don't know."

"Know *what*?"

Uncle Gavin nods to the empty chair. "Sit down."

"I don't want to sit down; I want—"

"*Ethan*," he says, and I sit down, staring at him.

Uncle Gavin exhales through his nose. "The police found Marisa less
than an hour ago," he says. "She was in her car. She's dead, Ethan."

I stare at my uncle. My mind has just gone blank, like a TV when
the power goes out. *Service interruption, please stand by.* "What?" I
manage.

"Her car was parked behind a warehouse off Fulton Industrial," he
says. "She was in the trunk. The police think she was strangled, but that's
not clear yet."

I lean back in my chair, stunned. Marisa is dead? Murdered? Horror
wells up in me, filling that mental blankness. But what is almost worse
than the news is a small voice at the back of my skull. *Lucky for you*, that
voice says. I want to vomit. "No," I say aloud.

Uncle Gavin leans in front of me and grips my upper arms. "Ethan,"
he says. "You have to tell me. Did you do it?"

I stare at him, eyes wide. "Did I—Jesus Christ!" I throw his arms off
me and stand up so fast the chair shoots back across the floor on its cast-
ers. "I didn't kill Marisa! Jesus. No. *Shit*." I can't think. I'm wheezing,
taking huge gasps of air. And suddenly I can't take in enough air. It's as
if my windpipe just shrank to the size of a pinhole. I stare at my uncle,
waving my hands. I can't breathe.

"Ethan." It's Frankie. He moves into my view, edging Uncle Ethan away. "Ethan, look at me. Look at me." I look at Frankie, my eyes wide, mouth gaping open. "You're hyperventilating," he says. "Just look at me and breathe in, okay? Breathe in, and then let a breath out. In, out." He takes my hands in his. "Here. Cup your hands together, okay? Yeah, like that. Now bend over and breathe into your hands, okay? Like that." I bend at the waist and lower my face into my cupped hands and do what he says. In, out, slowly, into my hands. In, out. After several breaths, the gray fuzzy feeling that was encroaching at the edges of my vision falls away, and I'm able to sit up and take in a slow, deep breath, then let it out.

"Thanks," I say weakly.

Frankie nods. I take in another breath, let it out. It's amazing that I've done this all my life, breathing, almost always without thinking about it, and then the second it seizes up, I'm helpless as a trout tossed up onto a riverbank.

Uncle Gavin is talking to Caesar about something. Marisa's phone—that's it. Because Marisa is dead. Someone killed her. The thought is abhorrent, but I find myself repeating it in my head, as if that will allow me to wrap my hands around it. *Marisa is dead. Someone killed her.*

And I have her phone.

Sweet Jesus.

I nearly hyperventilate again, but I bend at the waist and drop my head between my knees, dignity be damned, and concentrate on not passing out.

By the time I sit up, warily, and regain my bearings, Caesar has opened the microwave and is removing the phone, unplugging it and then turning it off. Uncle Gavin has put on a pair of black leather gloves he pulled out of his jacket pocket, and he takes the phone from Caesar. Frankie has a container of bleach wipes and pulls out a wipe and hands it to Uncle Gavin, who wipes every surface of the phone carefully. I watch all of this as if it's a slightly boring crime procedural on television.

"You're sure there's nothing?" Uncle Gavin asks Caesar.

"No," Caesar says.

My brain feels like it has congealed, conscious thought reduced to a slog, but I clear my throat to speak, and my uncle turns his dark eyes on me. "She knows . . . she *knew* what happened to my parents," I say. "To me and Susannah. Marisa knew."

As usual, I can't read the expression on Uncle Gavin's face. "She was disturbed, that woman," he says. "What happened to your parents was in the news. She must have done her research."

"She did," Caesar says. "We looked at her search history."

Uncle Gavin shakes his head. "Vulture," he says, his mouth turned down in disgust.

A thought emerges, like glimpsing someone skating through fog at night. "She had the name of one of the men who shot my parents," I say. "In her calendar. And another guy. The two that . . . got arrested running drugs."

His tone dark, Uncle Gavin says, "I saw her calendar, her texts. Her twits or whatever you call them. She was stalking you, Ethan. Trying to learn everything about you."

"But . . . she had their names in her phone," I say. "Maybe she called them—"

"Ethan," my uncle says. "How could she have done? One of them is in prison."

"Not Ponytail," I say. "Maybe she, I don't know, found him somehow—"

"Ethan," my uncle says again. "This woman lied to you. She took a job at your school to worm her way into your life and get some sort of . . . *thrill* from your own misery. She was a vampire, Ethan. She fed on what happened to you." He puts a hand on my shoulder. "And someone killed her, Ethan. It's a terrible thing, her death, but she was preying on you and your sister. You realize that, yes? And now her phone doesn't do anything good for you. If you take it to the police, what will they say? What will they think?"

He pauses and considers me. I know what he means—the police will want to question me, want to know why I have her phone. They will treat me like a suspect in her murder. Fear starts to wind itself around my throat and lungs, threatening to squeeze. I feel trapped, at the dead end of a dark alley. Uncle Gavin seems to be waiting. "What do I do?" I ask.

Uncle Gavin pauses, then says something to Caesar that I don't catch, and Caesar hesitates, but then he walks over to another table and retrieves something from it, handing it to Uncle Gavin. My uncle kneels and puts the phone on the concrete floor, and it's at this point that I realize that the object Caesar gave him is a hammer, which Uncle Gavin now holds poised above the phone. The icy numbness that gripped me earlier breaks and falls away, replaced by panic. "Hey!" I shout, but it's too late. Uncle Gavin brings the hammer down onto the phone. The first blow cracks the screen, the second shattering it. My uncle keeps at it until the phone is bent and twisted, the screen reduced to shards. Gingerly he picks up the ruined frame and plucks out a thin wafer from the wreckage—the phone's SIM card. He puts that on the floor and whacks it with the hammer until it is pulverized. He puts his free hand on the ground to help him stand up, his knees popping as he does. He winces. "I'm getting old," he says. He hands the hammer to Caesar, then turns to me, ignoring the fact that I'm gaping openmouthed at him. "No one will know you had that phone," he says. "If the police ask, you don't know anything about it. But when they come to you—and they will—you call my lawyer, Johnny Shaw, and then you tell them everything about your relationship with that woman. The truth. Just leave the phone out of it." He nods, once, then heads to the garage door with Caesar trailing behind. Frankie is already approaching with a broom and dustpan, ready to literally sweep the problem away.

# CHAPTER TWENTY

Frankie has already swept up and bagged the smashed phone when Caesar returns, pulling the garage door back down. It closes with a horrible crash—he must have pulled it down hard. I'm still leaning against the metal table, but I'm no longer numb. That tiny flame of anger inside me is still burning, and I'm doing my best to nurture it.

"We need to get back to work," Caesar says. He's talking to Frankie, but I know the words are directed to me as well.

"Sure," Frankie says. "I need to get rid of the phone case and dump this bag first, and then we—"

"I need to know what she meant," I say.

Frankie looks genuinely confused, but Caesar narrows his eyes, sensing a problem.

"What who meant?" Frankie says.

"Marisa," I say. "The two calendar entries about those men."

Frankie glances at Caesar, who is now on full threat alert—arms uncrossed, hands loose at his sides, head up and eyes on me. "Your uncle said she was crazy," Frankie says.

"She turned my life inside out," I say. "She went to bed with my sister to get inside my head. She—" I hear my voice rising and stop, take a deep breath. "I need to know why those men were in her calendar," I say. "I need to know for certain that it doesn't mean anything. Susannah is in a psych ward, Frankie. I barely stopped her from jumping off an overpass. I need to know what Marisa did, *everything* she did. I need to make sure she didn't do something that's going to come back and bite me in the ass. So Susannah doesn't try to hurt herself again."

Caesar sucks at his teeth. "Mr. Lester said no," he says.

That little flame of anger now blazes up, and I snap, "Fuck you, Caesar."

Caesar's nostrils flare and he steps toward me. Even though I can see he's angry and all the threat receptors in my lizard brain are pulsing bright red, I still notice how graceful he is, every movement a smooth economy of motion. Some detached part of me is curious to see what he will do, how he will hurt me. I stand up off the table. If I'm going to get beat down, I'd like to be standing first.

Frankie steps between us, still holding the trash bag with the smashed phone. "That's enough," he says firmly. He points a finger in my face. "Don't talk to him like that," he says. "Ever. Okay?" Before I can react, he turns to Caesar. "Don't do it," he says, his tone still firm but gentler. "He's hurt and he's worried about his sister, yeah? He's scared, too. Look at him. Look at him."

Caesar is looking at me, and I wish he wasn't, because Frankie's words have shocked me out of my detached anger and now I would like to keep living. Caesar's expression suggests he would like the exact opposite for me. Slowly, though, slowly, Caesar relaxes. Just barely. But it's enough.

"Okay," Frankie says, "okay," and he turns back to me. "You gonna be nice now?"

That anger starts glowing again, but with an effort I stifle it. "Yeah," I say. "I'm sorry, Caesar. I just . . . Frankie's right, man. I'm hurt, and I'm scared, and I'm pissed at my uncle for smashing the phone. I should be yelling at him, not you. I'm sorry."

Caesar's expression is stony, but he folds his arms across his chest and stands still.

"What do you want, Ethan?" Frankie asks.

I hesitate. "I need to know if you can hack into Marisa's phone records," I say. "Take another look at her posts, her calls, see if we learn anything. Maybe she called one of those men."

Caesar snorts, conveying an entire range of derision in a single sound. "You want me to hack into a major communication network so we can take a look at private phone records?"

"Can you?" I ask. "Can you do that?"

"It's stupid," Caesar says. "A stupid waste of time, and a stupid risk."

"Please," Frankie says. He reaches out and puts a hand on Caesar's forearm. "For me."

Something passes between the two of them, and realization breaks over me like a wave: the jealous vibes I got off of Caesar, this loft. I look at the two men and see them as they are, together.

Caesar looks Frankie in the eye for a few moments, then nods brusquely at him and walks past, not sparing me a glance as he sits back down at the laptop. "I'm going to need coffee," he says to Frankie. He's already typing.

Frankie heads for the garage door, and I follow him across the room. "Thank you," I murmur.

Frankie shakes his head. "Thank *him*," he says, indicating Caesar. "But wait until we come back with the coffee."

THE FRANKENSTEIN PROWLS through the side streets, now busier with lunchtime traffic. I sit in the passenger seat and glance at Frankie, feeling like we're back in high school and at the same time realizing that's not where we are at all. "You need a Starbucks?" I say. "I could find one on my phone."

Frankie shakes his head, downshifting as we approach a light. "Caesar has this one coffee place," he says. "It's not far."

We say nothing for a block or two, listening to the rumble of the car and the rush of the air conditioning and the passing traffic.

"So, you and Caesar," I say. "You guys are, ah . . ."

"Together?" Frankie says. "Yeah." He looks sideways at me, a short flick of the eyes, then back to the road. Except for the barest hint of tightening around his jaw, he looks unconcerned.

"Okay," I say, and we don't say anything else.

The coffee shop is called Gravy and has an industrial hipster vibe, flat caps and beards with iron machinery and butcher-block countertops. The barista, barrel-chested and bearded and dressed in denim and tweed, greets Frankie and starts making two lattes. I ask him to make a third and pay for all of them over Frankie's protests. We sit in a scarred wooden booth to wait for our drinks.

"It's a nice place," Frankie says. "Jamie's a good dude." He means the barista.

"Kinda looks like he's in Mumford and Sons," I say.

Frankie turns to look at Jamie, who is making our lattes at an enormous espresso machine that's straight out of a steampunk novel. Frankie chuckles. "Guess he does," he says. "Hadn't thought about it that way. Maybe he's the bassist. Nobody ever remembers the bassist."

"Paul McCartney," I say. "John Paul Jones. Lemmy from Motörhead."

Frankie raises his hands in mock surrender. "Point made." He leans back and looks around, as if considering whether to invest in Gravy. "Always wondered what it takes to open up a place like this," he says. "Do you think, 'I wanna open a coffee bar' and then go look for a location, or do you find the place *first* and—"

"So you and Caesar," I say. The words just burst out of my mouth. Frankie is startled, his eyes wide for a moment, but then he settles back in his seat with a rueful little smile. He actually looks relieved, as if glad this can be dealt with.

"Okay," he says evenly. "What about us?"

"Don't look at me like that," I say.

He frowns. "Like what?"

"I'm not a bigot, Frankie," I say. "I'm not scared of gay people. My neighbors are gay."

He raises an eyebrow. "And you have a Black friend, too, right?"

"Goddamn it, Frankie," I say, because now he's grinning at me. "I don't care if you're gay. Seriously. That's not the issue."

"Then what's the problem?"

"How come I didn't *know*?" I say, and although I hate how my voice sounds, an adolescent whine with a dash of outrage, I can't deny the pain behind my question.

He looks at me, the grin now gone, but his expression is more sad than angry. "You think I owe you an explanation? You're upset because I didn't tell you?"

"No to your first question," I say. "Yes to your second."

He nods, understanding. "You'd prefer a postcard from prison? 'Dear Ethan, missed you the last couple of Thanksgivings, hope your sister's okay, and by the way, I'm gay'? How would you have reacted to that?" He's still sitting back, arm over the back of his bench, like we're just two guys hanging out waiting for our coffee, talking about nothing important.

I think about his question for a moment. "I'd probably react the same way," I say. "But you wouldn't have seen me get upset. And when I would've seen you next, it wouldn't have been a thing at all." I lean forward. "Frankie, we grew up together, man. I had no idea, no sense at all. We talked about girls. Hell, you were as much in love with Sally as I was. So was all of that just . . . a lie?"

Frankie shakes his head, but whether in answer to my question or just as an overall reaction I don't know, because Jamie appears just then to drop off our lattes, interrupting the thread of our conversation, and neither of us picks that thread back up as we go out to the car and drive back to Caesar and Frankie's place.

CAESAR IS TAKING clean dishes out of the dishwasher and putting them into cabinets when we return with the coffee. He accepts his cup, sips from it, and gives a brief nod to indicate it's acceptable.

I look at his laptop, which is closed. "No luck?" I ask, my hopes sinking.

189

Caesar takes another sip. "Jamie is an artist," he says. He closes the dishwasher with his free hand. "Your girlfriend visited Fulton County Jail last week," he adds.

It takes me a second to process what he's saying to me. He doesn't smile, but there's a hint of one in his eyes. "You hacked into Fulton County?" I say, equally shocked and impressed. "That was fast."

"No," Caesar says, taking another sip. When he's finished, he says, "I backed up the phone data before Mr. Lester smashed the phone with a hammer."

Frankie gives Caesar a look that's both amused and annoyed. "And you didn't say anything earlier," he says.

"Wanted my coffee first."

"What was she doing at the jail?" I ask, not interested in Caesar's passive-aggressive coffee game. "Did she go see someone? When did she go?"

Caesar walks over to the laptop, lifts the lid, and presses a key. The screen comes to life, showing multiple open windows. "The things a smartphone can reveal about you," he says. "They're like GPS trackers, record all sorts of data unless you know what to turn off. Only goes back about six months, but that ought to be enough." He steps back and waves his latte-free hand at the screen, a ringmaster inviting me into the big tent.

I sit and look at the open windows. Each looks like a screen from an iPhone. One has a map of Atlanta dotted with several blue circles. Below the map is a list of the locations marked by those circles, along with the number of visits since a given date. "How did you do this?" I ask.

"It's what I do," Caesar says. He states it as a fact rather than a boast.

"It's what you do?" I say, looking up at him. "You hack, and you know things?" Caesar and Frankie both look blankly at me. "*Game of Thrones* reference," I say. "Never mind."

"I know what *Game of Thrones* is," Caesar says. "I lifted all that straight from her phone. It's all stored under your smartphone's privacy settings." He smiles, a thin curve of his lips. "What a delightful example of irony."

"I'll make sure to use that in my next English class," I say.

Marisa's phone has a few locations marked in the Atlanta area: the Archer School, no surprise; a Publix on Roswell Road; the Georgia World Congress Center, where we met at the conference; an address in Buckhead. And a single visit to the Fulton County Jail off Marietta Boulevard, dated Tuesday of last week. One of the same days she took off work.

"Why would she go to the jail?" I ask.

"Only one reason to go there if you aren't being taken there," Frankie says.

"Jay Gardner," I say. "In her calendar, dated last Tuesday. That's why she went to the jail. She went to visit him."

"Why?" Frankie asks.

"I don't know," I say. "Which is why I'm gonna to talk to the guy."

"You can't just roll up to the jail and talk to an inmate," Caesar says. "You have to make an appointment. And the inmate has to say yes."

"I'll do that," I say. "What about Sam Bridges, last Wednesday? Is he in jail, too?"

Caesar leans over again and brings another window forward, this one called **Significant Locations** with a listed history beneath. Sandy Springs, Chamblee, Dunwoody, and Marietta, all Atlanta suburbs, are there. He scrolls down, then stops at **Dahlonega GA**. One location is listed under Dahlonega, dated last Wednesday. Caesar clicks on it to reveal Monastery of Our Lady of Mercy. According to the screen, Marisa visited there from 9:48 AM to 11:31 AM.

"Same place she Googled," I say. "She actually went there."

"Looks like this Bridges dude went there too," Frankie says. "Least that's where she was gonna meet him. Guess he got out of prison."

I shrug. "One way to find out."

"Whoa," Frankie says, holding up a hand like a traffic cop. "This guy invaded your home, *güero*. You're just gonna drive to a monastery and ask to speak to him?"

"Not before I find out how to make a jail visit." I look at Caesar. "May I use your laptop to do that? And then I'll get out of your hair."

Caesar is clearly growing bored with me. "Go ahead," he says, flicking his hand at the laptop as if waving off a fly. "But make it quick. I have work to do."

It isn't until I turn back to the laptop that I realize what Frankie said. Not about Bridges invading my house. It was the first time today that Frankie called me *güero*. It's a small enough gesture, but it's enough to lighten my spirits a little.

THE WEBSITE FOR the Fulton County Jail looks like it's Nineties-era internet, and about as easy to navigate, but I finally manage to put in a request for a video visitation with Jay Gardner and set up an account on the secure channel website the jail uses. That way I can talk to him via video link from home. Now I just have to wait and see if Gardner will agree to talk or not.

While I'm doing that, Frankie and Caesar engage in a hushed but animated discussion on the other side of the loft. I can guess that they are arguing over me, but beyond that I don't know. I push back from the laptop and stand. "Done," I call out, and they both turn toward me, falling silent. "Thank you for your help, both of you. I'll get an Uber to a MARTA station."

Frankie glances at Caesar, then back to me. "You going to the monastery now?"

"Tomorrow," I say. "I need to check on Susannah first."

"I'll go with you," Frankie says. "To the monastery."

That simple offer eases an iron band around my heart, a band I didn't even know was there. Caesar sighs and looks at the ceiling.

"That's okay," I say. "I'll be fine."

"It's not a debate," Frankie says. "I can have Pablo cover for me at the bar."

Quietly, Caesar says, "Mr. Lester won't like it."

"Mr. Lester won't know what I'm doing," Frankie says.

"Uh-huh," Caesar says sardonically.

"Guys," I say, "really, it's okay."

"The man says he's okay," Caesar says to Frankie.

"I don't care," Frankie says.

Something in Caesar's face twists, just for an instant, but I see what it is—pain, and fear. His voice is low but urgent. "You cannot fix everything," he says.

"Not trying to fix anything," Frankie says. "I'm helping a friend."

Caesar's eyes are hooded, arms across his chest. "How many times did your friend come visit you in prison?"

That one sinks home. It's a punch in the gut, and no less effective because it's valid. Frankie wavers at that, glances at me. In that moment, I realize that he cannot come with me. As hard as it is for me to adjust to the idea of Frankie and Caesar as a couple, I have no desire to be a source of friction between the two of them. And yet some part of me shrinks at the thought of Frankie stepping back and away, tearing at whatever fragile bonds we've refashioned in the last couple of hours.

In the few moments I take to think about all this, though, Frankie straightens up and puts his shoulders back, less a posture of defiance than a man squaring himself to confront a difficulty. "I'm going with him," Frankie says.

For a few moments, Frankie and Caesar are in a standoff, each gauging the other's resolve. There's a molten anger in Caesar that he keeps contained, although I can see it in his eyes. In contrast, Frankie is solid, implacable. And then Caesar has turned and is walking to the garage door. "I'll let you out," he says, and it takes me a moment to realize he's speaking to me.

"You don't need to do this," I say to Frankie.

"A guy like this, you don't go see alone," Frankie says. "Don't care where he is. I'll pick you up tomorrow morning."

Caesar pulls the garage door open. The force with which he yanks it seems nearly enough to tear the door off its tracks.

As I walk out, I pause by Caesar, standing in the open garage entrance. "Thank you," I say.

The menace in his voice is like a deep bass note that penetrates to the spine. "If anything happens to him," Caesar says, "you and I are going to have words."

# PART III

I must become a borrower of the night
For a dark hour or twain.
—Banquo, *Macbeth* (3.1.26–27)

# CHAPTER TWENTY-ONE

When I get home, I let Wilson out and get him fresh water and food and then call Birchwood to talk with Susannah. The nurse puts me on hold for a few minutes until finally I hear Susannah's voice on the other end. "Hey," she says.

"Hey." I'm sitting on the floor of my living room, throwing a rope bone that Wilson chases and brings back to me with obvious pride. "How are you?"

"I'm in the psych hospital," she says. She sounds dispirited, not quite listless but definitely down.

"You should hear the Muzak they play when they put you on hold," I say. "It's like bad Kenny G."

"Isn't that redundant?" she says, and she chuckles. It's not much, but it's something.

"What's the worst thing about Birchwood?" I say. "You can tell me. The orderlies? The food? I bet it's the food."

She doesn't say anything for a minute. "I can't go to group," she says.

"Why not?"

"Dr. Ashan doesn't think it's a good idea."

Wilson puts his head in my lap, the rope bone in his mouth, and growls playfully. I take the rope bone out of his mouth, throw it across the room, and watch him bound after it. "Do I need to come up there and kick his ass?" I say.

"It's the same group Marisa was in," Susannah says.

"Oh," I say.

"Dr. Ashan thinks it might not be the best place for me to recover. So I'm in this other group." There's a rustling noise. "It's okay. Mostly I'm just tired."

I close my eyes. As annoying and infuriating as my sister can be, I can't bear to hear her like this—exhausted, caged like a tiger in a zoo.

"Thanks for bringing me clothes," she says.

"Sure," I say, latching on to that positive note. "You need anything else?"

She sighs. "I need to find an apartment," she says. "When I get out of here."

"I'll help you do that. But first you'll stay with me. Until you find a place."

"'Kay," she says. "I'd better go."

"Okay. 'Bye."

She hangs up, and after a moment I do the same. Wilson nudges my hand, and I look down to see the rope bone on the floor and Wilson looking at me with his little head cocked to the side. "Okay, boy," I say, and I throw the rope bone again, Wilson scampering across the hardwood floor to retrieve it and bring it back to me so I can do it again.

LATER THAT AFTERNOON my doorbell rings, causing Wilson to bark his head off, and even as I'm moving to answer the door, I know who it is. There are two of them: one, older and black, standing on my tiny front porch, the other, younger and white, behind him on the steps. They both wear the kind of off-the-rack suits worn by door-to-door salesmen and cops, and I'm certain they aren't here to sell me a new internet plan.

"Mr. Faulkner?" the older black man says. He holds up a badge. "I'm Detective Reginald Panko with the Atlanta Police Department. This is my partner Detective Klingman." Panko looks down at Wilson, who is cavorting at his feet. "Cute dog. May we come in?"

"Is this about Marisa Devereaux?" I ask.

The younger detective, Klingman, has a food stain on his tie and has been passing his hand over it as if he's embarrassed by it. Now his hand stops moving and his eyes widen slightly. No poker face on that one. But Panko looks calmly at me, no change in his expression. "What about Ms. Devereaux?" he asks.

"She was found murdered this morning," I say, and the quaver in my voice is real, as is the sudden prickling in my eyes. She may have tried to ruin my life and pushed my sister and my student to the brink of suicide, but I wanted her out of my life, not torn out of life altogether. "It's all over school," I add. It's true—about an hour ago Byron Radinger sent an all-staff email simply saying that Marisa Devereaux had died, that our hearts went out to her family, and that more information would be forthcoming. That set off a flurry of emails and social media posts by faculty and students alike, including a link to an 11Alive news report about a young woman found dead in the trunk of her car off of Fulton Industrial Boulevard.

Panko nods, gently, confirming my news. "We want to ask you a few questions."

I nod. "All right. But I'd like my lawyer present. If you want, we could meet him at a police station."

Detective Klingman is now practically gaping at me. Even Panko blinks. "All right," he says. "But you'll have to come with us."

PANKO AND KLINGMAN drive me to the nearest APD station, which is in Buckhead behind a giant PetSmart store. I sit in an interrogation room with Detective Klingman, who says nothing but reads his phone, occasionally glancing at me. I gaze at the wall, trying to stay calm, and wait for Johnny Shaw to arrive.

Shaw is older than my uncle and wears a gray seersucker suit and a regimental tie, like Andy Griffith in the old *Matlock* TV show. There's no folksy Southern charm about Johnny Shaw, though. When I called him earlier, he cut me off halfway through my explanation and told me to keep my mouth shut until he got to the station. Now, twenty minutes after I've arrived, he bursts into the interrogation room and barks, "Don't say a single word, Ethan." I raise my hands and shake my head. Shaw turns to Klingman. "I need a moment with my client," he says. Klingman reluctantly stands up and leaves the room, closing the door behind him.

"Hi, Mr. Shaw," I say. "Thank—"

"Save it," he says. "Gus had to drive me here. You know how hard it is to drive from downtown to Buckhead in rush hour?" He pulls out a chair, the legs scraping the tile floor, and drops into it. "Your uncle told me what happened," he says.

I look meaningfully at the closed door. It has a glass window, but currently no one is looking into the room.

Shaw shakes his head. "No two-way mirrors in here, just the glass in the door. And they wouldn't tape our conversation because it's protected by attorney-client privilege and they know I'd sue them six ways to Sunday." He leans forward, resting his arms on his knees, and lowers his voice. "Your uncle says you didn't kill the girl. That true?"

"I didn't kill her," I say, my voice somewhere between detached and disturbed.

Shaw nods, once. "They show you a warrant?"

"No."

"Good. They didn't arrest you, so they don't have anything on you. They may think they have motive, but that just makes you interesting." He scratches his nose. "Where were you the past two nights?"

"At home."

"Got a witness for either time?"

"No."

Shaw quirks his mouth. "So you tell them the truth. Answer every question unless I tell you not do, and do not give them any more information than they ask for. Understand?" I nod, and Shaw stands and opens the door, leaning out into the hall and calling out that we are ready.

Detectives Panko and Klingman conduct the interview, recording it on an iPhone that sits on a tripod in the corner. As they question me, I'm both hyperalert and a step removed from the entire proceedings because of how surreal this is, as if I've walked into an episode of *Law and Order*. Johnny Shaw sits quietly, eyes closed as if he's taking a nap.

Klingman starts by asking where I was the past two evenings, and I tell them I was at home, alone. Then I remember that last night around eight o'clock I took Wilson on a walk and saw my landlord, Tony, out power-walking. We waved at each other. Klingman writes this down, while Johnny Shaw cracks an eye open and glares at me, then goes back to being a statue. Then Panko picks up the questioning and asks me how I met Marisa. I tell them about meeting Marisa at the conference, then spending the night with her at the hotel.

"And then you hired her to teach with you?" Panko asks.

"I didn't hire her," I say. "The school hired her as a sub for my coteacher."

"But you weren't against hiring her."

Shaw's eyelids flutter, but he says nothing. "No," I say. "She mentioned our night together, said it had been fun, but we were both adults and this was about her doing a job."

"Did you tell anyone at work about your prior relationship?"

"It wasn't a relationship," I say. "We had a one-night stand before she was hired. But no, I didn't. Marisa was right—we were both consenting adults, it was our business, and as I wasn't going to be her supervisor, I didn't think I needed to share that with anyone else."

Klingman sits forward. I make an effort not to stare at his stained tie, but it keeps catching my eye, like a comma splice in a student's essay. "When did your relationship at work change?" he asks.

"When did we start dating? Maybe three weeks after she started at Archer."

"Who instigated it?" Panko asks.

"She did," I say. "I didn't really resist."

Klingman nods. "I saw a picture. She was real attractive."

There's a pause like an unspoken sigh at Klingman's observation. I'm aggravated by the bluntness of his words. It's the *was* that really bothers me, the past tense a crude reminder that she is dead. "Yeah," I say, my voice tight. "She was."

Panko frowns slightly at his partner, then shifts forward in his seat. "Mr. Faulkner, we understand that you broke up with Ms. Devereaux recently."

"Yes," I say.

Panko smiles slightly. "Can you elaborate a little for us?"

I let out a long breath and tell them how Marisa Googled me and found out about my parents, how she tried to get me to talk about them, and how she manipulated the Faculty Award vote. Klingman takes notes on a pad while Panko just listens. When I get to the part about confronting her in my classroom, Panko and Klingman both lean forward in their chairs.

"How did she react?" Panko asks.

"She asked if I thought she was only good enough to be my whore," I say. "Then she took off her shirt and her skirt and told me to fuck her right there, on my desk in my classroom."

Klingman is on the verge of gaping at me again. Panko raises his eyebrows. Even Johnny Shaw peeks at me. "Then what?" Panko asks.

"I turned my back on her," I say. "And then she left."

Klingman sits back and clears his throat. "So that was it?"

I shake my head. "She started impersonating me on Twitter."

"Yes, your head of school told us about your allegations," Panko says, looking at his own open notebook. "Including stealing your grade book and putting a picture of a naked woman in it for a custodian to find in

202

the hallway." He looks up at me. "And saying some pretty nasty things on Twitter, pretending to be you. Caused one of your students to attempt suicide."

I draw in a shuddering breath and let it out. Suddenly I'm exhausted. "Yes," I say.

Panko nods slowly. "If that had been me, I don't know," he says. He glances at Klingman. "I'd be upset."

Klingman snorts. "I'd be *pissed*," he says. "My girlfriend turns into a psycho bitch and gets me suspended from my job? I would *not* be happy."

Johnny Shaw opens both eyes, his glance sharp and keen, but he says nothing, just watches.

"I wasn't," I say. "I wasn't happy. She called to gloat, and I hung up and blocked her number."

Klingman nods, commiserating. "This was after you got suspended?"

"Yeah, I—" I stop, thinking. "No, sorry, that was earlier. It was last Saturday." I have to keep my timeline correct. The last time she called me was the last time I heard from her. That is the story. I resist the urge to wipe my palms on my pants.

Panko regards me from under half-lowered lids. "She contact you again after that?"

I think about the litany of texts Marisa sent to me on her own phone. *I'm going to eat your heart.* "No," I say.

"You sure about that?" Klingman says.

Could they know something? I hesitate but look steadily at Klingman, trying to turn my hesitation into a deliberate pause for emphasis. "Yes," I say. "I'm sure."

Klingman's eyes narrow. He doesn't believe me.

Johnny Shaw brings his hands together in a soft clap, startling all of us. "Asked and answered," he says. "What other questions do you have, gentlemen, because it's getting late in the day."

Klingman is annoyed and tries to land a jab. "Why'd you need a lawyer anyway, Ethan?" he asks.

Shaw stands abruptly, his chair legs squealing on the tile floor. "Because we are in *America*, Detective Klingman."

"Okay, counselor," Panko says, palms up and facing Shaw. "No need to get riled up. Mr. Faulkner, if you have anything else to share with us, please—" He makes an open gesture with his hands, welcoming anything else I have to say.

"I hope you find who did it," I say, surprising everyone in the room, including myself, with how forcefully I say it.

"Ethan," Johnny Shaw says, one hand on my shoulder, and I nod, throttling back my emotions. Shaw makes a show of looking at his watch. "If you don't have any more questions . . ."

"Actually," Panko says, standing up and wincing slightly as if his back hurts. "We wanted to ask if you would be willing to give us a DNA sample, just a cheek swab, help us rule you out as a suspect—"

"Absolutely not," Shaw says, his hand still on my shoulder and now gripping it as if my shoulder has somehow insulted him. "Not without a warrant."

Klingman makes one last attempt. "If it helps exonerate your client—"

"Do you know," Shaw says, voice rising to thunder pitch, "how many false positives there are on cheek swab tests? And if word got out to the press that the police were *conducting* a DNA test, forget the fact that you have no evidence whatsoever that my client had *anything* to do with Ms. Devereaux's tragic death? His career would be *finished*. You want a DNA test, you get a warrant and we pick the test and an independent lab."

There's a knock on the door, and it opens to reveal an older cop with a lot of brass on his uniform. He looks at me blankly, then waves Panko over to him. Klingman sits sullenly across from me as Panko and the cop talk, the cop doing most of the talking while Panko listens, but I don't really hear what the cop is saying to Panko. Instead I sit in that interrogation room, imagining the walls are made of metal bars and I can't leave. I'm having a hard time keeping my breathing steady, and I can feel my face flush. Acid is slowly burning a hole in my stomach. I need to go outside. I need air. And then I'm standing, Shaw's hand on my arm guiding me, and the cop with the brass on his uniform is gone and Panko puts a card in my hand and says to call him if I think of anything, that they'll be in touch, and then Shaw is leading me out of the room and down the hall past more cops and through three different doors until we exit the building into the warm, humid night that tastes of hot asphalt and exhaust, and I want to put my hands on my knees and bend over to catch my breath for just a minute.

"Ethan," Shaw says in a low voice, his hand like a vise closing around my upper arm. "Walk. Let's go. Just a few more steps. Breathe. That's it."

Dimly I register a black car and Shaw's gorilla-sized assistant, Gus, in a too-tight jacket and tie standing by the open door. Shaw pushes me into the car and I scoot across the back seat and drop my head down to my knees. Shaw gets in next to me, the door *whomp*ing shut, and then Gus gets in the front seat behind the wheel, the entire car tilting slightly from his weight, and then we are pulling away from the police station as if on smooth rails.

"You going to puke?" Shaw asks me, not unkindly.

I shake my head and take a long, deep breath, then another, and then I sit up, the dizziness momentary and then gone. "Thanks," I say. "Thank you. That was . . ."

"That was bullshit," Shaw says. "They've got nothing and so they try to pin it on someone. You're the ex-boyfriend; it's convenient. Once they find some physical evidence, they'll look somewhere else. But they'll probably get a warrant for your DNA—*Shit*," he says, pounding his fist onto the seat between us, his expression laced with anger and worry. "You blew your nose. What did you do with the tissues?"

I stare at him for a moment, then reach into my pocket and pull out the balled-up tissues. "Didn't see a trash can in there."

Shaw lets out a sigh. "Good. You throw that away, it's all the DNA they need. No expectation of privacy."

"But I didn't do it. So why not—"

He shakes his head. "I meant what I said back there. DNA evidence can be sloppy, and I don't trust the police to do this right. Look at O. J. What you need to do is go home and lay low. Don't make any out-of-state trips or anything. They know you're suspended from work, it's not a great look, but just sit tight. Don't talk to your landlord about the cops, and do *not* talk to a reporter."

"A reporter?"

"Pretty Buckhead girl gets killed and left in the trunk of her car? There's going to be reporters. If you think talking to Panko was hard, try seeing yourself on the nightly news." I must look horrified, because he smooths out his tone. "Look, if they get a court order for your DNA, I can raise a stink about the Atlanta PD's crime lab; they botched a serial rape case last year. I know a good lab; the police would rather outsource to them than send a DNA test to GBI, because that would take weeks."

Johnny Shaw continues trying to mollify me as we drive on through rush hour traffic, and I tune out his voice and try to process all of this, but it's like trying to process a storm when you are in the middle of it. Someone killed Marisa, and I'm a suspect. And I just lied to the police about when I last heard from Marisa. I realize I still have Panko's card in my hand. How would he react if I called and told him the truth about Marisa's phone and the texts? Then Susannah and Uncle Gavin, and Frankie and Caesar, would all get sucked into the same vortex of shit with me. I can't let that happen.

Before I know it, the car pulls up at the foot of my driveway, and I get out, then bend down to look at Johnny Shaw in the back seat. "Thanks for getting me out of there," I say to Johnny Shaw, reaching out to shake his hand.

He takes my hand in a strong grip. "Oh, I'm good, but maybe not that good," he says. "You oughta thank your uncle."

I frown. "My uncle?"

"You see the precinct captain come in at the end, talk to Panko? He told Panko to cut you loose."

"You're saying Uncle Gavin got the cops to let me go?"

Shaw drops my hand and shrugs. "They got to ask you their questions. It was enough." He leans back in his seat, and I take the hint and close the car door and watch as they drive away.

Wilson is overjoyed to see me and almost pees all over the doormat before I can get him out of the house and into the yard, where he starts sniffing the bushes for chipmunks. That night he sleeps curled up at the foot of my bed while I stare at the ceiling, everything about Marisa and my uncle and the police tumbling through my mind. I know that I need answers about what Marisa did, and I need to get them before the police decide to blow my life up even more. Tomorrow Frankie and I will drive to that monastery, Johnny Shaw's warning be damned, and see what we can find out. With that thought, exhausted and more than a little sick at heart, I fall mercifully asleep.

# CHAPTER TWENTY-TWO

Frankie picks me up when the early-morning light is washing from blue to gray and the birds are not yet singing. I step out onto my porch when he arrives, the Frankenstein rumbling and shivering the air. Wilson lets out a single *yip* from inside and then falls quiet. I hate leaving him alone again, even though my neighbor Gene told me he would let Wilson out and take him for a walk.

Frankie sits behind the wheel, one arm slung out the open window. He is wearing a crisp blue-and-white pinstriped button-down, the sleeves rolled back to his elbows, and dark jeans. Briefly I consider my own outfit—shorts, a clean T-shirt, and a hoodie for the cool morning. I look ready for the beach. "You going on a date?" I ask.

"We're going to a monastery," he says. "Wanted to show some respect." He glances at the sandals on my feet. I haven't seen Frankie's footwear, but I'm guessing he's wearing black loafers.

"You're dressed up enough for the both of us," I say. "Look, before we go anywhere . . . the cops came by yesterday. Questioned me about Marisa." Frankie just looks at me as I stand in the driveway, so I keep going. "They didn't arrest me, but they're clearly interested in me as a suspect. I'm still going to find out what Marisa did. But I don't want to

get you in any more trouble. If you don't want to take me to the monastery, that's cool."

Frankie looks at me, his expression unchanging. After a few moments
he says, "You wait to tell me until I show up to drive you there? You could
have called."

I stare at him. "I don't have your phone number."

"Could have called the bar."

He has a point. "Shit, Frankie, I'm sorry; I didn't want my uncle to
ask—"

A smile slowly unfurls on Frankie's face.

I stop. "You asshole," I say.

"Get in the car," Frankie says. "I told you I'd take you."

I get in the car, and Frankie slowly backs down the driveway. "Nice
neighborhood," he says. "How long you lived here?"

"Since college."

He says nothing after that, negotiating the driveway, but his smile is
gone. I know what he's thinking. I got to go to college and take classes
and party, all while he was sitting in an eleven-by-seven cell. I want to tell
him it wasn't really like that for me, that college was more about working
to build a new life and get away from my old one. But explaining that
I had it tough too would sound like the height of arrogant white male
privilege.

"How long you been working for my uncle?" I ask.

Frankie finishes backing out of my driveway, checks the mirrors, and
then puts the car in drive and pulls away from the curb. "Since I got out,"
he says. He looks at me to see my reaction, and to be honest, given that
I've worked hard to extricate myself from my uncle's life, my reaction is
complicated. Frankie's situation as an ex-convict is complicated enough
without adding my uncle to the mix. Ruben worked for my uncle for
years, doing God knows what kind of shady shit for him, then died of
a heart attack. And then Frankie stepped in to take his place. Was that
hard for Frankie? Did he feel indebted to my uncle, who had paid for

his defense lawyer? Or did he resent how his father had literally worked himself to death for the man Frankie now worked for?

Frankie must see something in my face, because he shrugs and says, "Hard to get a job when you get out of prison. Your uncle offered, and I knew how to work at Ronan's." He comes to a stop sign at Roswell Road, and even though there isn't any oncoming traffic, he doesn't turn onto the road but looks back to me. "If I've gotten between you and your uncle, or made you feel like I've taken your spot or something, I'm sorry."

That leaves me speechless for a moment. "No," I finally say. "You haven't. I got away from him years ago. I left. You haven't done anything wrong."

Frankie doesn't respond at first, instead waiting for an early-morning bus to roll past before turning onto Roswell. "Okay," he says.

We drive up to the Perimeter, and even though it's before rush hour, there's plenty of traffic, although it's moving swiftly for now. Frankie rolls up the driver's window before turning onto 285. I ignore the King and Queen Buildings rising up on our left. Ahead of us, the sky is beginning to crack open, a fiery light spreading across the horizon, and Frankie aims the Frankenstein directly at the rising sun, the V-8 beginning to thrum under the hood, finally getting to show off its paces a little.

WE TAKE THE exit for GA-400. The southbound lanes are heavy with traffic, but because we are heading north, Frankie can open up his car a little, and we move along at a brisk clip. The sun is now over the horizon, a golden star banishing the gray predawn to usher in a clear blue sky.

I've wanted to ask Frankie about Caesar but have hesitated, waiting for a good moment, then realize there is no good moment, only my own awkwardness to climb over. "Was Caesar okay this morning?" I ask. "With you coming with me and all?"

Frankie smoothly switches lanes to drive around a tractor trailer. "Don't worry about Caesar," he says. "He'll be fine. He's . . . protective. How's Susannah? Did you get to talk to her yesterday?"

I understand Frankie is changing the subject, but I don't fight it. "Yeah," I say. "I did. She's okay."

"Must be hard," he says.

I nod, my throat suddenly thick with sorrow. "I hate it," I manage to say. "I hate how she feels so . . . *diminished*. Like a light that's going out. Burning out."

"But she's getting help, yeah? Therapy and meds and everything?"

"Sure," I say. "But it won't cure anything. Just manages it."

"We're all just managing, *güero*," Frankie says.

THERE'S A WRECK that slows us down for a good half hour, but finally we turn off the highway, leaving the billboards and fast-food signs behind for a two-lane road. But it's still the modern world. Just five miles from the monastery, we pass a shopping center with a Publix grocery store, a Rooms to Go outlet, and a Pizza Hut, all moored in a shimmering black lake of new asphalt. Further on, we drive by a subdivision under construction, a paved road winding up into cleared lots of bulldozed red clay. Hispanic workers in denim shirts and straw hats stand around a half-completed ditch at the entrance to the subdivision, one of them looking blankly at us as we drive past. And ahead, on the horizon, I can just see the start of the north Georgia mountains, a set of blue ridges one after the other, rising up above the plains and receding into the distance.

Then a sign appears: Monastery Ahead—100 yards. A driveway to the left boasts another sign: Abbey of Our Lady of Mercy—Bless You. A yellow metal gate is pushed open to allow traffic, and Frankie turns in. Small magnolia trees line the driveway, which leads perhaps half a mile before bending to the right and out of sight. I don't see any buildings.

"Not what I expected," Frankie says, and I know what he means. I half-expected a high brick wall or a large church, not a driveway lined with magnolias.

We follow the curve of the drive to the right, and as it straightens, we can see the monastery a hundred yards ahead—a low concrete building with a wrought-iron gate in the middle, then a two-story building behind that, and a church with a steeple and simple crucifix that rises above all. On the left a grassy field slopes down to a pond. I can see gray and white geese strolling up from the water. To the right is a cracked and weedy parking lot next to another low concrete building with a sign that reads Abbey Gift Shop. Although it's not yet nine o'clock, there are already several cars in the parking lot, most of them dented older models of pickups and sedans. A group of people are waiting by the wrought-iron gate, maybe thirty or so adults, with children playing in the grass nearby.

Frankie pulls into the parking lot and kills the engine. Immediately, even through the rolled-up windows, I can hear the *wree-wree* of crickets in the surrounding woods. I open the door and get out, and when Frankie does the same, I point at the wrought-iron gate and we walk across the parking lot.

When we approach the gate, I can see that the gate has the word PAX wrought in the topmost part of it. The gate is closed, but I can see that it leads into an arched passageway that cuts through the building and opens onto a courtyard beyond. There's a cardboard sign on the wall next to the gate. Handwritten in black marker, the sign reads FOOD BANK. The people in line stir like blades of grass in a breeze and form a rough line. A bell tolls, and before it stops, a monk walks out of the building on the far side of the courtyard. He crosses the courtyard and walks through the passage to the gate and opens it. He wears glasses and a white hooded robe cinched around the waist with a leather belt. A black scapular, a rectangular piece of cloth with an opening for the head, lies over his shoulders. His white hood is pushed back from his head, which is gray and grizzled. He's wearing an old pair of grass-stained Reebok tennis shoes. The line of people shuffles forward, each person taking a number from a pad mounted on the wall by the left-hand door in the passageway before going through that same door.

Frankie and I get at the end of the line and slowly move toward the monk. When we finally reach him, I realize he's old, at least seventy. The monk gives numbers from the pad to a family of five, including two small boys, one of whom looks up at the monk and grins, showing off his missing tooth. "Thanks, Brother!" the boy says loudly.

"There you go, buddy, God bless you," the monk says, smiling, and the family goes through the door. When they open it, I can see it leads to a room with folding chairs. A sign inside the doorway reads, Only 28 people allowed at a time. I glance at the pad on the wall, which is on 29.

"I'm sorry," the monk says to me. "You can go in with the next group in about half an hour."

I smile in what I hope looks like embarrassment. "I'm very sorry to bother you, Brother," I say, "but actually I'm looking for someone who might be here. An old family friend? His name is Sam Bridges?" I don't know if it's a specifically Southern thing or not, but posing statements as questions tends to be disarming. I hope it makes me seem innocuous and in need of help rather than like someone seeking answers.

The old monk blinks behind his glasses. "Sam Bridges? I don't . . . ah, you mean Samuel. He's working in the bonsai shop today. Have you made an appointment through the abbot?"

Now I'm the one disarmed. I hadn't considered an abbot, let alone calling to make an appointment. "I—no, I haven't," I say.

The monk closes the door and extends his arm toward the door on the other side of the arched passage. "If you like, you can call his voice mail number from this phone over here and set up an appointment."

"I'm sorry, this is an emergency. I really need to speak with him today."

The monk's expression grows slightly stiffer. "Are you a member of his immediate family?"

"No."

"Then I'm sorry. You'll need to call the abbot." I don't know if he did this on purpose, but now the monk stands between me and the courtyard at the end of the passage.

"Ethan." Frankie puts hand on my shoulder. "How about I call and leave a message for the abbot. You go wait by the car." As he says this, with his back to the monk, he cuts his eyes to the left, then back at me and to the left again. The car is not to the left, but directly behind us across the parking lot.

"Okay," I say. "I'm sorry, Brother." The older monk shakes his head and smiles, as if denying that I owe him an apology, and then walks with Frankie over to the other door. I walk back out of the arch and look to the left, where Frankie indicated. Extending alongside the parking lot all the way to the gift shop is a fenced-off area with a closed gate. A sign reading BONSAI SHOP AND GARDEN hangs on the gate. Below it is a small sign: Please Do Not Enter Unless Gate is Open. Quickly I walk to the gate, push it open, and then shut it behind me.

Before me is another low building, but this one is wooden with a tin roof. One end is open so I can see inside the entire length of the building, which looks as if it was once a stable—on either side, what used to be pens are open to the center of the building. A few of the dividing walls between the pens have been removed. Sunlight streams in through glassless windows. In each area or pen, I can see a mound of soil and a stack of plastic plant trays. In some pens, I can see short rows of bonsai trees, each pruned and shaped into a unique twisted figure. The old monk said that Bridges is working in here today. I walk into the nursery, glancing into pens as I pass them.

At the far end of the nursery, two men step out of a doorway. Both stop when they see me. One is a monk, very old and humpbacked, dressed in white and black robes. "Can I help you?" he calls in a high, quavering voice.

The second man is wearing work clothes—khakis and a blue T-shirt—but his T-shirt is tucked in and his khakis are neatly pressed. The overall effect is of a man without a coat and tie dressing as best he can for church. Although the goatee has been shaved off, the acne scars are still on his cheeks. He looks at me with surprise but not recognition.

He probably didn't get a good look at my face that night. I was just a kid running down a hallway, trying to bring his father a pistol.

"Samuel Bridges," I say. The venom in my voice startles the men. It startles me. The hunchbacked monk cringes, while Bridges plants his feet as if awaiting a blow. "My name is Ethan Faulkner," I continue. "I met you before at my house, with your friend who wears a ponytail. And Kayla."

Astonishment washes across Bridges's face, then recognition, followed by something I wasn't expecting: guilt.

The old monk frowns, an ugly expression on his wrinkled face. "You shouldn't be back here," he says.

"It's all right, Brother Milo," Bridges says hoarsely.

We all stand facing each other, frozen by the enormity of the moment, depending on our point of view—Brother Milo from outrage, Bridges and me from other, more complicated emotions. We could be a Renaissance painting: the shocked monk, the guilt-stricken sinner, and the angry young man. All that is missing is the sad, cherubic face of an angel gazing down upon us from the heavens.

BRIDGES AND I sit outside the bonsai nursery on stone benches opposite each other. Frankie, who made his way back here after slipping past the monk at the gate, leans against a nearby wall, arms folded across his chest, his eyes never leaving Bridges, who, for his part, is doing a pretty good imitation of the Virgin Mary in the *Pietà*: head tilted toward the ground, eyes closed, mouth small and sorrowful.

"So, do you live here now?" I ask him.

Bridges opens his eyes, which are calm and clear. "Yes," he says. "Ever since I got out of prison. Right now I'm just working here, doing maintenance, landscaping, that kind of thing. Most of the monks are old; they need help running the place. But if things go all right, I'll go into my observership. Like a trial run. If the abbot and the vocation director like the progress I've made, they'll make me a postulant in a couple of months."

"And then you get a robe and sandals and everything?"

Bridges doesn't bat an eye at my sarcasm. "I wouldn't get to wear the religious habit unless I became a novitiate." He gives a thin smile. "And most of the brothers don't wear sandals these days."

"I'm guessing most of the brothers haven't murdered anyone either."

That one strikes home. Bridges winces, then hangs his head slightly. "It may not matter for much," he says, his eyes on the ground, "but I've never killed anyone. I've done horrible things, but I'm not a murderer."

"Bullshit," I say, and I like the reaction he has, the shocked jerk of the head, his eyes widening slightly, as if I've cussed at the altar. "You may not have pulled the trigger, but you came into my house with your buddy and my parents died." I lean forward, glaring. "I don't give a shit that you want to get close to God or whatever the hell you want to call this. You fucked up my life."

He nods, his lips pressed together, hands on his knees. "I know," he says, his voice thick with sorrow. "And I am sorry. Truly."

Leaning against the wall, Frankie makes a dismissive noise in his throat. Bridges glances his way, then back to me.

"I can't fix that night," Bridges says. "God knows I would if I could, but I can't. I told your girlfriend that, but it's better that you've come so I can tell it to you straight to your face."

Frankie stands up off the wall and uncrosses his arms. I'm leaning forward even farther, as if trying to hear. "What did—my girlfriend, what did she ask you?"

Bridges frowns, like he's heard a wrong note in a familiar tune. No matter what else he is, he's not stupid. "I thought you sent her here," he says. "Asked her to talk to me."

I look at Frankie, who shrugs as if to say, *Go ahead*, güero. "No," I say to Bridges. "I didn't."

Bridges's eyebrows knot together over that. Slowly, he says, "She told me that you were angry. That you wanted to know why I did . . . what I did. Did she tell you something different?"

"She . . . she actually didn't tell me *anything*, really—"

"She lied to you," Frankie says to Bridges. "Ethan didn't know you were here. She came out here on her own."

*Thank you, Frankie.* Confronted with a simple question, I didn't know how to respond, especially regarding the fact that Marisa is now dead. "Marisa lied to both of us," I say to Bridges, trying to swing the conversation back to her. "And I'm trying to figure out why. So please tell me what she asked you, what she said."

Bridges says nothing for a few moments. "I want to tell you a story," he says, then sighs and shakes his head. "I told her this, so I think I'd better tell it to you too."

BRIDGES USED TO live in the Florida Keys, he tells me, working on swordfish boats, shrimp boats, shark boats, anywhere that paid well. He often got paid in cash. One night, after two weeks of swordfishing, he was walking to his rented room with his pay in his pocket when three men jumped him. Bridges threw one of the men into the harbor, but the other two clubbed him down, and one pulled a knife. That's when another man stepped out from a nearby alley with a metal pipe in his hand, brained the one with the knife, and sent the other man running. The man with the pipe was thin and knotty, and when he smiled at Bridges, it looked like something a little kid would draw with crayons, all crooked and creepy when it was meant to be nice. But he had saved Bridges from being cut up and possibly stabbed to death, so Bridges took the man, whose name was Donny Wharton, to the nearest bar.

Turned out Donny was going to Miami and had a business proposition for Bridges, a little bit of risk for big money. Bridges was ready to leave fishing behind, and plus he felt obligated to Donny for saving him.

So the next morning, in Donny's car, a cherry-red Camaro convertible, they headed north.

"WHY ARE YOU telling me this?" I ask.

"I'm just trying to explain how I came into your life," Bridges says. "How I met Donny, and what happened with Marisa."

"Why should I give a shit about this Donny?"

Bridges looks grim. But then he sees something over my shoulder that gets his attention, and I turn around to look. A monk is approaching from the abbey, a tall sturdy man with a full, round face and a salt-and-pepper beard. He stops a few yards away from us. "Samuel," he says.

Bridges stands. "Dom Michael," he says. "My apologies. This is Ethan Faulkner and . . . his friend." He says this last with a lame wave toward Frankie. "Ethan, this is Dom Michael, our abbot."

Dom Michael appears to have little interest in either me or Frankie. His voice is both calm and penetrating, and almost manages to mask his irritation. "Samuel, I understand you have neglected to complete your duties in the bonsai shop this morning."

Bridges shifts his feet. "That's true, Dom Michael. I'm sorry."

As much as I don't mind seeing Bridges get in trouble, I need to keep talking to him, to learn what Marisa told him, and so I stand up from my bench. "It's my fault, Dom Michael," I say.

Dom Michael now considers me. "Mr. Faulkner, I understand that you asked one of our brothers to speak with Samuel and he directed you to contact me. Instead, you violated our sanctuary to find Samuel yourself. I have to ask you and your friend to leave."

I glance at Frankie, who has crossed his arms over his chest again, then back at Dom Michael. "I'm afraid I can't do that."

"Ethan," Bridges says in a low voice, "you ought to do what he says."

"Don't think so," Frankie says. He steps up beside me. "My friend needs to talk to this man."

Dom Michael frowns. "*This man,*" he says, "is a member of our community. And our community has rules."

"You know this guy just got out of prison, right?" Frankie says. "You want to know what he did to Ethan?"

The frown on Dom Michael's face darkens, but I also notice that he shows no surprise or confusion at Frankie's revelation. "I will not allow you or anyone else to violate this abbey," Dom Michael says, his voice stern and absolute. "If you won't leave, I'll call the police." He pulls out a cell phone.

Bridges looks alarmed. "Ethan . . . Dom Michael, please."

"Worried about the cops, *Samuel*?" I say. I register the sneer in my voice, and I don't like it, but I'm beyond polite manners at this point.

"Ethan," Frankie says warningly.

"What?" I turn to look at Frankie, and then my heart drops and I curse myself. Bridges is an ex-con, but so is Frankie. Even as I'm thinking this, Frankie shakes his head. "Not me," he says in a low voice only I can hear. "You. They're going to want to talk to you about Marisa. You don't need any cops pissed off at you right now."

It takes a moment for the truth of Frankie's words to get through to my head, as if static had been blocking the signal he was sending. He's right. But I don't have the answers I need.

"I'm sorry, Samuel," Dom Michael is saying. "But these men must leave."

"No," I say, loudly, cutting off Dom Michael and getting everyone's attention. "You don't—none of you understand." I turn to Dom Michael. "Both of my parents are dead," I say. "They're dead, and this man can tell me something about that, about *why*—"

"Ethan," Bridges says, and his face is mottled with emotion. "I just wanted to get her away from him; I didn't think that—"

"What are you *talking* about?" My voice is shaking a little, from anger or from grief or both, I don't know.

"I just—I needed to get Kayla," Bridges says, "take her somewhere she could get help. Try to get her away from Donny."

Kayla. The girl with the silver sandal. The girl Bridges demanded come out of our house. "Donny?" I say, staring at him. "What does Donny have to do with—"

"She started screaming," Bridges says—he hasn't heard me, has started his story and can't stop. "I just—I wanted to tell her it was okay, I'd help her, I wasn't going to hurt her. Then your dad . . . he swung at me. I don't blame him; I was storming into his house. We started fighting . . ."

Frankie's face looks pale, even a little green.

Dom Michael raises a hand to place it on Bridges's shoulder. "Samuel, you don't—"

"Then you came down the hall," Bridges says to me. "You fired that pistol, and it scared the hell out of me, out of both of us. I remember thinking you looked too young to be holding a gun. And then Donny came in . . ."

Ponytail. Jesus. Donny was Ponytail. I close my eyes. *The fuck?* One gunshot and my arm goes numb, and then a roar of shots, so loud in the front hall of my home, the burnt acrid smell of gunpowder, the blood—

"Ethan," I hear, and Frankie is next to me. "Sit down, *güero*."

"I don't want to sit down," I say. I open my eyes and see Bridges is sitting on his bench, his hands clasped in front of him. His eyes are wet.

"Don't you *fucking* cry!" I say. My heart is pounding and my chest feels like it's being squeezed, and I can't even register where I am on the emotional map anymore.

"I'm so sorry," Bridges says, tears running down his cheeks. "I told this to your girlfriend; I thought it would be easier. I'm sorry."

"What did she say?" I demand. "Marisa. What did she say? Did she tell you anything?"

"She said you hated me," Bridges says, his voice breaking. "That you wanted me dead and you hoped I went to hell." He's openly weeping now, trying not to sob. "I told her that I didn't know Donny had a gun, that I made him call nine-one-one. Marisa said—she knew it didn't matter, that she knew what I'd done, how I'd run back here after I got out of prison because I was a coward, that she knew all about me and Donny. When I saw you, I thought maybe—maybe it was another chance, that I could tell you I was sorry and you . . ." He slips off the bench onto his knees, his head hanging down. "I'm sorry," he sobs.

"You're *sorry?*" I say. I'm astonished at the anger coursing through me like a bright-yellow river. I want to punch Bridges in the face and then keep hitting him until there's nothing left that looks like a face. "You're sorry? You come into my house and attack my father, and then your friend comes in with a gun"—Bridges's face twists into a knot of pain— "and *shoots* my entire family, and my parents are dead and you're *sorry?* You think that makes it all better? You're sorry and it's all *better* because you've . . . I don't know, joined the *holy fucking men's club?*"

Frankie has taken a step back, his eyes wide. Dom Michael stands frozen, cell phone forgotten in his hand. Bridges looks shattered and continues to sob on his knees. I stare at him, considering whether I should kick him in the face. Then I turn and stalk off, leaving them all behind.

I DON'T KNOW how long I stand outside the monastery by the pond, watching the geese, waiting for my blood to cool. Presently I hear footsteps in the grass, and then Frankie stands next to me. He says nothing for a few moments. "You okay?" he asks finally.

"No," I say.

We stand there, looking at the water. One goose starts honking and raising its wings at another goose, and they flap and honk at each other, splashing and disturbing the surface of the pond.

"That's a metaphor for something," I say.

Frankie glances at me. "I don't know what you mean," he says.

"Neither do I," I say.

After a few more moments of silence, Frankie says, "Dom Michael didn't call the police. But he will if we don't leave."

"Okay."

Frankie waits a beat. "Bridges says he doesn't know anything else about Marisa."

"So this was a complete waste of time," I say.

"We know who this Donny guy is," Frankie says. "That's a start."

"Great. So now I know Ponytail's real name. I'll send him a fucking Christmas card." I pick up a rock and try to skim it off the pond. It skips the surface twice before sinking with a *plonk*. Then I turn and walk to the car, Frankie at my side.

"Bridges said Marisa knew all about him and Donny," Frankie says. "Or she told him she did, anyway."

"Yeah, well, Marisa was a pretty good liar."

"Okay, but how did she know about Bridges in the first place? She knew where to find him. She knew about Jay Gardner being in jail. How?"

I stop and shout, "I don't fucking *know*!" I'm loud enough to disturb the geese—they start splashing and honking again. I run my hand over my head, then rub my neck. "I'm sorry," I say. "I'm just frustrated. What the hell do we do?"

Frankie shrugs. "We find Donny, maybe we get some answers."

# CHAPTER TWENTY-THREE

THE DAY AFTER MY VISIT TO THE MONASTERY, SUSANNAH IS RELEASED on schedule from Birchwood, and I go to pick her up and take her home.

She's pale but smiling, even if the smile is as thin as the T-shirt she's wearing. Her mood is placid, a mountain lake unruffled by breezes or waterfalls or jumping trout. Clearly her meds have been adjusted. She hugs me, weakly, but not like she's fragile and would crumble in my arms if I tried to hold her. So I hold her for a few moments, rocking slightly in the lobby with the glossy magazines and maybe-faux birch furniture.

"What are you trying to do, dance with me?" she murmurs into my shoulder.

"I'm giving you a hug."

"Seriously, it's like the worst foxtrot ever."

I lean back and hold her at arm's length. "That's my sister."

"Are you crying?"

"It's spring. I'm allergic to pollen." I take the discharge papers from the nurse and thank her, then steer Susannah toward the front door. Outside, Susannah shades her eyes with her hand from the bright sunlight. She folds herself into my car and we drive away, me resisting an urge to flip off Birchwood in the rearview mirror.

"You were going to flip off the hospital," Susannah says. She's gazing out the passenger window, letting the passing scenery wash over her.

"I wasn't."

She turns her head to look at me. "It's spring," she says. "Spring break. You should be on vacation somewhere."

"I'm not going anywhere."

She nods and leans back in her seat, closing her eyes. In a reasonable imitation of Forrest Gump's drawl, she says, " 'Sorry I had a fight in the middle of your Black Panther party.' "

" 'You—are—a—toy!' " I say back.

" 'Mama always said life is like a box of chocolates.' "

"You have to quote a different Tom Hanks movie," I tell her. "You can't do *Forrest Gump* twice in a row."

"I just got out of the psych hospital," she says, eyes still closed. "You can cut me some slack."

WILSON IS FRANTIC with joy when Susannah steps into my house, leaping and barking and his tail wagging so fast it looks like a propeller. "Hi, doggy," Susannah manages, petting Wilson. "Good boy." She heads for the couch and sinks down onto it. "I'm going to lie down here for about a week, 'kay?"

"Good choice," I say. When she raises a quizzical eyebrow, I put my hand on top of my TV. "I downloaded every Tom Hanks movie ever made."

She raises up on her elbows. "Seriously?"

"Even *Joe Versus the Volcano*."

Susannah sighs. "You know how to make a girl feel special, Ethan."

We watch *Dragnet* because Susannah wants something funny, and then, after ordering pizza, we start *Apollo 13*. Yesterday I threw out all my beer and liquor, not wanting to tempt Susannah as alcohol and antidepressants are a terrible combination, but she doesn't even ask for a drink except for a Diet Coke. We gorge on Hawaiian pizza, Susannah's favorite, and call out favorite lines as we watch Tom Hanks on the screen.

The money quote for *Apollo 13* is coming up, as Kevin Bacon's character has just turned on the stirring fans for the spacecraft's oxygen tanks, one of which explodes. Susannah and I are leaning forward, eager to say the line aloud. What I don't expect to hear is the deep male voice behind us.

" 'Houston, we have a problem.' "

I jump off the couch and spin around, TV remote in my hand, while Susannah turns, stifling a cry. Caesar is standing in my living room behind the couch, hands in the pockets of his leather coat.

"Jesus Christ!" I yell.

Belatedly, Wilson starts to bark an alarm from his bed across the room.

"Might want to put the remote down before you hurt someone," Caesar says.

I glance at the remote in my hand, poised as if I'm going to throw it. I use it to pause the movie and then drop it on the couch. "The hell are you doing here?"

"Checking on you," Caesar says.

"How'd you get in?"

"Back door."

I glare at Susannah, who shrugs and holds up her hands in a *who, me?* gesture. "The best locks money can buy," I say to her acidly.

"Door was unlocked," Caesar says.

I open my mouth, then close it. Wilson takes this opportunity to scamper over, growling, and then rolls over shamelessly onto his back at Caesar's feet. Caesar crouches to rub Wilson's belly.

Meanwhile, Susannah is looking Caesar over. She turns to me and says, "So who's Shaft?"

I stare at her. "You did not just call him Shaft."

She tilts her head, considering. "No, he's more of a Hawk. From *Spenser: For Hire?* Avery Brooks played him?"

Blessedly, a knock on the front door interrupts her.

"That would be Frankie," Caesar says. His expression is unreadable.

I head for the door, but not without overhearing Caesar say, "Avery Brooks is all right. But I liked him better in *Star Trek*."

"Oh my God, I know, right?" Susannah says, her voice pitching toward fangirl excitement.

*Caesar's got a new best friend*, I think. I open the door to find Frankie midknock.

"What's going on?" I ask.

"Go inside," he says.

I stand in the doorway. "Not until you tell me what's going on."

"Frankie?" I hear Susannah say, and then she's beside me. "Hi."

Frankie stares at her. "Hey," he says. "How you doing?" His eyes flick to me, then back to her.

Susannah smiles, showing her teeth. "Fantastic. Just got out of the loony bin. Your friend Caesar likes *Star Trek*, which is amazing. We're watching Tom Hanks movies. Can I get a hug here, or what?"

Frankie chuckles and bends to hug Susannah, but over her shoulder he gives me a warning look. "You don't check your phone?" he says to me.

I silenced my phone and left it plugged up in my bedroom while Susannah and I watched movies. "I was taking a break," I say. "Catch me up."

"Suzie," Frankie says, one arm around Susannah's shoulders, "do you mind if I borrow your brother for a minute?"

Caesar is walking around my living room, glancing out the windows. Wilson trots behind him, head cocked in observation, his tail wagging.

"What are you doing?" I ask him. "Inspecting my house?"

"Something like that," Caesar says.

Wordlessly I turn to Frankie and hold my hands up, baffled.

"Guys, I want to watch Tom Hanks and eat pizza," Susannah says.

Frankie looks past me at Susannah, then back to me. "Caesar," he says, "did you know Ethan's sister is a huge Trekkie?"

Caesar is heading down the hall to my bedroom, Wilson at his heels, and his voice comes floating back. "I had an inkling. Girl has taste."

"What is he doing?" I ask.

"Probably checking your windows."

After a few moments Caesar reappears along with Wilson. "Looks good. As long as Ethan remembers to lock the doors."

I turn and look at the front door, then step over and turn the dead bolt. I can't be sure, but I think Caesar's mouth twitches.

"Suzie," Frankie says, "why don't you and Caesar hang out for a minute while I talk with Ethan?"

Susannah looks at Caesar, who raises an eyebrow in a perfect imitation of Spock.

"*Deep Space Nine* or *Voyager*?" she asks quickly.

Caesar grunts. "*DS Nine*, no question."

Grinning, Susannah takes him by the hand and leads him to the couch. "Go on, boys," she says. "Caesar and I have *loads* to talk about."

Frankie walks down the hall, and I follow him into my room. "What is going on, Frankie?" I ask.

Frankie glances at the bedroom doorway, then turns his gaze on me. "Sam Bridges is dead," he says.

"He . . . *what*?"

"One of the monks found him this morning, floating in that pond outside the monastery." Frankie is gauging me, seeing if I'm going to freak out. "He'd been stabbed. A lot."

I sit down on my bed. "Oh my God," I say.

"It's on the news," Frankie continues. "That's why I called. When you didn't answer, we came right over."

My mind is whirling. Sam Bridges, dead. Marisa, dead. I look up at Frankie. "Why did you come?" I ask. Then I'm struck absolutely still. Frankie sees the understanding in my face and nods grimly. "Someone killed him," I continue, "and you think that means I might be in danger."

"Just being careful," Frankie says. "But yeah. Caesar insisted."

Caesar insisted? It's a night of surprises. "God," I say. "Oh God, Frankie. What if it's my fault?"

"Easy, *güero*," Frankie says. "This isn't your fault."

"We go see him and ask about Marisa, and the next day someone sticks a knife in him? That's not a coincidence." I run my hands through my hair. Bridges tried to apologize for how he had ended up in my house that one horrible night. And I rejected him, essentially spat in his face. And now he's dead.

"It's not your fault," Frankie says again.

"So who would've killed him?" I ask. "Same person who killed Marisa?"

Frankie gives me a look like he's waiting for me to realize something.

"What?" I ask. "Do *you* know who—" I stop. There's one obvious choice. "Damn. You think it was Donny?"

"Makes sense," Frankie says. "He has the motive—get rid of any witnesses to what he did to your family. Plus Bridges probably had loads of shit on him."

I slowly nod my head. "Marisa starts asking questions and stirs things up," I say. "And we still don't know all that she knew, or how she—"

On my dresser, my phone buzzes with an incoming call. Frankie and I exchange a look. On the second buzz, I stand and walk over to the phone to look at the caller ID. I look at Frankie. "You told my uncle?" I say.

"Hell yes, I told your uncle. This is serious shit, Ethan. You need all the help you can get."

The phone continues to buzz, vibrating on the top of my dresser.

"You should answer that," Frankie says.

I level a dark look at him, then pick up the phone. "Hello?" I say reluctantly.

"Are Frankie and Caesar there?" Uncle Gavin asks.

"Yeah," I say, still looking at Frankie. "They're here. Susannah and I are fine."

"You've an interview with the Atlanta police tomorrow," my uncle says. "At one o'clock, downtown. Johnny Shaw will meet you there."

I stand there, trying to absorb what my uncle is saying. "Why?" I manage to say.

"They want to talk to you about the man you spoke with at the monastery. And they're trying to get a court order for your DNA."

There's a specific camera shot in film called a *dolly zoom* where the camera lens zooms out at the same time that the camera moves forward. Spielberg uses it in *Jaws*, when the chief is sitting on the beach and the shark strikes. The camera moves or dollies forward at the same time the camera lens zooms out, so you feel like you are both rushing toward and away from the screen at the same time. It's disorienting as hell, and it's exactly the way I feel now, talking on the phone to my uncle about meeting with the police.

"You are not being arrested," Uncle Gavin says. "It's an interview. So far Shaw's been able to gum up the works about your DNA, told a judge about the problems with the police lab. You go in and cooperate with the interview, that helps. Shaw has an independent lab to run the test, if it comes to that."

I nod and wet my lips with the tip of my tongue. "At the monastery," I begin, about to tell him what we learned, but I stop because Frankie is vigorously shaking his head no and waving his arms in a cut-off gesture.

"Call Johnny Shaw, Ethan," Uncle Gavin says. "He'll walk you through it all. It will be fine."

I let out a laugh that could easily be a bark or a sob. "Fine," I say. "Sure."

"Call Shaw," my uncle says, and then he hangs up.

I look at my phone for a few seconds, then lower it to the dresser. I'd like to lower myself to the floor, maybe lie there on the hardwood, but I have just enough dignity to walk over to my bed, where I sit down again.

"Why'd you wave me off?" I ask Frankie.

Frankie sits down next to me, carefully, like I'm a deer he's afraid he might spook. "You never know who might be listening to a phone call," he says.

I turn to stare at him. He looks back at me, calm but with a hint of worry in his eyes. "Are you saying I might be bugged?" I say. "My phone might be wiretapped or something?"

"More like your uncle's phone might be," he says. "The cops, the feds, he's always doing that dance."

I briefly imagine my uncle doing a little soft-shoe in Ronan's. Uncle Gavin, the Fred Astaire of crime. I'd laugh if I weren't afraid I'd descend into hysterics.

"Anyway," Frankie says, "when you talk to the cops, don't share anything unless you have to. Answer the questions you have to answer, but that's it—nothing else."

"They're going to want to know if I had anything to do with his death," I say.

"You were with me yesterday afternoon until I dropped you off here last night," Frankie says. "You have an alibi for later?"

"I picked up my sister after lunch today. But this morning? No."

Frankie dropped a hand on my shoulder and squeezed. "It'll be okay, güero. Johnny Shaw is good."

*He didn't keep you out of jail*, I think, but I don't say it aloud because it would be cruel and because it's not exactly a valid argument—Frankie confessed and took a plea deal. I plan on doing neither because I didn't kill anybody.

My phone vibrates again, trembling on the dresser. It's probably Johnny Shaw. I get up and pick up the phone, but it's not a call. It's an email alert, confirming my video visitation with Fulton County Jail inmate Jay Gardner tomorrow morning at nine o'clock.

I show my phone to Frankie. "Looks like I'm going to get all kinds of comfortable with law enforcement tomorrow."

"This is the guy Marisa went to see in jail?" Frankie asks.

I nod, looking at my phone. "And the guy I'm going to get some answers from tomorrow."

"SO MY BROTHER wants you to leave," Susannah says to Frankie. "So what? He's an asshole. Come on, stay, hang out, watch some Tom Hanks. It'll be fun."

From the doorway, Frankie smiles, shaking his head. "Sorry, but I've gotta get home. Caesar's going to stay, though." Across the room, standing in my kitchen, Caesar does not look excited at the prospect.

"Fine," Susannah sulks. "You go and we'll hang out with your stupid boyfriend." She turns her head. "Not that I think you're stupid, Caesar. Anybody who likes pre-Dominion *DS Nine* is obviously intelligent. I'm just annoyed that Frankie is leaving and that no one will tell me why we need someone else to stay here."

"Wait," I say, "did you call Caesar his . . . boyfriend?"

Susannah frowns. "What, you didn't know?"

"No, I know," I say. "I just—how did *you* know?"

She snorts. "Please. It's obvious. They're adorable."

"I need coffee," Caesar says, looking about as adorable as a hammerhead.

"Cabinet above the microwave," I say. Caesar glowers, then turns away and starts rummaging in the kitchen.

Susannah looks at me, grinning. "Adorable."

"Go watch Tom Hanks," I say, pushing her toward the couch. As soon as she's back in front of the TV, I turn to Frankie. "Is this really necessary?" I say in a low voice.

Frankie lowers his voice to match mine. "He's spending the night," he says. "I'd stay, too, but . . . I have some work to finish for your uncle." He sees the look on my face and rushes on. "Look, this Donny guy is dangerous. You call the cops, they might send a patrol car out, and that's *after* they interrogate you six ways to Sunday about Donny, how you know him, where were you this morning, all that."

"I know," I say, waving my hand like I'm dispelling smoke. "We went over it. It's fine. Tomorrow morning I'll go to work for my video chat with Gardner." Even though I'm persona non grata at Archer right now, it's spring break, so no one should be around to object.

Frankie says, "Caesar could help you set it up here—"

"In front of my sister?" I say, practically whispering. "No, thanks. She doesn't need to be any more involved in this than she already is."

Frankie nods and claps me on the shoulder. "Good luck. And call Mr. Shaw."

"I will," I say, and Frankie is gone. I shut the door, then lock it.

"Finally," Susannah says from the couch. "Come on, we were just getting to the good part."

Caesar materializes in the kitchen doorway—one second he wasn't there, and the next he is. "Tell me you have something other than a drip coffeemaker," he says.

"What do you want, an espresso machine?"

"A good French press would do. But if I have to I'll make do with this twenty-dollar piece of plastic and glass from Taiwan." He turns to go back into the kitchen, then stops. "I can't find the filters."

The machine has its own mesh filter—I hate the paper ones—so I go into the kitchen to show him. He's standing at the far end of the kitchen, the pantry all but blocking him from the den. "The filter—" I begin.

"I know about the filter," he says, his voice a low rumble. "Wanted to give you something." He holds out something in his hand. It takes me a second to realize he's holding a pistol.

I shake my head. "No thanks."

"Pretty sure this Donny character isn't interested in playing Chutes and Ladders," Caesar says. "This is just a little insurance."

"I'm not taking a gun," I say.

Caesar raises an eyebrow. "Not a Second Amendment supporter?" he says.

"A gun ended up killing my parents," I say. "Nearly killed me and my sister. So, no. I don't want a gun."

Caesar shrugs and pockets the pistol. "Your funeral," he says. "Now please tell me you at least have filtered water."

# CHAPTER TWENTY-FOUR

I CLOSE MY BEDROOM DOOR AND CALL JOHNNY SHAW, WHO ANSWERS on the second ring. The old lawyer reassures me that I am not being arrested, that the police simply want to hear my side of the story with Bridges. "Of course they want the DNA, which they're not getting," Shaw says. "Get there early, at noon, and you and I can talk and go over your story. It will be fine." I hang up marginally less anxious about the meeting.

The rest of the night passes uneventfully as Caesar brews a pot of coffee and wanders around the house, followed occasionally by Wilson, while Susannah and I fall asleep on the couch watching *Nothing in Common*. I wake up with a start around two AM to see Caesar standing in the corner, looking out the window into the front yard. He notices me and nods, then sips from one of my mugs. I glance over at Susannah and see her pale face, her eyes closed. She looks less like she's sleeping and more like she's enduring a nap—her eyes are rolling under the closed lids, and her arms twitch. I pull my fleece throw over her and stand up, yawning, then wave to Caesar and wander back to my bedroom, where I fall into a troubled sleep punctuated by chases and bright flashlights shining across dark fields.

I WAKE UP to find Susannah standing at the foot of my bed.

"Jesus," I say, sitting up.

"Not even close," she says.

A gray light seeps through my blinds. It's morning, then. I rub my eyes. "What's up?"

"I'm bored. Caesar's taking a nap on the couch. Poor man's exhausted. I kept him up all night."

"Naughty."

She rolls her eyes. "We were talking *Star Trek* and other geek lore, you moron."

"Any problems?"

She shrugs. "He likes *The Last Jedi*, but that's it." When I look at her, she sighs. "No, Ethan. No bogeyman tried to get me."

I get out of bed and head for the shower. "You take Wilson out yet?" I call over my shoulder.

"Pooped and peed and fed and now he's a happy little man. You have anything to eat?"

"Whatever you can find."

I shower and shave and put on my standard work clothes—I want to look professional when I go talk to the police. When I walk into the den, Susannah is on the couch, eating dry cereal out of a bowl and watching Tom Hanks play "Chopsticks" on a floor piano in *Big*. Caesar, his leather jacket removed, is typing on his phone.

"I have to go in to work," I say. "Shouldn't be gone long."

"Okay," Susannah says, waving vaguely in my general direction. Caesar grunts and continues typing on his phone.

"Need anything?" I ask him.

"Coffee," he says, continuing to type. "And a toothbrush. I forgot to pack one."

I PULL INTO my parking space at Archer with twenty minutes or so to spare before my scheduled video appointment. Spring break began yesterday, so the school is deserted—my car looks abandoned in the empty expanse of asphalt. The sky is overcast, the cloud cover low overhead. I use my key fob to get in through the front door. The halls are dim, the overhead lights turned off, although there's enough sunlight to see as I make my way to my classroom. I unlock my classroom door and push it open, allowing the stale air inside to escape. The overhead fluorescent lights are harsh, but although I'd prefer them off, I want Gardner to be able to see me clearly on the video connection.

Sitting at the desk in the front of my classroom, I open my laptop, log in to the video conference, and, with a click, agree to the parameters of the visitation and acknowledge that the jail officials can terminate a video at any time. Then I wait, sitting in my bright classroom, the desks empty, whiteboards cleaned, books stacked on the desk and the side tables, all waiting for students to return from break. I realize that if today goes badly—or even if it goes well—I may not return to Archer myself. That realization leaves a cold hollow in my stomach.

My laptop *dings*—my scheduled visitation is about to start. I sit up in my chair, wishing I had thought to bring a water bottle because now my mouth is dry. And then the open black window on my screen is replaced by a grainy video feed. There is a man in a dark V-neck T-shirt, seated in front of a white wall, facing me. His head looks like a squat rectangle, reinforced by the buzz cut. He has a long nose that looks like it might have been broken at some point. "Hey," he says, his voice tinny in my laptop's speaker. "You Ethan Faulkner?"

"Yeah," I say. "You're Jay? Gardner?"

The man nods, shifts in his chair. I wonder if he's chained to the chair—the angle won't let me see.

"So," Gardner says, "why'd you want to talk to me?"

"You had a visitor last week," I say. "I wanted to ask you some questions about that."

Gardner looks blank for a moment, then smiles. It's not pretty. "Yeah, she was hot," he says.

"What did she want?"

He opens his mouth, then shuts it. "Who's asking?"

"Just me."

His eyes narrow. "Why should I talk to you?"

"Why not?" I say. "You're bored, you're in jail. I bet she had a good story."

He rubs his hand over the top of his head. Not chained, then. "Why do you care?"

"She was my girlfriend. And now she's . . . gone." I stumble slightly on the last word, deciding at the last moment not to say *dead*. "I'm trying to find out what happened to her."

He frowns. "Look, man, that bitch—" He stops and looks to the side. "I'm sorry, Officer," he says to someone offscreen. "My apologies. I'll watch my mouth." He returns his attention to me. "Sorry. That *witch* was poking around, asking questions. Sticking her nose in."

"What did she want to know?"

"Man, I don't got to tell you a damn thing." As if to emphasize the point, he folds his arms across his chest and leans back in his chair, a signal as clear as a door slamming shut. This isn't going how I wanted.

"I know she asked about Sam Bridges," I say, trying to get a reaction.

Gardner mumbles something.

"Sorry?"

He leans forward. "I said, you don't know anything."

"I know you and Sam did time together," I say. "But he got out. Looks like you're back in."

"Man, forget this," he says, and looks to the side again. He's going to ask the guard to end the video and walk away.

"She knew about Donny Wharton too," I say quickly.

That gets Gardner's attention—his eyebrows scrunch together and he leans in toward the screen. "You know Donny?" he asks. His voice is different. It's hard to tell through the laptop speaker, but I'm a hundred percent sure Gardner isn't best buds with Donny. In fact, Gardner sounds worried.

"Oh, I know Donny," I say. "And so do you. And now my girlfriend's missing, and Sam—" I stop, as if I've misspoken and said too much.

Gardner's mouth is slightly open, like a kid watching a movie. "Sam what?" he asks.

"You see the news last night, Jay?"

"Oh, yeah," he says sarcastically. "Right after I played a round of golf and then had a dip in my Jacuzzi. No, I didn't watch the damn news."

"Sam's dead," I say.

He stares. "Say what?"

"Sam is dead," I say. I know this is being watched, maybe even recorded, and because I'm going to be sitting down with the police later this afternoon, talking about this might be a bad idea. But I need Gardner to give me some idea of what's going on, so I use the only thing I have—information that I hope shocks him into revealing something. "Someone stabbed him in the back," I say. "In a monastery, Jay. That's cold." I pause to let that sink in, and once it does—but before he can respond—I add, "And I think you can guess who did it."

It takes him a few seconds, but he gets there. "Whoa," he says, holding up both hands. "I don't know that. I mean, I haven't even *seen* Donny in, like, years."

"Uh-huh," I say.

"For real, man," he says, growing upset. "I ain't seen the dude since he and Sam drove into Cargill's to get rid of their—" He stops.

Now I'm the one staring at him. "Did you say Cargill?" I ask. "Brad Cargill?"

Gardner is trying to decide what he should say, and a saying of Susannah's pops into my head: *He looks like a monkey doing a math problem.* "No," he says, unconvincingly.

"You said they drove into Cargill's to get rid of something," I say. And then understanding drops like a quarter in a slot machine. Among his various enterprises, Cargill runs chop shops where stolen cars get stripped for parts. Bridges mentioned Donny Wharton's car yesterday. "They were driving a cherry-red Camaro convertible," I say.

Gardner's eyes bug out. "How'd you know?"

"I know a lot, Jay. I know that you and Bridges got busted for trafficking. I know they had to go to Cargill to take care of their car. And I'm guessing you told Marisa where Bridges was. But I need to know what else she talked to you about. And I need to know where Donny is."

He leans in close now, his features filling my laptop screen so I almost flinch. I can see his face is starting to gather a sheen. "She asked me if I knew him, okay?" he says. "About where he was. I told her I didn't know anything, and I don't. And I wish I hadn't even told her that. We're done, man." He looks to the side. "I'm done, Officer."

"Wait," I say. "Tell me—" Then the video feed cuts off, replaced by a message from the Fulton County Jail, thanking me for using their video service.

I sit back in my chair, frustrated. Marisa had already known something about Donny when she went to talk to Gardner. And she'd known about Bridges, too. She'd tracked both down like some sort of investigative journalist. *Why* she'd done it was due to her fixation with me, with what had happened to me. The question is, *how* did she know about those men in the first place? I think she died because she poked around in my life, just like Bridges died because she went to talk with him. Or because I had.

All bets are on Donny. And now Donny might be coming for me, or Susannah. And I know of one person who might know where he is.

I look at the time—it's over two and a half hours until I have to meet with the detectives and Johnny Shaw—and then I close my laptop, stick it in my workbag, and head to my car, thinking about the easiest route to Brad Cargill's garage.

ATL BODY SHOP is hardly different from when Frankie and I were last here to exchange envelopes with Cargill. The parking lot is still cracked with patches of gravel, and the building itself is still white, most of the bay doors pulled down. The maroon Honda with the windshield that Cargill redesigned with a wrench is gone, replaced by an equally dilapidated silver Ford Escort.

I walk into the nearest open bay, where a green Dodge is up on a lift. The concrete floor is oil-stained, the tangled snarl of a cord crossing from a compressor to the Dodge, where a man in a gray coverall is removing the tires with an air wrench. He looks up at me. "Yeah?" he says.

"Cargill here?" I ask.

The man puts the air wrench down on a workbench and grabs a rag from his back pocket to wipe his hands. "Who's asking?"

"Salvation Army," I say. "Is he here?"

The man stops wiping his hands, replaces the rag in his back pocket, and considers me for a minute. "In his office," he says with a jerk of his head, indicating the far end of the garage.

I nod and walk down the length of the garage, keeping to the side closest to the bay doors. Half the bays are empty, but there are some cars on the lifts and I want to keep out of the way. At the far end, someone put up Sheetrock across half of the last bay, put in a plate-glass window and a door, and turned the space into an office. Through the window I see Brad Cargill sitting at a desk, talking on a phone. There's one other mechanic at this end of the garage, bent over the open hood of a GMC pickup, and he glances up at me as I pass and walk up to the office.

"—don't *give* a shit what he *says*, he needs to show me the parts," Cargill is saying into the phone, as rawboned and pale as ever, a brand-new Atlanta United cap pushed back on his head, his feet in heavy work boots resting on his desk. He glances at me and continues talking into his phone. "I'm not ordering bad parts from anybody. Tell him that." He hangs up and leans back in his chair. "Help you?"

I stand there and let him figure it out. He squints in concentration, and then his eyebrows rise. "Well, well, Gavin Lester's nephew," he says. "All grown up. Took a sec, but the red hair did it. This is a surprise. Need help with your car?"

"Donny Wharton," I say.

Cargill frowns politely. "Sorry, who?"

"The guy who needed your help with a cherry-red Camaro convertible about twelve years back."

He's still frowning, but now he smiles. It's like watching a piranha try to be friendly. "I've fixed lots of Camaros," he says.

"He didn't want you to fix it. He wanted you to make it disappear."

Cargill's smile broadens. "Why, that sounds like you're suggesting something illegal. We don't do that kind of thing here."

I hold my arms out to the sides. "I'm not wearing a wire," I say. "Feel free to check."

Cargill brings his feet off his desk, the work boots stamping the floor with a *thump*, and stands. "George!" he shouts. He's still smiling, although it's a little fainter, which for some reason makes me feel good.

The mechanic who was working on the pickup appears. "Yeah?"

"Mr. Faulkner here says he's not wearing a wire," he says. "Let's confirm that." He sneers. "I'd hate to have somebody try to entrap me or illegally record my voice."

I shrug. "It's not illegal in Georgia. One-party consent makes it just peachy." Cargill's smile fades. "Thought you'd know that," I say cheerfully. "But I'm not recording anything."

The mechanic frisks me like he's done it before. Without being asked, I untuck my shirt and unbutton it, then open it and pull up my undershirt to show my bare belly. "Okay," the mechanic says to Cargill, nodding, and then he goes back out to work on the pickup.

"Empty your pockets," Cargill says.

I roll my eyes but empty my pockets—keys, phone, wallet, all in a tidy pile on Cargill's desk. He picks up my iPhone, looks at it, then gives me a smile that's a shade or two away from a snarl. "How's your uncle?" he says. "Any cancer or anything? He's gettin' older."

"My sister has a PhD in manipulation, so you playing with my phone and insulting my uncle aren't really doing it for me," I say. "Donny Wharton. I want to know where he is."

Cargill looks at me. "That a fact," he says. "Why?"

"Does it matter?"

He puts my phone down on the desk. "Might. Assumin', of course, I know who this Donny fella is."

I bite my tongue and wait. Guys like Cargill love to hear themselves talk and can't keep quiet.

Cargill laces his fingers and puts his hands behind his head. "One thing my daddy taught me was to never give away somethin' for free if you can get paid for it."

"Donny Wharton shot me, right here in the arm," I say, pointing to my right arm just below the shoulder. "Then he shot my sister, and then both of my parents. And then he and his partner Sam Bridges drove here in their Camaro and paid you to get rid of it for them. That's accessory to murder, *Brad*. No statute of limitations on murder. Even if it's accessory after the fact, you could be looking at serious prison time. So I'll pay you by not going to the police and telling them what I just told you."

Cargill hasn't moved since I said Donny shot my parents. He just keeps looking at me, although I can see in his face that he's working out the angles, seeing how many ways he could play this.

"I just want to know where the man is," I say.

Cargill unlaces his hands and sits forward, his skin almost milk white under the overhead fluorescents. "Somethin' else my daddy told me," he says. "If you're lookin' for revenge, first thing you should do is dig two graves."

"That's Confucius," I say. "And I just want to keep me and my sister safe."

He looks flatly at me for a few more moments. "I haven't seen him for a long time," he says finally. "Don't want to, either. Man trails bad luck behind him like a stink." He narrows his eyes. "And I'd think twice about threatening me, *Ethan*. If I ever wanted to hurt you, I wouldn't have Donny Wharton do it. It'd be worse."

I resist clenching my thumbs or stomping my foot or swinging for Cargill's jaw. Aside from feeling frustrated, I also think he's telling the truth. If he knew where Donny is, he'd play this out more, string me along like a cat toying with a mouse before he eats it. So I simply gather my keys and wallet and phone and put them in my pockets. On my way out of the office, I pause. "If Donny does show up," I say, "and anything happens to me or my sister? Either my uncle or I will find you. And you'd better hope it's my uncle who finds you first."

WHEN I GET to my car, I sit behind the wheel and take a few breaths. Then I check the time. Over an hour until my meeting with the police downtown. I call my house to check in on Susannah, and to apologize to Caesar for not getting him good coffee and a toothbrush.

The landline rings, then rings some more, and then goes to voice mail. I hang up, wait a few seconds, and call back. Susannah often screens her calls or ignores the phone altogether, but usually she answers after two or three tries.

No answer.

There are all sorts of reasons why she might not answer. She could be outside, walking Wilson. Or she could be in the shower. Although in both cases Caesar would likely have answered.

I call Ronan's. The phone rings, and then a happy female voice says, "Ronan's, how may I help you?"

"Frankie Gutierrez, please. Tell him it's Ethan Faulkner."

Another minute of waiting on hold and trying to ignore the rising sense of dread in my chest. I start my car to run the AC.

"Ethan?" Frankie says on the other end.

"Can you call Caesar?" I say. "No one's answering at my house."

"Hold on," he says, and then I hear indistinct sounds as he fumbles with his phone. Then in the background I can hear the rush of voices and plates clinking, the sounds of lunch hour. "You're on speaker," Frankie says, his voice echoing slightly. "I'm texting him."

I pull out of Cargill's parking lot and take a sharp turn onto North-side, heading north, away from downtown. "Hang up and call him," I say. "Then call me back." I disconnect and focus on driving. A minute later my phone rings and I answer, putting it on speaker.

"He's not answering," Frankie says. "Where are you?"

"I'm heading home," I say, pulling around a dump truck and then cutting back in front of him to avoid rear-ending a slow car in the passing lane. The dump truck honks, an irritated blast.

"Ethan, don't go home," Frankie is saying. "Call the police."

"I'll be there before they will be." I use my horn to encourage an SUV to move out of my way, then race under a light just before it turns red.

"Ethan—"

"Tell my uncle what's going on," I say. "I'll call you back." Then I hang up. I ignore the two times Frankie calls me back, instead seeing just how fast I can get my Corolla to go.

# CHAPTER TWENTY-FIVE

I REACH MY STREET ELEVEN MINUTES AFTER I HANG UP WITH FRANKIE, but instead of turning onto it, I drive around to the other side of the block and park in front of the house that borders my backyard. No one appears to be home. The entire street is quiet at midday—everyone is at work. The overcast sky has lowered even further, like an iron lid. I have a lug wrench in my trunk and I take it, closing the trunk as quietly as I can. Then I walk down the driveway, hoping there isn't a bored housewife or retiree peeking at me from behind closed curtains and dialing 911.

Thankfully these folks don't have a fence around their backyard, and I make my way easily through a backyard that's littered with kids' toys—a faded yellow plastic bat, a tricycle on its side, a large sandbox in the shape of a plastic green frog with its cover askew, a puddle of rainwater inside. I realize that I don't know the people who live here, not even their names. The thought makes me feel like even more of an intruder.

At the edge of their backyard is a stand of trees, old pines dotted with a few tall oaks, along with a fair amount of undergrowth—an effective wall of foliage that stretches down the center of the block, separating the houses that already face away from each other. I step carefully into the trees, watching where I put my feet. The last thing I want to do is step on a copperhead. A small cloud of midges dances around my head, and

I wave them away with one hand, the other gripping the lug wrench as I try to navigate around the trees.

After a few yards, I see Tony and Gene's house appear through the trees, a wall of brick and glass with an oiled hardwood deck spanning the entire back, a radar dish and two solar panels crowning the roof. I angle to the right, stepping over a small drainage ditch that runs down the entire length of the block. Just then my phone vibrates in my pocket, and I nearly drop the lug wrench as I snatch at my phone, trying to keep it from ringing. It rings once before I can get it, and I see it's Johnny Shaw. I reject the call and mute my phone and put it back in my pocket. In that short pause to deal with my phone, the mosquitoes have found me, and I slap the back of my neck as I continue stepping through the undergrowth.

Then my own house looms ahead, the tiny strip of fescue that masquerades as a backyard, the dilapidated garage to the right. The back door to the kitchen is shut. I tighten my grip on the lug wrench and prepare to step out of the trees when I see something in the grass to my left. Then I'm out of the trees and I walk over to the thing in the grass and drop to one knee. It's Wilson's rope bone. My heart sinks with dread. He rarely takes it outside, and he never leaves it in the yard. I stand, peering into the trees that loom at the edge of the yard. "Wilson," I call in a stage whisper.

"That his name?" a voice says.

I stand and spin around, the lug wrench in my hand. A pistol pointed at my face from two yards away stops me. The man holding the pistol has shaved his head, but I recognize him the way you recognize a familiar nightmare. Ponytail. Donny Wharton.

"Not a sound," Donny says. He motions at me with his free hand, the one holding the pistol unmoving. "Drop that."

I drop the lug wrench onto the grass next to Wilson's rope bone.

Donny smiles tightly. "Good boy," he says. A red rage spurts through me and I ball my fists, causing Donny to move the pistol closer to my forehead. "Easy," he says. "Come on. Over to the garage."

I walk toward the garage, keeping my eyes on him. He's wearing a khaki shirt and dark-green work pants, like someone working for a lawn service company. Which, I realize, would be a great way to blend into a neighborhood. "Where's my sister?" I ask.

"She's fine," Donny says. "Having a little time-out. So's her bald black buddy."

My heart sinks at hearing about Caesar. "Did you hurt my dog?" I ask, trying to keep my voice from shaking.

"Fucker ran away," he says. "Gave him a good kick. Wouldn't stop yapping."

I am at the point where I'm willing to take a bullet to the face if first I can take a swing at this guy, but as if he can read my mind, he takes one step away from me, his pistol still trained on my forehead.

"Marisa," I manage to say. "Why'd you kill her?"

He shakes his head. "That bitch," he says. "Sniffing after me like a bloodhound. You and your sister, though, you've been following me for years."

We walk around the corner of the garage, and I see a BMW backed up to the entrance of my garage. My heart, already low, drops another foot when I recognize the car—it belongs to Tony, my next-door neighbor. I stop. "What did you do to Tony?"

Donny presses the muzzle of his pistol against the back of my head, a cold circle that may very well be the last thing I feel. "Didn't tell you to stop," he says.

"This is my neighbor's car," I say. "What happened to him?"

"Nothing," he says. "I stole it out of his garage." He taps me on the back of the head with the pistol. "Get in the trunk."

"No."

He jams the pistol into the back of my head hard enough to leave a bruise. "I won't ask again."

"You're going to drive way out somewhere and shoot me and dump me in a ditch," I say. "Might as well shoot me here."

The pistol doesn't let up. "One last chance," he says, and he sounds bored, as if I'm failing to amuse him.

I want to move; in fact, part of my brain is screaming at me to move. It's not that I'm paralyzed, although finally seeing Ponytail after all these years is terrifying. *The fuck?* he said, and then blew my family away. I've replayed that scene in my head so many nights, my bedsheets twisted and sweaty, my pillow hot as a brick from an oven. It's like my own personal zombie has finally shown up at the door, grinning and savage, ready to eat me. Maybe it's because I know he will kill me, but I'm not going to do what he wants me to. He may hit me over the head with his gun and throw me into the trunk, but he'll have to do that. So I stand facing the trunk of the car and don't make a move.

With a muttered curse, Donny shoves me to the side, his pistol tracking me. "Your sister's in here," he says. "So you need to get in, or I'll start hurting her. Don't need a gun for that, but I'll use it if you force me to." He reaches for the trunk latch.

"Don't hurt my sister," I say.

He lifts the trunk lid to reveal my sister lying on her side, mouth gagged, hands tied together in front of her. Her eyes are open and she stares directly at me.

Donny smirks. "You people live in a different world," he says, and he reaches for Susannah's eyes.

A red star ignites in the trunk. Susannah rises up, the star burning in her hands, and she thrusts it into Donny's face. With a cry he stumbles back, away from the roadside flare, one hand raised to his face and the other bringing the pistol around. Before he can bring the pistol to bear on Susannah or me, I tackle him, and we fall to the concrete, me on top, the pistol knocked away and skittering into the corner of the garage.

Donny's nose is an angry, raw red and his right cheek is charred and he is screaming and bucking underneath me. His burnt face smells like a hot dog dropped into an open fire. I nearly gag at the stench. Then he pops me in the ear with his fist and I fall off him, then scramble to my feet. He is weeping and cursing, the right side of his face like a bloody flank steak that's been pressed to a hot grill, but he pulls out a switchblade and staggers toward me. I back into the garage and grab the lid of a recycling can, holding it in front of me like a shield. The switchblade stabs through the thick plastic of the lid, inches from my face, and then Donny withdraws it and stabs again and again frantically, so all I can do is hold up the lid. I try to duck and kick at him, and he swings down, cutting with a white-hot heat across the top of my right arm.

I step back, glancing past Donny at Susannah. She has dropped the flare to the concrete and is sitting up in the trunk, trying to untie the rope around her wrists. Then Donny thrusts the switchblade at my face and I duck just in time, the blade slicing the right side of my head above the temple. First it's ice-cold, and then the cut burns. Blood flows down the side of my head, threatening to run into my eye.

I crouch and then thrust forward and up with the lid, catching Donny on the chin and shoving him back. It gives me enough time to wipe the blood out of my right eye, but then he bellows and advances again, his switchblade stabbing in the gloom of the garage. The plastic lid has several holes in it. I try to let him stab the lid and then use the lid to wrench the knife away, but he's too fast, plunging the knife down again and again. I grope behind me on the wall, looking for anything to hit him with or throw at him. My hand seizes on a broom handle.

He swings down hard with the switchblade, slicing straight through the lid and gouging my left hand, which is gripping the lid handle. His switchblade is buried in the lid handle. He angrily shakes it to free the blade, and I let go of the lid. When he flings the lid to the ground, I thrust the straw end of the broom straight into his face, hard, knocking his head back.

With a yell, I run forward, using the broom to help me shove him back and out of the garage. My left hand is slick and doesn't quite work, so I can only swing the broom with my right hand. I hit him once with it, and then he tears it out of my hand and throws it away. Bleeding in three places, I step back as Donny raises the knife, his burnt face hideous with a rictus grin as he comes at me.

There is a sharp *thock* and Donny's head snaps to the side and he collapses, revealing Caesar behind him, a loose brick in his hand. Caesar's other hand is clutched to his belly, which is clearly bleeding, and his left eye is swollen shut, but he still manages to raise an eyebrow.

"You look terrible," he says.

Behind him, Susannah finally gets through her knots and tries to climb out of the trunk, half falling to the concrete. Then she runs to me and grabs me in a hug. "I'm sorry," she babbles, "I'm sorry, I'm sorry."

Caesar steps over to the car and sits down, making even that movement look graceful, his back against one of the tires. "I need an ambulance," he says.

Blood is running down my right arm, the right side of my head, and my left hand, but somehow I disentangle myself from my sister and manage to get my phone out of my pocket. "Call nine-one-one," I tell Susannah, thrusting the phone at her. As she does, I take a better look at Donny. The back of his head is bloody where Caesar hit him. I glance at Caesar, who is looking at me. "Why were you in prison?" I ask.

He blinks slowly. "This is what you need to know right now?" he says. "While I bleed to death in your driveway?"

"Just before the police come," I say.

He looks at me for another moment or two. "My sister's husband was beating her," he says. "So I threw him out a window."

I nod. "So if you killed . . . Donny here," I say, stumbling over Ponytail's actual name, "that might be problematic for you, from a legal perspective."

Caesar looks at me. "It was self-defense," he says.

"I know," I say. "And it is much appreciated. But you have a record." I crouch down and pick up the brick that Caesar dropped. "So when the cops come, I'm the one who hit him." I look down at Donny, lying still on the concrete, his skull crushed. I think I see his eye twitch. I can't be sure.

Caesar frowns. "They'll be able to tell that you didn't—"

I raise the brick and bring it down hard onto Donny's head. The impact shocks my arm up to the shoulder and I drop the brick, but now Donny's blood is on my hand, and there's another gash in the back of his skull, and his eye is definitely not twitching now.

# CHAPTER TWENTY-SIX

THE FOLLOWING NIGHT IS SATURDAY, AND I'M SITTING AT HOME, stitched up like the creature in *Frankenstein* and watching *Saving Private Ryan*, when my phone rings. I pause the film and see who's calling this time—Frankie, or my uncle, or Johnny Shaw, or Detective Panko, who has already left a message about meeting first thing tomorrow morning to talk about Sam Bridges and Donny Wharton. When I see it's my sister, I answer and say, "I'm watching your most favorite war movie."

"Bitch," Susannah says at the other end.

I smile. "You moved in okay?" She's living in a halfway house near Birchwood for now. Baby steps.

"I'm all good," she says. "How's your neighbor?"

Tony was less than thrilled that Donny had stolen his BMW and locked my sister inside it, and when he was certain the police no longer needed access to it for evidence, he was going to sell it and get a new Tesla. But mostly he was glad that we were alive and okay.

"Tony and Gene brought me cookies and wine," I say. "I think they're a little excited from their brush with real-life crime, although they'll never say so. I thanked Tony for keeping roadside flares in the trunk of his car."

"Glad they weren't hurt. Hey, I think I left a bag over there—can you look around for it later?"

"I'm not bringing your stuff to you. I'm recovering."

"Okay, Gimpy. Dinner next week?"

"Only if you're buying," I say.

We hang up, and I automatically look over at Wilson's bed to see if he needs to go outside. Then I remember, just as I have a dozen times every day since, and a terrible sadness punches me in the heart. Wilson has vanished with no sign. I've combed the neighborhood, walked the woods behind my house, even looked in the storm sewers. It's as if Donny Wharton spirited him away, one last *fuck you* from beyond the grave.

I sit there for a few moments, letting the sadness wash over me, and when it recedes a little I pick up the remote and continue watching the movie, although now it's not distracting me as much as it was before.

DETECTIVES PANKO AND Klingman look dour when I arrive for our meeting downtown, but I'm curiously unconcerned. Maybe escaping death at the hands of Donny Wharton has made me feel invulnerable. Or maybe I'm just done feeling anxious about something I know I didn't do. Johnny Shaw sits next to me in his gray seersucker suit but doesn't say much other than to restate my constitutional right to have a lawyer present.

Panko and Klingman both hammer away at me about talking to Bridges at the monastery and then my online meeting with Gardner. Of course, they especially want to hear about Donny. I rest my injured hand, wrapped in gauze and an Ace bandage, on the table between us like a piece of evidence. We go over Bridges and Gardner and Donny again and again, and I tell the truth about everything except Marisa's phone and how Caesar really hit Donny in the back of the head, not me. It's essentially a long oral quiz, and just as boring.

The only interesting bit comes near the end of our interview, when Klingman stretches and grudgingly asks me if I'd like some coffee. When I decline, he grunts. "What I'm still surprised by," he says, "is how you knew to talk to Gardner and Bridges in the first place."

"Marisa mentioned their names at some point," I say. "I put two and two together."

Panko raises an eyebrow. "That's some good math."

I shrug. "Google is a fabulous thing."

I know at this point, based on what Caesar said before, that the police must have access to Marisa's phone records and have in all likelihood read her texts to me. Once again I am thankful that I never replied to her.

"It's a funny thing," Panko says, looking at me. "We never did find Marisa's phone."

I say nothing. Johnny Shaw looks like he's taking a nap.

"Can't locate it through apps or cell towers, either," Panko continues. "My guess is somebody destroyed it."

I look straight back at him. "That is weird."

We look at each other for another moment, long enough for Shaw to open an eye and gaze at us, and then Klingman has a few more questions to ask.

As Klingman is stacking his notes and closing file folders, I say, "So Donny Wharton killed Marisa and Sam Bridges."

Klingman pauses. I notice he has on the same tie he wore when we first met, although the stain is gone. Klingman glances at Panko before saying, "I can't speak to anything specific connected to an ongoing investigation."

We shake hands, and Johnny Shaw and I take the elevator down to street level and walk outside. The downtown streets are busy, cars crawling around a lane blocked due to a county crew repaving, the stink of asphalt hanging in the air.

"What happened with the DNA test?" I ask Shaw. "I walked in thinking there'd be a lab tech waiting to swab my cheek."

"They don't need it anymore," Shaw says. "They found other evidence."

"What did they find?"

Shaw shakes his head. "Don't worry about it." He squints at the traffic, looking for a cab—Gus is on vacation this week, and Shaw doesn't trust ridesharing. I rode MARTA here, but instead of walking to the station, I hesitate.

"What Klingman was saying in there," I say to Shaw. "When I asked if Donny killed them both. What did you think about his answer?"

Shaw blows his nose and tucks his handkerchief back into his pocket. "Officially, it's boilerplate that keeps him from having to share anything," he says. "Unofficially?" He looks at me pointedly. "Donny Wharton killed them both." He raises his hand, conjuring a taxi to the curb.

I MEET COLEMAN at a Starbucks near my house, and we find a table among half a dozen patrons wearing earbuds and staring at their laptops. Coleman is horrified and fascinated in equal measure by my injured hand. I tell him I fought with a home intruder and it's all okay now. "How's Sarah?" I ask. "Is she still in the hospital?"

Coleman smiles. "Went home two days ago, as a matter of fact. She's okay."

I close my eyes and sigh with relief. "That's good," I say. And it is. Guilt still batters away at my heart, but at least Sarah's okay. I take a breath. "I need to tell you about Marisa," I say.

I tell him the abbreviated version of me and Marisa, how she became infatuated with me and stirred up my past. I gloss over Donny and Bridges as much as I can, but I do reveal that Donny was the one who caused my stitches. I say nothing about her phone.

When I stop talking, Coleman is floored. "So this Donny character, *he* killed Marisa?" he asks.

"Yeah."

Coleman lets out a low whistle. "Are you all right?" he asks.

"I'm thinking about resigning, actually." Just saying the words feels like a stone rolling over my heart.

Coleman raises his eyebrows. "Why?" he asks.

Now I stare at him. "The students must think I'm some sort of stalker creep," I say. "I can only imagine what their parents must think. And Byron and Teri can't be comfortable with me teaching there anymore."

Coleman pulls out his phone, swipes at his screen a few times, and then holds the phone up. "You ought to see this."

I peer at his screen to see a picture of what looks like a poster board with my name in the center, surrounded by handwritten notes—*We love you, Mr. Faulkner! English teacher extraordinaire! Thou are the nonpareil!*— and a cloud of signatures, including Mark Mitchell and Sarah Solomon. That stone I felt in my chest rolls away as if from the mouth of a cave, letting in sunlight. "What is this?" I ask.

"It's from your AP English class," Coleman says. "Sarah wanted them to sign a card in support of you. They had to get a poster board." Coleman smiles down at the picture. "I saw Sarah just before she was discharged from the hospital. She'd already figured out that it was Marisa Devereaux on Twitter. 'I knew it wasn't Mr. Faulkner,' she said."

The image of the picture on his phone blurs, and I wipe tears away with my good hand. I'm a high school English teacher who likes poetry, I often tell people—I cry at everything. But hearing what Sarah said makes me want to sob. "That's really nice," I manage to say.

Coleman nods. "I think you'll find Byron and Teri are willing to welcome you back to school," he says. "If you want to come back."

I laugh at that, a short bark through my tears. "What, back to *that* place? With those kids? Good God." I wipe my eyes again. "But . . . I *have* to resign. Don't I? I mean, I was having sex with Marisa at school. She manipulated students to get me a teaching award. She got *murdered* because she got wrapped up in my shit."

Coleman thinks for a moment, brows knit together. "I can understand having mixed feelings about the Faculty Award," he says. "Which, I have to tell you, is going to be awarded to Betsy Bales instead. And having sex with another teacher at school is probably not compatible with the highest principles of workplace behavior. But this Donny character killed Marisa, not you. And everyone's figured out Marisa Devereaux was manipulative and tried to ruin your career. Unless the police are going to arrest you for her murder, I don't see the school having a problem." He puts a meaty hand on my shoulder. "As a priest, I talk to a lot of people who feel guilty. If you feel guilty about something, don't try to make up for it by punishing yourself in some other way, like quitting your job." He squeezes my shoulder, then smiles gently. "That's not how it works."

CAESAR IS SITTING up in his hospital bed and talking with Frankie when I walk into the room. "Hey," Frankie says, hugging me. "Man, you got cut up, *güero*. You okay?"

I hold up my bandaged hand. "Another inch and he would have sliced open my radial artery. The doctors assure me that would have been bad." I step over to the bed, where Caesar looks faintly ridiculous in a hospital gown. His head and left eye are swathed in gauze, as is his abdomen. According to the police, Donny waited outside my house until Caesar took Wilson out to pee. Frankie already told me that Donny clocked Caesar in the face with a paver from the yard, breaking his eye socket, and then Donny still had to stab Caesar three times, once in the liver, before he could get through him and into the house. Caesar is lucky he didn't bleed to death.

"How are you doing?" I ask.

"Aside from the fact that they won't let me have coffee, and the food is revolting, and they wake you up in the dead of night to give you a sleeping pill, I'm fabulous," Caesar says.

"I'm sorry," I say.

Caesar grunts, closing his right eye. "I'm the one who got jumped and didn't protect your sister." He cracks his eye open. "I'm sorry about your dog."

I nod. Donny had beaten and stabbed Caesar nearly to death and then gone into the house to grab Susannah, who had been asleep, so neither of them saw what happened to Wilson. I'm about to make some dumb joke to lighten the mood, because I don't want to start weeping about Wilson again, when Caesar grabs my right hand. "I'm sorry," he says. "I didn't protect your sister."

"Hey," I say, "it's okay; you were—"

He pulls me toward him, his grip like iron. "I mean it," he says. "And thank you, for what you did. With the brick."

Frankie hovers behind me. "Take it easy," he says to me. "He needs to rest."

"He has an orbital fracture and a lacerated liver, and I'm pretty sure he could still kick my ass," I say.

"Damn straight," Caesar says. "Now listen to Frankie and get out so I can get some rest." He releases my hand and leans back, closing his eye. I flex my hand to make sure it's still working, shooting a look at Frankie to make sure he sees.

"Yes, my boyfriend is a badass," Frankie says.

I nod and walk out the door, but not before I see Caesar, his eye still closed, slowly smile.

I'm at the elevators when I hear Frankie call my name, and I turn around to see him walking down the hall. "What's wrong?" I say when he reaches me.

"Nothing," Frankie says. "I just . . . I wanted to tell you—about me and Caesar."

The elevator dings and the door opens, and two nurses step off the elevator, then stop because we're blocking them. I usher Frankie to the side to let them pass and find myself standing by a window that looks out onto a ventilation shaft. "Okay," I say to Frankie.

"You know he saved my life," Frankie says. "And when he did that, I immediately wondered what he wanted. Everybody in prison wants something. But he just seemed to want to do what he thought was the right thing, helping me. And we became friends, got close. But that's all we were, in there. It wasn't until we both got out . . ." He trails off and looks at me hopefully.

"Yeah," I say, nodding. "Okay."

"Okay," he says. "So, he got out first, right? A month before I did, turns out. And when he was gone, I was so . . ." He looks out the window, as if the words he is searching for will be hovering right outside in the ventilation shaft. "I wasn't just lonely. It was like part of me had walked away with him. It felt—it felt like I was dying inside, you know?" He wipes his face with his hands and looks back at me. "And when I walked out of that place, there he was, leaning up against this Cadillac he'd rented, waiting for me. And when he opened his arms to give me a hug, I just walked straight through that hug and kissed him. We stood there in front of God and everybody, kissing in the prison parking lot."

He laughs, then glances at me to see my reaction. I smile back at him, nodding, and he grins a little. "He said, 'Are you sure?' Like asking me if I'd ordered what I really wanted off the menu or whatever. And I was. I was sure." Frankie lowers his head a little, eyes still on me. "I'd never felt that before. I didn't lie to you when we were growing up. I wasn't hiding anything. Hell, I don't even know if I *am* gay. I mean, I still find women attractive. But the only man—the only *person*—I feel this way about is him. And I'm good with that."

I reach my uninjured hand out and grip his shoulder. "You don't owe me an explanation," I say. "And you don't need my blessing or anything. But you have it."

Frankie grips my shoulder in return, and then he pulls me into a hug, pounding me firmly on the back. "You're such an asshole, Ethan," he says in my ear, and then laughs, like a long-held dread unspooling.

We stand there locked in an embrace like long-lost comrades, reunited at last.

THAT EVENING I'M trying to make spaghetti with my good hand when the phone rings, and I answer and put it on speaker. "Hello?" I say, stirring the marinara.

"Mr. Faulkner?" a man says.

"Speaking." I lift the lid on the stockpot, but the water for the pasta isn't boiling yet.

"Mr. Faulkner, my name is Steven, and I am calling on behalf of Mr. Jackson Devereaux," the man says.

I nearly drop the lid. "Marisa's father?"

"Exactly," Steven says. Now I recognize his voice from when I first called Marisa's house. "He would like to know if it is possible for you to meet with him tomorrow afternoon," he continues. "Say three o'clock?"

"May I ask what this is regarding?" I say, mostly keeping my voice steady.

"I believe he would like to share some private information with you, sir. That's really all I can say."

I stare at the unopened box of spaghetti on the counter. "That would be fine," I say.

"Excellent. Shall I text the address to this number?"

"Perfect."

"Tomorrow at three, then. Good evening."

I hang up and stand in my kitchen, looking blankly at my sink, until the water finally starts to boil.

THE HOUSE ON Habersham Road is a brick mansion that would look right at home in Gatsby's neighborhood, set on a hill of manicured lawn with rosebushes that I have no doubt are tended by a host of gardeners. I roll up the cobblestone drive in my Corolla and park out front, conscious that my car needs a wash. I am wearing a blazer and slacks but decided in the end to forgo a tie.

Steven answers the door, an ageless butler-secretary type in a light-gray suit and salmon-pink tie. He ushers me inside to a foyer with a marble floor wide enough for dancing, leads me through the foyer and past a sitting room or two, turns left, and stops outside an oak door. He knocks and cracks the door enough to insert his head and murmur my name, then opens the door wide and gestures for me to enter. Behind the door is an oak-paneled office with leather furniture and a desk that is far neater than my uncle's. A man stands from his chair behind the desk, silvering hair brushed into place, a strong jaw, broad chest and trim waist fitted into a navy-blue suit, no tie, the white shirt unbuttoned at the collar. "Mr. Faulkner," the man says. He moves around the desk and shakes my hand. "Jackson Devereaux. Thank you for coming. Can Steven get you anything? Water, juice, coffee?"

"No, thank you."

Devereaux looks over my shoulder. "Thank you, Steven," he says, and I hear the door shut behind me with a discreet *click*. Devereaux returns behind his desk and sits, and I lower myself into a leather club chair.

"Mr. Devereaux, please let me say first that I am so very sorry for your loss," I say.

He nods in acceptance. "Thank you," he says. "Marisa's mother and I have been devastated." He claps his hands together and leans forward onto his desk. "I wanted to apologize to you as well, Mr. Faulkner. I understand you and Marisa were . . . involved."

I feel my face redden, although I'm not surprised. At this point the police have found Marisa's website in addition to her phone records and have no doubt shared them with her parents. "We were coworkers at Archer," I say carefully. "And we did date, for a time."

"I'll be frank, Mr. Faulkner," Devereaux says. "Marisa was disturbed. She's always been rather sensitive." He unclasps his hands and sits back in his chair. "There was an incident at her previous school, in Connecticut. She began a relationship with another teacher, a young man named Todd. She became infatuated. Her mother and I thought it was just first love, but . . . it did not end well. She thought Todd was flirting with another teacher and stole his phone to check his texts. The school's HR and legal departments got involved. Todd contacted me directly, complained that Marisa was harassing him, prying into his private life, his family." He gazes intently at me. "Todd demanded that I pay him to not press charges."

*Poor dumb Todd*, I think. "That's unfortunate," I say.

Devereaux nods as if I have hit the nail on the head. "Yes," he says. "Marisa called us, frantic. The school was considering terminating her contract for unprofessional behavior. She wanted us to help, hire a lawyer, sue the school. It was ridiculous, of course. Her mother and I told her we would do no such thing. We argued; she said hurtful things to her mother." He pauses, then sits up a bit straighter in his chair, forging ahead. "Her mother was distraught, got behind the wheel when she shouldn't have. There was a terrible accident, another driver died, and my wife suffered a traumatic brain injury. She has recovered, thank God, at least somewhat. But in those first weeks after the accident . . ." He pauses again, his eyes for the first time becoming a bit unfocused. After a moment he sighs and shakes his head. "It was horrible. Marisa came home, to help."

*And to leave Todd and her previous school behind.* "I'm so sorry," I say.

Devereaux dismisses that with a short wave of his hand. "I thought we could help her if she came home, get her back on the right path. And for a time, things were . . . not fine, but manageable. She was going to therapy." He glances at his desk, then back at me. "And then she met you."

Neither of us says anything for a minute. Several possible responses come to mind, and one by one I dismiss them. I don't much like Jackson Devereaux, his calculated businesslike response to his family's tragedy. I remember what my mother used to say about parents, that when parents are upset or angry they are mostly just reacting to their own fears about their children's struggles. But I find myself wishing Devereaux would react differently.

"Mr. Devereaux," I begin. "Your daughter and I . . . for a short time, at the beginning of our relationship, it was good. I cared for her."

Devereaux considers me across his desk. "My daughter was very good at getting people to do that," he says. He says it in a way that makes me feel like a sucker. "She was ill, Mr. Faulkner. I don't expect you to have realized that, not at first. She was good at hiding it." He opens a drawer and takes out a calfskin notebook and places it on his desk. "I know from the police that she ferreted around in your life, tried to find some problem she could solve for you." He closes the drawer with a quiet *thunk*. "I apologize for that." He opens the notebook, and I see it's actually some sort of checkbook. Devereaux picks up a pen and writes a check. "I wanted to show you how sorry my wife and I are for your troubles with Marisa." He tears out the check and holds it out to me.

Slowly, I stand and take the check and sit back down to read it. There are far too many zeros. I look back at him. "I can't accept this," I say.

"Nonsense," he says. "I know you suffered an injury to your hand from the same man my daughter was . . . investigating." He says this last word with distaste.

"You mean the same man who murdered your daughter."

Again he waves my comment away. "Take the check, Mr. Faulkner."

"I could buy a brand-new hand for this and have money left over."

He nods. "Consider it payment to cover your emotional trauma." He glances at his watch, then places his hands on his desk, a CEO closing a deal, and stands.

I pause, then stand and place the check down on his desk. "I won't accept it," I say. "You should donate that to a worthy charity. In Marisa's name."

Devereaux frowns. "I want this to be a clean break here, Mr. Faulkner," he says.

I give him a tight smile. "You don't need to worry," I say. "You won't hear from me again. I'll show myself out."

I leave him standing there, the check on top of the desk, and find my way down the hall and through the foyer. As I head for the front door, I pause. There is a woman in the front sitting room, wearing a monogrammed bathrobe and sitting on a couch. A younger woman in pressed nursing scrubs is standing next to her, murmuring something. The woman on the couch is at first glance beautiful, pale blonde hair and blue eyes, but there is something slightly vacant about her expression, a slackness in her jaw, her eyes dull. She has Marisa's mouth and nose, I realize, and for a moment I can't breathe.

Marisa's mother turns her head to face me, the nurse glancing up but still murmuring into her ear. There is a look of confusion in her eyes now, confusion and sadness and loss. I bow my head to her. After a moment, she bows back, and her eyes shine with tears. I go out the door and close it behind me, then make my way down the steps to my car.

# CHAPTER TWENTY-SEVEN

On Monday, when I get home from the grocery store and walk through my front door, there's a rustle of movement from the kitchen. I put my grocery bag on the floor and pick up the fireplace poker. Then Susannah walks out of the kitchen, a bag of chips in one hand, and gives a breathless little cry when she sees me. "Jesus, you scared me," she says.

"I scared *you*?"

"You're the one carrying a poker."

I set the poker back down on the hearth. "You broke into my house. Again."

"*Au contraire, mon frère.*" She reaches into her pocket and holds up a key.

"You had a key made? When did—" I shake my head. "Never mind."

She puts the key down on the coffee table, along with my bag of chips. "Key's all yours. You find my stuff yet?"

After I get the groceries out of my car, we conduct a sweep of my house, and Susannah is poking around in my bedroom when I find a plastic Target bag under my couch. "Think this is it," I call to her, and I open the bag to find a short stack of T-shirts, haphazardly folded. Then I pause and look closely at the T-shirt on top, and my breath stops, cold realization like an icicle through my brain.

265

Susannah is coming down the hall and saying, "Good, 'cause I hate shopping and didn't want to—" She stops when she sees me kneeling on the floor, holding a T-shirt. "Ethan?" she says.

I hold up the T-shirt. It's black, with the words *Get Up the Yard* slashed across the front. "Where did you get this?" I ask, my voice hoarse.

She's very good. It's only a flutter of her eyes, a slight catch, that gives anything away. Then she shrugs. "Bought it at a concert," she says. "Athens, I think."

"Susannah."

She looks back at me, arms across her chest. "What?" When I don't say anything, she frowns. "Seriously, what is—"

"Marisa was wearing this when she walked out of my house," I say. "The last time we saw her. Before she died."

Susannah pauses for only a moment, no more than to count *one*, but that pause tells me everything. "I must have bought a couple," she says. "Impulse purchase. I was drunk; the band was—"

"Don't lie to me," I say.

"Ethan, seriously, what—"

"*Don't!*" I shout. "Just . . . don't." I drop the shirt and feel myself sag and hang my head, as if I'm observing myself from far away. "What did you do?" I whisper.

Susannah says nothing, and then she is out the front door and gone. I stay there, kneeling on the floor of my living room, too stunned to move. It's only when I wonder where Wilson is, and why he isn't trying to lick me to death, that the tears come.

RONAN'S IS BUSY for a weeknight—I can see through the front windows that customers line the bar and the tables are full, and I can hear the noise as I enter the service door and walk down the short hallway to the stairwell. I climb the risers one at a time deliberately, gathering myself, and then I'm standing on the faded blue carpet runner in the upstairs hallway outside my uncle's office. I open the office door without knocking.

Uncle Gavin is sitting behind his desk, which has its usual assortment of papers, wrappers, file folders, and other assorted junk. "Ethan," he says, like he was expecting me.

"I just walked right up here into your office," I say. "You might want to rethink your security. Since you're in a dangerous line of work and all."

Uncle Gavin picks up a tablet that sits on a stack of invoices on the corner of his desk and holds it so I can see the screen. It shows four different video feeds, including the service door entrance and the hallway outside his office door. When he's sure I've seen it, he puts the tablet down again. "I'm quite happy with Caesar's security," he says. "What's on your mind?"

His matter-of-factness is infuriating. I want to sweep everything off his desk and onto the floor, then maybe overturn the desk for good measure, never mind that the desk is massive enough to take four people just to move it. For a moment I stand there, clenching and unclenching my fists.

Uncle Gavin pulls open a drawer and retrieves a bottle of whiskey and two glasses, then shoves a stack of file folders to one side so he can put the glasses down on his desk.

"I don't want a drink," I say.

He pours one glass, then another. "You need one."

"No thanks."

He holds a glass out to me. "It's a twelve-year-old peated single malt from Ireland. Be civil."

I take the glass and drink, the whiskey smooth and smoky with a touch of raw heat at the back of my throat. I take another sip and sit down. "There. Civil."

Uncle Gavin *hmph*s and drinks from his glass, setting it down on his desk. "Is Susannah all right?" he asks.

I laugh, a sad, ugly sound. "No," I say, "she's not all right. You know that." I finish my glass in one go and put it down on the desk.

As usual, my uncle's face is unreadable. "Talk sense," he says.

"Sense?" I shake my head. "Okay, here's 'sense.' Susannah killed Marisa."

Uncle Gavin sits back in his chair. "Donny Wharton killed Marisa," he says.

I rest my face in my hands, suddenly exhausted. "My sister did it," I say. "I know she did it."

Uncle Gavin's chair creaks as he shifts in it. "Your sister was in the hospital when Marisa died," he says.

"Then she got out somehow," I say, annoyed. "It's not like she didn't have the motive. Marisa slept with her to get back at me. You know how Susannah would react to being used like that. She got out of the hospital and found Marisa and killed her." I look up at my uncle. "And then she called you to help her."

Uncle Gavin says nothing but takes another swallow from his glass, looking past me at some spot in the near distance only he can see. I wait.

"She was never in the hospital," Uncle Gavin says. "At Northside."

I frown. "I dropped her off. I saw her walk inside and talk to the nurse." Then understanding hits me, and I collapse back in my chair like a sigh. "She never actually got admitted, did she?"

"She told the nurse you were an abusive boyfriend and she was trying to get away," my uncle said. "The nurse let her walk in and then walk right out the back door." He finishes his glass, pours himself another, then raises an eyebrow at me. Wearily I nod, and he refills my glass. We sit sipping whiskey. It's excellent, but the warm glow forming in the pit of my stomach is doing nothing to make me feel better.

"Your sister," my uncle says, and then he sighs. "Do you remember when I told you about those two men in Jacksonville? One of them was the man who fought with your father that night. Bridges, the one at the monastery."

I nod. "You brought me a newspaper article. Bridges and Gardner were arrested for drug trafficking."

"You threw it away. The article."

I shrug. "I guess so."

"Your sister took it out of the trash and kept it," he says.

I can't think of a response at first and just stare at my uncle instead. Someone down in the kitchen is shouting about an order for a table of twelve. "Why?" I ask finally.

"She came to me," my uncle says, "when she was about to graduate from high school. You were in college. She showed me the article and asked me if I knew where those men were. I told her they were still in prison. Then she asked me if I knew where the man you called Ponytail was."

My heart feels as if it's pounding in my throat. "Did you?" I ask.

He sips his whiskey again. "I had an idea," he says. "Susannah wanted to find him. I told her no, tried to talk her out of it. She . . . wasn't persuaded." He gives me a faint smile. "She told me she would go look for him with or without my help." He shrugs. "I thought she might be safer if I helped her."

I stared at him. "What are you saying? That she was . . . on some sort of *vendetta*?"

"She blames herself for what happened to you and your parents," he says. "You went running down the hall to give your father his pistol. She was angry with you, thought you were dismissing her. So she tripped you."

I'm running down the hall, the gun in my hand, my father and Bridges struggling, my mother and Kayla crying out. Susannah scowls at me from her doorway. She sticks out her foot. I trip and fall, the gun in my hand going off. And then Ponytail comes in with a hand cannon and shoots, and there's blood and screams. I shut my eyes and raise my hand as if to blot the memory out. "It's . . . she didn't—"

"Doesn't matter," Uncle Gavin says. "She thinks it was her fault. That's her perception, so that's her reality. And she was going to do what she could to make it right."

I open my eyes and look at my uncle, horrified. "Are you saying that for the past few years, she was looking for Donny Wharton?"

"She was looking for justice," my uncle says. "Or whatever version of it she could find."

*Nashville*, Susannah told me when I asked where she had been. *Cleveland for a little while. Saint Louis. Wanted to head out west, maybe Montana.* Had she been following Donny, tracking him from one town to another?

"You said you helped her," I say, my voice sounding as if it is coming from far away. "What do you mean?"

Uncle Gavin puts his glass down, then gives it a quarter turn on his desk. "I tried to help her find him," he says. "Sent her money if she needed it. She would check in every month—it was my rule; she had to call at least once a month. Sometimes she'd call and just say she was fine, then hang up. Other times she would need cash wired to some town in the middle of nowhere, or ask me if I had any contacts in Kansas City, or Saint Louis, or Biloxi." He shakes his head. "Here in Atlanta, I know lots of things, the right people to call. Out there . . ." He sighs again, gives his glass another quarter turn.

"What happened with Marisa?" I murmur.

He holds the glass still and looks down into it. "Susannah called me late that night," he says. "She needed help. I couldn't send anyone; I had to come myself. She was on Roswell Road, all the way up near Dalrymple in the parking lot of some strip mall. Most of the businesses were shuttered. I drove up there and pulled into the parking lot, and she was standing at the far end of the strip, as far away from the main road as she could be. Almost didn't see her, but she called when I turned into the lot and told me where she was. She took me behind the building to the service bays. There was a red Audi parked in one. Marisa was in the car, sitting behind the wheel." He turns the glass another quarter turn. "She was dead."

I drink the rest of my whiskey, my hand shaking ever so slightly, then put the glass down and drop my face into my hands again. *Suze,* I think.

"Susannah told me what Marisa had done to you, to her. Marisa found that article about those men from Jacksonville in your sister's backpack. That must be how she learned their names. I don't know how your sister found her, but she got Marisa to agree to meet her after . . . the situation at your house. They met, and argued, and Marisa told her what she'd done, how she was looking for Donny Wharton and the others." My uncle looks directly at me, and for the first time ever his face is completely unguarded—he looks old, old and tired, like a rock face etched and worn down by wind and weather and time. "Your sister told her to stop, and Marisa started yelling, going berserk, tried to claw out your sister's eyes. So your sister hit her, in the throat. She told me she just wanted to shut her up. Instead, she crushed her windpipe."

*My sister killed her*, I think. *Murdered her.* I want to tell my uncle to stop, to not tell me anymore, and yet I'm drawn to listen, to hear, no matter how sick it makes me feel.

"We put Marisa in the trunk of her car, and I drove it onto 285," he says. "There's an industrial district on the Chattahoochee south of Six Flags. I left her car behind one of the warehouses down there, tucked behind a dumpster. If I'd had more time, I could have maybe made her vanish, but this was the best I could do. Susannah followed in my car, picked me up, and we left. Then I drove her to Birchwood and she checked in."

I stare at the blue carpet on the floor, trying to discern some pattern in the threads. "What about fingerprints?" I say. "Hair, all of that?" I look up. "Jesus, Uncle Gavin, you could both go to prison. Get the death penalty."

He actually smiles. It holds more sorrow and bitterness than humor, true, but he smiles nonetheless. "I know how to clean a car," he says. "But they found hair. Just not mine or Susannah's."

I look blankly at him, and he looks back at me, waiting for me to figure it out. It doesn't take too long. *They found other evidence*, Johnny Shaw told me. "Donny Wharton's," I say. "You . . . you planted his hair in Marisa's car?"

"Your sister did," he says. "She'd been following Donny Wharton a long time. Had some of his hair in an evidence bag in her backpack. I asked her why and she said she didn't know, just thought it might come in useful someday." He says this last as if he's proud of her.

"Wait," I say, because realization has washed over me and I'm struggling for air as if I've been pulled underwater by a sudden riptide. "You lied to me," I continue. "You . . . you already *knew* Susannah had killed Marisa when I came to you. You *fucking* asked me if *I'd* done it." Uncle Gavin begins to open his mouth, and I talk over him. "Don't you tell me not to curse in front of you, Goddamn it. You don't get that option. How long were you going to string me along?" Then another wave of realization hits me. "Did Susannah fake *everything*? The suicide attempt, *all* of it?" I grip my head as if that's the only thing keeping it together.

Uncle Gavin gets up from his chair and makes his way around his disaster of a desk until he is standing next to me. "I lied because I was protecting Susannah," he says. "No one could know. Not even you. She wanted to tell you about what she'd done, but I said no. And I'd do it again. I let Caesar check Marisa's phone to make sure there wasn't anything connecting either your sister or you to her death. I didn't want to drag you into it any more than you already were." He lets out a heavy sigh. "I didn't count on Frankie and his loyalty to you. It's as deep as any that he has to me." He puts his hand on my back, just below my neck, and while part of me wants to shove it away and scream in his face, I stay there in my seat, head in my hands, my uncle's hand heavy on me. "Your sister wasn't faking. She would have jumped off that bridge if you hadn't been there. She told me that after you saved her, she was going to commit herself at the hospital. But when she heard about your student who took those pills because of Marisa, I think it was the last straw. She felt she had to do something." Uncle Gavin pauses. "But I *am* sorry, Ethan. I'm sorry I lied to you. I was doing what I thought was best."

I take my hands from my face, take a deep breath, and let a shaky breath out. "I know," I say, and I do. I know my uncle was trying to protect us. It's not enough for me to forgive him, not yet, but I know why he did it.

Uncle Gavin squeezes my shoulder, then withdraws his hand. "Where is she now?" he asks. "Your sister?"

"I don't know," I say. "She left."

And we have nothing else to say.

# CHAPTER TWENTY-EIGHT

THE LAST SATURDAY OF SPRING BREAK, I WALK DOWN MY DRIVEWAY to my mailbox. It's late afternoon, and the sun touches the clouds and sets them afire as it lowers in the west. Birds are singing, trees are budding, and tender shoots of grass are poking out of the ground, rejoicing that winter is finally gone. My hand still looks like someone went after it with a chain saw, but the gauze and bandage are off and the skin held together by the stitches is healing, pink as a newborn's.

I open my mailbox, and there with the catalogs and other junk mail is a white envelope with *ETHAN* handwritten across it.

Sitting on the front porch of my house, I open the envelope. It contains two pieces of paper. One is a letter, and I read that first:

*Dear Ethan,*

*I'm sorry. And I'm okay, or will be.*

*She was like a cancer, a virus that would find a place inside of you and just grow and grow until there wasn't anything left but her. I'm not sorry for that.*

*I've found everyone I wanted to find. Now I just have to find myself. (Insert barf emoji here.) The last person I've left here for you, if you want.*

*You're my brother. Always. Even if you don't like Dirt Plow. I mean, seriously, what the fuck is wrong with you?*

*Please don't try to find me.*

There is no signature.

The second sheet of paper, to my surprise, is a poem:

*The ancient Norse, white-haired, eyes lashed with frost,*
*dreamt the world as a mighty tree of ash,*
*its branches reaching to heaven, its roots*
*bound in the darkness of the underworld,*
*while humankind scrambled upon the bark*
*of the trunk, not knowing which way they went,*
*toward heaven or into hell. In my dreams*
*I see a tree as well, a living oak.*
*From roots to crown one half is green and young;*
*the other half burns, charred limbs, black bones,*
*the flames red tongues that lick the living side.*
*I do not know which vision I accept.*
*In both are yoked together life and death.*
*Yet only one springs from my own dark thoughts,*
*and so I claim it as my very own*
*as one would claim one's offspring, darkling child.*
*Instead of crawling toward my final doom*
*I choose both green and flame, to suffer each.*
*Yet at the end one only will remain.*
*But shall I claim your ever-living half,*
*or shall I grasp at last the burning branch?*

The poem is signed *S.*

I sit on my porch and sip cold beer from a bottle and read my sister's poem again. A tree half-alive and green, the other half burning. Life and death, green and flame. *I choose both green and flame, to suffer each.* That's my sister. I raise my beer. "To Suzie," I say, saluting the setting sun, and I drink, then brush the tears from my eyes.

My phone rings, and the screen says it's my vet. God. They have been so kind about Wilson having gone missing, even offering to send me meals, which I've declined. Now they've probably found half a bag of kibble I've left with them and they're calling to ask me what to do with it. I put down my beer and answer the phone, not wanting to deal with a voice mail, and there's an explosion of babble on the line. It's Nora, the purple-haired girl who runs the office, and it takes me several seconds to get her to slow down so I can understand.

"She brought him in," she says, breathless, nearly hysterical, as if she's close to tears. "Said she was your sister; she found him on *Craigslist*—can you believe that? Someone in Brookhaven found him in their yard—how did he get all the way to *Brookhaven?*—they were looking for the owner and posted an ad on Craigslist, and your sister just walked in here and dropped him off, she wouldn't stay—"

I stand. "What are you saying? What—"

"It's Wilson, Mr. Faulkner," Nora says, and she's definitely crying. "She found Wilson."

I run for the car.

WILSON IS FILTHY and he has a scratch on his nose and his ribs are bruised on one side where the vet thinks someone kicked him, but when I enter the exam room where the vet is checking him out, Wilson raises his head and gives this little howl, and both the vet and I burst into tears. When I crouch to get to Wilson's level on the exam table, he licks the tears off my face and pats at me with his paws.

After petting Wilson and baby-talking him for about half an hour, I leave him at the vet so they can give him a thorough checkup and observe him overnight. Nora can't tell me anything else about Susannah, just that she came in holding Wilson, handed him to an astonished Nora, and told her about finding him through a Craigslist ad before vanishing while the staff all gathered around Wilson. My best guess is that when Donny attacked Caesar, and most likely kicked Wilson in the process, Wilson hightailed it out of the yard and just kept going until he was lost. My feelings toward my sister right now defy easy explanation, but her tracking down and returning Wilson to me is a peace offering, and I accept it as such.

It's not until I get home that I remember the letter, which I tossed onto the passenger seat of my car when I jumped in to drive to the vet. Sitting in my driveway, I look at her letter again. *The last person I've left here for you, if you want.* I look at the back of the letter, then the back of the poem, and then the envelope. There it is: a third piece of paper, a thin, yellow strip that looks like it's torn from a sheet on a legal pad. I pull the piece out—it's about twice the size of the slip you find in a fortune cookie—and on it, in the small block lettering that Susannah sometimes uses, is a street address, followed by one word: *Kayla*.

WOODBINE DRIVE IS in Marietta, a few miles northwest of the Perimeter across the Chattahoochee River. It's part of the suburban tracts that surround Atlanta, subdivisions with cul-de-sacs and winding streets lined with pine trees and oaks, an occasional magnolia dropping its seed pods like organic grenades. It's a landscape of mowed front yards, basketball goals in the driveway, trampolines and gas grills and block parties and an occasional backyard pool. The houses are split-level ranches and modest Colonials, in contrast to the regal piles of brick and stone alongside the newer and gaudier McMansions in Buckhead.

That Sunday afternoon, well after church services are over and the faithful have mostly returned home, I turn onto Woodbine Drive and roll slowly down the street, looking for number twelve. And there, at the far end of the street, on the left just before the cul-de-sac, I find it: a dark-gray two-story stucco house with white trim and a red door, sitting back on a fringe of ivy that decorates a brick walkway.

There's a swath of grass from the walkway to the curb, and a woman and a small boy are playing in the grass. The boy is three, maybe four, towheaded and kicking a soccer ball to the woman. The boy is not kicking the soccer ball very far, but each time he kicks it, the woman claps and cheers and the boy grins, and the woman gently kicks the ball back to the boy.

I pull up to the curb, and the woman straightens up and shades her eyes to look at me. When she stands up, I realize she's pregnant, just a few months along but with a definite baby bump. "Can I help you?" she says.

I look at her face, her brown hair floating in wisps at her temples, and try to see the younger woman with stringy blonde hair who stumbled into my home one night all those years ago.

"I'm sorry," I say. "I was . . . looking for someone."

She smiles. "Who you looking for?"

I'm thinking of a reply when the front door opens and a man walks out, wearing a green polo and blue jeans and flip-flops, a Georgia cap perched on his head. The towheaded boy cries, "Daddy!" and runs to him, flinging himself against the man's legs.

"Hey, buddy," the man says, dropping a hand on the boy's head. "You playing soccer with Mommy?" He looks up and sees me at the curb, then walks down the yard toward me and the woman. "Sheri?" he says, his tone questioning but not alarmed.

"This fella's looking for someone," the woman says.

The man nods and stands next to his wife, their son still clinging to his father's leg.

"I don't think she lives here anymore," I say.

"Well, we moved in, what, two years ago?" the man says, looking at the woman.

"Three, right after Billy was born," she says, smiling at the towheaded boy. She rests a hand on her belly.

"Yeah, three," the man agrees, smiling. "I don't remember the folks who lived here before, though. Friends of yours?"

I shake my head, smiling. "It's all right," I say. "Sorry to bother y'all."

The towheaded boy is looking up at me. "What's your name?" he says suddenly.

"Billy," his father says, laughing and shaking his head.

The boy looks at his dad, frowning. "You told me to be friendly," he says.

"Sorry about that," the man says, and he sticks out a hand. "I'm Tom. This is my wife, Sheri, and our son Billy."

I shake his hand. "Nice to meet you all." Then I reach out to shake Sheri's hand. "My name's Ethan."

She takes my hand and gives it a firm squeeze. "Nice to meet you, Ethan," she says, and that's when I see her, like the child hidden in every adult's face.

"Y'all have a good afternoon," I say. "Nice to meet you, Billy."

Billy nods solemnly at me.

"Hope you find your friend," Tom says.

"That's okay," I say, putting the car in gear. "I don't think she exists anymore." And I pull away from the curb, leaving Tom behind, a slight frown on his face. When I circle around the cul-de-sac and pass them going the opposite direction, Tom and Billy are playing with the soccer ball, having already forgotten me. But the woman stands apart from them, staring at me, her mouth open in recognition. I wave good-bye, then drive away.

As I drive out of the suburbs, I hear on the radio a report about a woman found dead on 285, in the breakdown lane. It's the third body found on the interstate in the past month. The police have no leads on whoever the murderer is, but the press have already dubbed him the 285 Killer. I turn the radio off and drive in silence. At a stop sign, I wave at a boy with a leashed golden retriever who crosses the road in front of me, and he waves shyly back and hurries through the crosswalk, the retriever trotting by his side. I make a note to take Wilson on more walks once he gets home.

I drive on, and the road crests a hill and then I merge onto the highway, a river of asphalt carrying cars into the city. Ahead of me, on the horizon, Atlanta's towers rise like spires. It's a welcome sight. It means home. And yet somewhere out there, a man is plotting another death on the highway that encircles the city. There are always men like him, like Brandon Cargill and Donny Wharton. But my sister is out there in the world as well, and Frankie, and Caesar, and Coleman and Teri Merchant and Betsy Bales. And Uncle Gavin as well. That must be worth something, a starshine to counter the darkest impulses of our hearts. There are good people in the world. I hope to be one of them. I think of Kayla, with a new name and a new family. I hope I haven't scared her. I hope she goes on to have a good life with Tom and Billy and her unborn child. She deserves that. We all do.

# ACKNOWLEDGMENTS

Second novels are rumored to be difficult to write. I'm here to confirm that rumor is true. Writing a book is rarely easy, but this one was a bear. I hope you enjoy it.

Many thanks to my agent Peter Steinberg at Foundry Literary + Media for his unwavering support and for believing in me. Jenny Chen at Crooked Lane Books has championed this book from the get-go; not only did she see the heart of the story I was trying to tell, but she also helped me discover the best way to construct that story. She and the rest of the folks at Crooked Lane are outstanding, and I'm so grateful to them.

I'm also so very grateful to Holy Innocents' Episcopal School for celebrating and supporting me in my second career as an author, as well as allowing me the opportunity to continue in my first career as a teacher. To my students, who push me and challenge me to be a better teacher and who never cease to amaze, embarrass, and delight me—thank you, and it will all be on the test.

There are too many authors for me to thank properly, and I fear I'll inadvertently leave someone out, but the following deserve my special thanks for their encouragement, advice, and friendship: Brian Panowich, Jami Attenberg, Emily Carpenter, Patti Callahan Henry, Jonathan Evison, Ben Loory, Joshilyn Jackson, J. T. Ellison, Caroline Leavitt, Ed Tarkington, Morgan Babst, Daren Wang, Tim Johnston, Susan Rebecca White, Emily Giffin, Lynn Cullen, Julia Franks, Mira Jacob, Hank Early,

Mary Laura Philpott, Marsha Cornelius, Linda Sands, Jason Sheffield, Wiley Cash, Dunn Neugebauer, Sheryl Bryant Parbhoo, Clifford Brooks, David Abrams, David Williams, Marilyn Baron, Zachary Steele, Rob Aiken, George Weinstein, Roger Johns, Anna Schachner, Robyn McCord O'Brien, Soniah Kamal, Carmen Deedy, Scott Gould, Elizabeth Colton, Amanda Kyle Williams (RIP), Georgia Lee, T. M. Brown, Angie Gallion, and Julia McDermott.

Thank you to Robin Hoklotubbe, Kelly Moore, Karin Glendenning, and all other librarians who promote authors and their books and reading in general; to Joy Pope, Kate Whitman, Alison Law, and all the other folks who tirelessly support the Atlanta literary scene; to Susan Rapoport, the wind beneath my wings; and to Gary Parkes, Jake Reiss, Nora Ketron, Frank Reiss, Kelly Justice, Doug Robinson, Niki Coffman, Justin Souther, Charlie Lovett, and indie bookstores everywhere (go to www.indiebound.org to find and order books from your local independent bookstore).

And finally, and most of all, to my number-one promoter, my editor-in-chief, the mother of our two incredible boys, and my best friend—to my wife, Kathy Ferrell-Swann. You were right. And I love you.